MW01073650

JUDGMENT
DAY

JUDGMENT DAY

LAST BOOK OF
THE CHIMERA CHRONICLES
TRILOGY

Jill & Tom
Thanks for joining
me on this journey

ROB JUNG

HAWK HILL
LITERARY
AN IMPRINT OF INGRAM

Judgment Day

A Psychological Thriller

Last Book of the Chimera Chronicles

Copyright © 2022 Rob Jung

Publisher: Hawk Hill Literary, LLC, an imprint of Ingram

All rights reserved. No part of this book may be reproduced, stored or transmitted by any means or in any form—whether auditory, graphic, digital, mechanical, electronic, photocopying, recording, or otherwise, or conveyed via the internet or through a website—without written permission of both publisher and author, except in the case of brief excerpts used in critical articles and reviews. Unauthorized reproduction of any part of this work is illegal and is punishable by law.

This is a work of fiction. Names of characters, places and incidents are either the product of the author's imagination or are used fictitiously. Living persons or historical characters portrayed in this book are portrayed in fictional circumstances and settings.

Cover Design by Jun Ares.
Interior Layout Design by Spellbound Publishers.
Inquiries should be addressed to: Hawk Hill Literary, LLC 13274 Huntington Terrace Saint Paul, MN 55124 Voice and Text: (612) 812-6060

Paperback ISBN: 978-1-7366108-3-1
E-book ISBN: 978-1-7366108-2-4
Library of Congress Control Number: 2022919140

Printed in the United States

ALSO BY ROB JUNG

Cloud Warriors

The Chimera Chronicles Trilogy:
The Reaper
The Sower

AUTHOR'S NOTE

My novels arise from actual historical events. The Chimera Chronicles Trilogy is a saga of *The Reaper,* a painting by Spanish artist Joan Miro that disappeared from the Spanish pavilion at the end of the 1937 Paris Exposition. It is around that still-lost work of art that this three-part story revolves. *Judgment Day* is the last installment of that story. It is entirely fictional, as are the characters, except in the case of living or historical characters who appear in fictional settings.

Rob Jung

We are, who we are,
because we stand
on the shoulders
of a thousand yesterdays.

DEDICATION

To my youngest daughter, Dr. Ashley Junghans-Rutelonis, psychologist *par excellence,* without whose oversight, guidance and input this book could not have been written.

NEW YEAR'S EVE, 2014

The metamorphosis from self-confident business executive to defenseless little girl had been instantaneous the moment Magnolia Kanaranzi saw him. She gasped as she crumpled from the stool into a heap on the floor. Her silk, ivory-colored skirt twisted around her legs, and the matching blazer rode up her back. Mascara rivulets streaked her pale face.

She looked small and vulnerable lying there, but it was her soft whimpers of "mommy" between sobs that struck Hamilton Blethen's heart. He could hear his own voice bleating the same futile lament in reply. Tears streamed down his dark brown cheeks, tears for himself and for her, knowing that her forlorn cry would bring to her no more solace than they had for him.

A sudden movement at the door pulled his attention from the devastated woman on the floor. He looked up as two police officers pushed their way around his wheelchair and walked toward Magnolia. A male officer kneeled down beside her. Speaking softly, he said, "You are under arrest for the murder of Lorraine Blethen." Hamilton heard the click of the handcuffs and watched as Magnolia Kanaranzi, Senator-elect from the State of Massachusetts, was lifted to her feet.

After five and a half years, his grandmother's murderer had finally been found, and in the process, after 36 years, Hamilton had finally succeeded in finding his estranged mother.

He had not expected them to be the same person.

ONE MONTH LATER

The Montreal Express whistled forlornly between the skyscrapers of downtown Boston, whipping snowflakes helter-skelter against the conference room window of Taft, Hartman and Lowinski, Attorneys at Law. Inside, Napoleon Taft was confronting his newest client, Senator-elect Magnolia Kanaranzi.

"Senator, they have the testimony of this guy, Otto Bonhoffer, who has admitted killing your mother, saying that you hired him to do it. They also have the person who was with him who will testify that the daughter of Lorraine Blethen hired them to kill her. And they have the packing slip that was used to gain access to the victim's home, bearing your name. Your birth name, Mary Blethen."

"I didn't hire them, or anyone, to kill my mother," Magnolia Kanaranzi repeated, her voice rising. "They're trying to frame me."

"Bonhoffer wasn't under arrest. He came forward on his own."

"Isn't that the best evidence that I'm being framed?" she countered. "Someone who I don't even know, and who was not even a suspect, pops up out of nowhere and accuses me of hiring him to kill my own mother?"

"He also says you hired him to kill Aaron Feldman."

"That's obviously a lie."

"So, who is framing you? What's their motive?"

"It has to be political," Magnolia answered. "I flipped a Senate seat. I'm a woman."

"Senate seats get flipped all the time," Taft countered, "and the flipper doesn't get charged with murder. We're going to have to come up with something better than that."

"It's my word against his," she snapped back. "Why would I kill my own mother?"

"You hated your mother. You left home the day you graduated from high school," Taft responded, irritation creeping into his voice. "You have a history of violence. You shot a man just two months before you were arrested."

"I was never arrested or charged for that," she shouted. "Aaron Feldman was a sleazy, lying son-of-a-bitch…"

"He was a campaign worker who disappeared, allegedly because you hired Bonhoffer to take care of him," Taft interrupted flatly.

"I shot the bastard in self-defense!" Magnolia screamed.

"You told the police you have no memory of shooting him or of what happened that night!" Taft bellowed back. "You can't have it both ways. They'll crucify you on the witness stand if you try to make that claim now."

"I'm not being tried for shooting Aaron Feldman."

"But his shooting will be fair game at your trial, particularly if you testify," Taft replied more softly. He paused to regain his composure and looked squarely at Magnolia. "Even if you don't testify, they'll bring it up in Bonhoffer's testimony to prove you are the kind of person who hires people to kill someone who crosses you."

Sleet ticked against the conference room window and the muffled sound of howling wind gusts settled over the room. Magnolia glared at her celebrity lawyer. She didn't need to be reminded that the facts of her case were unfavorable. She had hired Taft, reputably the best criminal defense attorney in the country, to obfuscate that and to work his wizardry with the jury. He was being paid to get her acquitted, not to argue with her.

Magnolia also knew the motive behind her arrest for murdering her mother was not political. While it was true that she had never met Otto Bonhoffer, she knew who he worked for: Henri Hawke, a Barcelona habitue and Magnolia's French-born fixer. Hawke had been instrumental in ruthlessly clearing the way for her rise to the top of Kincaid Media. She should have parted ways with him long ago, but in the last decade he had performed enough "jobs" for her that their fortunes had become inextricably intertwined, and there always seemed to be more situations that needed *fixing*. If she knew only one thing, it was that if one of them stumbled, they would both fall, and that made Bonhoffer a problem.

When she first announced her intention to run for the Senate, Hawke strongly argued against it. He saw her election, and the intense public scrutiny that came with it, as a huge risk for both of them. She did it anyway and pulled off an upset win over a two-term incumbent. In the process, she had hired Hawke again to help clear obstacles in her path. This included getting rid of Aaron Feldman, a job that Hawke's henchman, Bonhoffer, unfortunately botched.

Now, with her arrest, it appeared that Hawke was trying to separate himself from her. She was certain he was behind Bonhoffer's false confession. *I'm being fixed by my own fixer, and this will not stand,* she pledged. *Taft will have to do his job without knowing all the details. If he's as good as advertised, that should be no problem.*

"Follow the money," she hissed, breaking the silence. "You'll see that I never paid anyone named Otto Bonhoffer." She gathered her things and stood up to leave. "If he did what he said he did, find out who paid him!" *Let Hawke wrestle with that little problem!*

As she left, Taft moved to the window and gazed out at the swirling snow, deep in thought. *Who did she pay,* he wondered? After a few minutes he sat down and peered across the conference room table at his young assistant, Laura Avery. She had a photographic memory and a talent for being virtually invisible during meetings with difficult clients. She also was smart enough to sit quietly and wait until Taft was ready to talk again.

"Now there's a piece of work," Taft said, gesturing in the general direction Magnolia had gone. "It's amazing that so much venom can be contained in such a small package."

Avery raised an eyebrow and shook her head. "How do you defend someone like that?"

"Everyone is entitled to the best representation that money can buy," Taft answered with a smirk. "And that's us."

"That's cynical," she replied.

That was another reason Taft liked working with Avery. She was direct and to the point. She was not intimidated. Some day she would be a great defense attorney.

"Maybe a little cynical," he admitted, "but let's not kid ourselves. The legal system is rigged in favor of the rich. If Magnolia Kanaranzi was a pauper, she would be pleading guilty with some overmatched public defender representing her. She'd spend the rest of her life in jail."

"Doesn't it bother you?"

"You mean the unfairness of the system or having clients who are, shall we say, incorrigible? "

"Both."

"We're not here to overhaul the legal system. We're here to provide the best representation we can," he responded in a mock professorial voice. "As for difficult clients," he continued, "you never ask them if they did it, and you never take cases to trial that you might lose. That way you can sleep at night while at the same time build your reputation as a winner."

"You think she did it? Killed her own mother?" Avery asked.

"Don't care, and neither should you," Taft said firmly. "Our only job is to figure out how we can best represent our client to get the best outcome for her, which will mean getting the best outcome for us. Right now, based on what we know, taking this case to trial is not in our best interest."

"Should we follow the money, as she suggested? We could get her bank records."

Taft chewed the inside of his cheek as he thought. "Let the prosecutors waste their time on that," he said finally. "Someone with Kanaranzi's resources will have accounts in places we've never heard of, buried under three aliases. It will be impossible to know if she paid Bonhoffer, or anyone for that matter. Let's start by finding a reason to oppose extradition. The last thing we want is to try this case in Minnesota."

Four hundred miles south of Boston, the reverberations of Magnolia's arrest were being keenly felt.

"What if they declare her insane?"

"Worse yet, what if she stands trial, and they find her guilty?"

Senator Brad Styles planted his elbows on the arms of a blue rattan chair and leaned into a tripod formed by his fingers, upon which he rested his forehead. He closed his eyes and muttered to no one in particular, "It doesn't matter. We're screwed either way."

The arrest of the newly-elected United States Senator, Magnolia Kanaranzi, had set off a firestorm of political maneuvering in

Washington, D.C., and in no place more so than in the backyard of the Georgetown home of U.S. Senate Minority Leader Bradford Styles of Michigan. Styles was midway through his third term and was highly regarded as a problem solver. However, nothing in his experience had prepared him for this current problem. In fact, there was nothing in the history of the United States that remotely resembled the conundrum he faced.

Styles straightened up and looked at the pale, thin man seated to his right. "What's the Justice Department saying, Harvey?"

"They're saying that the only way to get rid of her is by resignation or by two-thirds vote of the Senate," responded Harvey Findley, Styles' veteran Chief of Staff.

"Does the fact that she wasn't sworn in before she was arrested make any difference?"

"Nope," Findley said, shaking his bald head. "There's no distinction. Once elected, the only way, short of resignation or death, is by vote of the Senate."

"The state has no say in it?"

"State law determines how a vacant seat is filled, but the law is clear that removal of a duly elected U.S. Senator is governed by federal law," Findley answered. "Article 1, Section 5 of the Constitution. It's called the expulsion clause."

"Maybe they can't remove her, but it didn't take them long to kick her to the curb," Styles responded ironically. "The Governor couldn't authorize her extradition fast enough."

"That's because that asshole wants to appoint himself to replace her, and then we'll be down to 41 seats." The third member of the troika, rotund Senate minority whip Gus Steinberg, stood in the center of Styles' backyard patio giving off his usual combative vibe. "We can't afford to have her removed. If we lose that seat, then it would take only one more vote and there goes the filibuster. We'll be castrated like a harem guard. We might as well kiss the U.S. auto industry good-bye."

Styles and Findley winced at Steinberg's colorful hyperbole and the painful truth of his words. Without the filibuster they would have no check on the agenda of the majority, the most immediate concern being a pending bill that would eliminate tariffs on foreign automobiles. To Styles and Steinberg, whose constituencies relied heavily on the U.S. auto industry for jobs, the pending bill was an abomination that would put U.S. automakers at a staggering disadvantage.

That possibility alone elevated the task of saving the Massachusetts Senate seat to crisis proportions, particularly because at least one member of their caucus, Utah Senator Marilee Wintheiser, who had broken from the caucus on other legislation, had threatened to cross over on the tariff-repeal bill. If the Massachusetts' seat was lost, that thin margin would be gone and any additional crossover would give the opposition the 60th vote that would negate a filibuster, and with it would go the last line of defense against the repeal of auto tariffs. James Madison's warning of the "tyranny of the majority" would come to pass.

Rather than respond to Steinberg, which he knew would only bring another tirade, Styles punched the speed dial number of his Capitol office. "Get the Massachusetts' party chairman on the line, please, and then patch me in. Thanks." He hung up and turned back to Findley.

"This early, with a full term to serve, wouldn't there be a special election to fill the seat?"

"Every state is different," Findley answered. "I'm sure the state party chair will know."

"We can't rely on some party flunky…"

Before Steinberg finished, Styles' phone rang. "Cheryl Belton is on line for you, sir."

"That was quick," Styles intoned, relieved to be spared the bluster of the Senator from New York.

"Hello Cheryl. Brad Styles here." They exchanged pleasantries for a moment and then Styles cleared his throat. "I've got Senator Steinberg and my chief of staff, Harvey Findley, here with me. We've been talking about the situation with Kanaranzi's Senate seat. We've got a couple of questions for you. Hold on. I'm going to put you on speaker phone."

He fumbled with his phone for a second and then continued on speaker. "If Kanaranzi is removed from office, what's the process for filling her seat? Does the Governor appoint someone, or do you have a special election?"

"Both," Belton said. "The Governor has the power to appoint an interim Senator, but a special election must be held 145 to160 days after the seat is vacated."

"So, he could appoint himself, or Metzger, or anybody."

"Correct," Belton answered. "Although I don't think the Governor would appoint Metzger. He lost to Kanaranzi and was pretty much discredited in the process. The Governor might appoint himself, or any one of several up-and-comers. Regardless, whoever is appointed has a five-month head start on the special election and will be tough to beat."

"Have you got anyone lined up to run in the event that the Kanaranzi seat is vacated?"

"There are always people wanting to run, but on such short notice to raise money and get a name out, it will be difficult to win. We don't have anybody with the name recognition of the Governor, or Metzger, or for that matter, a couple of their state legislators."

Styles shook his head and exhaled loud enough for Belton to hear. What she couldn't see was his craggy, weather-worn face scowling in frustration. "Better send out your search party, Cheryl," he said. "Find the best person you've got and convince all the pretenders to drop out.

We can't be splitting support among multiple candidates. This is critical. The filibuster rule, and our ability to hold the line against the garbage they're trying to cram down our throats, are at stake. Hell, the whole future of the country is at stake."

"Perhaps if she resigned and endorsed somebody…"

"No. No. No," Steinberg cut in. "We don't want her to resign. At least not yet. We just need you to have someone lined up and ready to run in case they succeed in having her expelled."

"If you need help," Styles interrupted, "use Harvey. As I said, this is critical. Find a candidate, and if you need us to, we can put pressure on anyone who won't cooperate to get out of the way."

"The press is having a field day with this," Steinberg growled after the call ended. "They're playing up the public demonstrations and the outcry for Kanaranzi's resignation."

"I know," Styles responded. "Harvey, you need to get someone to convince Magnolia not to buckle under the pressure."

"Or maybe convince her to plead temporary insanity," Steinberg barked. "If she's convicted, there's no way we can oppose a motion for expulsion. We'll be toast at the next election. But, if she's acquitted because of temporary insanity, we can argue that her actions, under those circumstances, don't rise to the level of moral turpitude that should cause her to lose her seat. Similar to the Langer case back in the 40s."

"Interesting theory," Findley growled, "but how do you prove temporary insanity when the murder happened six years ago, *and* she hired someone to do it. She didn't do it herself. I've never heard of an insanity plea where the accused hired someone to do their dirty work."

For once, Steinberg didn't have an answer.

They fell silent, pondering the implications for their party, the country, and their own political futures. A chilly wind whipped around them, announcing a coming storm and providing impetus to wrap up the backyard meeting.

"I still want someone to meet with her," Styles said as he stood up, unfolding his gaunt, 6-4 frame from the chair, feeling every one of his 68 years. "Just to show that she has our support and to suss out where her head is at. Maybe explain to her how critical her seat is to maintaining the filibuster…"

"And encourage her not to resign," Steinberg finished the sentence.

"And get a reading on whether she's fit to stand trial," Findley interjected.

Styles cocked his head, directing a wordless question to his chief of staff.

"There are rumors that she's gone wacko since the arrest," Findley responded carefully meeting Styles' gaze. "She spent almost a month in the hospital. If she's found unfit to stand trial, the whole thing would be dismissed, and we won't have to worry about a conviction."

Steinberg nodded. "That would be easier than proving insanity six years ago. I like it."

"Wouldn't it be better to have her stand trial?" Styles asked. "If her case is dismissed, we're still going to have a fight on our hands to keep her from being expelled."

"If she goes to trial, we can tell the press we are letting the legal process take its course," Steinberg interrupted, "and argue that any effort to expel her until then is premature. In the meantime, it will give us a year or two to prepare for the special election."

"And, who knows," Styles said, his face suddenly showing optimism. "Maybe she'll be acquitted."

"Except the actual murderer is apparently going to testify against her," Steinberg added sardonically.

The three men hunched their shoulders against another bitter wind gust, perhaps a harbinger of their future political prospects, and shuffled toward the back door of Style's opulent Victorian townhome.

"I'll go see her myself," Findley said as they entered the house.

"Good idea," Styles agreed. He shook Steinberg's hand. "We may be screwed, but we won't go down without a fight," he assured his party whip.

"Walk with me to my car," Steinberg said as he and Findley walked out the front door onto the sidewalk. They made an incongruous pair: Steinberg's Oliver Hardy to Findley's Stan Laurel. The New York Senator stopped beside his chauffeur-driven Mercedes. "Letting our future be determined by a trial court is not smart, but I'm not sure your Pollyanna boss has the stones to handle it the way it needs to be handled."

Findley looked up at him with steely, cold eyes. "Keep your nose out of this, Senator," he said in a low, dark voice. "I've got this, and it's better that neither you nor Brad knows how it goes down. You're familiar with the phrase 'plausible deniability'?"

Findley didn't wait for the shock to disappear from Steinberg's face, nor for what, undoubtedly, would be a braying response.

Fucking amateur, Findley thought as he walked away.

MAGNOLIA

Magnolia was aware of her memory lapses. When she thought about them, which wasn't often, she concluded they were most likely due to alcohol. She had made a conscious effort to cut back on her alcohol consumption, but the events of the last three months had challenged her assumption that alcohol was the culprit.

The mental fog around the whole Aaron Feldman thing was disturbing. A search on the internet had satisfied Magnolia that temporary amnesia is not uncommon, particularly when a person is faced with extreme trauma. It is a defense mechanism your psyche involuntarily activates to protect you. The shooting of Feldman fit that explanation and so too did her arrest, but hiring someone to kill Feldman? That was a calculated act, not an unexpected traumatic event. It didn't make sense that she couldn't remember it.

Unless, of course, the whole thing is fabricated; part of Hawke's plot to take me down.

There were other things—little things—like the kitten called *Houppette*. Why couldn't she remember where it came from; how had it ended up in her penthouse? And "firing" a campaign volunteer. She had no recollection of doing that, and she had made a fool of herself later when asking for his help.

She got up from the chaise and walked across the expansive penthouse living room, stopping for a moment to enjoy the lights of Boston's inner harbor before pouring herself a cognac, neat, at her built-in, mirrored bar. Notwithstanding her best intentions, Magnolia's liquor consumption had definitely escalated since she found herself exiled to Pier 4, freed on a million-dollar bond, but not free at all. The paparazzi were permanently stationed at the Pier 4 entrance, and they followed her relentlessly whenever she left the building. The traditional media was not much better, but thank God for Samantha Jones, her former press secretary who had stayed loyal. Samantha handled the media crush with veteran skill and coordinated with Magnolia's lawyers on when, and what, to communicate to the press.

Magnolia tested the cognac with a sip, then strolled to the kitchen and placed it on a warmer, lighting the candle beneath the tilted snifter. She stood watching the flame for a minute, twirling the snifter and waited until the candle warmed the cognac just enough to release its aroma.

Back on the chaise, she thought about the meeting with Taft. He had come with the highest of recommendations, but appeared to be more interested in preserving his reputation than fighting for her. She needed to light a fire under him, or change attorneys. If she fired him, she would lose in the court of public opinion. Switching attorneys in midstream is always bad, particularly if you fire one of the country's most notable attorneys. It would make headlines and cast doubt on her innocence.

And she hadn't killed her mother. Even if she had, she couldn't plead guilty or enter into a plea agreement. It would disqualify her from holding political office, from being a U.S. Senator. She would never agree to anything that could allow that to happen.

So, what would motivate Taft? Money? Women? She was sure he had more than enough of both of those. *Position? Power? Would being chief of staff to a U.S. Senator be enough? Probably not. A Federal Court appointment?* Magnolia was not sure she had the political capital to orchestrate one at this time, plus it would be a massive pay cut for Taft. *What else? Threats? Blackmail? Not good to threaten your own attorney, but blackmail?*

A smile crept onto Magnolia's face.

Henri Hawke, I have a job for you. The last one you'll ever do.

She reached for her burner phone.

The next day, Magnolia sat in the same chaise, dressed to impress in a Veronica Beard velvet pantsuit, her slender legs crossed to display Valentino Garavani gold sneakers. Across the white-carpeted living room, facing her and a splendid view of Boston Harbor, was a pale, bald man who did not appear to be in awe of either his hostess or the grand surroundings of her Pier 4 penthouse. Harvey Findley might look like the 90-pound weakling who gets sand kicked in his face, but he had seen it all in his 30 years as Brad Styles' chief of staff, and the experience had vulcanized him. He was neither awestruck nor intimidated by new money or the nouveau privileged.

"I've had to fight for everything I've ever gotten in life," Magnolia declared. "I didn't become president of a media empire, and a U.S. Senator, by backing down. I've never been a quitter, and I won't quit now."

Findley looked at the small woman, trying to see beyond the bravado of her words. "We didn't think the political gibberish of the media would intimidate you," he said. "We, Senator Styles and I, on behalf of the entire caucus, want you to know that we are behind you one hundred percent."

Magnolia's cobalt blue eyes flashed as her shoulders rose and fell in an exaggerated shrug. "That's comforting, but how does that benefit me in this trial?" Her tone reflected no trace of gratitude.

"We have far-reaching influence," Findley offered.

"Well, use some of it to convince my lawyer to get a backbone and stop this extradition thing." Magnolia's anger began to rise like the incoming tide. "I did not kill my mother, and, contrary to the scurrilous rumors being spread about me, I am not incompetent, nor incapable of making rational decisions."

Findley had heard of her collapse when she was arrested and knew she had spent more than three weeks in the hospital. For the moment, however, her reactions seemed quite normal: angry at the situation in which she found herself, claiming innocence, and defending her sanity which, whether true or false, would be expected.

"You understand how critical it is to hold on to your Senate seat," he said, moving the conversation away from her legal struggles. "So far, we're confident they can't get the 67 votes required for expulsion, but to prevent any of our votes from wavering, and perhaps to persuade a few more to vote in your favor, we'd like to have you examined by our own psychiatrist."

"I…" Magnolia started indignantly.

Findley held up his hand. "We can use his opinion until you're acquitted to show that you are both legally competent and intellectually stable. Politically, it would be literally impossible to expel you from office in the face of such an opinion."

"I hate psychiatrists," she snapped. "And don't *ever* raise your hand to me or interrupt me again."

"I apologize," he said soothingly, while thinking: *She'll be her own worst enemy on the witness stand.* "I didn't mean to offend. Please remember that we are on the same side here."

Magnolia stared at him, hostility heating the air around her body.

"I'm no big fan of shrinks, either," Findley continued with his appeasing tone, "but that's the way the game is played." He shrugged. "My concern, like yours, is that you do not get removed from your seat. A report from our *independent* psychiatrist will assure that. No one in our caucus will vote to expel you in the face of that report, and maybe your lawyer can use it to defend you at trial. The more psychiatric reports you stack up on your side, the better your chances."

Magnolia didn't move.

"Plus, we can talk to your lawyer and impress upon him that it is neither in your best interest nor in the best interest of the United States to have you extradited to Minnesota to stand trial."

Her eyes flashed in anger.

"Fine!" she snapped. "Set it up."

Findley nodded. "I know you're not happy," he said, "but trust me. I've been doing this for decades."

He excused himself and left. Magnolia did not see him out.

"I don't trust you any farther than I can throw you," she muttered to the closed door. "I'll prove my innocence, and it won't be because of you."

She glanced at her phone. She'd missed a call from a number she didn't recognize, but the prefix identified it as coming from Barcelona. *Must have been Hawke. Damn.*

"Personally, I don't give a shit whether she's a lunatic or a serial killer. What I need is a report from you saying that she is sane, stable, and intellectually and emotionally capable of carrying out her duties as a U.S. Senator."

"You know I can't guarantee that," replied Walter Robbins. He looked across his battered desk at Findley. "The best I can do is give you my opinion after I examine her. You know psychiatry is not an exact science."

"Neither is politics," Findley answered evenly. "I've met with her, and she certainly seems competent to me. By the way, I don't want you opining on her guilt or innocence. That's to be left for the court to decide. You might want to say that in your report."

"You do your job, and I'll do mine. I promise I'll give you my honest opinion. And I won't say anything about guilt or innocence."

"One more thing, Robby," Findley said quietly. "I need to know about her loyalty. Can her loyalty be counted on? This is just between you and me. I don't want it in your report."

Robbins looked at Findley quizzically.

"Here's a little history that may give you some perspective," Findley added. "When Magnolia was young, she was in a lot of trouble, drugs and sex stuff, and a guy named Arthur Kincaid bailed her out. She went to work for him and served as his right hand for over 30 years. Ultimately, she took over his business when he died. That was a decade ago. The real question is if we bail her out of her current mess, can we count on that same level of loyalty that she gave to Kincaid?"

"I remember Kincaid from years ago," Robbins said thoughtfully. "I think he was an ambassador or something. This information is helpful, but that's no guarantee that you can count on the same kind of loyalty now, nor that I can make a determination on whether *you* can. As I said, all I can do is give you my honest, professional opinion."

"You can't be wrong on this, Robby. The stakes are too high."

HAWKE

A look of disdain settled on Henri Hawke's round face. The meager salad in front of him was not part of his culinary proclivities. It would not have been allowed on his table or in his kitchen if not for his physician. *Lose weight, indeed,* he thought indignantly. He carefully set his fork down in its proper place beside the salad plate.

At five-foot-five and 180 pounds, Hawke considered himself to be at the pinnacle of physical prowess. He could dance until dawn at the clubs; his stamina of legendary stature. He could climb the steps to the *Magic Fountain of Montjuic* without breathing hard. Of equal importance, his corpulence enabled him to consume large quantities of absinthe or Pernod or fine brandy without visible effect. He was quite at peace with his weight.

But his physician, a gloriously beautiful woman of Swedish descent named Eva – a full head taller than Henri – had reminded him that he had just celebrated his 60th birthday. It would be wise to lose weight, lower his cholesterol, and reduce the stress on his heart. He had told her that just being in her presence caused stress on his heart.

Hawke picked up his fork and reluctantly speared a lettuce leaf. He did not want to disappoint Dr. Eva. Some day he would take her dancing.

As he poked his way despondently through the salad, he thought about a call he had received earlier. The message had simply said, "Call me. I have a job for you." The fact that he received a call of any nature from Magnolia Kanaranzi was perplexing.

He assumed she blamed him for her current legal predicament. She would be right, of course, but perhaps she did not know it was Bonhoffer's confession that had led to her arrest.

It was unlikely. Magnolia was a perceptive woman who understood how these things worked. She would understand why he had done it. They both knew their decade-long association, which had been mutually enriching, would come to an end someday, most likely in an ugly fashion that could end tragically for both of them. He had just been the first to act, making sure that only one of them would suffer the tragedy. She would have done the same to him, given the opportunity.

Hawke pushed the few bites of remaining salad around his plate. There was no doubt Magnolia was laying a trap for him, but he had matched wits with the best and each time come away unscathed and a bit wealthier. For him, it was like a game of chess. He always needed to think at least one move ahead of his adversary. To do that, he had to deduce his adversary's next move.

He replayed her voice message several times, listening for voice inflections, but he heard nothing that might be a tell. He would return her call shortly. Failure to do so would be tantamount to an admission of his culpability, and he needed to maintain deniability. Plus, he wanted to know what she was thinking. The phrase, *keep your enemies closer,* crossed his mind. He set the phone down on the table and finished his salad. Tomorrow he would call Magnolia. He did not want to appear too eager. Tonight, he would rest easy and dream of Dr. Eva.

Hawke picked up the salad plate and ate the last crust of bread. He rinsed the plate and placed it in the dishwasher. The appliance was one of the few luxuries in his otherwise austere, one-bedroom flat. The other was a robotic vacuum. Both gadgets were a product of his fastidious nature, a compulsion that applied both to the cleanliness of his flat and his professional assignments. He scraped the linen table cloth with a stainless steel crumber, efficiently guiding the recalcitrant bread crumbs into the palm of his hand and dumping them in the trash. Then he hooked a stool with his foot and guided it to the front of his lime green *Galanz* refrigerator, circa 1958, to reach the half-empty bottle of *Remy Martin Louis XIII* stored above the fridge. He poured three fingers into a snifter and sat it at a 45-degree angle on a warmer. He lit the tea light and waited for the flame to warm the spirit.

Ah, it is such a rich reflection of life. The flame that warms the spirit. The spirit that warms the heart. He gazed at the amber liquid. *When all else fails, it brings peace. Merci, good doctor, for not forbidding me this elixir.*

His soliloquy finished, Hawke removed the cognac from the heater and swirled it, taking in its strong aroma of caramel and smoke. He couldn't repress a confident chuckle. *Perhaps she really does have an assignment for me. If so, it will be a six-figure fee, and one can never have too many of those. Perhaps I will collect the fee while adding another nail to Magnolia's coffin.*

A neighborhood Yoigo store provided cheap, pre-paid phones. Hawke bought a half dozen, all with caller ID and recording capabilities. He would use these to communicate with Magnolia from now on. He needed to get rid of the phone on which she'd left her message.

He checked his watch, calculated the time in Boston, then dialed Magnolia's number. His call wasn't picked up. He left a message.

"Magnolia, it is so good to hear your voice," he said in his syrupy, heavily accented voice. "I am so sorry for what you are going through, but happy to hear that you are still in need of my service. It suggests that your circumstances may not be so dire as the news media reports. I look forward to your return call."

He dialed a second number.

"Isabella? I am sorry to remove you from the amiable Florida climate, but I must send you to chilly Boston. Ms. Kanaranzi again needs our attention."

HAM AND TONI

Ham leaned forward, the tip of the brush that was clenched between his teeth touching the canvas. A fine frost-green arc, approximately an inch long, appeared as the brush tip moved in unison with his head. He repeated the effort four times, then pivoted his wheelchair and deposited the brush in a can partially filled with water. He turned back to look at the canvas. The first of the arcs had already dried. It blended into the elegant gown worn by the woman in the painting, providing the initial effect of faint shadows caused by folded fabric.

His studio, located on the top floor of their three-story brownstone, was the only calm place in the house. Through the open studio door, he could hear people moving about on the floor below, packing in preparation for their move back to Minnesota, back to where he had grown up, gone to college, met his wife Toni, and had been beaten within an inch of his life.

The assault had put him in a coma for weeks, in the hospital for nearly a year, and in a wheelchair for the rest of his life. It happened a week after his grandmother was murdered, and the investigation by local police was cursory at best. Perhaps it was because at the time he was the prime suspect in his grandmother's murder, or perhaps it was because of the color of his skin. Regardless of the reason, the person responsible for the beating had never been identified.

Remarkably, Toni stuck with him through it all. She even proposed to him at a time when he was struggling to recover, when most partners would have bailed out of the relationship. The adversity had welded them into a solid team.

Now they were moving because Ham had accepted a position as a roving lecturer with MnSCU, the umbrella organization governing 37 colleges and universities located in Minnesota. His job included teaching week-long seminars focused on art forgery and forgers, a subject with which he had become well-acquainted. In the decade before the attack left him a quadriplegic, he had been one of the country's premier art copiers.

The job opportunity stemmed from an invitation Ham and Toni had accepted from Jim Benson, an old friend and mentor of Toni's from her time in the art history doctoral program at the University of Minnesota. The invitation to give a series of lectures on art forgery ironically came at a time when Ham and Toni were embroiled in a scandal claiming they had sold a forged painting to the Boston Museum of Visual Arts, Toni's former employer. The lectures were a rousing success, and Benson reached out to Ham and Toni about a full-time position. A week later, they were planning their move.

Coincidentally, they were moving back to Minnesota at the same time his estranged mother was facing extradition to Minnesota to stand trial for murder.

The tail of Ham's faithful golden retriever, Barca, drummed the floor as Toni stuck her head through the doorway. "They'll be done packing in about an hour," she said. "What do you want me to order in for dinner?"

"Pizza," he said. "The usual."

"Perfect," Toni replied as she walked across the room to pet Barca. "We can eat in front of the TV. That and the couch are the only things left in the living room." Barca rolled on his back so Toni could scratch his belly.

"When are they moving the furniture?"

"The day we leave. They'll move it to the storage unit in Minneapolis until we find a permanent place." Toni looked up from Barca's tummy, and her eyes drifted to the painting in front of Ham. "That's coming along nicely," she said, standing up.

Ham cast a critical eye toward his work.

"You're amazing," she said. "Don't be so hard on yourself." She leaned over and kissed his cheek. Her frizzy orange hair tickled against his skin. Ham leaned his head against Toni, feeling her warmth. They stayed that way for a moment."

"I'll go order pizza," she said, breaking the mood and turning to leave. "Oh, I almost forgot. Magnolia is holding a press conference tomorrow night. I just heard about it on the radio; thought you'd like to know. Speculation is that she is going to resign her Senate seat."

EXTRADITION

The cozy theater was packed, as planned. Scores of reporters, both local and national, were squeezed in with hundreds of supporters who had been recruited to fill the gallery. Hundreds more with opposing views and picket signs lined Commonwealth Avenue outside the theater. Uniformed police strolled up and down the street, making sure peace was kept.

Napoleon Taft tapped the microphone.

"Ladies and gentlemen, members of the press, thank you for coming today. My client, and your duly elected Senator, Magnolia Kanaranzi, has been in seclusion since her arrest. You can only imagine the shock and the trauma she has suffered from being charged with arranging the murder of her own mother.

"Senator Kanaranzi worked her way from the lowliest station in life to the pinnacle of the media world—a man's world. She has been a champion of women's rights throughout her journey…her struggle… and it was that steadfast adherence to the precept that women are equal, entitled to equal pay, equal treatment, equal respect, that was a primary reason she was elected as your United States Senator.

"To even think that someone as committed to the rights of women as she is could murder another woman is beyond belief. And for that woman to be her own mother…" Taft let the sentence dangle as he slowly wagged his head from side to side, a look of utter disbelief on his face.

"But enough from me," he continued. "The time has come for Senator Kanaranzi to speak out; to tell you her side of the story." He turned to the woman seated on a folding chair behind the podium. "Senator."

Magnolia slowly rose and walked to the bank of microphones amid flashing lights and buzzing from the crowd. She was stunning, despite intentionally dressing her petite frame conservatively to avoid giving the ever-critical media something else to criticize. Her silver-white hair was perfectly styled, and her nails were manicured to match her cerulean blue eyes. She stepped up on the riser and nodded slowly, acknowledging those in the theater.

"I did not love my mother," she started, her voice resolute.

The crowd collectively inhaled, shocked by her words.

"I didn't love her, but I respected her," Magnolia went on. "She had a hard life. She was a single mother, which made her a social outcast, particularly in the small town where we lived. She worked many jobs, including the farm I was raised on. She raised me. We didn't always get along, but I believe that it's because of the values she instilled in me as a youngster that I have succeeded in life.

"She was a strong woman with strict rules; rules I chafed under as a teenager. I left home after I graduated from high school, and we seldom spoke after that. The lifestyle that I chose, a decade of drugs and alcohol, was not something she could tolerate nor is it a choice of which I am proud. But when I showed up at her door with a child, she took that child in and raised him.

"Eventually, I came to my senses. I went to talk to her about my son, to take him back, but my mother did not believe I would be a good influence on my child, or that I was in a good position to raise a child. I could not disagree, and so by mutual agreement, I stayed out of my child's life and stopped communicating with them both. It was the most difficult choice I have ever had to make. To help temper my pain, I became absorbed in a new career. Eventually, my mother, and my child, faded from my life but never from my memory.

"When I learned of her passing, it had been more than a decade since I had last spoken to her. Unfortunately, I did not learn about her death until long after the funeral. I regret not being there. I regret not having a chance to say good-bye."

Magnolia paused, and members of the press started to yell questions. She held up her finely manicured hand to silence them.

"As I said at the beginning," she continued once the hubbub subsided, "I didn't love my mother, but I didn't kill her, or hire anyone to kill her. I do not know this criminal who is accusing me of this. I have never met this person, and I have certainly never hired him to do anything for me, much less kill my mother.

"Why this person would come out of nowhere, six years after my mother was murdered, admit to killing her, and then claim that I hired him to do it…it's incomprehensible. We can only speculate on his motives, but I am here to tell you I am innocent."

Cheers and standing applause from the gallery erupted and lasted for several minutes.

"Now I'll take questions," she said as the applause subsided.

A cacophony of questions rained down on her. She answered a few of them then excused herself. The press conference was over.

"Very good," Taft greeted her as they walked to a waiting car. "Nice touch, with the questions at the end. You showed them you aren't afraid; have nothing to hide. That always boosts credibility." He graced her with a dazzling smile.

Magnolia, exhausted from the stress of the news conference, just shook her head. "That's nice, but how does any of this make a difference?"

"Because legal defenses to extradition are generally ignored," Taft answered, "but the court of public opinion can have a miraculous effect on a judge's attention span or a Governor's willingness to cooperate. If the media reports the actual news, and not a bunch of speculation or opinions, it will give us a chance."

"What I hear you saying is that this was a Hail Mary," Magnolia sighed.

Hamilton sat in his wheelchair in the back of the theater, waiting for the crowd to clear. Toni nodded toward the stage. "It almost makes you want to believe her," she said, her emerald-green eyes flashing.

Ham understood why his wife loathed Magnolia Kanaranzi. They had clashed over a painting, Joan Miro's *The Reaper*. The conflict had cost Toni her job at the Boston Museum of Visual Arts, but it was more than that. For their entire marriage Toni had dealt with Ham's depression from being abandoned by his mother. Until recently, Ham's mother had only been an abstraction. Now that they knew Kanaranzi was his mother, Toni had a living target upon which to unleash her own frustration and anger.

Nevertheless, Toni's words made him wince. For the first time in 36 years, he allowed himself to think that maybe he hadn't been discarded like a bag of garbage. Maybe his mother did care about him and had abandoned him out of concern for his well-being.

He wanted to believe her. "She admitted I exist," he said earnestly. "That's a start. I'd like to meet her in person."

"You mean when she isn't being arrested for murder?" Toni regretted saying it the moment the words came out of her mouth. Ham's head dropped. "I'm sorry," she said.

"She's still my mother," Ham's voice cracked. "I need to know if she meant what she said today."

Their Uber came and they rode in silence until they arrived at 76 Worcester Street.

"It's weird that we're moving back to Minnesota at the same time they're trying to extradite her there," Ham said, breaking the silence while they waited for the driver to get his wheelchair from the back of the vehicle.

"No such thing as coincidences," Toni responded, "but with all the things we need to do in the next few days, maybe you should wait until we're back in Minnesota before reaching out to her."

Ham nodded. "I'm going to find out when the extradition hearing is. If she gets sent back to Minnesota, I'll wait. If she isn't extradited, then I'll try to meet her at the hearing or at least set up a time to meet with her before we leave."

"Magnolia was quite impressive at that press conference," Findley mused. "She certainly sounds like she has all her wits about her."

"I didn't see the press conference before I met with her, but I saw a recording afterwards," Dr. Robbins said. "It confirms what I observed in our session. There is nothing wrong with this woman's intellect or her ability to reason or communicate. I can write you the opinion letter you requested. She is entirely capable of fulfilling her duties as a Senator. She sure dislikes psychiatrists, though."

Findley chuckled. "I failed to warn you about that. I had a helluva time convincing her to meet with you."

"It doesn't matter. Once she found out I wasn't going to delve into her childhood, she thawed a little, and we got along fine. I will say this: she is extremely intelligent and accustomed to being in charge. She'll be a real firebrand in the Senate."

"If she ever gets there. What about the other thing; the loyalty question?"

Robbins shifted uncomfortably and scratched the back of his neck. "That's a little more difficult to determine. Her personality type tends to see things in black and white. She's very passionate about certain things – equal pay for women, gay rights, etcetera. As long as you're on her side of the issues that make her passionate, there is no doubt about her loyalty. And, if you support her on those issues, you can likely count on her loyalty on issues of which she is ambivalent or has no interest. The problem will come when you are on opposite sides of an issue of which she's passionate. It's unlikely she'll change her mind to your point of view for the sake of loyalty."

"And what if we cross her on an issue that's important to her?" Findley asked. "Will she hold a grudge, or can she let it slide and move on to the next issue?"

"I'd say she's likely to hold a grudge. She's not used to being second-guessed or having her opinions disregarded. In my estimation, there would be long-term effects if that were to happen."

An hour later, Findley was on a secure phone with his boss, reporting the results of his meeting with the psychiatrist. "According to Robbins, she's a lot like everybody else in the caucus, passionate about a few things and willing to go along on most everything else. There is a concern that if we have to ditch one of her pet projects it will spill over, but she's smart. She'll learn quickly."

"Sounds good," Styles responded. "Will Robbins issue an opinion that there's nothing wrong with her that would prevent her from carrying out her duties as a Senator?"

"We should have his opinion tomorrow. I'll distribute it to everyone in the caucus."

"And to the three, maybe four, across the aisle who have indicated reluctance to vote for expulsion," Styles added.

"Have you heard from Belton? Have they found a candidate?" Findley asked.

"Not yet. You need to follow up on that."

The more Findley learned about Kanaranzi, the more he thought, given the opportunity, she'd be a valuable member of the caucus. And she had won an election. Who knows what kind of candidate they'd get from the state party apparatus? Belton didn't sound confident they could field a winner.

Findley needed to find out which judge was handling Kanaranzi's trial and who had made the judicial appointment. It wouldn't hurt to give the judge a nudge in the right direction.

Magnolia scrambled into the bedroom, tossing clothes and towels out of the way as she searched for the ringing phone. Without a housekeeper, her penthouse, and particularly her bedroom, had begun to resemble a landfill. She found the phone on its last ring and tapped "accept."

"Hello."

"Magnolia. It is you. I have missed hearing your beautiful voice," purred Henri Hawke at his smarmy best. "I'm glad that we finally have connected."

"Hello, Henri. Thank you for calling me back. How are you?" she asked sweetly.

The question put Hawke on guard. She never asked, or cared for that matter, how he was. "I am doing well, but the more important question is, how are you?" he parried.

"You know about the murder charge."

"I do. I watch international news, and you have been a constant presence. I saw the highlights of your press conference. You were impressive."

"Thank you. We're fighting extradition," she said. "They want to send me back to Minnesota to stand trial."

"And that would be bad, why?"

"Because the trial would be in a small town. Conservative people. Built-in bias against wealthy Easterners. It would be much easier to find a sympathetic jury here in Boston where I'm known for more than a murder charge."

"And you called *me* because you think I can help?" Hawke asked feigning surprise.

"Are you available? I'm in a bit of a time crunch."

"Of course, I am always available to help you," Hawke responded in a playful tone. "Just remember, the difficult I do immediately. The impossible takes just a bit longer." He laughed at his own joke. "What is it you wish me to do?"

"I want you to blackmail my lawyer."

"What? Say again?" The playfulness was gone.

"I want you to blackmail my lawyer," Magnolia repeated slowly. "He needs to be motivated."

"How is it that you hired a bad lawyer?" Hawke responded, intentionally sounding concerned.

"He's supposedly the best criminal defense lawyer in the U.S., but he's become extremely passive in his approach to this extradition matter, and he's making noises that suggest he thinks I should take a plea deal."

Hawke was silent for a time.

"You still there?" Magnolia asked.

"Yes. Thinking. Thinking that this is not such a good idea; blackmailing your own lawyer. Even if we *motivate* him, there is no guarantee the judge will rule in your favor. Why not solve the problem more directly and motivate the judge instead?"

Magnolia smiled at how well she knew Hawke. He had done exactly as she had expected. He had made the plan his own and selected the judge as the target. In so doing, he had assured his own demise. "Can you be in Boston tomorrow?" she asked.

"*Oui*, Madam. I will call you when I get in, but first there is the matter of my fee."

"We can meet at my place," Magnolia countered. "We'll discuss the project, and I'll deliver your fee. Does $50,000 plus expenses cover it?"

"Under ordinary circumstances, yes, but a judge is involved, and one that is presiding over a case of very high profile. That puts any action I might take very close to the glare of the public spotlight. Under these circumstances, my fee is $100,000 and I'll cover my own expenses. You can wire it to my usual account. I'll book my flight as soon as the wire is confirmed."

Again, exactly as Magnolia had anticipated. "I'll wire it right away," she said.

"I assume you are under surveillance" Hawke said.

"Yes, I assume I am."

"Then we shall meet someplace discreet. When I get in, I will call you on this phone and send a car for you."

"Fine."

She massaged her temples after the call ended. Hawke's abundant caution was a tip-off that he suspected she was setting him up. But all his subterfuge would not save him. He'll never see it coming. *It's worth a hundred K to take down the smug little prick.*

The black SUV worked its way through the residential streets of south Boston, then picked up I-93 south. Twice it exited, only to return to the interstate a few blocks later. The driver, wearing sunglasses and a long-billed chauffeur's hat pulled low, checked constantly to see if they were being followed. They took the exit to Highway 3A.

"Where are you taking me?" Magnolia asked impatiently. "How much longer?"

"To meet Monsieur Hawke, of course." The driver replied. She spoke with a Spanish accent.

"I meant what location?"

"I will know in a few minutes," she answered. Magnolia looked at her watch: 3:10 p.m. Before she could ask another question, the driver's phone buzzed. "*Hola.*" The one side of the conversation Magnolia could hear was mostly grunts and head-nodding, then "*Adios.*" The SUV veered to follow a sign that read, "Hancock Street".

"Now can you tell me where we're going?" Magnolia asked in irritation.

"We'll be there in just a minute," the driver said. Less than five minutes later the SUV parked in front of a small bistro they had passed just minutes earlier. The driver opened the door for Magnolia.

A sign on the bistro door read, "Closed for Private Party."

Magnolia turned to the driver. "There must be some mistake," she said, motioning toward the sign.

"It is correct," the driver said, pointing at the door. "Go in. He's waiting for you."

Cautiously, Magnolia opened the door and stepped inside the dark restaurant. There were 50 or 60 empty chairs around a dozen tables. A bartender, visible behind a glass divider, was watching sporting events on multiple television sets mounted behind the bar. She could see a cook prepping food in the kitchen, bopping his head to the music from his headphones. Otherwise, the place appeared empty.

Magnolia's eyes adjusted to the dimly lit room as she scanned it a second time. Hawke appeared out of the shadows in a back corner. He rose to greet her. "Welcome to our little party," he said.

"Quaint little spot," she replied, taking a seat at the table, opposite Hawke.

"Secluded, if inconvenient. One cannot be too careful. Would you like something?"

She asked for a glass of Sauvignon Blanc, preferably from New Zealand. Hawke went to the bar, giving Magnolia an opportunity to check the table and chairs for bugs. She found none.

"I must apologize," Hawke said moments later as he handed Magnolia a glass of wine.

"For what?"

"For Otto. I do not know if you know this, but he confessed to killing your mother. I am so sorry."

The apology caught Magnolia completely off guard. Bonhoffer was supposed to be the invisible 800-pound gorilla in the room, and Hawke had just pulled back the curtain. "I know he confessed to killing my mother, but why would he implicate me?" she asked, trying to sound perplexed while mentally scrambling to understand Hawke's strategy.

Hawke raised his eyebrows apologetically. "I do not know why he implicated you, or why he killed your mother," he said. "What he did…has done…he did on his own."

"But what would be his motive?"

"I do not know, although, in recent months I have seen signs of, shall we say, instability. I was about to terminate him when he confessed."

"Aren't you worried?"

"About what?"

"Him turning on you?"

A self-confident smirk spread across Hawke's round face, making Magnolia think of the Cheshire Cat.

"What is it you would like me to do for you?" he asked, changing the subject.

"Does that smile suggest that he will be taken care of?" Magnolia asked, refusing to let go of the Bonhoffer topic.

"I am sure I do not know what you mean," he said, the smirk morphing into a broad smile. "And what of this new assignment?"

"I would like you to do a background check on this man," she said, letting the issue of Bonhoffer go. Taking a picture out of her briefcase, she said, "This is Winthrop Stewart. He is the judge sitting on my case. His personal information is on the back of the photo. I want to know everything about him, including where every one of his skeletons are buried. And I need to know quickly because the extradition hearing is coming up next week."

"And what do you want me to do with this information?"

"Just gather it, and we can get back together on Sunday to discuss it further," she said.

"Very well," he agreed. "Three days should be sufficient."

Magnolia finished her wine, and Hawke escorted her to the waiting SUV.

"Until Sunday," he bowed slightly as she got in. "I will call you."

Magnolia's mind raced as she rode back to Pier 4. *Was Hawke telling the truth? Did Bonhoffer confess on his own without Hawke knowing? But why? Did he actually kill my mother? Would he confess to it if he hadn't done it? Was it to frame me, and who would want to frame me other than Hawke?*

She nodded, agreeing with herself, then stopped, a concerned look crossing her face. She ticked through a mental list of people related to her business, people she had crossed or double crossed. She did the same for the political side of her life. The list was long. *Whoever it is, what have they offered him that was enough for Bonhoffer to confess to a six-year-old crime? And how would they have even found him? Hawke has to be behind this.*

But she was no longer so certain.

Hawke returned to the table in the dark corner and sipped the last of his Pernod. *Little fool,* he thought. *Play innocent with me! She had to be wearing a wire, but she got nothing from me but an apology; nothing to implicate me in her mother's murder.*

On the other hand, she had not said anything incriminating about herself either. He took the pen from his vest pocket and slid the recorder button to "off." He would try again at their meeting on Sunday.

He swirled the last few drams of the Pernod as his thoughts drifted back to a phone call six years in the past. Like the call last Friday, it had come as a surprise. It had been less than two weeks after Arthur

Kincaid had died, and just four days after Magnolia had threatened, then fired Hawke.

Hesitantly, he had answered. She spoke as if nothing had happened, as if she had no recollection of firing or threatening him. Instead, she wanted him to do another job. She needed her mother "removed."

The job was one of the least risky he had ever been asked to arrange. So easy, in fact, that he could not refrain from asking her why. Magnolia, her voice immediately turning angry, had responded that Lorraine Blethen was a bad person, an obstacle. Hawke presumed she meant an obstacle to her ascent to the control of Kincaid Media, just like a previous "removal" for which she had hired him.

Bonhoffer had taken care of the project within a week, and legal authorities had never linked any of them to the crime.

However, his recollection of that phone call was clear as crystal. *Does she really not remember hiring me? Or is she acting, playing the innocent, pretending to be shocked that Bonhoffer implicated her in the murder. Surely, she expected to be recorded. Perhaps she anticipated the apology. Is she really that good?*

On Sunday he would find out.

Hawke chalked his cue and carefully set a bridge on the red felt. "Seven ball in the side pocket," he announced, then deftly stroked the cue: a click, and then the pleasant sound of the ball settling into the leather mesh pocket. The cue ball traveled the length of the eight-foot table, kissed off the cushion and rolled to a stop behind the eight ball, giving Hawke a straight shot at a corner pocket.

"I know you didn't come all the way to Boston to spend the afternoon losing money to me playing nine-ball," Hawke chided his opponent. "To what do I owe the pleasure?"

"The pleasure is all mine," a well-tanned Todd Vanderbilt laughed. "When I learned you were in the States, I couldn't resist the opportunity to take your money."

Hawke lined up the eight ball and called his shot, but this time, as the eight-ball dropped, the cue ball drifted too far, resting against the rail, leaving him a difficult shot on the nine.

"That's what I mean," Vanderbilt chortled, picking up his beer from a nearby high-top.

Hawke studied the table, walked to the opposite side and tilted his head. "I could play it safe," he mused, as if to himself, "but what is the challenge in that. I suggest we double the bet. If I make the shot, I win. If I miss, you win. You won't even have to make the nine."

Vanderbilt smiled. "Call your shot."

Hawke lined up the cue ball and announced, "Nine ball off the rail and into the side pocket." Stroke, click, bump and there was that sound again as the nine-ball nestled into the side pocket.

"Lucky shit," Vanderbilt groused. "Again? Double or nothing?"

"Let me enjoy my victory for a moment," Hawke chuckled, holding out his hand, "and feel some of that Washington, D.C. green."

Vanderbilt grudgingly pulled a money clip from his pocket, peeled off two hundred-dollar bills and handed them to Hawke.

"It is definitely *my pleasure*," Hawke chided, stuffing the bills in his pocket. He boosted himself up onto a tall stool and took a sip of espresso. Vanderbilt sat on the stool across from Hawke. It was two hours before the Carrie Nation Cocktail Club would open to the public. They were the only people in the billiard room.

"You didn't get that tan in D.C.," Hawke observed. "Florida?"

"Caribbean," Vanderbilt answered. "I've got a place in St. Thomas, and we spent January there. Ever been there?"

"No. I usually do not emerge until after dark, so the sun and I are strangers," Hawke joked. "I must keep a pale complexion to maintain my mysterious image. Besides, the Caribbean is too far away when I have the Mediterranean on my doorstep."

"Speaking of mysterious, I have a little mystery for you to solve, if you're interested," Vanderbilt said.

Hawke tilted his head, a quizzical look on his face.

"I got a call from a contact high up in the D.C. food chain. He's looking for a little help. I thought of you."

"And it is this D.C. person who is the source of the mystery?"

Vanderbilt nodded. "The mystery is how do you convince a judge to deny an extradition request."

"Isn't extradition fairly automatic?"

Vanderbilt nodded again.

"Ah, then a great mystery indeed. To solve such a mystery would come at great expense," Hawke said, trying to buy time to let his brain process what Vanderbilt had just said.

"The mystery has to be solved in five days," Vanderbilt said. "The good news is the mystery is right here in Boston."

"What a lovely coincidence. And I shall be in Boston for another week. Give me the clues, and I'll tell you if I can solve your mystery… and at what price."

They settled on $75,000 as Hawke's fee for convincing The Honorable Winthrop Stewart to deny Minnesota's request to extradite Kanaranzi. Hawke would notify Vanderbilt of the wiring instructions once he had settled on a method to solve the mystery. "If, after a bit of investigation of the good judge, I do not believe it is possible to solve the mystery, I will let you know and there will be no charge. As an accommodation to an old friend," Hawke said.

He lost the next nine-ball game, his mind elsewhere busily making plans.

Hawke and Magnolia met again late Sunday afternoon at a coffee shop in Cambridge, after another long, circuitous drive from Pier 4. Magnolia was dressed in jeans and sneakers and wore tinted glasses. She looked like a student with her hair tucked up under a baseball cap. Hawke was uncharacteristically dressed in a herringbone tweed jacket and matching flat cap. He was already seated with his back to a wall as far from the barista as possible. His college professor charade was completed by an open laptop in front of him.

"You should order something," Hawke suggested, raising his mug as Magnolia approached the table. "We need to look like regulars." She looked around. There were, perhaps, a dozen other patrons.

"What have you found out?" she asked a few minutes later as she put her cup on the table and sat down.

"Your gentleman friend has quite the history," Hawke said, turning his laptop so the screen faced Magnolia. A photo of Judge Stewart and accompanying story was on the screen.

"I hope you've done more than search the internet," she scolded. "*I* could have done that."

"You will not find this picture or the story on the internet," Hawke replied, unruffled. "Only a very small portion of the information I have for you is public knowledge."

"Well?"

"First, Judge Stewart has aspirations. He is the Chief Judge of the District Courts. He desires to be appointed to the Supreme Judicial Court. I tell you this because this makes him vulnerable.

"Second, while in college young Mr. Stewart impregnated two different women, both of whom had abortions. Both abortions were paid for by Stewart's family. One of the women was a fellow student from a prominent family. The other was a 40-year-old assistant professor. There are insinuations that in neither case was the sex consensual, and both required a substantial six-figure payoff.

"To the best of my knowledge, these events have been kept secret from Stewart's wife, whom he married after law school and with whom he has three children. The youngest still lives with them. The two older children are students at expensive colleges, but the Stewarts, by all appearances, live a frugal, unremarkable life.

"There is no history of any further indiscretions of a sexual nature since he has been on the bench. His reputation as a judge is estimable, although he takes great care not to render decisions that might be reversed on appeal, and he appears to avoid conflict wherever possible. He is generally popular with the other District Court Judges.

"Finally, his political persuasion is opposite of you. He was appointed by Governor Rowland and is a friend of your current governor."

Hawke picked up his coffee mug and took a sip, making a face because it was cold. He turned the laptop back so the screen faced him.

"Do you have a plan?" Magnolia asked.

"Of course."

"It had better be more effective than the Feldman project."

"I had nothing to do with that. It was totally Bonhoffer."

"I hired..." Magnolia snapped, the decibel level beginning to rise.

Hawke interrupted, placing an index finger over his lips. "It is not only corn that has ears," he said.

Judge Winthrop Stewart was a creature of habit. He woke up at 5:30 a.m. every morning, ran three miles through the Fens, and then peddled a stationary bike for a half hour while reading the morning newspapers and drinking a smoothie of yogurt, avocado, honey, chia seeds, and two raw eggs, a recipe he had personally concocted. After a steam and a shower, he had coffee with his wife and daughter, then left for court at exactly 8:00 a.m.

On this particular Tuesday morning, scattered snowflakes floated in the air, harbingers of the heavier snowfall predicted to start later in the morning. He was already a half mile into his run and had yet to see another runner. *Wimps,* he thought as he rounded a bend in the running path. Ahead, a woman in running gear lay crumpled on the grass between the jogging path and the parkway. She was not moving. He sprinted to her. "Are you alright?" he asked.

The woman didn't respond, so he retrieved his phone from a pocket and dialed 9-1-1. Suddenly a black SUV pulled up at the curb. A man rolled down the passenger window and asked in a thick accent, "Can I be of any help?"

As Stewart looked up, the woman on the ground said, "I'll take that."

He looked back down. Aimed directly at his chest, was a very business-like handgun. Her other hand snatched his phone out of his hand. "Get in the car," she ordered, in a calm Spanish-accented voice. Stewart's mind raced, trying to think of any ruling he'd issued that might make him a target of a cartel or Hispanic gang.

"I…"

"Get in the fucking car or I'll shoot you right here," she snarled, getting to her feet. She jerked open the rear door of the SUV. Stewart frantically looked around for help.

"Now!"

The judge, with a shove from the gun barrel in his back, lurched into the back seat. He righted himself and was shocked to see the man who had offered him help a moment ago was now sitting next to him in the back seat. A black fedora was pulled low to obscure the man's face. The woman shut the door, walked to the front of the SUV and got in the driver's seat. She pulled away from the curb. The whole incident had taken less than a minute.

"Sorry to disrupt your morning run, Your Honor, but I need your undivided attention, and circumstances dictate the need for haste," the man said. The silky voice's accent was not Hispanic, but a mix of French and something Stewart couldn't identify. Short and rotund, the man held a handgun, a smaller caliber than the one used by the woman but nevertheless imposing. "There is a small business proposition that needs to be discussed. It will take only a few minutes, and we will have you back on your run in no time."

"Do you realize what you're doing, who you're kidnapping?" Stewart hissed, anger replacing shock.

The man cut in. "No. No. No. Not kidnapping. Just inviting you to an unscheduled business meeting. The longer you protest, the longer it will be before you're back to your morning routine, so please listen."

Stewart glowered at him. "I'm listening."

"There is an extradition hearing before you this Thursday, involving a newly elected U.S. Senator. You will deny the extradition."

"Why would…"

The man raised his gun. "Listen."

The judge sat back in the seat.

"There are valid legal reasons that this case should not be removed to Minnesota, and I'm here to provide you an incentive to listen closely to those reasons.

"I have in my possession statements from two women you impregnated. They attest to the fact that your family paid them large sums of money for abortions and for their silence. Those statements will stay in my possession as long as you rule against extradition on Thursday. I'm sure I do not need to remind you the undesirable impact the release of those statements would have on your chances to be appointed to the Supreme Court, not to mention the betrayal, grief, and distrust it would cause your wife and children.

"The sworn statements are what I choose to call your negative incentive. But there is also a positive incentive; the sum of $75,000 has been deposited in your bank account in the Cayman Islands."

Stewart looked shocked. "I don't…"

"Oh, but you do. It was opened in your name just in time to receive the wire transfer." The man handed Stewart a folded slip of paper. "Here is the account information and a link you can use when you get home to confirm that the funds are deposited and available for your use. No one needs to know about this account except you and me and the bank, and they are very discreet…unless I tell them not to be."

The SUV turned off the parkway and stopped a half block from the jogging path.

"Are we understood?" the man asked.

"I will not be bribed or threatened…"

"What you do is entirely up to you, but you are an intelligent man. I'm sure you understand the consequences."

The woman opened the SUV door, her body shielding from onlookers the gun she kept pointed at Stewart. "Get out," she ordered.

As Stewart slid out the door, the man's words followed him. "We'll be watching with great interest what happens on Thursday."

"My phone?" Stewart asked.

"We'll keep that," the woman said with a wicked smile. "Perhaps we have more to learn about you."

Stewart stared at the monitor in his study. Just as the kidnapper had said, the funds were deposited in a bank account bearing his name. If it was just the money, he could deal with it. He'd report it, have the account investigated, and find out who these people are. But the statements from the two women were something else. He hadn't thought about that for years. He had insisted on the abortions. There had been drugs involved in the first episode, a one-time affair in which he had been physically aggressive. And the second; he just shook his head miserably. Considering his pro-life rulings in abortion cases, at best he would be branded a hypocrite. It would cost him the Supreme Court for sure and maybe his District Court seat. He didn't even want to think about what it would do to his marriage and family.

He got to work uncharacteristically late, and he spent the day distracted. He abruptly adjourned at 4:30 p.m. and returned to his office and a pile of phone messages. One was from the office of the local U.S. Attorney. *This day continues to be full of surprises,* he thought. He returned the call, but it was after hours, and he got a voice message.

When his wife asked him that evening what was bothering him, he just said "tough day" and mentioned the odd phone message from the U.S. Attorney. He did not mention his disturbing meeting in the black SUV.

He slept fitfully that night and decided to skip his morning run, spending an extra half hour on the stationary bike instead. He arrived at the courthouse early and returned the call to the U. S. Attorney's office. The call was brief. Stewart hung up, thought for a moment, then placed a call to Napoleon Taft.

"Counselor," he began when Taft picked up the call, "this call is a bit out of the ordinary, but I thought you should know that I just received a courtesy call from the U.S. Attorney letting me know that if your client is not remanded to Minnesota for trial, he intends to bring federal charges."

Two hours later Taft sat in an anteroom across the hall from the courtroom, drumming his fingers on the table. He checked his watch, then compared it to the clock on the wall. Both indicated it was less than 15 minutes until the extradition hearing was to start, and Magnolia was *in absentia.*

"Check the courtroom again," he said to Avery. "We can't make a decision without her."

The call from Judge Stewart had added yet another ingredient to the already complicated stew in which the extradition of Magnolia simmered, putting the normally confident Taft on edge. His argument, based on interpretation of Article IV, Section 2, of the U.S. Constitution, was already on life support. At best, it might give Stewart something to hang his opinion on, if the judge was inclined to deny the extradition request. But federal prosecution brought with it the specter of incarceration without bail and, even worse, opened the door to a death-penalty sentence if Magnolia were to be convicted.

Taft was no longer certain that opposing extradition was a good idea.

In any event, he couldn't make that decision without consulting with his client who, with only minutes until the hearing, had yet to make an appearance.

His assistant returned, shaking her head. No sign of their client.

If she doesn't show, he'll grant extradition, Taft thought, *but he'll also have to revoke her bail and issue a bench warrant, making her a fugitive.* The ramifications for future proceedings were unpredictable, and none of them were good.

With two minutes to go before the hearing was to start, Taft stood up. "Let's go," he said to Avery.

At that moment the anteroom door opened and Magnolia calmly walked in, followed by her press secretary, Samantha Jones, a Black woman a full head taller than the Senator. Jones apologized for being late.

"Magnolia, we have a new problem," Taft said. "Ma'am, I'll have to ask you to leave so I can discuss it with my client. Laura, please tell the clerk that we need a couple of minutes before the hearing starts."

As soon as they were alone, Taft filled Magnolia in.

"The fact that they are threatening to bring federal charges, when there are state charges already pending, is a pretty strong indication that they think they have a strong case," Taft said. "There's a chance they might not seek the death penalty, but why risk it? I advise you to waive extradition."

"You've already got me convicted!" Magnolia flared.

"You need to understand the implications of this," Taft interrupted. "Facing a federal judge and federal prosecutors is a whole new ballgame. There won't be any deer-in-the-headlights from this group. They handle cases of similar magnitude all the time, and the publicity that will accompany a trial here in Boston will be sensational. Some prosecutor may want to use it as a springboard to become attorney general, and it certainly won't be good for your political career."

Taft's last statement got Magnolia's attention, but the glare on her face remained. "It's my recommendation that we withdraw our opposition to the extradition," he repeated.

Magnolia didn't respond.

"C'mon. We've got to go in."

As soon as they entered the courtroom, Magnolia saw him, Hamilton Blethen, sitting in his wheelchair at the end of the front row. She hesitated, then walked slowly forward. As she passed him, her head turned to look at his face.

Transfixed, she bumped into the gate that separated the judge, jury box, and counsel tables from the gallery; her eyes remained locked on him until the impact with the gate broke the spell. She reached down, pushed open the gate, and, with a youthful step, walked to the counsel table and sat down, settling on the chair like a feather. A pleasant expression washed over her face.

Judge Stewart was announced, and everyone in the courtroom stood until he took his seat behind the bench. The clerk called the case.

"We're here on Defendant's petition to deny extradition," he said. "Counsel, are you ready to proceed?"

"A moment, Your Honor to confer with my client, please," Taft said.

Stewart nodded, and Taft turned to Magnolia, whispering, "Do you agree to withdraw our petition?"

Magnolia looked at him and smiled. "I think that would be great," she said. "I'd love to go back to Minnesota."

"Are you okay?" he asked.

"I'm fine. Great."

Taft stood up. "Your Honor, at this time Defendant withdraws her petition and waives extradition. We request that, considering the circumstances, she be given 48 hours to put her affairs in order before she is bound over."

The judge addressed Magnolia directly. "Senator Kanaranzi? Do you agree to waive extradition?"

She looked uncertain.

Taft whispered, "You have to answer the Judge."

"What was the question?"

"Do you agree to waive extradition?" the judge repeated.

"Oh. Yes. Of course."

Defendant's waiver meant he didn't have to deny extradition. Withdrawal of the petition left him nothing to rule upon. Judge Stewart exhaled in relief. He realized he had been holding his breathe.

As the hearing wrapped up, his thoughts wandered. *Will it make any difference to the kidnappers that she voluntarily waived extradition? Kanaranzi is still going to Minnesota to stand trial, and the people that didn't want that to happen might not care about the legal nuances. I'll give the money back. Maybe that will satisfy them.*

But The Honorable Winthrop Stewart had no idea how to contact the kidnappers.

48 HOURS

It was his enduring hope, rekindled at Magnolia's press conference, that had propelled Ham to attend the extradition hearing, but she had gaped at him like he was a circus freak. His hope now lay dashed in figurative splinters on the courtroom floor where his glazed eyes were fixed.

"Are you all right?" Ham looked up at the uniformed bailiff standing on the other side of the half-wall. "You need a ride or something?"

"Oh. No. I'm going to catch a cab."

The bailiff nodded and turned away. Hamilton didn't move. Sadness clung to him like a cocklebur as he thought back over his life... all the way back to when he was four years old and his mother walked away. She had discarded him and never looked back. Now, 36 years later, nothing had changed. Everything she said at the press conference, about the pain she felt for abandoning him, was nothing but B.S. Even when she passed him on her way out of the courtroom, she had refused to look at him, discarding him once more. She obviously doesn't care, or, worse yet, she saw him only as a grotesque reminder of her past.

A tear seeped out of one eye and cut a path down his dark cheek.

"I've got to lock up." The bailiff was back. Hamilton glanced at the clock and realized it had been a half hour since the extradition hearing had ended.

"Sorry," Ham said apologetically. "Could you help me on with my coat?"

The bailiff lifted Ham's coat off the back of the wheelchair and helped Ham get his arms in the sleeves, then tucked the back behind him as he leaned forward. The bailiff stepped back, then realizing he wasn't finished, leaned forward and fastened the Velcro straps that held the front of the coat shut.

"All set?" he asked, standing up.

"All set," Ham replied. "Thanks." He moved the joy stick, and his wheelchair did a one-eighty, then headed toward the courtroom door.

"Here, let me get that," the bailiff said, hustling past Ham to open it.

"Thanks. You're a godsend. Nice to know there are still people like you."

The bailiff smiled at the compliment as Ham wheeled out of the courtroom.

Magnolia's head moved in short, sharp jerks, as if she was seeing the back seat of the car for the first time. *How did I get here? What happened?*

"We should spend a few minutes when we get back to my office to talk about what happens next." Taft was sitting next to her. The car wove its way slowly through Boston traffic.

"I…I'd rather not. I'm not feeling well," Magnolia responded.

Taft turned to look at her and thoughtfully nodded. "We'll take you home, and we can talk about it tomorrow. Just remember, you have 48 hours to get everything in order before you have to turn yourself in."

They rode in silence until Taft spoke again. "You do understand what happened at the hearing today, though, don't you?"

"Of course," she said curtly. She tried to force herself to remember. She remembered walking into the courtroom, and seeing…what? A wheelchair? And a man…dark-skinned. *Her son.*

Then…nothing. *He was there. I know it. Why can't I remember anything after that?* She sat with her hands folded in her lap, not wanting to admit that she had no recollection of the hearing.

Magnolia scanned *The Globe* the following morning until she found a short story in the local section. "Kanaranzi Waives Extradition" the headline read. The story went on to say that the judge had given her 48 hours before she had to report to the Suffolk County sheriff where she would be bound over to Minnesota authorities for extradition back to the state where she has been charged with conspiracy to commit the murder of her mother, Lorraine Blethen.

She snatched the phone off the table and dialed Taft. "Tell me why we waived extradition," she demanded.

There was a pause on the other end. "Because the Feds were threatening to bring charges if you weren't extradited," Taft answered in a tone that suggested he was puzzled by Magnolia's question. "Not doing so would expose you to the death penalty."

"Is it too late to change my mind, to withdraw the waiver?"

"The judge has already issued the order," Taft answered.

"So, what happens now?" she snapped.

"We have a two o'clock appointment at the sheriff's office tomorrow. Come to my office at one, and we'll go there together."

This time it was Magnolia that paused. "What happens then?" she asked, her voice more contrite.

"A law officer from Minnesota will take you into custody, and you'll leave for Minnesota. I can't go there with you, but I'll send Laura."

"I presume we're flying?"

"I expect so. I don't think they would drive. The logistics of a two-day trip with you in handcuffs would be difficult," Taft answered.

"I will *not* be handcuffed like a common criminal!" Magnolia declared. "I will *not* be stared at by the common riffraff like I'm some zoo animal. Do something about it."

She could hear Taft's audible sigh.

"Those things are beyond my control," he said. "Once you're bound over, the Minnesota law enforcement will make those decisions. I can make a request, but they don't have to follow it."

The thought of running crossed Magnolia's mind. She didn't have time to liquidate her stock holdings, but she could get her hands on several hundred thousand dollars in cash within 24 hours. *I could catch a plane. Hawke could get me a new identity. Work my way across the border to Mexico or South America.*

But she knew it was unrealistic. It would be giving up everything she had worked for: the Senate, Kincaid Media, her fortune. It would also be seen as an admission of guilt, and deep in her heart, she knew she was innocent.

"What about a private plane?" she said. "Kincaid Media has two jets, and I'm still the biggest shareholder of the company. I'm sure I could get access to one of those."

"I can ask," Taft said carefully. "How many people do they seat?"

"Eight. Ten. Something like that," she answered. "Unless the press is coming along, it should be big enough, and I, or rather, Kincaid Media, will pay for it."

"No press," Taft said. "I'll ask. If they can save the cost of commercial airline tickets, they might go for it."

Magnolia's phone buzzed, indicating she had another call. It was her press secretary.

"I have another call I have to take," she said to Taft. "I'll call you later to confirm the private plane."

She hung up and picked up the call from Samantha.

"Cheryl Belton would like to talk to you," she said. "She'd like to do it in person, if possible. I told her that was unlikely, but that I'd call you."

"What does she want?"

"Wouldn't tell me."

"Hmm. Now, what would the state party chair want to talk about that would require an in-person meeting?" Magnolia mused. "I'm sure it's not to deliver a going away gift."

"If I were to guess, I would guess she's going to ask you to endorse a successor," Samantha said.

"Call her back. Tell her if that's her purpose, I have no intention of resigning nor of endorsing anyone to succeed me. If that's not her purpose, give her my number and tell her to call me. On another subject, I'm being delivered to the cops tomorrow at 2:00. Set up a news conference at the Suffolk County Sheriff's office at 1:30 and have our own camera crew there. We can use this to show how I believe in the rule of law and that I will be vindicated. Have our crew shoot everything. We'll put it in the archives. We'll find a use for it later."

Now, Magnolia thought after hanging up, *what should I wear tomorrow, and what should I pack?*

She was busily filling two suitcases, a carry-on and a large cosmetic case when her phone rang. Caller ID said it was Cheryl Belton.

"What in hell happened?" Vanderbilt's voice was shrill.

"It appears that she voluntarily waived extradition," Hawke answered. "She has not returned my call, so I do not yet know why she changed her mind."

"You didn't know she was going to do that?"

"No," he answered. "Apparently, neither did Judge Stewart. My courtroom observer said the good judge looked surprised and his skin color went from gray to pink. He looked relieved."

"So, you think he was going to rule against extradition?"

"My observer said it appeared that is how he intended to rule. Magnolia's action caught him off guard. It may have allowed him to escape an ethical dilemma."

"What about the money?" Vanderbilt whined.

"The money was used."

"All of it?"

"Every cent," Hawke said. "I was not keeping any for myself. It did not seem right to take money from an old friend, unless it is over a game of nine ball."

"I want it back," Vanderbilt fumed, not acknowledging Hawke's humor. "He didn't even have to rule on the extradition."

"Retrieving it would be messy," Hawke reminded him. "It's not likely he'll give it up voluntarily, and we could risk being exposed. I think it would be wise to leave it as is."

"I'm not accustomed to giving away $75,000 for nothing!"

"Oh, come now," Hawke scolded soothingly. "In your line of business, $75,000 is chump change. Your clients squander more than that on military toilet seats. Think of this as a deposit for future favors. It is always good to have a judge in your pocket, particularly one that is likely to be sitting on the state Supreme Court soon, perhaps, even on the U.S. Supreme Court at some future time."

Vanderbilt was silent for a long time.

"What's to stop Stewart from going to authorities and saying that someone tried to bribe him?" he asked. "He could make himself look like a hero."

"He will not do that. Money is not the only leverage we have over Judge Stewart. There are past indiscretions that, if made public, would ruin him. Trust me. He will not go to the authorities."

The last thing Vanderbilt felt at the moment was trust for Hawke. He was sure that the smooth-talking Frenchman was scamming him and keeping the money for himself.

"What kind of indiscretions?" he probed.

"The kind young men make when alcohol and testosterone are mixed," Hawke answered.

"I want specifics. I paid you for specifics."

Hawke rolled his eyes. "You are being petulant, my friend. For the record, you did not pay me for details. You paid me to convince Judge Stewart to rule against extradition. I did that, but because of circumstances beyond our control, that ruling was taken out of his hands. That is not my failing. What I *will* provide you is a link so that you can see that the entire fee is in an offshore account in Judge Stewart's name."

Vanderbilt was still grumbling as they ended the video call.

Hawke knew it would not be the last time he heard about this. He would send Vanderbilt an account statement with the bank name and account number redacted. It would infuriate his OCD friend, but it would also prevent Vanderbilt from accessing the account. Eventually he would get over it. After all, it was not his money. And, eventually, Hawke *would* close the account and move the money.

So naïve, these Americans. Thinking I would create an account without a back door.

His bigger problem, for the moment, was Magnolia. He was not concerned about the $100,000 she had paid him. He had performed his part of the bargain and earned his fee. *She* had voluntarily changed the outcome, and that was the problem. She had become erratic. Erratic people make mistakes. Mistakes, in Hawke's line of business, have dire consequences.

"Good God! What was she thinking?" The distress in Styles' voice was a thin veneer over his anger. "She has no understanding of what she's done."

Findley stood in his boss's office, waiting for the words and emotions of the Senate Minority Leader to subside. "It's unfortunate," Findley said after a moment. "I wish Belton had consulted with us before asking Magnolia to resign. Particularly since I had assured Magnolia, we would have her back. But…," Findley raised his index finger to emphasize his point. "…there may be an opportunity here."

"How is that possible."

"First of all, I'm quite certain that Belton's overture was turned down flat. If I read Magnolia correctly, her first reaction was hostile. Her second would be a sense of betrayal, followed by a mix of anger and sadness. What better way to assure the new Senator's loyalty than to come to her aide at her darkest hour?"

"And how would we do that?" Styles asked.

"You would have to do it, personally," Findley answered. "Belton's ill-advised action killed any credibility I might have with Magnolia, but if *you* were to reach out to her with assurances of support *and* a promise that Belton will be removed as the head of the state party, I'm sure she would be forever grateful."

"I don't have the authority to remove a state party chair," Styles objected.

"But you do have influence with the national party. They can bring pressure on her to resign."

"Belton made a mistake, but I'm not sure it's enough to marshal the support of the national party to force her resignation. Besides, some of the national committee might actually agree with her that Magnolia should resign."

"Brad, this is not your garden variety mistake," Findley countered. "This one has national implications." He stopped and fixed the minority leader with a serious look. "You can persuade them that we need a united front on this. We can't have loose cannons running around with their own agenda, threatening the very existence of the party…of the nation."

Findley let the words sink in, then continued, "Particularly if their own agenda wants an elected Senator removed so that they can take her place."

"What?"

"There's a rumor that Belton tried to get Magnolia to resign so that she, Belton, could run for the vacant seat."

"What?" Styles sputtered, stunned at his chief of staff's revelation. "Where…"

"That rumor," Findley interrupted, "will make its first public appearance in the five o'clock news cycle."

Also appearing in the five o'clock news cycle were snippets of Magnolia's press conference. Dressed in blue Armani to accent her eyes with matching Jimmy Choo spiked heels that made her four inches taller than her five-foot-nothing height, she again declared her innocence and her belief that justice would prevail.

What wasn't on the evening news, although it was captured by her own film crew, was Magnolia's shock when her phone was confiscated, and she was informed that she could not take her luggage.

Firmly guided by a no-nonsense female deputy sheriff from Minnesota, Magnolia was led to a waiting police SUV, taken to Logan Airport and guided onto a Delta Airlines plane for the flight to Minnesota. Handcuffed.

INCARCERATION

"All rise."

The bailiff stood stiffly, as starched as his uniform, and announced the arrival of Judge Susan Weber. Judge Weber swept into the courtroom, her black robe billowing behind her like smoke from a tire fire. She stopped for a moment, posing, peering over her gold-framed pince nez glasses at the packed gallery; then, with a flounce, settled into the over-sized leather chair behind the bench. She fixed the defense attorneys with a cold stare and leaned closer to the microphone.

"Please be seated," she commanded. "Calling case number 17-CR-1327, *State vs. Magnolia Kanaranzi.* This is a First Appearance. Counsel, please note your appearances for the record."

"Lawrence Bunch, County Attorney for Goodhue County, for the people, your honor."

"Napoleon Taft for the defense, your honor. With me is my colleague, Laura Avery."

The mention of Taft's name caused a stir in the packed courtroom. His notoriety as one of the most adroit and cunning criminal defense attorneys in the country, along with his leading-man good looks, added yet another layer of excitement to what the media, in its usual hyperbolic over-reach, was calling

"The Trial of the Century." It was only fitting, one news channel talking head proclaimed, that Taft was the leader of the defense team in the first-ever murder trial of a U.S. Senator.

Weber rapped her gavel against the top of the bench. "There will be no outbursts or disorder from the gallery," she barked, "or I'll clear the courtroom. If Mr. Taft's presence proves to be too much of a disruption, we will hold this hearing in chambers!"

Taft acknowledged the statement with a nod to the judge. It was not the first time a small-town judge had felt the need to establish their superiority in a trial made notable by Taft's presence.

Magnolia sat between Taft and Avery and sized up the judge: arched eyebrows over piercing dark eyes, kinky salt-and-pepper hair that appeared to defy taming, and a voice with sharp edges. At age 60, she was a contemporary of Magnolia but they looked nothing alike.

Ordinarily, Magnolia's out-spoken advocacy for women's rights and gender equality would earn her favor from a woman judge, but this judge was unpredictable. "Weber is a bit unconventional," Taft had understated it.

Weber ran her courtroom with an iron fist and a penchant for the dramatic. Having her as the presiding judge in what likely would become a clash between alpha females troubled Magnolia. If they had been on equal footing, she would have relished a head-on battle with the pretentious judge, but these circumstances required cunning, not confrontation.

A confident smile crept across Magnolia's face. She was good at cunning.

The noise from the gallery subsided, and Weber informed Magnolia of her rights and the charges.

"You are charged under Minnesota Statutes, Section 609.175, Subdivision 2, subsection 2, and Subdivision 3, subsection 3, with conspiracy to commit murder in the first degree. Do you wish to enter a plea at this time?"

Taft stood up. "We wish to enter a plea at this time and waive the Rule 8 hearing, your honor." Magnolia, whose hands were restrained in handcuffs chained to the belt of her navy-blue prison uniform, struggled to stand. Taft placed a hand under her elbow.

"How do you plead?" Weber asked, looking directly at Magnolia.

"Not guilty," Magnolia stated defiantly.

The Judge flipped through papers on her desk, leaned over and said something to the clerk, and then returned her attention to the lawyers. "My first open date for an Omnibus Hearing is March 5th. Does that fit on your calendars?"

"I am available," Bunch answered.

"I will be in trial that week, and the next, your honor," Taft answered.

"Under our rules, Mr. Taft, we have to set a hearing date within 42 days of today. That means we have only until March 15 to hold the hearing." The judge's tone was one of sarcastic annoyance. "It is lucky for your client that there are multiple lawyers in your office. I will set the hearing for Friday, March 13, at 2:00 p.m. Either you, or one of your associates, will need to be present. Mr. Bunch, does that work for you?"

The tall, gaunt county attorney nodded.

"And for you?" she said, directing her question to Taft.

"Yes, your honor," Taft said with a staged smile. "We will make it work."

"Now, as for release of the prisoner," Weber continued, "I am setting bail at one hundred million dollars."

"What!" Taft bellowed. "That's ridiculous…," he gasped before composing himself. "That is unprecedented, your honor."

Weber cut off his protest. "There *is* no precedent for this trial. The defendant is a U.S. Senator. She has immeasurable wealth. She has international connections and far-ranging influence. She is definitely a flight risk. In addition to that, four months ago, she allegedly shot and killed a man; shot him eleven times. *Allegedly*, she first hired someone to kill this same man, but that attempt failed. Why that case has not been prosecuted, I do not know, and it is not my concern. What *is* my concern is that the charge in this case has allegations that, if proven, are uncomfortably similar. There's a pattern here that leads me to believe that the Defendant is a flight risk. For those reasons, bail is set at one hundred million dollars. This hearing is adjourned."

Weber rapped the gavel hard against the bench's wooden surface, rose, and left the courtroom in a flurry.

Taft turned to the prosecuting attorney. "We're going to appeal that," he snarled as he pushed documents into his briefcase.

"How do we get a different judge?" Magnolia hissed through clenched teeth.

"Let's get you out of here first," Taft replied. "Then we'll deal with the judge."

"I have $10 million I can get my hands on quickly," Magnolia said. "I can bond out of this."

"No one's going to issue a $100 million bond, even if you could come up with half of it. Weber knew that when she set bail."

Two deputies approached the table, interrupting the conversation. "Time to go," one of them said. Magnolia turned on them but suppressed an angry retort before it came out. She exhaled. *Cunning, not confrontation,* she thought. She forced a half smile.

"I'll meet with you tomorrow," Taft called as she was led out of the courtroom.

The tunnel leading from the courthouse back to the jail was a half-block long, but it felt like a mile. Its bleak, gray cement block walls, gray concrete floor, and harsh lighting lent a stark, hopeless feeling.

"They should paint the floor green," Magnolia said. "Like in that movie, *The Green Mile.*" The two deputies who sandwiched her didn't respond. Their footsteps beat a staccato click-click-slap rhythm; the deputies' heels countered by the slap of the flip-flops Magnolia wore as part of her prison uniform. The sound echoed, bouncing back at them at the point in the tunnel where it turned left into more dreariness.

Although it took less than five minutes, it felt like an eternity before the deputies guided Magnolia through the reddish-brown metal door and into the women's section of the jail. Several inmates, lounging in the day room, stared at Magnolia as she was led through the common area.

Another of the reddish-brown security doors was unlocked, and Magnolia entered the A Unit where Goodhue County housed the occasional celebrity who ran afoul of the law within its borders. A third security door was unlocked, and Magnolia entered her personal space, a room approximately 12-feet square with a single bed, stainless steel sink and toilet, designated wall area (gray, of course) where photos or other mementoes could be attached, and a narrow, frosted vertical window which let in a bit of natural light. Goodhue County did not pamper its celebrity inmates.

Free of her handcuffs and the deputies, Magnolia sat on the edge of the sparse mattress. *I had Hawke go after the wrong judge,* she thought unhappily.

"I should probably go visit her."

Toni had watched her husband struggle for years over his abandonment by his mother. "You…we…have enough on our plate right now, don't you think?" she said.

They were in the process of cramming the contents of their three-story Boston brownstone into the two-bedroom apartment they had rented as a temporary Minneapolis landing spot. The unpacking and continual clutter ratcheted up the stress they were already feeling from moving across the country with a wheel chair and a golden retriever, and looming on the horizon was Toni's search for a job, Ham's preparation for his new duties as traveling art lecturer for the Minnesota State University system, and the search for a permanent home.

The cherry on the top of the stress sundae was the unresolved issue of *The Reaper.* While they had put physical distance between themselves and the klieg lights of the Boston arts community, the specter of litigation over the authenticity of *The Reaper* hung over their daily lives.

In Toni's opinion, adding another confrontation, or disappointment, between Ham and his mother was an additional stressor they didn't need.

"Do you think she'll even agree to see you?" she asked when Ham didn't respond. "She's never wanted to before," she added gently.

Ham let out an audible sigh and shook his head. He wanted to lash back at his wife, but what Toni said was true. He had been abandoned by his mother, then known as Mary Blethen, at age four. He had gone nearly 36 years without knowing the slightest thing about this mother, until a private investigation firm he had hired had dug up evidence that media mogul Magnolia Kanaranzi, one of the richest and most powerful women in New England, was his mother.

The first time they met face-to-face was the day she was arrested. She had fallen to the floor, curled into a fetal position, and plaintively cried out for help from her mother, the very person whom she was accused of killing. He wondered if her breakdown was because she saw him. Was having a dark-skinned, illegitimate child more than she could bear?

She spent several weeks in the hospital following her arrest. No visitors had been allowed, but now she was in the Goodhue County Jail in Red Wing, only an hour's drive south of Minneapolis.

"She's never been in prison before," Ham shrugged in response to Toni's question. "She might want someone to talk to."

"Oh, Ham. Don't do this out of guilt. You have nothing to feel guilty about. *She* abandoned *you*." Tears welled in Toni's green eyes, feeling her husband's pain.

He turned his wheelchair, looking for a place to be alone with his thoughts, but in the tiny apartment there was no place to go. He spun his chair back to face Toni, her usual dazzling freckled smile now a mask of sadness. "I'm going to take Barca for a walk," he said.

At the sound of his name, the golden retriever got up and ambled across the room, sitting at attention beside Ham's wheelchair. Toni helped Ham put on his coat and hat, then clipped the leash to Barca's collar. She opened the apartment door.

"I love you," she said softly as Ham wheeled through the doorway.

He nodded. "I love you, too." Barca obediently followed the wheelchair out of the apartment, his head down, instinctively feeling the anguish felt by his humans.

The bright sunshine and sharp February air pushed the gloom away. Ham squinted, wishing he'd brought his sunglasses. Barca used the first available snowbank to relieve himself.

"What do you think I should do, old boy?" he asked his shaggy companion. "Do I even want to know her? Is she really evil, or does she just hate me? How can she hate me? She doesn't even know me. Maybe she hates what I represent, a sordid past that she wants buried."

They rolled down the sidewalk, steam curling up from every word as Ham continued his monologue with Barca as his audience. By the time they circled the block they were both ready to go inside, but Ham paused to give Barca another opportunity to take care of business. Instead, Barca found interesting things to sniff in the snow.

"C'mon old boy. Time to go in." Barca looked up and wagged his tail. "*You* know me, don't you, old boy." Ham reached out and ruffled Barca's fur. The big dog returned the affection by putting his chin on Hamilton's knee, his brown eyes looking up at his master with unquestioned adoration.

"Barca has advised me that I need to visit my mother," Ham said as he accepted Toni's help with his coat. "I need answers to questions, and the only way to get them is to confront her."

Toni poured them both a cup of apple cider from the kettle steaming on the stove, then sat at the table opposite Ham.

"Can I suggest something?" she asked.

"Of course. What?"

"Don't think of it as a confrontation. Think of it as a chance to get acquainted with a long-lost relative. Think of it as an exciting opportunity, not as something to dread."

An appreciative smile spread over Ham's handsome face. "You are the best," he said.

"We're screwed."

Taft had just gotten off the phone with the Chief Staff Attorney for the Minnesota Court of Appeals. "The Court of Appeals has turned down our request for an emergency hearing," he said. "They don't think this is an emergency since we can't demonstrate any real threat of physical danger to Magnolia. We have to proceed under Rule 120."

"We can have a petition filed by tomorrow," Avery offered. "The State has to respond in seven days."

"I understand what the rules say," Taft admonished his young associate, "but without an emergency designation we won't get a hearing for weeks, and then there'll be briefing schedules, probably another hearing for arguments, and then the Court of Appeals has months before it has to make a decision."

"Can't we file a habeas corpus in federal court?" Avery asked.

"That only works after a state court appeal is denied."

"But we *were* denied expedited relief."

Taft stopped for a moment to consider Avery's words. Snowflakes fell outside the window of the office provided by the Minneapolis law firm Taft had hired as local counsel. Street lights were starting to flicker on. He disliked winter, even more so in Minnesota where darkness came before six o'clock and the weather was unrelenting. He also didn't understand law offices that were almost empty at this early hour. In Boston, at Taft, Hartman and Lowinski, the place hummed with activity until at least 9 p.m., and it was normal to see lights on in offices long after midnight.

"Call back to the office," he said. "Get someone to research whether that's enough to file a federal writ. Tell them we need the answer by tomorrow morning. Also, get someone to start looking for a bonding company that might issue a $100 million bond, maybe Lloyd's. And, we need to figure out how to approach Magnolia with the competency question."

"She's not going to like that," Avery said.

"That's why I'm going to have you bring up the subject," Taft answered. "She'll take it better from you than from me."

Avery bit her lip, scowling. "She's going to understand that if she's found incompetent to stand trial, she's going to end up in a psych ward someplace, and if they ever let her out, she'll have to stand trial anyway."

"Better that than a conviction and a prison sentence for murder."

"You mean keep from losing," Avery muttered. At that moment, Taft decided Avery's time with Taft, Hartman and Lowinski was short.

Later, back in his hotel room, Taft channel-surfed between 24-hour news networks. Among the top stories was speculation on whether the majority party was going to start a proceeding to have Magnolia expelled from the Senate.

Oh, God, he thought, *I hope she's not watching television.*

"We're not going to be able to get you out of here right away," Taft told Magnolia when they met the next morning. "The Court of Appeals turned down our request for an emergency hearing. We need to go through the regular appeal procedure." The two of them and Avery were at the Goodhue County Jail, jammed into a tiny room with barely enough room for a small table and four folding chairs.

"What's that mean?" Magnolia asked.

Taft shifted uncomfortably on the metal chair. "Probably a couple of months," he said, downplaying what was likely to be a much longer process. "It will depend on how quickly the court will schedule a hearing on our petition to reduce bail. We'll be filing it this afternoon. Meanwhile, we're trying to find someone who will post a $100 million bond."

"So, I'm stuck in this hell hole!" Magnolia bellowed. "I'm…I'm…"

"I'm afraid so," Taft cut in. "We're doing everything we can, but the Court of Appeals didn't see this as an emergency, so we're stuck with taking the longer route."

"If this isn't an emergency, then what the...," Magnolia stopped, realizing that her ranting wouldn't change anything. "What if we get a statement from the Senate Minority Leader that my vote is critical," she said after a moment. "Would that raise it to the level of an emergency?"

Taft bowed his head for a moment, massaging his forehead with his fingers, thinking. "If it was a vote on an issue of national security, it might," he said looking up. "But just saying your vote is critical, by itself, I don't think will be enough. Unless there is an actual vote of that magnitude coming up, or we can find someone to underwrite the bond, I think you need to reconcile yourself to being in here for a while."

"Contact the office of Senator Bradford Styles," Magnolia said, directing her order to Avery. "Ask for his chief of staff, Harvey Findley. Harvey said they were willing to help. Maybe there's something they can do. In fact, have Harvey call me."

Avery nodded. "I'll make the arrangements."

"And contact Samantha Jones. Tell her to register as a visitor and to set up an email account with the jail. I still need to communicate with the outside world. Everything doesn't stop just because I'm stuck in here."

They sat silently for a moment.

"Are we done here?" Magnolia asked.

"We need to talk about trial strategy," Avery said, looking at Taft.

"What's to talk about?" Magnolia snapped. "I'm being framed. Find out who's doing it!" She stood up to leave.

"One option we should consider is how to avoid the trial," Taft cut in.

"You mean a plea deal!" Magnolia barked. "I told you. I won't agree to a plea!"

"Not that," interjected Avery. "There is another way to avoid trial. We could raise the issue of your competence to stand trial."

"I am not insane!" Magnolia shouted.

"No. No. No one is saying you're insane," Avery assured her. "Competence to stand trial is a question of whether you can knowingly participate in your own defense. We could argue that the stress created by the events of the last several months has put you temporarily in a mental state that prevents you from participating in your own defense."

"You said 'temporarily.' That means I would still have to stand trial when that *temporary* problem goes away, right?"

"That's true, but it would let this press frenzy settle down before you stand trial, and it would give us some time to work the public opinion angle," Avery said. "And, it's likely you'd get a different judge when you came back."

Magnolia's face lit up at the last statement as she sat back down at the table.

"We would have to get a medical opinion to support our claim," Avery added, "but that shouldn't be difficult."

"I'd have to see another shrink?" Magnolia's eyes darted around the tiny room as if searching for a way out.

Avery nodded. "You can handle this," she said. "We'll choose the psychiatrist or psychologist and give him specific instructions on what areas to question you. You'll know in advance what he's going to ask you. Besides, you're smarter than any psychiatrist."

Magnolia knew that Avery was just stroking her ego, but the inflection in her voice suggested that the result of any psychiatric visit would be predetermined. This allowed Magnolia to relax enough to weigh the pros and cons of delaying her trial.

"Think about it," Taft said. "You don't have to decide right now. We'll talk again tomorrow."

There was confidence in Magnolia's stride as she returned to the day room. Lunch was being served, and she took a seat at a table on the outer edge of the room. She stared in disgust at the food tray that was placed in front of her. She pushed the tepid food around with a plastic spork, the only eating utensil provided, lost in her thoughts about the possibilities that delaying her trial might provide. She was startled when she realized there was someone standing beside her.

"You have a phone call," the guard said, loud enough for everyone in the day room to hear. "It's from some senator." Furtive glances from the other inmates made Magnolia uncomfortable as the guard led her out of the day room to the secluded room ordinarily reserved for attorney phone calls. "Take it in here," he said, unlocking the door. "You've got 20 minutes."

The senator turned out to be Harvey Findley.

"How are you faring, Senator Kanaranzi?" Findley asked.

"How do you think?" she responded coldly.

"Your legal counsel asked me to call," he said, ignoring her answer. "What can we do for you, Senator?"

"You've heard this impertinent judge set my bail at one hundred million dollars."

"I've heard."

"And the appeals court has refused my request for an expedited appeal."

"Yes. We were sorry to hear that."

"I think a letter from Senator Styles saying I need to be released because my vote is critical would be enough to convince the appeals court to expedite the appeal."

Silence.

"Are you still there?" she barked after a moment.

"I'll talk to the Senator," Findley responded, "but I can't think of any vote coming up in the next week or two where a vote would be critical, except for a possible vote on your expulsion, and you couldn't vote on that even if you were here."

"Aren't *all* Senate votes critical?"

"We like to think so, but in this context, I think a vote would have to be on something like impeachment or national security."

"You told me you were willing to help," Magnolia snapped.

"I'll do what I can," Findley repeated. "I'll also talk to some of our big donors and see if they would be willing to back a bond."

The phone call took far less than the allotted 20 minutes. Magnolia returned to the day room in a foul mood, exacerbated by the removal of all of the food trays, including hers. She went to the Seg Unit and retrieved the jail-issued credit card out of her tote, then bought a bag of chips from the vending machine. Back in her room, she ate chips and water for lunch and listened to the radio, a station that featured 1960s and 70s music. As the smooth harmony of The Righteous Brothers crooned *Unchained Melody*, Magnolia's dismal world took on a mellow glow.

The radio station must have had a short play list, because when Magnolia awoke from an unplanned nap, the third song she heard was, again, *Unchained Melody*. She day-dreamed through the afternoon, staying in her room doing crossword puzzles until she was interrupted by a rapping on her door.

"You have company for a couple days," one of two guards standing in the A Unit anteroom said, "but don't get chummy with her. She's in lock down."

"Why?"

"Disciplinary segregation," the other guard answered. "Something you might get familiar with, if you get another call like the one today. That was a one-time thing. The captain okayed it as a courtesy, but in the future, you get *no* incoming calls except from your lawyer. I don't care if it's the President."

She heard the outer door's lock click into place as the two guards left. *What call,* she wondered?

Curious, she walked the few steps to the closed door of the other Seg Unit room. She knocked. "Can you hear me?"

There was no response. She knocked again. "I know you can hear me knocking," she said. She put her ear to the door. There was a voice, muffled but audible.

"What you want?"

"Are you okay?"

"Hell, no, I ain't okay."

"Are you hurt?"

"What?"

"Are you hurt?"

"No, I ain't hurt. What do you care?"

"I thought maybe I could call someone for you if you were hurt."

"You ain't too smart, are you? Or is that some special deal you got with the *captain*, like phone calls."

"I don't know any captain."

There was a pause.

"Why have they got you locked up?"

"Pack a cigarettes in my cell."

"I thought you couldn't smoke in here."

"Can't. That's why I'm locked up," she snarled.

"How'd you get cigarettes?"

"The Mooch. She can get you 'bout anything."

Another pause.

"You can get your ass in a lot of trouble talkin' to me through the door. You be in lock down too if they catch you."

"Oh. Sorry." Magnolia went back to her room and closed the door.

"Guest count in five minutes," came the voice over the intercom. "Rise and shine. Breakfast at 7:00. Today's menu: oatmeal and brown sugar, fruit cup, milk, and coffee. And for you gourmets who don't like oatmeal, there is the ever-popular dry cereal. Today's work schedule will be posted on the kiosk in the day room, and for you lucky people having visitors, that schedule will be posted there, too. There will be church service this morning at 10:00 and the daily AA meeting tonight at 7:00. Have a wonderful day, and remember, you're a guest of Goodhue County where it's always friendly, so be nice to your neighbor."

It was the fourth morning in a row that Magnolia had woke up to the good neighbor spiel. She was sure that if she ever met that voice in person, she'd choke him. She dragged herself out of bed and sat on the edge, reaching for her socks. The outer Seg Unit door lock clicked, followed by "Cell check." A female guard stuck her head in Magnolia's room without knocking. "Morning," she said, then withdrew and closed the door.

Magnolia disrobed and gave herself a quick sponge bath, shivering in the cool morning air. She put on clean underwear, fresh pants, and a tee shirt. Still chilled, she added a long-sleeved overshirt. Squinting into the hazy metal mirror, she tried to make sense of her short, silver hair, running her hand through it, noticing that her roots were starting to show.

She wondered what kind of color-enhancing shampoo was available at the commissary.

The anteroom door lock clicked again, signaling the end of overnight lock down. Magnolia went to the day room for breakfast, taking her usual seat by herself. Another inmate, who looked like everyone's grandmother with gray hair and a round plump face, motioned to Magnolia; it seemed a visual invitation to join her and two others sitting at a table in the middle of the room. Magnolia hesitated, then thinking that it was an opportunity to learn more about how the jail worked, got up and walked across the day room to join them. She sat next to the woman who had motioned.

The food trays were delivered. After the server left, the woman spoke to Magnolia out of the side of her mouth. "Wanted to introduce you to Mooch," she said, not moving her lips. She nodded toward one of the women across the table.

"Real name's Doris," the woman said in a raspy voice, "but everybody calls me Mooch." She appeared to be about 50 with a face ravaged by meth use.

"And I'm Renee," the woman next to her whispered. She was the youngest of the three by at least 20 years and once might have been considered pretty. "Mooch can get you anything."

"You were askin' about me the other night?" Mooch said.

Magnolia struggled to recall. "I heard about you. Just wanted to meet," she said, faking it.

"Darla here thought you might need something," Mooch said, nodding toward the grandmotherly woman sitting next to Magnolia.

"No. I don't need anything right now," Magnolia said. "How do you get stuff?"

"Been in and out of this place half my life," Mooch answered. "I work in the kitchen and the laundry. Don't get in any trouble. They trust me."

"What do you charge?"

"Depends what you want."

Magnolia nodded. She listened as the subject changed and the other three women lectured her on the dos and do nots of jail life. They told her which guards to avoid, and which were friendly.

"I've been in a couple of other jails," Renee said. "This one ain't bad. Food's even pretty decent." Darla stuck out her tongue and shook her head in disagreement.

"We understand you're in here for killin' yer old lady," Mooch said. "Been all over the news. A *you ess senatore* accused of murder. First ever. You're quite the celebrity."

"I didn't kill her," Magnolia shot back, surprised at the bluntness of Mooch's statement.

"Ain't nobody in here guilty," Darla chuckled. "Welcome to the club."

"Why are you in here?" Magnolia asked. "You look like you should be at home in a kitchen baking cookies."

"Weren't cookies," Darla laughed. "It was brownies. Everybody liked 'em 'cept the cops. They objected to my ingredients."

Mooch and Renee both smirked, apparently having heard Darla's explanation before.

"How do you get a job in the kitchen or the laundry?" Magnolia asked Mooch.

"Don't get into trouble, and be around for a while. There's a waiting list."

"Are there any other jobs for inmates?"

"Nope."

"Any opportunities to get outside?"

"Man, you are a rookie," Mooch chided. Renee and Darla smiled knowingly and shook their heads.

After the trays were cleared, Magnolia went to look at the posted schedules. None of the other women bothered. A 2:40 p.m. visit with Samantha Jones was listed. There was nothing about a meeting with her lawyers. She approached a guard. "I'm supposed to have a meeting with my lawyers this morning. How do I find out when that is?"

"Someone will come and get you," the guard replied.

"Do we even tell her about the *habeas corpus?*" Avery asked as she and Taft trudged into the Goodhue County Jail.

"We have to," Taft replied. "It's an option, even if it's a bad one. Canons of ethics requires us to point out all options, give her our advice, and then let her make the choice." They passed through security and went to the meeting room to wait for Magnolia, tossing their coats on the back of the extra folding chair.

"Have you heard from Senator Styles' office," was the first thing Magnolia said after the door was closed.

"Not a word," Taft answered. "Did they call you?"

Magnolia nodded. "Findley called but I doubt they'll do anything," she said. "How about a bond. Did you find anyone who would issue a bond?"

"No one," Avery said. "We tried every company that issues large bonds, and none of them would touch it unless you could put up $100 million in collateral."

"If I had $100 million, I wouldn't need a bond."

"It's frustrating," Avery agreed.

"So, we wait?"

"There is another option," Taft cut in, "but it's not a very good one. We could seek a writ of habeas corpus from the Federal Court. If we prevail, the court could set a new bail, but there are risks. Filing a habeas corpus petition would be like kicking a sleeping dog. It's possible, in fact I would say it's likely, that if we seek habeas corpus from federal court, the U.S. Attorney will bring separate charges against you."

"Can they do that?"

"Yes. In all probability the state action would be dismissed, and you would stand trial in federal court."

"And face the same issues that we faced in Massachusetts?" Magnolia asked.

"Yes. You could be held without bail and the death penalty comes into play," Taft reminded her. "Just as importantly, our research indicates that sentences here, in federal cases, have been on average more severe than in Minnesota state courts. Plus, you would be transferred to a federal prison. The population in those prisons is made up of hard-core criminals, and the rules are harsh. You'd have less freedom than you have here, and it's possible you could become a target. And another thing. We can't be sure that the federal court would even agree to hear the petition. Ordinarily, you can file in federal court only after the state court has denied your appeal. It's an open question whether denial of a request for an expedited hearing is sufficient. My advice is stick with the devil that we know and continue with the appeal in state court on the bail issue."

Magnolia thought for a moment. "We can always do the habeas corpus thing in the future, can't we?" Both Taft and Avery nodded. "Then let's wait, but what about this hearing that's set for the middle of March. Is there something we should be doing for that?"

"We have to disclose our evidence and witnesses, and we're getting that ready," Avery said, "and the County Attorney needs to do the same, but none of that typically happens until a week before the hearing so we've got time. What we *do* need to act on is whether we're going to seek a competency hearing. That has to happen quickly."

"No. I'm not going to do that," Magnolia said. "First, I am not incompetent. I can participate in my own defense. This conversation proves it. Second, even if we were to do it for strategic reasons, and I were to be found incompetent to stand trial, it would probably get me expelled from the Senate. I'm not going to risk that."

Avery nodded in sympathy, showing her understanding of Magnolia's reasoning.

"Besides," Magnolia went on, "this jail is not so terrible. I was in a lot worse 40 years ago. I can handle this."

Later that afternoon, Magnolia sat in the visiting room before a blank monitor, waiting for her visitor to appear. Samantha had proven to be the most loyal among Magnolia's campaign staff, and the two had become, at least in Magnolia's mind, friends. In a world where she could trust few, Samantha had become her closest confidant.

The screen came to life, and Samantha's face appeared.

"Who thought it would ever come to this," Magnolia said, trying to inject a little levity into the electronic visit. "Thanks for meeting me. Where are you?"

"Back in Boston," Samantha answered. "How are you?" The two exchanged pleasantries and miscellaneous information until Magnolia got around to the main reason she requested Samantha's visit.

"It looks like I'm going to be here for a while," she started, "maybe two or three months. I need you to act as my pipeline to the outside world. I'd like you to visit me every week about this time to fill me in on what's going on, particularly in the Senate. I'll probably have several things I'll ask you to do each week. I've told my lawyers to prepare a power of attorney giving you control of my financial accounts and authority to act on my behalf. The first thing I want you to do is to increase your salary by half."

"That's not necessary," a shocked and embarrassed Samantha interrupted.

"It is, and don't worry; you'll earn it," Magnolia answered ominously. "The second thing I want you to do is to check my account here at the jail daily and make sure there is always a thousand dollars in it. And, I want you to monitor what's going on in the Senate."

"Do you have a contact for me at the Senate?" Samantha asked.

"Start with Brad Styles' chief of staff, Harvey Findley. He will be able to direct you to someone, but double-check everything you hear directly from Harvey. I don't completely trust him."

They talked for another 10 minutes until Magnolia looked at the clock and realized their 20- minute visit was about over. "One last thing," she said. "I would like you to move into my penthouse."

"Whoa!" Samantha exclaimed in surprise. "Really?"

"Yes. I don't like it sitting empty, and I know you'll take care of it."

"I'll have to think about that," Samantha said. "I've got a lease."

"Check into it, and we'll talk next week."

A minute later the screen went black.

Magnolia spent the next hour in the day room, signing up for library time, watching Renee and another woman trying to play ping pong, and sitting with Darla watching a soap opera on TV. She noticed a new inmate, bent and emaciated, also watching TV. Magnolia knew that the jail provided minimal, basic hygienic needs for indigent inmates at no cost. She guessed that this woman was one of them.

The soap opera didn't hold Magnolia's attention for long. She eyed a guard standing near the Seg Unit entrance, one that the three women had identified as a guard to avoid. She checked the wall clock. Fifteen minutes to pre-dinner lock down, and she would have to walk past the guard to get to her cell. She looked again at the new inmate and made a decision.

"Excuse me," she said, walking directly up to the guard. "How would I go about putting money in the accounts of indigent women inmates?"

The guard looked shocked, either by the question, or the audacity of an inmate asking it.

"I don't know," he said. "Why?"

"Because I'd like to do that."

"What for?" he asked suspiciously.

"To put them on the same level as the inmates who can afford to get things from the commissary," Magnolia replied. "Can you help me find out?"

"I don't know how to do that, but the program director probably would."

"Thanks," Magnolia said with a smile. "I appreciate your help."

The guard nodded. The puzzled look on his face was replaced with just a trace of a smile.

Back in her room, as she waited for the lock-down announcement, Magnolia turned on the radio and laid down on her bed. The station was playing the same tired song list. Eventually, *Unchained Melody* made its way around the loop. She slipped into the familiar song, a feeling of happiness enveloping her. She barely heard the announcement that lock down was over and dinner was ready. As she left the Seg Unit, the guard gave her a slight nod of recognition. *That was nice,* she thought.

She saw Darla sitting at her usual table. She walked over, said "hi" and sat down. Mooch came and sat with them, acknowledging them both with a nod.

Renee, the last to arrive, greeted them. "Hi, Mooch. Darla. Magnolia."

"My name's Mary."

The three women looked at each other, puzzled. Mooch said, "Rich bitch got two names," and began shaking her head in amusement.

The attack was instantaneous. Magnolia was across the table and on top of Mooch before anyone else moved, knocking her off her seat and pummeling her with both hands. Despite being mismatched in size, the element of surprise gave Magnolia an immediate upper hand, and before Mooch's size advantage turned the tables, the guards moved in and broke up the fight. Magnolia fought against the guard to get at Mooch, but the guard who had been standing by the Seg Unit restrained her. Mooch's nose was bloody.

The next few minutes were a blur. Magnolia remembered struggling as she was dragged away, then being pushed into her room and hearing the lock bolt click into place.

Then, silence.

There was no mistaking the orange-red Afro. Particularly when the person wearing it had pale skin.

He followed the woman through the store at a distance, careful to keep at least an aisle between them, until he was certain that it was Toni Chapereaux. He considered approaching her, but remembered the last time they had seen each other she hadn't let him in her house. Instead, he slipped out of the store and stationed himself at the corner of a parking lot a half-block away. He had a clear view of the entrance to Whole Foods.

Fifteen minutes later, Toni came out of the store carrying two bags. She crossed Washington Avenue and walked south on Hennepin. As soon as she disappeared behind the corner building, he sprinted across Washington Avenue and peeked around the corner of the building. She was nowhere in sight.

That's okay, he thought. *I know where she buys groceries. I've waited three years. I can wait a little longer.*

"I called this morning to set up a time to visit my mother," Ham said, wheeling up to the table for lunch, "but they said she is in lock-down and can't have visitors."

"Did they say why she's in lock-down?" Toni asked.

"They wouldn't tell me, and they couldn't tell me how long she'd be there."

"Hmm. I'm sorry." Toni put a bowl of tomato soup in front of Ham, with a straw in it. She broke some crackers into his soup, then into her own bowl. "Want a pickle?" she asked as she put a glass of milk, also with a straw, beside Ham's soup bowl.

"Sure."

She speared a pickle out of the jar with a long skewer and put it on a plate, letting the end of the skewer stick out over the edge so Ham could grasp it with his one semi-functional hand.

"Guess who I saw today," she said as she sat down. "Remember Todd D'Anselmo?"

"That creepy guy who was in your grad student program?"

"Yeah. I saw him at Whole Foods. It's weird, but I'm pretty sure it was him."

"Did you talk to him?" Ham asked. The thought of D'Anselmo being anywhere near Toni made him uncomfortable.

"Oh, heavens no," Toni exclaimed. "He's the last person I want to get reacquainted with. Remember that day he showed up at my apartment, and I couldn't get rid of him?"

A dark expression settled on Ham's face. "Yeah, and I remember seeing him leave my building late one night. I'm sure he stole pictures out of my desk. Did he see you?"

"No. I don't think so."

They ate their soup in silence, until the buzzer indicated someone was at the front door of their apartment building. They both jumped and then laughed at each other.

"Yes?" Toni answered over the intercom.

"I have a delivery for Ham and Toni Blethen," the voice said.

"Just put it by the door. I'll come down and get it."

A few minutes later Toni was back carrying flowers.

"Who're they from?" Ham asked.

"Let's see." Toni took off the outer wrap, revealing an arrangement of lilies and roses in pink and white. She opened the card. It was from the Monet Detective Agency, the all-woman P.I. firm that had discovered the truth about Magnolia Kanaranzi. "Well, isn't that nice. It says 'welcome home'."

Magnolia tried desperately to remember what had happened. She was sitting on the stool in her cell, peering at something called a Rules

Violation Report. It stated she had attacked another inmate. She could either sign it, admitting she was guilty, or refuse and go to a hearing.

She looked up at the guard who had brought her the report. "You say there's a video of this?" she said. The guard nodded.

"Can I see it?"

"No. Only the Sergeant looks at it."

"That's bullshit," Magnolia flared. "Someone's trying to frame me, and this is just one more thing."

The guard shrugged like he'd heard it all before. "Sorry. You either sign the report or you don't. Up to you."

"I need to talk to my lawyer before I sign anything."

The guard hesitated, then shrugged. "I'll see if we can get him on the phone. I'll come and get you if we do."

An hour passed. Then another. Magnolia had nothing to do but simmer and think. *Charged with attacking another woman…I didn't… but a video…and eye witnesses…all part of the frameup…No memory of any of it…Conspiracy to commit murder…my own mother…I didn't do that…Did I block that out too? I hated her…but she was my mother. God, they must think I'm a monster…is my mind playing tricks, again? What's wrong with me? No. No. It's all a conspiracy…Senate seat probably gone if word of the attack gets out…of course it will get out…but I won't…Solitary confinement…for how long? I'll be in danger when I get out. Maybe if I apologized…for what?…It's a frame job. I didn't attack her, and I didn't kill my mother…I'll take Hawke down with me if I go… That sonovabitch…Will I live long enough to get to trial? …Will I live long enough to see my son?*

Her cell door clicked, and the guard stepped in. "Your attorney's on the phone."

She followed him, relieved to be out of her cell and away from her spiraling thoughts. As they passed through the day room, inmates she didn't know glared at her. Renee looked at her with a "WTF" look, and Darla looked away. She didn't see Mooch. It was a long walk to reach the room with a secure phone. For the first time since she'd been arrested, Magnolia felt fear.

"What happened?" Taft asked.

"I don't know. They say I attacked an inmate; a woman named Mooch. They have a video. Now they want me to sign something, a Rules Violation Report, where I admit I did it. I don't remember any of it."

"Did they ask this Mooch woman to sign something, too?"

"I don't know. I don't think so. The report says the attack was unprovoked."

"Did she get hurt? This Mooch?"

"The report said she got a bloody nose."

"Did you get hurt?"

"I skinned my shins. Apparently, I lunged over a table at her. And my left hand hurts."

"Like it's broken?"

"No. Like it's bruised."

"And you don't remember anything."

"No. I've tried, but I don't even remember going to dinner last night. That's when this supposedly happened."

"I recommend you sign the report," he said after a long pause. "Under your signature, write an apology to Mooch and to the jail administration. In that apology say you don't remember the attack and have no idea why it happened. This will give us a plausible reason to bring a competency motion."

"You keep bringing that up," Magnolia snapped. "I hate it."

"What happens if you attack somebody during the trial, a witness or the prosecuting attorney?" Taft asked pointedly. "It'll seal your conviction, and they'll send you to prison for life."

Magnolia ground her teeth. "I would never attack anybody in a court room."

"How can you be sure? You can't even remember what happened last night."

"ALL RIGHT!" she screamed. "I'll go see your shrink just to prove I'm not crazy."

"Thank you." Taft sighed; the tension deflated. "We'll notify the court tomorrow. On second thought, hold off on signing that report for the moment. I'll send Laura over to look at it tomorrow morning and have her ask to see the video. After she's reviewed everything, she can advise you on whether or not to sign the report."

Magnolia abruptly changed the subject. "I want you to add another lawyer as co-counsel." Her words caught Taft completely by surprise.

"What? Why?" he asked, nonplussed.

"Because I trust him."

Taft bristled. "Maybe you should change legal counsel if you don't trust me."

"Don't be ridiculous. I want you to remain as my primary defense attorney. This other lawyer has been my personal advisor for a long time. I want him added because it will give me the opportunity to talk to him."

"Who's the lawyer?"

"His name is Henri Hawke."

"Does he handle criminal defense, and where does he practice law?"

"Yes, and Barcelona. He's a lawyer in both Spain and France."

"He can't practice U.S. law, even if he was admitted here."

"I understand that," Magnolia said impatiently, "but they claim I hired a foreign national to kill my mother, so we should be allowed to have a foreign attorney."

"One, that makes no sense, and two, the guy who claims you hired him is from Germany."

"Henri speaks German, along with six other languages, and as I said, I want him as my personal adviser to give me another perspective."

"Then have him register as a visitor," Taft said pointedly.

"Visitor conversations are all monitored," Magnolia answered. "Lawyer conversations, like this one, are not. I want my conversations with Henri to be private and privileged."

"I don't need some European lawyer second-guessing me," Taft complained.

"Perhaps you might learn something from him," Magnolia said curtly. "Regardless, I want to add Henri. Please call him and ask him to register as a guest and set up an appointment so we can discuss it."

"You can't have visitors. You're in lock down," Taft reminded her.

"Then you'll have to convince him to join our team as co-counsel." Magnolia had the upper hand, and she knew it. "It shouldn't be difficult to convince him. Tell him I've personally made the request." She gave him Hawke's office phone number in Barcelona. "There's a seven-hour time difference between here and Barcelona. Call me tomorrow after you've talked to him."

She ended the call, pleased with herself. *Keep your enemies closer,* she smirked.

Mooch sat at the table, not eating. "Can't taste anything," she said in response to a question from Darla.

"You look a sight," Darla said, referring to the tape over Mooch's broken nose and the black swollen eyes. "Little shit packs a punch. What you suppose set her off?"

"No idea," Mooch said, "but she'll get hers."

"Watcha gonna do?"

"Nothing. I got people who owe me. I won't touch the bitch."

"Maybe that's what started it," Darla offered blithely. "Maybe she didn't like being called a bitch."

"Hmmm. We'll see."

COMPETENCY

Hues of copper and magenta reflected off the state capitol dome as the sun rose, promising another clear, cold March day. Less than a mile to the south, in the downtown Saint Paul office of the Monet Detective Agency, the three women who comprised the agency were huddled over coffee and crullers, discussing whether or not to cooperate in the murder trial of Magnolia Kanaranzi.

"I thought when we gave the information to the Goodhue County Attorney – what's his name?"

"Bunch. Lawrence Bunch," Ronni Brilliant cut in.

"Once we gave the information to him, I thought we were done with this," said Carrie Waters, the youngest of the three.

"It's never that simple," sighed Holly Bouquet, the tacit leader of the agency. "One of us, probably Ronni, is going to have to testify at the trial."

"All the more reason not to talk to the attorney," Ronni said, less than happy with the request they had received. Ronni, a transgender woman, had been an early supporter of Magnolia Kanaranzi's run for the U.S. Senate because of her advocacy for women's and LGBTQ+ rights. That all changed when the agency took on Hamilton Blethen as a client.

As Ronni's investigation began pointing toward Kanaranzi as the probable estranged mother of her client, Ronni suddenly found herself the target of a gaslighting campaign that escalated from psychological warfare into physical attacks on her sister, her partner Carrie, and eventually, on Ronni herself. What should have been a routine investigation to locate a missing person turned into Magnolia Kanaranzi's eventual arrest for the murder of her own mother.

"They're going to force us to talk to them, one way or the other," Holly reasoned. "If we don't do it voluntarily, they'll subpoena our records. If we cooperate, we can at least control what to show them."

"Have you talked to Bunch since we got the request?" Ronni asked.

"Maybe we should hire our own attorney," Carrie interjected.

"Let me talk to Bunch, first," Holly replied, "to see if there is anything he doesn't want us to show…"

"Or tell," Ronni interrupted.

"…Kanaranzi's lawyers. My personal opinion is that we don't have anything to hide, so there's no reason to ramp this up by hiring a lawyer."

"Bunch may see it differently," Ronni groused.

The sun crept high enough to penetrate the conference room, illuminating the framed copy of Claude Monet's painting, *Water Lilies,* that adorned the wall. Ronni took a moment to take in the tranquil scene. The agency had derived its name from the painting, a visual anagram of Brilliant, Bouquet, and Waters, a name they could not use because Carrie Waters did not have the qualifications to be a licensed private investigator. Notwithstanding, her psychic abilities made her an important part of the agency, and, as far as Ronni and Holly were concerned, an equal partner.

For Ronni, the painting helped take the edge off her sometimes-caustic personality. "Okay," she sighed, looking at Holly. "You're right. Let's comply with the request, if it's okay with Bunch."

"Who's going to deliver the documents?" Carrie asked.

"I'd *love* to," Ronni replied sarcastically, "but if I am going to testify, meeting with her attorneys now would give them a chance to unofficially cross examine me. Holly should be the one to deal with Kanaranzi's lawyers. She's the only one of us who wasn't physically attacked by Kanaranzi's henchmen."

Holly got a return call from the Goodhue County Attorney later in the morning.

"They want you to voluntarily turn over your files?" Bunch queried. "You didn't receive a subpoena?"

"No, just a phone call requesting to look at our investigative file on Kanaranzi," Holly responded.

"What's your client say?"

"He has no objection," Holly said. "He still hopes that Kanaranzi will acknowledge him as her son. He thinks showing her lawyers our file might somehow help with that."

"Hmm," was Bunch's noncommittal response. "They're going to get your files one way or the other. Maybe if you do it voluntarily, you'll get some insight into how they plan to defend her. You need to make a list of everything you show them and make sure that you leave with everything you brought."

"Will do," Holly answered.

"And, if you have any conversation with them about the case or your files, make sure you record it."

With no objection from Bunch, the meeting with Kanaranzi's legal team was set. Unfortunately, on the day of the meeting, Holly was sick with the flu.

"Coming out of both ends," was the way Ronni put it. "We should probably postpone."

"I can handle it," Carrie volunteered. "I did a lot of the investigation, and my broken ribs are healed. I hold no grudges."

They debated the issue, finally calling Holly to cast the deciding vote.

Carrie Waters waited in the reception area of the posh Minneapolis law office, a box of documents on the carpeted floor beside her. A woman about the same age as Waters, wearing an unadorned three-piece business suit and sensible heels, walked across the reception area and extended her hand. "I'm Laura Avery," she said. "You must be Holly."

Waters rose and took the proffered hand. "Carrie Waters," she said. "Holly couldn't make it. She has the flu."

Avery led Waters into a small conference room. "You're from the Monet Detective Agency?" she stated more than asked. "Interesting name."

"Long story," Waters responded, but offered no further explanation. She set the box of documents on the table in front of her. "These are originals," she said. "You can make copies of what you need."

For more than an hour Avery meticulously looked through the documents while Carrie sat and watched. Finally, Avery gathered up most of the documents, put them back in the box and slid it across the table to Waters.

"I want copies of these," she said, indicating a one-inch pile of papers on the table next to her.

After the copies were made, Waters confirmed that all the originals had been returned to her. She started to leave.

"I'd like to ask you a few questions about these documents, if you don't mind," Avery said politely, stopping Waters halfway out of her chair. Avery took a few pages off the top of the stack, and without waiting for Waters' answer, placed four artist renderings of a woman's face on the conference room table. "Can you tell me where you got these sketches?" she asked.

Waters paused. "I'm happy to discuss the documents, but I'll need to record the conversation." The control in her voice belied her hands shaking under the table.

Avery nodded. "Of course. A copy of the recording would be beneficial for us as well."

Waters nodded, employing all her self-control to still the tremor in her hands. She took a small recorder out of her pocket, laid it on the table between her and Avery, and clicked the on button.

"Are you going to test it to see if it works?" Avery asked, a tiny smirk crossing her face.

"Uh, yeah. Good idea," Waters answered, silently kicking herself for not thinking of that first. Having determined that the recorder was in working order, Waters pushed the on button again.

"Are you ready now?" Avery asked.

Waters nodded.

"You have to say it out loud so the recorder can record it," Avery chided.

"Yes. I'm ready," Waters answered, now red-faced and embarrassed.

"All right. This is Laura Avery speaking. I am about to ask questions of…," she nodded toward Waters.

"Carrie Waters."

"We're looking at four sketches of a woman's face," Avery continued. "Ms. Waters, where did you get these sketches?"

"A police artist named Eldon Koskinen did them for us," Waters responded, leaning over the table to look at the drawings.

"And why did you have a police artist make these sketches?"

"We were trying to determine whether Mary Blethen and your client were the same person."

"My client being?"

"Magnolia Kanaranzi."

"Where does this police artist work?"

"The Saint Paul Police Department."

"Have you or Eldon Koskinen ever met my client?"

"No. I haven't, and I don't believe he has either."

"Ever talk to her?"

"No."

"Ever seen a picture of her?"

"Yes."

"Are the pictures used by this artist to draw these sketches among the documents you brought today?"

"Yes." Waters flipped through the box until she found the stock photo from the Kanaranzi campaign. "Here it is," she said, handing the photograph to Avery.

The questioning went on for another 20 minutes, Avery asking about each document until there was only one left. She picked it up and showed it to Waters. "Tell me what this is," she said.

"It's a memo I wrote after an interview with a man named Albert Freeman."

"Your memo says that Mr. Freeman was a janitor at a high school where Mary Blethen went to school."

Waters nodded, then caught her mistake and replied with a clear, "Yes."

"Do I understand this correctly," Avery continued, "that Mr. Freeman has dementia?"

"Yes."

"Was he suffering from that affliction the day you interviewed him?"

"Yes."

"So, it would be safe to say that you can't be sure that anything he said during that interview was reliable."

"Mr. Freeman was hypnotized when I interviewed him," Waters said, "and a person in a hypnotic state, even a person with Alzheimer's disease, can remember things from their past with accuracy."

"Are you a licensed hypnotherapist?"

"Hypnotists aren't required to be licensed in Minnesota," Waters responded, "and I don't practice hypnotherapy. I hypnotize people to help them remember things from their past. I don't use hypnosis to heal, so I don't have to be licensed."

"Are you a psychologist?"

"No."

"Where did you learn hypnosis?"

"I'm pretty much self-taught. I took online classes and read a lot. I also practiced as much as possible. I did take one in-person class at a local community college."

"Are you certified?"

"No. For my purposes, there is no reason to be certified."

"What are your purposes?"

"As I said, to help people remember things from their past. Sometimes, I use those memories to trace people and on the rare occasion to solve a crime."

Magnolia sat on her bed, her back against the wall with her knees propped up in front of her, watching *The Devil Wears Prada* on her county-issued electronic tablet. It was her last day of lock down and about the hundredth movie she'd watched. Breakfast had come and gone, her laundry had been picked up, and she'd showered. Showering had become a daily highlight, one of only two times during the day she was allowed out of her cell. The other was an hour in the afternoon to exercise. She dreaded that exercise hour. It was the only time she could possibly come in contact with the other prisoners, which made her vulnerable to reprisal for her attack on Mooch.

So far, nothing had happened in the week since the attack, but once lock down was lifted and she was back in the regular prison population, Mooch's revenge would lurk at every turn. She had requested that protective custody be continued after her lock down expired, but she had not yet heard if her request would be granted.

When the movie ended, Magnolia got up and paced back and forth across the 12-foot distance between her cell walls. It was a self-imposed daily regime. Together with the scheduled exercise hour, it was her attempt to keep herself in tolerable physical condition. She did crosswords and Sudoku to keep her mind active. Unfortunately, there was nothing she could do about her makeup, hair, or nails. The commissary didn't have makeup or nail polish, and the shampoo that was available was not designed to cover up the dingy gray hair roots that grew longer each day. She wondered if she made a personal apology, and paid enough, Mooch might get her the right shampoo. And maybe some clear nail polish.

Her flight of fancy was interrupted by a knock on her cell door. A guard stuck her head in. "You've got a call from your attorney." Magnolia followed the guard through the empty day room to the room designated for attorney-client phone calls. She was pleasantly surprised by the voice on the other end of the line.

"Magnolia," Hawke said in his oily accent, "I am pleased that you wish me to be your co-counsel, but I am not sure how much help I can give you in that role."

"Hello, Henri," she answered curtly. "I'm not doing this for your legal expertise, but I may need to talk to you from time-to-time. This is the only way to keep those conversations confidential."

"I understand completely," Hawke oozed. "So, tell me why did you elect to have your trial moved to Minnesota?"

"Because the U.S. Attorney in Massachusetts was threatening to bring federal charges."

"Would that not be...how do you call it...double jeopardy?"

"I'm told that the same charge can be brought both by the state and federal government, and it's not considered double jeopardy," Magnolia answered. "Plus, the death penalty is possible with federal charges."

"By moving to Minnesota, you have avoided federal charges?"

"Yes. At least from the U.S. Attorney in Massachusetts."

"So, what can I do for you?" Hawke inquired, changing the subject.

"I need you to do some more background checks. This time on three people: State Court Judge Susan Weber, Goodhue County Attorney Lawrence Bunch, and the U.S. Attorney for the State of Minnesota."

"Are the other two from Minnesota, also?"

"Yes."

There was a long pause.

"There is the issue of my fee," Hawke said.

"Consider this part of what I paid you for earlier."

"That is not how I see it," he replied.

"You should *see* that our fortunes are very much tied together," Magnolia said. Her voice was dead calm.

Hawke hesitated. "Very well," he said lightly. "I shall do this for you, but then we are even. Any further services will require an additional fee."

"There is one other thing I would like your thoughts on," Magnolia said, without acknowledging Hawke's statement. "Taft is pushing me to see a psychiatrist. He wants to have me declared mentally unfit to stand trial. How do you think I should play this?"

"Let me think on it. Perhaps overnight. I'll call you back tomorrow. Is that satisfactory?"

Hawke hung up the phone and rubbed his chin thoughtfully.

Their fates were indeed intertwined. If she went to trial there would be a better than even chance his role in her mother's death would come to light; possibly even the other matters he had handled for her. The best outcome for him would be for Magnolia to take a plea deal. Or maybe, to be committed to a mental institution. Or to disappear. Permanently.

If she had been in a federal prison, Hawke was sure he could arrange the latter, but in a county jail? Probably not. *Perhaps I should give Minnesota's U.S. Attorney a little nudge to bring those federal charges.*

As he pondered his dilemma, his phone rang. He didn't recognize the number. "Hello."

"He resigned. The fucking judge resigned," shrilled the voice on the other end of the call.

"Please explain. What judge?"

"Winthrop Stewart resigned," Vanderbilt screamed.

Hawke paused. "He seems to be quite unpredictable," he chuckled.

"Bullshit! This is not funny! Did you have something to do with this?"

"I did not."

"I want my money back," Vanderbilt bellowed. "All of it."

"My dear friend," Hawke said, turning on his most soothing voice. "I did what you paid me to do, but there are some things that are even beyond *my* control."

"You get paid to control what other people do," Vanderbilt bellowed. "I want my money back."

"I will give you something better," Hawke replied without hesitation.

"What the hell could that be?"

"Information."

"Information." Vanderbilt repeated sarcastically.

"Yes, information about your recently elected Senator that the people who hire you would dearly appreciate knowing," Hawke teased. "I give you this information as a courtesy, and then you will stop hectoring me about money. Deal?"

"Tell me what it is, and I'll decide whether it's worth it," Vanderbilt snapped.

"My friend," Hawke effused, "you do not understand our respective bargaining positions. I have made you a reasonable offer. In fact, an offer that was unnecessary since I owe you nothing. But out of camaraderie I have made it. Now you have thrown it back in my face?"

Hawke stopped and let his words dangle in the air between them.

"I am a forgiving person," Hawke continued. "I will ignore your insult this one time and restate my offer. If it is not accepted, you will get neither the information, nor the money."

"This better be good," Vanderbilt grumbled after a lengthy pause.

"I want to hear you say it."

"What?"

"I accept."

"Fuck you…I accept."

Hawke took a long time to answer. When he did, the pretentious tone of his voice was gone, replaced by a serrated, icy edge. "Magnolia's defense team is moving to have her ruled incompetent to stand trial, *and* she is about to be charged in federal court with conspiracy to commit murder. I'm sure your people will want to get out in front of this before it becomes public knowledge."

Vanderbilt's audible sigh confirmed that he'd heard the information

At the moment, Brad Styles hated his job. He had run for office to make a difference, to pass legislation that would make the world a better, safer place. More and more he found himself at the center of partisan squabbles that had nothing to do with benefitting the country, but were only about power and who would wield it. *Maybe this will be my last term,* he thought. But he knew it wouldn't. He was as much a part of the process, and the problem, as anyone else.

"What's the bad news today?" he asked his chief of staff by way of a morning greeting.

"He-who-would-be-king says he won't bring up the vote to remove Kanaranzi if we back the tariff bill," Findley said, referring to the Senate majority leader.

"Fuck him," Styles responded. "He knows we can't do that. What's the head count on the expulsion issue?"

"We're solid," Findley replied. "Since we've circulated Robbins' opinion letter, I've heard that there might be a couple votes from across the aisle to oppose expulsion. No way he can get 67 votes."

Styles exhaled. "That's good. What's the latest on Magnolia's situation?"

"Judge set bail at $100 million," Findley said. "They've appealed it, but that will take at least a couple months to be heard. She's going to be in jail for a while."

"At least she can't get into any more trouble there."

"I talked to her a couple of days ago," Findley continued. "She wants me to get an affidavit from you saying her vote is critical on something, anything. She was grabbing at straws, trying to expedite her appeal on the bail."

"What did you tell her?"

"I said there aren't any critical votes coming up, but I would talk to some of our supporters to see if any of them are willing to back a $100 million bond."

"Have you? Did they?"

"No. We're better off to leave her where she is for now," Findley said.

"Should we be rethinking this?" Styles asked. "We may have to consider whether we'd be better off with someone else. Take our chances on a new election. Call Belton and see if they've found a candidate."

"And encourage her to run," Findley added with a touch of sarcasm, "so she doesn't suspect we started the rumor? I think we're better off with the status quo at the moment, but I will have someone in the party call her to inquire."

Less than three hours later, the status was no longer quo.

"The source is indisputable," Findley told Styles. "If they find her incompetent to stand trial, we'll have a tough time holding on to the 34 votes we need to prevent expulsion. Even if they don't find her incompetent, and a federal charge is brought, it gets a lot more difficult. We need to find a replacement for Kanaranzi."

"Have you called Belton yet?" Styles asked.

"I haven't had time," Findley replied. "I've been scrambling, trying to measure the impact of the incompetency thing. Some of our support is wobbling; feeling that just the request to have her ruled incompetent is going to make it difficult for them to oppose her removal."

"Has this hit the news cycle yet?" Styles asked.

"Not yet. There's a hearing scheduled for March 13. That's probably the first time the press will get wind of it."

"That gives us about three weeks. Get in touch with Belton and the national committee chairman. Set up a meeting for tomorrow. In person. Here. Tell them it's urgent, and tell them to keep their mouths shut."

Thanks to Judge Weber's grant of the request for protective custody, Magnolia was accompanied by a guard as she went to take Hawke's return phone call. The presence of a guard did little to shield Magnolia from the glares of the other inmates as she passed through the day room. Darla refused to acknowledge her, and Mooch, whose back faced her, did not turn around. Renee was gone, having "transitioned through the Goodhue County legal system" according to the guard. Magnolia wasn't sure what that meant, but didn't press the issue.

"Where will these meetings with the psychiatrist take place?" Hawke asked as soon as Magnolia picked up the phone.

"I don't know. Why?"

"With movement there are opportunities," he said. "Perhaps you could speak to your Mr. Taft and have him arrange to have your meetings outside the prison."

"Are you saying what I think you're saying?" Magnolia queried.

"I am only suggesting that you might like some time outside the prison."

"It's a jail, not a prison," Magnolia corrected.

"Outside the jail then. A little fresh air and a bit of freedom would be good for your health." There was a smile in Hawke's slippery voice.

"That's not a good idea," Magnolia answered. "Going outside the jail will draw the attention of the press. If the opposition becomes aware I'm being examined by a shrink on the issue of competency, they'll jump on it like a fly on garbage. They'll use it to start the process to expel me."

"I would not spend too much time worrying about your Senate seat," Hawke deadpanned. "Your political *friends* in Washington are ready to…how do you say in America…throw you under the autobus."

"I don't believe you! How do you know that?"

"My sources in Washington tell me that your party officials are actively seeking a new candidate," Hawke said. "There are rumors that once they find a viable candidate, they will cease opposing your expulsion."

Magnolia sat in silence, stunned. It explained why she hadn't heard from Findley. *They want my loyalty, but they're stabbing me in the back. Bastards!* Her anger quickly shifted into attack mode.

"Contact my press secretary, Samantha Jones," she ordered. "Tell her to set up a visit with me as soon as possible. You and she will need to work together."

"Does this Ms. Jones person know of your past activities?" Hawke asked.

"No, but she is loyal and believes I'm innocent. I want her to visit me so I can vouch for you. As I said, the two of you will need to work together on things like rearrangement of my personal finances. We need to get started right away."

"A three-cornered conversation will be clumsy and slow," Hawke speculated. "Do you have access to a library?"

"What?"

"A library. Does the prison…jail, have a library from which you can borrow books?"

"Yes. Why?"

"Tomorrow, I want you to get a copy of *The World Almanac* for the year 2013."

"And?"

"When this Ms. Jones person meets with you, she is going to tell you that I have purchased ten lottery tickets for you. She is going to give you the numbers for each ticket. You are going to write them down in the exact order in which she gives them to you."

"I don't need to win the lottery. I need the two of you to take care of my existing finances."

"Each lottery ticket has six numbers," Hawke continued, ignoring Magnolia's comment. "You will break the lottery numbers for each ticket into two three-number series. With ten tickets, you will have 20 three-number sections. The first number in each section is a page number in the *2013 World Almanac*. The second number is a line on that page. The third number is a word in that line. So, if the three-number series is 39, 13, and 6, the word will be the sixth word in line 13 of page 39.

"I will call you a day or two after your visit with Ms. Jones. As a test, you will repeat back to me the 20-word message I've sent you. By using this method, we will be able to get messages to each other without needing to involve Ms. Jones in things of which she does not need to know. I will present this to her as a game that you and I have played for years. The game's goal, as far as Ms. Jones is concerned, is to see which of us wins the most money."

Magnolia nodded to herself. "I get it. This is for things other than rearranging finances."

"Precisely."

"What if I can't get a copy of the *2013 World Almanac*?"

"If you can't get 2013, get the most recent year you can. You can tell me what year when we talk again, after your visit with Ms. Jones. Also, if you can't get 2013 you can ignore the numbers she gives you. We'll do another test with the almanac that you do get."

"And what if we win the lottery?" Magnolia chided.

Hawke chuckled. "I shall buy Goodhue County and set you free."

As they were about to end the call, Hawke changed the subject. "One other thing. The judge who was sitting on your case in Boston has resigned. I thought you'd like to know."

"Did you cause that?" Magnolia asked in surprise.

"His decision to resign was entirely his own," Hawke assured her. He neglected to mention that the Cayman Islands bank account was empty. Hawke had helpfully removed the $75,000 as a "humanitarian gesture" to save the good judge from temptation.

Hawke chuckled silently as he hung up, quite pleased with himself.

The initial shock had worn off, and her brief pity party lasted less than the time it took to walk back to her cell. Magnolia sat on her bed rubbing her temples and fuming about how to get even with the bastards who were trying to take away the U.S. Senate seat she had fought so hard to win. She hadn't risen to the top of the heap by lamenting over the past or dwelling on things she couldn't control, but this was different. All of them would suffer for this, especially the ones who had promised to support her.

She needed to confirm what Hawke said. Initially, he had not wanted her to run for the Senate because of the attention it would draw, but she had run contrary to his advice. Having been elected, she couldn't think of any reason Hawke would now benefit from her expulsion from the Senate. Nor was he likely to start a rumor that he knew she could easily vet. Still, she didn't trust him, so she had to be sure. She would have Samantha arrange a visit with Findley and confront him with the rumor. His reaction would tell her whether the party had abandoned her.

A tap on the door interrupted her thoughts. "Dinner" said a voice from the other side. A food tray was slid through the slot on the bottom of the door. "You have a visitor tomorrow," the voice said, "at 1:30. I'll come and get you."

"Thank you," Magnolia replied. She looked down at the food tray. "What is this?"

There was no answer. The guard had either left or was too embarrassed to answer. Maybe she didn't know what it was, either.

Magnolia put the tray on the table, sat down on the stool and pushed the glop around with her spork. Elbow pasta, beans, onions, chunks of tomato, corn, and meat lumps of an unidentifiable source, were mixed together in a thick sauce. A dinner roll, a plastic container of sliced peaches, and a carton of milk completed the evening's fare. At least she'd have bread and peaches to eat.

She began eating, and her thoughts returned to Hawke's revelation and how, if true, it changed everything, not just her status in the Senate, but her trial strategy, too. Proving her innocence might be impossible; it was her word against a mountain of evidence. Her rejection of Taft's suggestion to take a plea deal might have to be reconsidered. But she was innocent, and for now, she could not reconcile herself to pleading guilty to a crime she didn't commit.

On the other hand, avoiding a trial had its appeal. Without the Senate seat to worry about, the incompetency strategy might be her best option, although, *God, how I hate shrinks.* When her mother had forced her to "go to counseling" as a teenager, Magnolia already knew she was the smartest person in the room. *Namby pamby gasbags who spouted platitudes and think everything is a result of your childhood. A waste of time!*

But she could play their game. She could be incompetent if that's what was needed. Hawke, without saying it, had made it clear that Magnolia would never spend time in a mental institution. *Where should I spend the rest of my life,* she pondered as she stuck a spork full of food in her mouth.

Magnolia looked down at the tray. Without thinking, she had eaten half of the glop. *That's pretty good,* she mused, surprised. And then she remembered a conversation over dinner one night in the day room, back when she was still welcome there. *Hot dish!* Apparently, a Minnesota tradition.

She finished eating the other half of the mixture. *Not too bad, but hot dish? The French word, cassoulet, was much more appealing.*

The following morning, Magnolia fidgeted while she waited for her 1:30 visit with Samantha. Pacing back and forth in her cell, she daydreamed about places she would like to spend the rest of her life. It would be someplace out of the United States. She loved Barcelona, but she was too well-known there. Ireland was too wet, and anything close to the equator was too hot. Her rhapsodizing kept going back to a little village in southern France, St. Cirq Laopopie. She and Kincaid had visited there once. The village was built high on a cliff overlooking a river and was the evolution of an 11th century medieval fortress. Quaint, with steep cobblestone streets and open-air markets, it would be a perfect place to reinvent herself. It was isolated from the incessant news cycles, yet within a few hours of both Paris and Barcelona. Her French was passable, and she could easily come up with a new name that suggested French lineage. Perhaps she'd be a Canadian citizen from Quebec, moving to France to be closer to her roots. Maybe a bit of plastic surgery to alter her appearance. This time, her new name wouldn't come from a highway sign.

At 1:20 the guard came to escort her to the electronic visiting room. Magnolia braced herself, hoping she wouldn't see Mooch. She knew the guard was there to keep them separate, but she found herself perspiring. What if the guard looked the other way? What if Mooch, or one of her cronies, jumped her?

She got to the room without incident and slid into the seat in front of a blank monitor. No other inmates were in the room, a function of the protective custody order.

The monitor sprang to life and startled Magnolia. She gasped softly and stared into the screen, wide-eyed and dumbstruck. Staring at her through the screen was not Samantha Jones but another dark-skinned person. A man.

Magnolia pulled back from the screen. A rosy complexion appeared out of nowhere. Her left eye twitched, and she blinked. "Do I know you?" she asked. "You look familiar."

It was the first time Ham could remember being alone with his mother. Even though they were geographically separated by miles, the electronic visitation network brought them face-to-face. She looked small and fragile in the too-big prison uniform. Her eyes were a striking cobalt blue. Her hair was silver with roots that were black and gray from lack of attention. Her facial features reflected European ancestry, far from his East Indian features and dark brown skin. Naturally black hair was the only common trait between them.

I must have gotten all my genes from my father, he thought.

Her question sounded almost whimsical. Was she trying to deal with the situation by being humorous? Her expression, now with a slight smile that made her look years younger, showed no trace of levity.

"Thanks for seeing me," he said.

"What do you want?" she asked, more curious than hostile.

"I thought you might like some company; someone to talk to," he answered.

"That's nice." Her face lit up. "Are you some kind of social worker?"

"No," he answered, his optimism tinged with confusion. "I'm related to you, and I'd like to get to know you."

"Really?" She sounded genuinely surprised. "I didn't know I had any relatives. I'm an only child, and my mom died years ago. I never knew my da…," her expression changed as she stopped in mid-sentence.

"You're not one of those con artists who goes around taking advantage of people who are all alone, are you?"

"No," Ham blurted. "You're my mother, and...."

"I'm not your mother, and I'll never be your mother!" Magnolia snarled.

Ham reeled, as if the force of her response and cataclysmic change in her demeanor had blown him backwards. He tried to grasp what had just happened.

"Let me phrase that differently," he countered, struggling to overcome his shock. "I'm your biological child, and I thought it might be nice to get to know each other."

"I don't know you, and I don't want to know you." Her reply was cold, heartless. She stared at him, then blinked. "*You* are that art forger who sold my museum a fake painting, and it cost me a million dollars."

His mind reeled from the second unexpected assault. "It isn't a forgery," he parried defensively. "It's the original *Reaper;* it was painted by Miro, not me."

"I know it's a forgery because I hired you to paint it!" she shrieked.

"Arthur Kincaid hired me to paint a copy of *The Reaper,*" Ham struggled to keep from shouting back at her. "When he died, the deal was canceled, costing me a million-dollar commission. You ordered that cancellation. I think you regretted that decision later after you learned I'm your son. You agreed to donate a million dollars to the museum to purchase *The Reaper*, even though you thought it was a forgery, because you knew I would get the million dollars you cost me by cancelling the deal. What you don't know is that I never painted a copy of it. I inherited the real *Reaper* from a relative of my wife who actually worked at the 1937 World Exposition where the painting was displayed."

"Wrong! Wrong! Wrong! I have no son. And I had no idea who the seller of *The Reaper* was until after the museum bought it, and I'd put up a million dollars. Your story about inheriting the painting is pure fantasy. There is not a court in the world that will believe your lies."

Ham nodded, a grim look on his face. "But you don't deny that it was you who had Kincaid hire me to paint *The Reaper*," he said. "Why did you cancel my commission in the first place?"

Magnolia stood up and shouted at someone in the room just out of camera range. "Get me out of here."

"Why won't you admit you're my mother!" he shouted desperately as Magnolia walked away and disappeared from the screen.

Ham sat deflated as the monitor went blank. He had messed up, allowing his temper to get out of control. He thought he had prepared himself, but when the subject of *The Reaper* came up, she'd gone wacko, and he'd lost it. Tears ran down his face.

"I'm going to try again," he told Toni later over a plate of spaghetti at Cossetta's. "We got off on the subject of *The Reaper*, and she's really angry because she thinks we sold the museum a forgery. But she didn't deny that she was behind Kincaid hiring me to paint a copy of it. She didn't pick any random artist. She picked me. The only logical reason is that she felt guilty about abandoning me and wanted me to get a million dollars. What I don't understand is why she cancelled the deal after Kincaid died."

Toni, who had spent the afternoon on eggshells waiting for her husband to explode, was both relieved and surprised at Ham's attitude. "So, she acknowledged you as her son?"

"Well, no, not exactly," he explained. "She denied being my mother, but I think she was really talking about performing the role of a mother. She didn't deny I was her biological child."

"Well, that's something." Toni grimaced. "Why don't you mail her a copy of the order from the French court that awarded you the painting? Maybe *that* will convince her the museum's *Reaper* is authentic."

Ham nodded. "Great idea. If we can at least get on speaking terms maybe we can have a conversation about why she cancelled the deal. And why she abandoned me."

"My persistent, hopeful husband," Toni said, reaching across the table to hold Ham's hand. "I love you for that, and I'll help you any way I can, but it's possible she will never agree to talk with you."

"I've thought about that," Ham answered. "But, when we first started talking today, it was…it was…pleasant. But when the painting came up it was like she changed into a different person. If we can just get *The Reaper* issue out of the way…," Ham trailed off. As much as he didn't want it to, the prospect that his mother was mentally ill had momentarily crossed his mind.

They sat, each with their own thoughts, until Toni broke the silence. "I got a job offer today."

Her quiet words snapped Ham out of his trance. "Wow. That's great," he said. "Wait. Is that why you took us out to dinner? To celebrate? And I've been all wrapped up in this thing with my mother. I'm sorry."

"Nothing to celebrate, yet," Tony answered. "I haven't accepted it, but it is an intriguing offer. Only one problem. It's in Winona."

"Winona? That's two, three hours from here."

"As I said, that's the problem."

"Who's it with?" Ham asked.

"The Minnesota Marine Art Museum," Toni answered. "It's a new museum, less than ten years old. It focuses mostly on art inspired by water. Apparently, it's gone through a series of expansions, and they're looking for an event manager and education assistant."

"That sounds like a big step down from assistant curator of the Boston Museum of Visual Arts," Ham said, referring to Toni's previous job.

"I'm not exactly a hot commodity in the art industry right now," she offered. "We've still got the issue of *The Reaper* hanging over our head. Until that's over, I'll be happy just to have a job, and this sounds like it could at least be interesting. And, guess what? I tried to call Jim Benson today to ask him for a letter of recommendation, and he's not at the U anymore. He's teaching at Winona State University. "

"That's part of MNSCU, right?" Ham asked. "So, what's next?"

"I have an interview in Winona next week. Want to go on a road trip? We can tour the museum and maybe Jim and Melissa will show us the city."

"Winona's way in the southeast corner of the state," Ham mused. "If we settle there, it means a lot more travel for me."

"I know," Toni said softly, looking down at her half-eaten pasta. "I haven't said anything before," she continued, "but I'd like to get out of the Twin Cities. I don't feel comfortable here. It brings back memories. I'm always looking over my shoulder. And we could buy you a new van."

"Is it because you think you saw that Todd character?"

Toni shrugged. "Maybe. Whatever it is, I don't feel comfortable."

Magnolia met with Samantha the following morning.

"I got a call from some French guy who called himself Onree Hawk," Samantha began. "He said that he and I are supposed to work together on your finances and investments. He also gave me ten lottery ticket numbers he said he bought for you."

"Henri is an old friend," Magnolia replied. "He's been one of my advisers on legal and financial issues for a long time, even before I was the CEO of Kincaid Media. I need the two of you to work together on my finances, particularly on off-shore issues. He's an expert on foreign investment and banking, but only you have my power of attorney. He has no authority to act on his own. He can only advise, and I want his recommendations run by me before you implement them."

"Of course."

"What have you decided about moving into my penthouse?" Magnolia asked, purposely turning the subject away from Hawke.

"I still have eight months left on my apartment lease…," she stammered.

"Just pay it off," Magnolia interrupted. "Take money out of my personal account. I really would like you to live in the penthouse until I'm out of here. After I get out, we'll make the necessary arrangement for you to buy a place of your own."

Samantha looked down, embarrassed by the generosity.

"Just do it," Magnolia insisted. "I'll have my lawyers get in touch with the Pier 4 management so there won't be any issues with you moving in."

Samantha looked up. "Thank you," she said softly.

"Thank you!" Magnolia repeated back to her. "On another subject, have you had any conversation with Harvey Findley?"

"I left a message for him after our last meeting, but he hasn't returned my call."

"Call him again. If he doesn't answer, leave a message that I need to talk to him immediately. Tell him he can't call me. The only way we can have a conversation is to set up a visit like this one. You can help him handle the logistics. Call him every day, two or three times a day, until he answers your call."

"What's going on with Kincaid Media?" Magnolia asked, changing the subject.

"The stock has fully recovered," Samantha said.

"That's good. I still have shares in that blind trust. Anything else?"

"Nothing in the media. The company is keeping a low profile," Samantha answered. "What about these lottery ticket numbers?"

"Oh. Those." Magnolia laughed, sounding nonchalant. "It's a little game Henri and I play. He's much more into it than I am, but it gives him pleasure so I play along. Do you have the numbers?"

Magnolia returned to her cell and sat down with the *World Almanac* to decode the lottery ticket numbers. When she was finished, the message read, "Hope you are having nice day flowers are out and it's beautiful here this time of year your friend." She squelched the urge to draft a reply. She would just talk to Hawke tomorrow.

Lunch was delivered, and with it came the information that a meeting with Taft had been scheduled for 2:30. She picked at her food and wondered what bad news this meeting would bring.

"We filed a motion this morning, raising the issue of your competency to stand trial," Taft told her. Magnolia rolled her eyes and exhaled loudly to make sure Taft understood her dislike for the idea. "A telephone hearing with the judge and prosecuting attorney has been set for tomorrow."

"Do I need to be there?"

"No," Taft continued. "They can't deny the motion. The hearing is about scheduling. The judge will appoint a psychiatrist to examine you. The prosecutor may request his hand-picked psychiatrist be appointed, also. We'll tell them who our expert will be. That's all we'll talk about."

"You mean I am going to have to sit through this B.S. with *three* shrinks?" Magnolia complained.

"No. Sorry. I wasn't clear. There will only be two; ours and theirs," Taft responded, "but I expect you will have multiple sessions, at least with our guy. I've retained a forensic psychologist named Bishop Pollock. He's highly regarded in the Minnesota judicial system."

"When does this start?"

"The schedule will be set in tomorrow's phone conference, but likely as soon as we can get on Pollock's schedule."

"What about the prosecutor's psychiatrist? When will that happen?" Magnolia asked.

"You'll have a session with the court psychiatrist after Pollock submits his report. That's how it works in most jurisdictions, but we'll have more clarity after tomorrow's hearing."

"These are in person, right?" Magnolia asked.

"Yes. At Pollock's office in Rochester. About an hour's drive, I'm told," Taft said. "With travel time, each session will take about a half a day. You'll be able to get out and get a little fresh air. Of course, you'll have a guard with you at all times."

"I assume I'm paying for all of this."

"Including the guard, the driver, and a charge for the car," Taft confirmed.

Magnolia nodded and sighed. "Okay. It will be worth it to get out of here, even if it's just for a little while."

"You'll have to waive your constitutional right to a speedy trial," Taft added. "This process is going to take a few weeks, and the omnibus hearing that was scheduled for mid-March will be delayed until all the psychiatric reports are in."

"Speedy trial?" she laughed. "Fast or slow won't make any difference."

Before breakfast the next morning there was a knock on Magnolia's cell door. The lock clicked, and a guard stuck her head in. "Your attorney's on the phone," she said.

"Which one?" Magnolia groaned, stretching.

"I don't know. I didn't take the call. Get dressed and come with me." Minutes later Magnolia entered the attorney meeting room. "Just pick up the phone and say who you are," the guard said. "The operator will connect you." The door lock snapped shut behind her.

As Magnolia had suspected, the caller was Hawke.

"The sound of your voice brightens my day," Hawke gushed in his usual smarmy manner.

"Where are you? What time is it there?" Magnolia asked.

"I am in Paris, and I have just finished my lunch. It is 1:55 in the p.m. Why do you ask?"

"Because it's 6:55 in the morning here. You got me out of bed, and I am about to miss breakfast," Magnolia scolded. "In the future, please do not call before 4:00 p.m. your time."

"Ah, my apologies, mademoiselle. I shall abide by your wishes in the future. Did you get my message?"

Magnolia read the decoded message.

"Excellent!" Hawke exclaimed. "And what of your psychiatric appointments?"

"The psychologist's office is in a city near here called Rochester. It's about an hour's drive. I assume that is where the sessions will be."

"Ah, the day is full of good news."

For the next fifteen minutes Hawke gave her the results of his background checks on the judge, the county attorney, and the U.S. attorney. "These Minnesota people are not nearly as scandalous as your Washington politicians," he concluded. "Your judge is a little... what shall we say...erratic. Perhaps unpredictable is better. The county attorney may have some political aspirations, but there is little among any of them that we can leverage."

"Without force," Magnolia prodded.

"Do not say such things," Hawke admonished.

"Don't go soft on me now," Magnolia laughed.

Hawke veered away from the subject. "I will need to know the address of the place where you will be *visiting*. Perhaps you can give that to Ms. Jones, and she can forward it to me. By the way, neither of us won anything this week."

Late that afternoon Magnolia received a call from Taft.

"It went as we expected," he said. "We've been allowed 30 days for Pollock to examine you and file his report. The State has 15 days after that for examination and filing her report. A hearing will be held in 60 days where the judge will rule on your competency to stand trial."

"The other psychiatrist is a woman?"

"Yes. Her name is Amanda Pappenfuss," Taft answered. "We're doing a background check on her. All the psychiatric sessions will be held at the jail. The judge wouldn't agree to have your sessions at

Pollock's office in Rochester. That's the only part of the hearing that didn't go as we planned."

Magnolia felt the bile rise in her throat. "Have you passed this information along to Henri?"

There was a pause at the other end of the line. "I'll have Laura do it," Taft said. "We've got a call in to Pollock to set up your first session. I'll let you know when, as soon as we find out."

Findley sat on the couch in Styles' office, waiting patiently for the Senator to finish his morning briefing. A federal judicial appointment, committee activity on the tariff bill, and a laundry list of constituent requests topped the agenda for the day. Findley hung back as the last staff person filed out.

"You were uncharacteristically quiet this morning," Styles said, cocking his head as he looked at Findley, turning his statement into a question. "What don't I know that I should be worried about?"

"Kanaranzi," Findley responded.

"Now what?" Styles grimaced.

"I got two phone calls saying she *needs* to talk to me," Findley exhaled loudly.

"So, talk to her."

"Why does she *need* to talk to me? And what do I say to her? That we're looking for another candidate?"

"I thought she couldn't make calls except to her lawyer."

"The calls were from her press secretary."

The Senator nodded, his lips pursed. "What would Magnolia *need* from you?"

"It could be about the bail, but more than likely she's gotten word that we're looking for someone to fill her seat."

"Has she gone forward with that incompetent-to-stand-trial strategy?"

"I have no new information about that. There's been nothing in the media."

"So, call her and tell her we've heard a rumor that her competency to stand trial is being brought into question," Styles said. "Tell her that if that happens, we won't have the necessary votes to prevent her expulsion…"

"And that we are fully behind her," Findley completed the Senator's sentence, "but we need to be prepared if we lose the expulsion fight. We're just being prepared…like boy scouts."

"Don't go overboard. No one is ever going to call us boy scouts," the Senator chuckled. "Is there any indication that anyone on The Hill is aware of this competency thing?"

"Not so far, but as soon as word gets out, this is going to unravel quickly," Findley said. "Belton is the best option we've got at the moment to run for the open seat. I think we need to start lining up behind her."

"Do it," Styles said. "Or, rather, do both. Call Magnolia and tell her we're just covering our asses in case we can't hold together the necessary votes to keep her in office, and then get on the phone with the national committee to start ramping up support for Belton."

Findley gave Styles the Boy Scout salute. "Yes, sir," he said in his best mock-military style.

"Screw you," Styles laughed.

"Your press secretary has been telling me about all the humanitarian work you've done," Findley said after he and Magnolia had exchanged pleasantries through the visitor monitor. "Did you really…"

"Why are you looking for someone to take my place?" Magnolia cut in.

Findley hesitated, momentarily mesmerized by her blazing blue eyes. "There's a rumor that your lawyers have filed a motion to have you declared incompetent," he finally said. "Is that true?"

"I don't like it, but they say it's our best strategy," Magnolia answered.

"I was afraid that was what you were going to say. It's possible we'll lose some votes because of the competency question. If you're declared incompetent to stand trial, or even if word gets out that your lawyers are proposing that defense, there will be an immediate move to start an expulsion proceeding, and we may not be able to defeat it. We had to start strategizing. We're just trying to be prepared."

"I am not incompetent, no matter what the court decides," Magnolia spat. "Your own psychiatrist confirmed that."

"I know, but a court ruling of incompetency is likely to change minds in the Senate, and it will only take a couple to flip, and then we lose the expulsion vote."

"Can you send a copy of your psychiatrist's report to my lawyer? Maybe it will change his mind." Magnolia gave him Taft's contact information. "And send him a list of the Senators who might switch their votes."

"What would you do with that list?"

"I still know people with influence," she said. "They might be able to convince them not to switch."

"I'll have to think about that."

Findley's answer told Magnolia all she needed to know. She knew that he would never send that list. Hawke was right.

And each and every one of them is going to pay.

Bishop Pollock got Carrie's name from Laura Avery.

"I've been retained to psychoanalyze Magnolia Kanaranzi," he said. "I understand you know a great deal about her early life. I'd like to talk with you about that if you are willing."

"Why are you psychoanalyzing her?"

"I've been asked to render an opinion on whether she is mentally fit to stand trial."

"Who hired you?" Carrie asked.

"Ms. Avery's law firm."

Carrie paused. "What happens if she's not fit to stand trial?"

"She'll be committed to a mental institution for treatment."

"For how long?"

"Until it's determined she *is* fit to stand trial."

"I'll have to check with my partners," Carrie said. "I'll get back to you."

Two days later Carrie was sitting at a local coffee shop, across the table from Pollock, sipping a latte. "My partners aren't wild about my talking to you," she said. "It cost us a great deal to investigate Magnolia Kanaranzi and find out who she really is…and what she did…but our client said I should talk to you, so here I am."

"Your client?"

"Magnolia's son, Hamilton Blethen."

"Well, thank Mr. Blethen for me, and thank *you* for meeting with me," Pollock replied. "You and your client should know I have no bias in this case. I am being paid to be impartial. It's much easier to reach an accurate diagnosis if you know a person's history, and Ms. Kanaranzi's history is shrouded in mystery."

Carrie smiled. "You're telling me? I spent months investigating her. We had to dig to connect the dots because someone made a big effort to erase her real life and replace it with a fictional one."

Pollock pursed his lips, nodding. "Mind if I record this?" he asked.

Carrie nodded her consent, then went on to relate the story of Mary Blethen growing up and going to high school in Zumbrota; how she had been brutally raped when she was 14, got involved in drugs, began running with a rough crowd, and left town the day she graduated from high school. She disappeared after high school, caught up in drugs and petty crime.

"She had a child. She literally left him with her own mother when the kid was four. Just dropped him off and never came back. She must have been desperate because she hated her mother," Carrie related. "That's how we got involved. The child, our client, hired us to find out who killed his grandmother. The second part of our job was to try and help him find his estranged mother whom, by that time, he hadn't seen or heard from in over 35 years. It turned out that by finding one, we solved the other."

"You said someone went to great lengths to erase her past. Can you tell me more about that?" Pollock asked.

"Her high school records in Zumbrota disappear after eighth grade, plus records of her run-ins with the law after high school were deleted. Instead, a whole new set of records were created in Sturgis, South Dakota, and in Las Vegas, for a girl named Mary Stumpf. These records showed that Mary Stumpf changed her name to Magnolia Kanaranzi while she was living in Las Vegas. We now know Mary Stumpf doesn't exist, and it was Mary Blethen who changed her name. It took us a long time to figure that out."

"Do you know who changed the records?"

"It wasn't relevant to our investigation. We assume whoever it was, was hired by Magnolia."

"I understand you learned that Ms. Kanaranzi had been raped in high school through an interview with a man who has Alzheimer's. Tell me about that."

"His name is Albert Freeman. He was a custodian and dance teacher at the high school. Apparently, he found Mary…Ms. Kanaranzi… after the rape and took her home. According to Freeman, her mother blamed Mary and accused Freeman of raping her."

"Was Freeman ever charged?"

"He didn't do it," Carrie answered. "It was a high school student who raped her, and I don't think charges were ever brought. The student was the son of a very influential person."

"Did you learn that from Freeman?"

"Initially, yes, but I confirmed through other sources. No charges were brought against Freeman or anyone else. Believe me, if Freeman had been responsible, he would have been prosecuted."

"You said her mother blamed Ms. Kanaranzi," Pollock said. "What was the relationship between them?"

"We learned that Magnolia and her mother didn't get along very well, but it seemed that the relationship got worse after the rape. I can tell you that her mother, Lorraine, wasn't particularly well-liked, and not just by her daughter."

"The memo you wrote after your interview with Freeman said that you hypnotized him. Tell me more about that."

For the next half hour, over a second latte, Pollock and Carrie discussed hypnosis, its uses and limitations, techniques, and subject susceptibility. It was clear that they concurred on most aspects.

"Have you ever worked with a psychologist?" Pollock asked as the conversation wound down.

"I don't do hypnotherapy," Carrie said, "but on occasion, I share information with a psychologist who uses it to treat a patient. Kind of like what we're doing here."

"Have you ever gone out to dinner with a psychologist?" Pollock asked next. It caught Carrie completely by surprise.

"Ah…ah…no."

"Would you like to?" he asked, smiling.

"I don't think that would be a good idea," she said. "Not until this case is over."

Carrie sat in her old blue Subaru, stunned. *Wow.* She wasn't sure whether she should be flattered or repulsed. Pollock was at least 25 years older than she was, and he had a PhD. Carrie had barely finished high school. *Yet he was hitting on me. Isn't that a violation of some ethical standard? Maybe he's just trying to get more information from me. But he didn't have to ask me out to dinner to get that? He's not ugly. Maybe a little overweight, but so am I. More than a little. But he still asked me out. Maybe he was hypnotized.*

She giggled at her own humor. She decided she was flattered.

The vintage Pontiac Trans Am emitted low guttural exhaust notes as it glided south, crossing the Mississippi over the Hennepin Avenue Bridge, passing Whole Foods, then making a right at Washington Avenue and continuing west into the toney North Loop district of Minneapolis. At Second Avenue North it turned left, and again a block later, doubling back on the route.

He had made this loop two or three times a day in the past two weeks, hoping to catch sight of the woman he knew as Toni Chapereaux. After three years, his thoughts of her had waned to no more than two or three times a week, but seeing her in the Whole Foods Market had brought his fantasies back in lurid detail.

She had been on foot when she left Whole Foods the last time he saw her. She had to be living close by. He knew if he persisted, he would find her again. Until then, his fantasies would sustain him. Todd D'Anselmo could be a very patient man when necessary.

Bright sunshine glinted off the pristine black car and off the gold firebird painted on its hood as he rolled toward the intersection of Hennepin and North Third Street. He scanned the area. A mixed-race couple strolled on the Third Street sidewalk, hand-in-hand. An elderly woman pushed a shopping cart on the other side of the street, going the opposite direction. A man in a wheelchair sat in a small grassy area set back from the corner, holding the leash of a large dog.

D'Anselmo's gaze swept north and then south on Hennepin as he came to a stop. The building next to the grassy area was a parking ramp. "Shit!" he blurted out loud. How had he missed that? Maybe she had just walked into the parking ramp, got in a car, and driven away. Maybe she didn't live near here after all. "Shit!" he repeated.

He checked his rearview mirror. There was no car behind him, so he sat for a moment at the intersection, processing the information. *Most downtown parking ramps are attached to an office or an apartment building*, he thought. He peered down Hennepin, trying to see what was on the far end of the parking ramp halfway down the block. The space appeared to be vacant.

He turned right on Hennepin, and a small surface parking lot materialized halfway down the block. The building served by the small lot was set back from the street. A sign on the entrance said "Atrium Apartments." He turned into the lot, parked, and went in. The interior door, not surprisingly, was locked. He scrolled through the electronic directory of residents. First names were designated by letters. He didn't see anyone named Chapereaux. He buzzed the management office.

"Hi," he said when a woman answered. "I'm looking for an old friend, and I've been told she used to live here. Hoping she still does. Her name is Toni Chapereaux." He spelled the last name for the woman. "It might be under Antoinette. That's her first name."

"Nobody by the name of Chapereaux here," the woman said after a pause. "How long ago did she live here?"

"Within the last three years."

"Hold on a sec."

As D'Anselmo waited the outer door opened and the man in the wheelchair he'd seen on the corner came in. After a buzz, the inner door opened automatically.

"C'mon, Barca," the man said to the dog trailing him.

D'Anselmo kept his back to the man, waiting for him to pass through the vestibule and for the inner door to close. Then he slowly turned his head and watched the man in the wheelchair and the large golden dog make their way toward elevators. A smug smile crept onto his face.

"No one named Chapereaux has lived here in the last three years," the woman said over the intercom.

"Thanks anyway," D'Anselmo said. He stood for a moment. *What was the man's name? The dog's name was Barca.* He remembered that. *It must be the same guy. What is his name?* They had met at a jazz club. The guy wedged his way in between Toni and him. He was a painter. They had talked. Kind of a prick. Toni had introduced him as her boyfriend. *Hamilton!* Last name is…*Belton.*

Close enough.

He scrolled through the directory again. There was no *Belton*, but he did find *H and A Blethen.* D'Anselmo's smirk faded. "I should have killed the son-of-a-bitch when I had the chance," he muttered.

Magnolia had asked for a bigger table on the pretense that she needed more space to spread out as she wrote a book about her experiences. Now she sat with pen in hand, poised over a piece of notebook paper, searching the *World Almanac* for words. An hour later, finished, she double-checked her work. *First session Monday will send itinerary next week correct on Senate support move funds off shore need to be liquid.*

The lack of punctuation and cryptic grammar would give Samantha a heart attack if she knew. Magnolia half-smiled at the thought. It was too bad she had to take advantage of the young woman in this way, but Samantha would be richly rewarded.

An hour later they were talking.

"I'm scheduled to move into your penthouse next week," Samantha paused, "if that's still all right with you."

"Absolutely. It's the best news I've heard all day."

"Did Mr. Findley get in touch with you?"

"Yes. Thanks for setting that up. It was most informative."

"It doesn't sound like there's going to be an expulsion vote," Samantha went on. "From what I heard, they don't have the votes."

"I hope you're right," Magnolia answered, sounding optimistic for the benefit of her press secretary. "Any news about Kincaid Media?"

"No. Still quiet."

"I want you to get in touch with my broker," Magnolia directed. "I want to sell my shares in the company. Have him set it up in a way that draws the least attention and has the smallest impact on the company's value, probably in smaller blocks spread out over several weeks. If he asks, tell him I need funds to pay for my legal defense. He'll need to get the shares out of the blind trust, or terminate the trust, whichever works. If there are any legal issues, get in touch with my personal lawyer, Artemis Blazing. You've dealt with him before, and you have my power of attorney so you can sign whatever is necessary. Talk to Henri about where the sales proceeds should be invested. I'd like to have all this done in less than three months. Quicker, if possible." Magnolia paused and sighed dramatically. "And here are the lottery numbers for Henri when you talk to him. Tell him I've had a lot of time to think, and I'm certain these are my lucky numbers." She smiled mischievously.

"I'll make sure he gets these," Samantha laughed, "and I'll get on the stock sales as soon as we're done here."

"And set up a visit with Artemis. There are a few things he needs to do."

"Should I let him know what it's about?"

"Just tell him there are some estate planning issues I want him to take care of," Magnolia answered.

For the next several minutes, Samantha passed along gossip about various members of Boston's upper crust, one of whom served on the museum board with Magnolia.

"That reminds me," Magnolia said. "Check with Meredith Glenn and see what the museum plans on doing with *The Reaper*."

"Oh, speaking of *The Reaper*," Samantha said, "Can you read this?" She held a newspaper clipping up to the screen.

"I can't read the newsprint," Magnolia said, squinting at the screen. "What does it say?"

"That the Minnesota State university system has hired the guy who sold *The Reaper* to the Boston of Museum of Visual Arts."

"Hired him to do what?"

"To be a traveling lecturer. You'll never guess the subject."

"What?"

"Art forgery."

"You're talking about Hamilton Blethen, right?"

"Yes."

"Well, he certainly should know his subject."

Magnolia returned to her cell, to find mail on the table. The return address on the envelope simply said "Blethen" with a Minneapolis address. The note inside was from Toni Blethen.

> *Senator Kanaranzi,*
>
> *I know you suspect my husband of painting and selling a forgery of Joan Miro's "The Reaper." Enclosed is an order from a French court awarding the painting to Hamilton Blethen as part of the settlement of the estate of Monique Picard.*
>
> *Monique Picard worked at the Paris Exposition in 1937 where Miro's painting was exhibited. Her husband*

worked for the man who acquired the painting after the Exposition was over. The painting was given to Mr. Picard as a gift, and Monique inherited it when he died.

Monique Picard was my aunt. She met Hamilton at a family reunion, and they formed an instant bond. At the time no one knew she owned "The Reaper." When she died several years later, we learned that she had left the painting to Hamilton in her will. That was the first time that anyone in our family knew she owned it. There was litigation, brought by one of my cousins, claiming Monique's will was defective, but as you can see from the court order, the judge ruled in Hamilton's favor, finding Aunt Monique's will, and her bequest to Hamilton, to be valid.

I hope this will convince you that the painting purchased by the Boston Museum of Visual Arts is the original, and that Hamilton is not a forger.

Sincerely, Antoinette Blethen

Magnolia sat down on the chair and unfolded the papers that accompanied the note. One was a certified copy of a court order in French. The second was the same order in English. Magnolia's French was good enough for her to determine that the English translation was accurate.

She put the papers down on the table, shaking her head, trying to reconcile what she had just read with the facts as she knew them. She walked across her cell and laid down on her bed, staring at the gray ceiling.

PSYCHOBABBLE

"I'm not safe in here," Magnolia said as she sat on the front edge of the metal chair, leaning toward the table that separated her from Bishop Pollock. Although restraints fastened her ankles to the chair legs, her legs bounced up and down in a rapid, agitated rhythm. Pollock could feel the vibration and see the staccato twitching of the sleeves of her blue prison shirt.

"Why do you think you're not safe?" he asked.

"The inmates hate me."

Pollock pursed his lips. *She'd be an easy target. She's rich and famous and a U. S. Senator. She's the perfect mark for some psychotic prisoner or a lifer looking for a trophy to enhance their cred.*

"Why do you think the inmates hate you? Have you been threatened?"

"One of the inmates has put out a contract on me."

Pollock cocked his head, a questioning look on his face.

"Supposedly I hit her. Broke her nose."

Pollock thought he detected a bit of pride in Magnolia's last statement. "It's my understanding that you're in protective custody," Pollock continued.

"That looks good on paper, but a guard could leave a door unlocked or just happen not to be outside the door where they're supposed to be," she said. "Some inmates have special...um...privileges. They've been in here so often they've become friends with the guards. They could probably persuade them to look the other way."

She hunched her shoulders and squeezed her elbows tightly against her body. Her manacled hands, palms up, were secured by a chain attached to a metal ring on her belt. "I can't defend myself or even run. Could *you* protect me if someone came through that door right now?"

"I have this buzzer to call a guard," he said, holding up a hand-sized electronic device.

"And if the guard's not right outside the door it could be too late… for both of us."

It had never occurred to Pollock that he might be in danger from an outside source. He looked around the small, institutionally sparse room and rubbed his chin in thought. "Do you feel safe enough right now to answer a few preliminary questions?" he asked, concern creeping into his voice.

The rhythm of her bouncing legs picked up tempo.

"Is the guard outside the door?" she asked.

Pollock got up, opened the door and looked out. There was no guard in the hallway. He turned to her and shook his head. She squeezed her elbows tighter to her body again and shuddered.

"I'm scared."

Taft and Lawrence Bunch sat across a massive desk looking at Judge Susan Weber. Court had adjourned for the day, and they were in chambers because of Taft's emergency motion to allow his client to be examined at a site outside of the Goodhue County Jail. On one end of the desk sat a monitor. Pollock had joined the meeting electronically at the request of Taft, with Weber's permission.

"So, you're telling me," Judge Weber said, addressing Pollock directly, "that you can't make a professional diagnosis if you have to question, or counsel, or whatever you call what you do, the defendant at the jail facility where she's currently incarcerated. Is that correct?"

Pollock nodded his concurrence. "Not with the necessary degree of professional certainty, Your Honor. Her fear could affect any or all of her answers. It could prevent her from remembering things. It could make her act out in ways that, if she were not fearful, would otherwise never happen."

"Mr. Bunch," the judge turned to the County Attorney. "Your thoughts?"

"The prosecution opposes the defense's request to have the sessions held at Dr. Pollock's office," Bunch stated. "That's a drive of at least an hour each way, and the defense has stated that there will be multiple sessions. Neither the jail staff, nor the Goodhue County Sheriff's Office, has sufficient staff to cover that kind of extraordinary treatment. There is always the risk of escape or accident or some intervening event. And, there is no precedent for the request being made. This has never been allowed in Goodhue County, especially not for a murder suspect. We respectfully request that you deny their emergency motion."

"Is there any realistic basis for the defendant's fear?"

"No, Your Honor," Bunch answered. "She is under protective custody. She is always under guard. She's as safe as she can possibly be."

"That's exactly the point," Taft interrupted. "'Safe as she can possibly be.' I can give you a long list of defendants, some from this state, who were in protective custody while in prison but who were attacked, maimed, and at least in one case, murdered. Safe 'as can possibly be' is not safe. It may be *safer*, but it is not safe."

"If I may, Your Honor," Pollock interjected, "legal arguments notwithstanding, fear is a valid emotional response. It does not have to arise from some actual threat. It may not seem logical to others, but if it is perceived, it is real in the mind of the perceiver. I observed Senator Kanaranzi this morning. She was afraid. She fears for her safety. She doesn't think the guards can, or will, protect her."

"So, you're claiming that she should be transferred out of Goodhue County Jail to another facility because she's afraid?" Judge Weber snapped. "If that was the standard, I'd have to move every f…every prisoner to another facility. But about this claim that fear will interfere with your ability to issue a professional opinion." She turned to Bunch. "Have you asked Dr. Pappenfuss if there is any medical basis to support a claim of that nature?"

"I…I haven't been able to reach her," Bunch stuttered.

"Get her on the phone right now," Weber ordered.

"I only have her office number," Bunch answered.

"She's a psychiatrist. She'll have an emergency number. It will either be her personal number or the number of someone who can get in touch with her. Get her on the phone!"

Less than ten minutes later, Dr. Amanda Pappenfuss was on speakerphone, listening to Bishop Pollock talk about fear as an impediment to diagnosis.

"Dr. Pappenfuss, do you agree with Dr. Pollock or not?" Weber asked when Pollock was done.

"I do," she said. "If the subject is fearful and perceives she is in danger, it can certainly alter how she responds, which could result in an erroneous diagnosis."

"In your opinion, will changing the location of the interview to some place outside the jail correct that problem?"

"We have no way of knowing that, Your Honor," Pappenfuss replied, "but if the source of the fear is at the location, it might. It might take two or three sessions to determine if it solved the problem, but it certainly could."

The Judge rocked back in her chair and rested her chin on her clasped hands. "Thank you both," she said to Pollock and Pappenfuss. "You may both hang up and go about your evening. You have been most helpful." After they hung up, Weber called her court reporter into chambers. "I'm ready to issue an order."

"First, let me preface my order by saying that this case is without precedent. We are all a part of living history that will be dissected, studied, reiterated, criticized, and acclaimed for centuries. We must not shrink from the duty that this monumental event imposes upon us, nor step back from the level of excellence that it requires of us. This unprecedented trial calls upon us to think in terms of historical significance and to make decisions of unparalleled gravity.

"With that in mind, I am hereby granting Defendant's motion to move the psychiatric sessions outside of the Goodhue County Jail on the following conditions: that all examinations be held in Red Wing at a site agreed upon by Drs. Pappenfuss and Pollock, the Defendant will bear the burden of all costs related to and arising from this Order, and my previous Order is amended to extend the time periods for psychiatric examinations and exchange of reports by an additional 30 days."

She turned to the attorneys. "Anything else?"

"Can we have the defendant come and go through the courthouse, Your Honor?" Taft requested.

"Any objection, Mr. Bunch?"

"None, Your Honor."

"Fine. Do you want it in the Order?" she asked Taft.

"No. Your order will become public soon enough, and I don't want the press camped out at the courthouse door waiting for her. Could we get her some clothes other than her prison uniform? Maybe some sunglasses and a hat. Something to make her less identifiable."

"Mr. Bunch, would you please talk to the Sheriff's Department and get that taken care of?"

Coming from Judge Weber, it wasn't a question.

Magnolia received a call from Taft and Avery the next morning.

"Your sessions will be at the St. James Hotel," Taft said. "It's convenient and it's comfortable. We're planning for the first session on Monday. We'll let you know over the weekend as soon as we get logistics figured out. You will get different clothes to wear. After we're done here, you and Laura can go over a list of what you'll need. We'll want to avoid the press, so pick out something lowkey. Think of it like a costume party where you don't want to draw attention to yourself because you don't want anyone to know who you are."

"Where's this hotel?" Magnolia asked.

"Just a few blocks from the jail," Taft answered. "A car will pick you up at the courthouse and take you to the hotel."

"How long before the media knows about this?"

"Probably within a week. I'm sure some nosy reporter will look at the court file and find our competency motion and Weber's Order. We made sure the order didn't say where in Red Wing the sessions would take place, or that you'd exit the jail through the tunnel to the courthouse."

"They'll figure it out soon enough."

"We tried to get you out of there altogether, transferred to another facility," Taft said, adopting Pollock's argument as if it was his own.

"But the Judge wouldn't buy it. She said fear is not a basis for switching facilities."

Magnolia snorted. "She needs a little fear in her life."

"They're saying my best chance is to plead incompetence so I don't have to stand trial."

The look on Samantha's face was one of shock. "That's insane," she blurted.

"Really?" Magnolia responded, a note of humorous disbelief in her voice.

"Sorry. That wasn't meant to be a pun," Samantha blushed. "It's just that it doesn't make any sense. You didn't kill your mother. And what happens to your Senate seat if they find you incompetent?"

"We're dealing with all that," Magnolia answered, trying to calm Samantha with words that she wasn't sure were true. "Have you talked to Harvey Findley lately, or anyone else in Washington?"

"I left another message for him, but I haven't heard back. I've kept a close eye on the news, but there is nothing there except the occasional op ed piece about the filibuster rule. What's going to happen now with the incompetence thing?"

"I'm going to see a shrink who will issue a professional opinion on whether I am competent to stand trial. If he o-pines I'm incompetent, my lawyers are supposed to make sure it's worded in a way that gives the opposition limited basis to argue that this should be sufficient to expel me."

"Wow," was all Samantha could muster. "That's a real gamble."

"Life's a gamble," Magnolia answered. "I've won more than I've lost. I'm counting on this to be another win. Speaking of gambling,

I have numbers for you to give Henri. Maybe I'll win the lottery this week," she chuckled.

"I'm examining a U.S. Senator," Pollock said firmly. "I can't have my examining room looking like a bedroom or the lobby of a brothel. The setting must be comfortable and serene without a cacophony of…," he looked dispassionately around the room. "Of this."

The venerable old hotel had hosted the famous, the infamous, and the highly-sensitive over its 150-year existence. Accommodating a U.S. Senator and a petulant psychologist was little more than business as usual for its staff, and in the fashion of world-class hoteliers, the hotel management had responded to Pollock's insults and brusqueness with grace and dignity.

Nonetheless, Pollock muttered to himself as he and the hotel's assistant manager watched two maintenance men disassemble a massive king-size bed. It would have been much easier if they had just let her come to Rochester where his comfortable and well-appointed office put his clients at ease and made assessing them simpler.

The room he finally settled on was on the mezzanine floor of the hotel where all of the rooms were named after famous Mississippi river boats. This room, the Delta Queen, overlooked the river, with large windows, a high ceiling, and wallpaper with wide vertical stripes in neutral colors that gave the room an airy, pleasant feel. Two microfiber seafoam green wingback chairs replaced the bed and were set in front of the windows, angled to face each other. Between them was a table with bottles of water, soft drinks, and coffee.

The maintenance men hauled the bed out of the room, followed by the assistant manager who assured Pollock that if there was anything else that was needed…anything…he would personally be available to attend to it.

"Chairs in the hallway by the door," Pollock said. "The guards will need something to sit on." In minutes, two comfortable chairs flanked the doorway.

Pollock checked his watch --10:20-- forty minutes until the Senator was due. He sat down, then immediately got up and walked to the window. He gazed out at the river, gray and frothy from the swift current caused by the spring snow melt. He looked down and realized he was wringing his hands. He turned and went into the bathroom, giving it a quick visual inspection to make sure everything was in order. Ordinarily unflappable, Pollock was surprised at his own nervousness.

More than a decade had passed since Pollock was first hired to analyze a woman charged with murdering her abusive husband. The woman had carried out her plan to shoot her husband, but then she dragged the body out of their house on to the driveway where she proceeded to mutilate the body by running over it multiple times with the family's large SUV. The murder itself was the culmination of a series of traumatic events suffered by the woman that "tipped her over the edge"—the proverbial last straw, so to speak.

Although Pollock couldn't opine with medical certainty that she was insane when she planned the murder, or even when she pulled the trigger, he was professionally certain that by the time she had finished her last passage over her dead husband, her sanity had been ground away under the tread of the SUV's tires. She had been catatonic since the murder and was, in Pollock's opinion, incapable of rationally participating in her own defense.

The judge was persuaded, and Pollock soon became the go-to psychologist in the upper Midwest whenever a defendant's legal competency to stand trial became an issue.

This was his tenth or twelfth such case – he had lost count – but it was, by far, the most consequential. Pollock's notoriety would go from regional to national if he diagnosed the first U.S. Senator to be tried for murder as incompetent to stand trial and the judge agreed with him. He could envision winding down his practice and traveling the country as *the nation's expert*, charging fees commensurate with his national stature.

He was so close to grabbing the brass ring.

But within that reverie an ethical dilemma tugged at his conscience. Working with a criminal defendant on an issue of competency, with its subsequent requirement that he testify in court as an unbiased professional, prevented him from taking on the defendant as a client for treatment purposes. Finding someone to be mentally incompetent without the ability to help them heal made this part of his practice onerous. It left him feeling empty, like he'd only done half the job and violated the oath he had taken.

And what if she isn't incompetent? What if she fabricated her condition? Is her adamant opposition to the suggestion that she might be incompetent and her outspoken dislike for psychologists just a ruse? Will I be able to tell the difference? Does it make any difference? Everyone expects me to find her incompetent. And if I don't? Defense attorneys will stop calling. I won't be the "go-to" guy anymore.

The chance at the brass ring would disappear.

He checked his watch again. 15 minutes. He left the room, locked the door behind him, and took the elevator to the main level in search of a double espresso.

FIRST SESSION:

Pollock's first observation of Magnolia related to her size: She was barely five feet tall and one hundred pounds. In his brief meeting with her at the jail, they had been seated and he had not realized she was so small. His second observation was that she did not look at all like the scared woman he had seen in the jail. She appeared confident and defiant, despite the shackles that limited the movement of her hands and feet. Her silver-white hair was artfully styled, and her navy-blue prison uniform looked starched and pressed. She spoke like a person accustomed to exercising authority.

"Are these manacles necessary?" she asked, directing the question at both Pollock and the guard who had escorted her into the room.

The guard looked at Pollock.

"You'll be outside the door during the entire session?" Pollock asked.

The guard nodded. "I'll be right outside this door the entire time."

"Then I see no reason for her to be restrained."

The guard unlocked the shackles and handcuffs. "I'll have to put them back on when we leave."

"Fine." Magnolia sat down opposite Pollock.

"Senator Kanaranzi, you are looking well. How are you feeling today?" Pollock asked formally while he turned on his recording device.

"Much better now that those things are off," she answered. "My clothes haven't arrived from Boston, yet. I'll be more presentable the next time we meet."

"Our last meeting was so short I feel like I should reintroduce myself. My name is Bishop Pollock. I'm a forensic psychologist who has been hired by your lawyers. We're going to spend some time together over the next week or two. May I call you Magnolia?"

"You may call me Senator Kanaranzi or Madam Senator," she replied curtly.

"Very well," he said, absorbing the rebuff without reaction. "Is this room acceptable to you? Do you feel safe here?"

She looked around the room. "This is fine. Any room outside the jail is fine."

Pollock nodded and jotted a note on a pad that was balanced on his knee.

"I have been hired to determine whether you are capable of participating in your own legal defense. You have agreed to this session and any additional sessions that I deem necessary to form a medical conclusion in that regard. This session, and any subsequent sessions will be recorded, but the recordings will only be used by me. They will not be shared with anyone, including your lawyers. Does that comport with your understanding of why we're here and do you consent to my recording our sessions?"

"I'm here because my lawyer says it will look bad if I don't cooperate. Personally, I think your profession is a bunch of malarky; you and your ilk are all charlatans, and this exercise is a waste of time and money. But yes. I agree and understand."

"Very good. Let's get started then," Pollock began in a pleasant tone. "First, I'd like you to take an MMPI test. It will help give me some base lines to work from. Is that okay with you?"

Magnolia shrugged her acceptance, and he handed her a booklet and a black pen.

Pollock settled back in his chair. "I'll give you time to finish that later, but, for now, let's start with something recent. I'd like to hear about your election to the Senate."

The question accomplished exactly what Pollock had hoped. For the next half hour Magnolia recounted the highs and lows of her Senate campaign, from the solicitation of her candidacy by the state political party to the election night celebration of her victory over incumbent Senator David Metzger. When she finished, Pollock offered her water and asked if she'd like to take a break. She demurred.

"You mentioned debating Metzger," Pollock resumed. "I understand that in your second debate there was a heated exchange related to your changing your name. I'm interested to know more about your name change."

Kanaranzi glared at him. "That's none of your business," she said. "I don't see how changing my name has anything to do with my ability to participate in my own defense."

Pollock shifted effortlessly. "Tell me about Aaron Feldman. I'd like to know more about your interactions with him."

Fire lit up Magnolia's eyes. "He's a traitor," she spit out.

"What role did he play in your campaign?"

"He was supposed to be my policy adviser, but it became clear as the campaign moved forward that he was not qualified for the job."

"What did you do when you realized that?"

"First we moved him to another position, but eventually we had to terminate him."

"Describe Feldman for me, so I can get a better picture of him."

"He was a fat slob. He waddled rather than walked, and he sweated so much that he left stains on my upholstery."

"It sounds like he was quite unpleasant to be around. How did it happen he was hired by your campaign?"

"He came highly recommended. He supposedly had other talents besides being a policy wonk. He allegedly was good at…what did they call it…opposition research?"

"Was he? Good at opposition research?"

"He was a liar and a cheat. He outlived any usefulness to the campaign when we found out he fabricated a situation that was meant only to embarrass my opponent."

"When you realized he was no longer useful, what did you do?"

"We had to publicly apologize to Metzger. We terminated Feldman."

"There was a rumor that you hired someone to kill him. I certainly know that most rumors are just that; rumors. Tell me about that one." Pollock delivered the incendiary question in a monotone voice, trying to soften its impact.

"That's absolutely untrue." Magnolia slid forward until she was sitting on the edge of the chair, leaning toward Pollock. The knuckles of her hands, locked onto her knees, turned white; her lips curled back in fury. "There were a lot of rumors started by Metzger. None of them were true."

"Political campaigns have become such nasty things," Pollock agreed, "and you were stuck in the middle of one, but we know Feldman *was* killed."

"I said I didn't hire anyone to kill him!" Her voice was low and ominous. To Pollock it said more than her words.

"Okay." Pollock stopped, poured a glass of water and slowly, deliberately took a drink. After a moment he resumed. "I understand Feldman threatened you."

"Is that a question?" she snapped.

"Did Feldman threaten you?" Pollock asked carefully.

Magnolia took a deep breath, collected herself, and then answered through clenched teeth, "The bastard broke into my home and tried to blackmail me."

"What…"

"He had a gun."

"That must have been…?"

"He kicked *Houppette.*"

"Who is *Houppette?*"

"A cat…kitten."

"What did you do after he kicked the kitten?"

Magnolia's face went blank. "I don't know."

SESSION NOTES – DAY 1, MK/BP.

1. *No indication of fear. Dismissive. Fabricated?*
2. *Quick, intense temper.*
3. *Temporary amnesia vis a vis AF. Real?*
4. *Kicked the cat. Follow up. Empathy?*

SECOND SESSION: FOLLOWING DAY

"I don't remember anything after…," Magnolia trailed off.

"After Feldman kicked your kitten?"

"She wasn't my kitten."

It was the second day of analysis, and Pollock had chosen to probe the issue of temporary amnesia, but Magnolia's answer surprised him. He cocked his head, a quizzical look on his face. "If it wasn't your kitten, how did it happen to be in your penthouse?"

"Maybe she belonged to my housekeeper. I had a French housekeeper."

"That would explain the kitten's name," Pollock said. "Although you speak French, too, don't you?"

"*Oui. Vous parlez francais?*" Magnolia responded.

Pollock made a note in his pad, ignoring her question. "Did you give your housekeeper permission to have a cat?"

Magnolia shifted in the chair as if it suddenly had become uncomfortable. "No. I don't allow my housekeepers to have pets," she said.

"Did you like *Houppette*?"

"What a stupid question. Of course, I liked *Houppette*. She was a little white furball. Who wouldn't like her?"

"But you don't know how the kitten got in your penthouse."

Magnolia stared at Pollock. When she didn't answer, he pressed on, knowing he was venturing into volatile territory.

"Apparently, Feldman didn't like the kitten," he said. "What's the first thing you remember after Feldman kicked *Houppette*?"

"What difference does it make!" Magnolia exploded. "I've had enough of this!" She stood up as if to leave. He had pushed the right button. There were voids in Magnolia's memory, and she became angry when she couldn't remember, when she wasn't in control.

"We still have most of this session left," he said, casually looking at his watch. "We can talk about something else."

She hesitated, then flung herself back onto the chair. The presence of the police outside the door kept her from leaving, and while Pollock could force her to stay, he couldn't force her to cooperate. For the next 15 minutes they were like two prizefighters – jab and parry, bob and weave – until Pollock asked a question about Arthur Kincaid.

For the rest of the session Pollock listened as Magnolia spoke of the man who had been her savior and mentor; the man who had rescued her from a life of drugs and crime and elevated her to a level of trust that eventually led to her becoming his successor at the top of the media empire that bore his name.

"It was a platonic love relationship," Magnolia declared. "Something someone like you wouldn't understand."

"I'd like to understand," Pollock said. He took her wordless stare as affirmation to continue. "Can you remember back to the time when Kincaid arranged a job for you in Las Vegas?"

"Of course, I can remember. He actually arranged for a job at a casino while we were on the road between Sturgis and Las Vegas."

"That was in 1976?"

She nodded.

"And he dropped you off in Las Vegas and left you there?"

"He stayed for a few days and helped me find an apartment and get settled. He gave me enough money to tide me over until I got my first paycheck."

"And this was a completely platonic relationship – between you and Kincaid?"

Again, the death stare. He moved on.

"How long after he left you in Las Vegas before you saw him again?"

"I only saw him twice in the three years I was in Vegas," she answered, "but we talked a lot, particularly at the beginning."

"Because a truly platonic relationship is so unusual, I'd be interested in what you talked about in your frequent conversations."

Magnolia exhaled in unison with a slight nod of her head, as if she had made a decision.

"I was a drug addict," she said. "I called him for support, when I was tempted to use. It happened a lot in the beginning; less as I recovered. Without Arthur, I would never have gotten clean."

"How did he help you?"

"By listening. And encouraging me; making me believe in myself."

"So, you got clean and you got a promotion at the casino, and you were living the good life when Kincaid showed up three years later and asked you to leave Las Vegas and be his personal assistant."

"Remarkable. You managed to remember all that."

Pollock ignored her sarcasm. "Can you tell me about the other time Kincaid came to Las Vegas to see you?"

"Why should I?"

"Because it may help me better understand the relationship you and Arthur had."

"Why would I care whether or not you understand our relationship?"

"Being able to handle a long-term, sometimes distant relationship of the type you describe, is indicative of your ability to handle complicated, extended situations such as a trial. It's important for me to know as much about your relationship with Kincaid as possible."

The look on Magnolia's face conveyed that she considered Pollock's statement as bullshit, but with a small, disgusted shake of her head, she answered. "Arthur came to Las Vegas because I was in trouble."

"Can you tell me about the trouble you were in?"

"I had been charged with aggravated assault, and he came out to help me."

"Tell me about the assault."

"A guy tried to force himself on me, and they said I beat him up with a fireplace poker."

"Who is 'they'?"

"The police."

"Who was the 'guy'? Did you know him?"

"He was a customer at the casino. I'd seen him a couple of times. Seemed like a nice guy. He had a simple name: Tom or Bob or something like that. He was staying at the hotel. Anyway, he asked me out to dinner, and I accepted. I was still a dealer then and was barely making ends meet. A free dinner was tough to turn down."

"If you are willing, tell me about the assault."

"He pushed me up against a wall and groped me. I resisted, and the next thing I remember is standing over him with a bloody poker in my hand."

"And the police charged *you* with assault?"

"He was a lawyer in town for a convention. The local chamber of commerce doesn't like it when a convention-goer gets beat up by the hired help, no matter what the reason. Neither does the casino."

"Then what happened?"

"Arthur flew out from Boston and got the charges dropped. He also made sure I kept my job."

"Going back to the assault for a minute; were you afraid?"

"I don't know. Probably. No, I was just angry that this asshole thought he was entitled to…to…molest me."

"You said you were accused of hitting Bob or Tom, or whatever his name was, with a fireplace poker. Where would you have gotten the poker?"

"I don't know," she said, her voice becoming a little unsteady.

"So, you don't remember hitting him with it?"

"All I remember is that it was all bloody! I had both hands around it, and it was all bloody."

⤳

SESSION NOTES – DAY 2, MK/BP

1. *MMPI: INTJ. Validity scales within normal parameters.*
2. *Likes to illustrate superiority – French.*

3. *Empathy? Beyond pet? Pursue further.*

4. *Memory lapses/kitten, assault.*

5. *Physical threat triggers violence/amnesia. Check for seizures.*

The media descended like vultures as the squad car pulled up to the jail entrance. At least a dozen reporters, with microphones in hand, shouted questions at Magnolia as she got out of the car. Three television trucks were parked in the lot. The secret was out.

"How do you feel about having your competency questioned?"

"Who's the psychologist you're seeing?"

"What about your Senate seat? Do you think they'll try to expel you?"

The questions cascaded, overlapping. Lights flashed. Magnolia raised her arms, crossing them in front of her face as if to protect herself from the barrage. The guard pushed aside a reporter and led Magnolia up the sidewalk and into the detention center entrance, pulling the door shut behind them.

Magnolia's head was spinning. *Why haven't my clothes arrived yet? How did I look on camera? I need to talk to Samantha. And what now? I need to talk to Taft. I can't be harassed every time I leave the jail. Henri will know what to do.*

When she got back to her cell there were two suitcases and a cosmetic case on her bed. She flipped open the suitcases. They had obviously been rummaged, and the person responsible had not bothered to refold the clothes. *Where will I hang everything?* She glared at the few hooks in the cell. And pressing? *God, it will be worse going out in clothes that look like I slept in them. I may just as well wear the prison rags.* She pressed the intercom button and waited.

"I can have them taken to the laundry," the guard said. "They can press them there. That's the best I can do."

"You're kidding, right?" Magnolia snapped. "I have outfits that cost thousands of dollars, and you expect me to let a prison laundry take care of them?"

The guard shrugged apologetically. "It's not a problem we've had to deal with before, Ma'am. I'll see if the program director can help you out."

"What about a place to hang them?" Magnolia asked. "Could I get a portable rack so I can at least hang them up?"

"I'll see what I can do, see if the captain has any ideas, but don't get your hopes up. This is way outside what's usually allowed."

Magnolia wanted to be mad at the young guard, but his sympathetic tone and I'm-so-sorry eyes were disarming. He left the Seg Unit, and Magnolia felt sad. *He's doing the best he can within the rules,* she thought. She looked at the two open suitcases, and at the bottles of makeup haphazardly strewn around the table. For the first time, she felt like she might cry.

An hour later the intercom squawked. "Senator, you have a phone call from your attorney. I'll be there in two minutes to get you." The same young guard escorted Magnolia to the phone room. She learned his name was Seth and that he'd spent his entire life, all 26 years of it, in Red Wing, Minnesota. His family was one of only a handful of Black families in the small river city.

Taft and Avery were both on the phone.

"The press knows about the shrink," Magnolia said. "They ambushed me when we got back from today's meeting. You've got to put a stop to that."

"There's nothing we can do legally," Taft answered. "First Amendment, freedom of the press and all that. It will be in the news cycle for 24 hours and then it will go away. I think it's something we'll just have to deal with."

"*We* won't have to deal with it. *I* will," Magnolia complained. "And it won't go away because the Senate won't let it go away. There is going to be an attempt to have me expelled because of this, and that will keep it in the news cycle for weeks."

Taft was silent on the other end of the line. "You may be right," he finally acknowledged. "We could move the sessions back into the jail, or we could try to play cat and mouse with the press, moving the time and location around, but that's likely to keep their attention for even longer."

"What about moving the trial to a different location?"

"The press is going to be wherever you are," Taft responded. "They're always a nuisance, but that has never been cause to change the venue of a trial. We just need to ride it out. Don't respond to their questions, and their interest will eventually dwindle."

"Fine," Magnolia snapped, "but if I am going to have to face those vultures every day, I can't look like road kill. I need my clothes cleaned, pressed, and properly taken care of, and I need my makeup done. I need to look like a Senator, not like a fugitive."

"We'll see what we can do," Taft said.

"One last thing," Magnolia interjected. "Please have Henri call me."

The office of Napoleon Taft was lushly appointed. This was apparent even through the narrow view of the computer monitor. Pollock amused himself by trying to guess the value of each item in the office while he waited for the notorious criminal defense lawyer to appear for their scheduled Skype meeting.

Taft's antique desk was huge, stacked with neat piles of files. The chair behind it, empty for the moment, was of burgundy leather tufted with matching burgundy buttons and with arms trimmed in bronze nail heads. Pollock could see framed photographs of Taft with celebrities and politicians on the credenza behind the chair. On the wall above the credenza was a large painting of a racing yacht in rough seas. It looked very much like a Winslow Homer painting. Pollock wondered if it was an original.

If the painting looked like a Winslow Homer, the man who slid into the seat behind the desk looked like Clark Gable – wavy black hair with salt and pepper temples, perfectly trimmed mustache, golden tan, and dark, piercing eyes.

"Thanks for waiting," Taft said. He settled into his chair, his elbows on the arms, and leaned forward toward the monitor, fixing Pollock with an intense stare. "Are you making any progress with our client?"

Hypnotic, flitted through Pollock's mind, *like a snake;* then, shaking himself loose from those mesmerizing eyes, he began his report.

"Not surprisingly, her MMPI shows her to be an INTJ," he said.

"What's that?"

"It's a test to … "

"I know what an MMPI is," Taft barked. "What do the INTJ letters mean?"

"They indicate she is goal-oriented, intuitive, judgmental, impatient and arrogant; confident to the point of being arrogant. Less than two percent of the population falls into this category," Pollock concluded.

"How does that help us?"

"It doesn't, *per se,* but it will help explain some of her actions and decision-making."

"What else?"

"I may have discovered something to make your incompetency argument plausible," Pollock said. Taft's eyes lit up. "I've only had two sessions with her, but I've found significant gaps in her memory. Not just forgetfulness but complete blackouts where she has no recollection of things that occurred, important, significant things."

"Is that enough to say she is unable to participate in her own defense?" Taft cut in.

"There can be several explanations for blackouts of this nature," Pollock said, ignoring the interruption. "One explanation could be a physical problem, like epilepsy or cardiomyopathy. While these might cause a delay in the trial, they have never been, to my knowledge, the basis for finding a person incompetent.

"However, the blackouts could also be caused by a psychological condition, such as Dissociative Amnesia or Dissociative Identity Disorder, which used to be called multiple personality disorder. If, in fact, she has D.I.D., we can make a strong case that she is not able to knowingly participate in her own defense."

"How long will it take you to determine if she has D.I.D.?"

"Could be one more session, could be 20, but I first recommend that you have her examined by a medical doctor to rule out a physical issue as the reason for her memory loss. I recommend that you have her seen at the Mayo Clinic."

"I'll see what I can do," Taft said, "but the judge is determined to move this case forward. I may have to come back to you for an affidavit on why we need more time."

THIRD SESSION

Two hours after the call with Taft, Pollock was sitting opposite Magnolia. The prison uniform had been discarded in favor of a light blue, fashionably tailored business suit, and the flip flops had been replaced by dark gray pumps with a three-inch heel.

"Ready?" he asked as he turned on his recording device.

"I suppose," Magnolia said with a sigh.

"In going back through my notes from our first two sessions, I noted that there are a few times when you can't remember..."

"My memory's fine," she snapped.

"...like when you were assaulted in Las Vegas, or how *Houppette* became your cat. Are you aware of any other times when your memory has gone blank; when something happened that you found out about later, but can't remember even though you were there?"

"My memory's fine," she repeated, emphasizing each word.

"What about the Aaron Feldman incident. You were absolved of any wrong-doing in that matter, but you admit you don't remember what happened."

"Isn't it normal for people to block things, bad things, terrible things, out of their memories?"

"It happens sometimes, but it isn't considered normal, per se," Pollock responded. "It's a defense mechanism that prevents the person from processing a traumatic event."

"Isn't that how you make your living? First you dictate what is *normal*, and then you charge people a bundle for therapy if they don't fit your stereotype?"

"That might be a cynic's viewpoint, but psychological disorders are every bit as real as physical ones," Pollock replied, "and complete loss of episodic memory, as you have described it to me, could be a symptom of a serious mental health concern."

"And I think you're full of bullshit," Magnolia snapped. Her clothes may have changed, but her attitude hadn't.

Pollock paused to collect himself, realizing he had almost allowed himself to be drawn into an argument with his patient. *Very unprofessional*, he scolded himself.

"I acknowledge your skepticism about psychotherapy, but I'm really interested in your memory lapses. It might be a symptom of a serious medical problem such as epilepsy or a heart condition. I would like to ask a few more questions, if you're willing," Pollock said, deftly moving the session back on track.

The "heart condition" comment caught Magnolia's attention. "How does a memory lapse arise from a heart condition," she inquired, her voice still as sharp as a razor.

"Lack of blood flow to the brain can cause memory loss and can lead to early dementia. Your blackouts could be a symptom."

A look of concern replaced the hostility in Magnolia's face. She leaned forward. "Are you serious about this?"

"Yes."

"Then shouldn't I be examined by a heart specialist instead of sitting here and listening to you?"

"You're right, you should be, and I will recommend that you be examined, but the more information I can give to the heart specialist, the more thorough and complete his diagnosis will be. It might be very helpful if you could recall any other episodes like the ones we've talked about where you've had memory blackouts."

Magnolia shifted uncomfortably in her seat and looked out the window toward the river. For a few minutes she appeared to be lost in her own thoughts. Pollock waited.

"There have been a couple," she finally said, still looking toward the river. She closed her eyes and stroked her eyebrow with middle finger of her right hand. Again, Pollock waited.

"I lost a couple of days in Barcelona when Arthur died," she said, turning back toward Pollock.

"I'm sure that was a very traumatic event," Pollock said when Magnolia paused. "Having the events of the first few days be a blur after the loss of a loved one is not uncommon."

"This wasn't a blur," Magnolia corrected. "I found Arthur in the hotel, and I clearly remember making phone calls to tell people of his passing. I remember making all the arrangements to have his body returned to the States, and I remember discussions with his lawyer, but after that I remember nothing until a Kincaid Media board meeting back in Boston. That was three or four days later."

"And you have no memory of what happened during those three or four days?"

"None."

"Do you recall any other times like this?"

"Not for that long, but I do occasionally have mornings when I wake up and can't remember the previous evening. I've always thought that was from too much alcohol."

"Tell me about specific times when that happened?"

Magnolia rested her head on her thumbs, using the fingers of both hands to massage her forehead. Finally, she sat back and shook her head. "It hasn't happened in quite a while. I don't remember any specifics, just a vague recollection of not knowing anything about the previous evening. Luckily, I never ended up in bed with someone I didn't know."

The last line was delivered without humor, but Pollock smiled anyway. *Anything,* he thought, *that might melt the ice.* "Think back to the first time you are aware of a blank spot in your memory," he said.

"That might be difficult," she said. "I was heavy into the drug culture in the 70's. There were a lot of days, I am sure, when I didn't remember anything."

Again, Pollock smiled. "I'm sure there were some of those, but I'm talking about times when you weren't using drugs. What about when you were in high school?"

The traces of pleasantness that had crept onto Magnolia's face faded. "I was into drugs in high school."

"Did you have memory lapses or blackouts from high school?"

"I remember high school. It was the worst four years of my life."

"So…"

"So… I am not going to talk about high school. I washed that all away, along with the drug scene, when I changed my name. That was 40 years ago. How does that have anything to do with my ability to defend myself in this trial?"

⌇

SESSION NOTES - DAY 3, MK/BP

1. *Admission of additional memory lapses.*
2. *MK becoming more cooperative. Slowly building rapport.*
3. *Medical records request delayed. Follow up!!*
4. *Blocking high school. Source? Pursue.*

The first ten minutes of their weekly virtual visit was spent figuring out clothing issues. "I went out in my Armani two-button suit today, the light blue one, and it was wrinkled. I looked like a vagabond," Magnolia whined.

"I'll hire someone to take care of your clothes," Samantha assured her. "We'll move your clothes, and any others you want from your wardrobe, to the hotel. Every day we'll have your clothes for the day delivered to you. Do you think the jail will agree to that?"

Magnolia nodded. "I'm sure they will. They don't want to deal with my clothes, and the jail staff has actually been pretty decent."

"It will take a couple of days…"

"I'll manage until then," Magnolia interrupted. "I don't have a session until next Monday, so I won't be leaving the jail. Have you talked to Henri?"

"He's funny," Samantha said. "He talked mostly about his love of dancing. I told him I am six feet tall and uncoordinated. He said he is five-six, which makes us a perfect fit, and that he'll teach me to dance the next time I go to Barcelona."

"Henri is legendary in the Barcelona clubs," Magnolia mused. "Did you talk at all about investment strategies?"

"He has a structure in mind for the stock sales proceeds, but he prefers to discuss that with you in person. He mentioned attorney-client privilege. He also said I should close out all your investment accounts and bank accounts except for the one that I use to pay your expenses."

"Do that," Magnolia nodded, "and put the money in that account for the time being. I'll have instructions on what to do with those funds when we meet next week. How're things going in your new home?"

"I'm still trying to wrap my head around the fact that I can look out at Boston Harbor through my entire living room wall."

"I never tire of that view. It's why I bought the place."

"I can't thank you enough...," Samantha started. "How is the psychotherapy going?"

"No more talk about that," Magnolia said, ignoring Samantha's question. "It gives me peace of mind to know that you're there. Did you talk to Meredith Glenn at the museum?"

"She hasn't called me back. I'll try her again tomorrow."

"How are the Kincaid Media stock sales going?"

"I checked just before I got on this call. We've sold less than five percent so far. Your broker is very reluctant."

"Have Henri call him," Magnolia said. "He can be very convincing."

"Oh, wait! I have numbers for you," Samantha said as their meeting time waned. "And Henri said you were right. Those were lucky numbers you gave me last time. He said you won money."

"Did he say how much?

"Four dollars."

They burst out laughing. For Magnolia, it felt good to laugh.

Hawke called two hours later.

"*Mon cheri*, I do hope this finds you well."

"I hear you've been trying to seduce my press secretary."

"*Non. Non. Non.* I only invited her to dance," Hawke guffawed, "but, *l'amour,* one must never pass up the opportunity."

"You are an old lecher," Magnolia chortled. "Not so much *l'amour* as *soif,* or as we would call it here in the States, lust."

"Ah, you know me too well *mon amie,*" Hawke replied, "but you did not want me to call to discuss the seduction of Ms. Jones. What can I do for you?"

"You have a plan for my investments?"

"I do. Untraceable. Untaxable."

"And your fingers are in it how deeply?" Magnolia asked matter-of-factly.

"Only ten percent, and once that fee is paid, I have no access."

"Three percent, and how can I be sure?"

"Because I will personally introduce you to the bankers, and then you can make any changes you like. Seven and one-half percent."

Magnolia shook her head. "That's too much. I'll agree to a flat million, and you pay all the expenses involved in my meeting the bankers. When do you expect that might happen?"

"In due time. First, we must know your itinerary. Then your assets must be liquidated and transferred. Then we will make arrangements for your meeting. One million, and we each pay our own expenses."

"Fine. Speaking of assets, thank you for the lottery winnings," Magnolia said. "I assume I can trust you with $4.00. Did you win anything?"

"*Non,*" Hawke lamented in faux disappointment. "Perhaps next week."

"I have sent you new numbers," Magnolia responded.

"I am your humble servant," Hawke intoned.

"One more thing," Magnolia said. "I need your wisdom on an issue. The paparazzi has become aware that my competency has been brought into question. Each time I leave the jail, or return, I am besieged. Your thoughts?"

There was a long pause before Hawke answered.

"If you wish to spend a little money, we can create an on-going distraction that will leave the paparazzi in the dark as to your comings and goings. It would likely only be successful for two or three weeks until they catch on. Perhaps by that time it will no longer be an issue."

"How much money?"

"Perhaps a hundred thousand dollars or two?"

"Which is it? One or two?"

"Two. And putting people in place to create such a distraction might have ancillary benefits."

"I'll authorize Samantha to make a transfer to your account."

"Perhaps she could deliver it in person?"

The next morning Magnolia woke up in a sour mood with a headache and a vague awareness of dreams she couldn't remember. Her morning shower didn't help, nor did the prospect of a session with Pollock, or running the gauntlet of the news media.

In keeping with a suggestion by Hawke, she was back in her prison blues. Her regular clothes lay scattered about her cell, wrinkled, adding to her bad mood, and then breakfast was delivered: over-cooked scrambled eggs that were cold with toast the consistency of cardboard. This was truly going to be a shitty day.

At nine o'clock there was a rap on her cell door. "Time to go," a voice from the other side said. It was Seth, and he had a twinkle in his eye as Magnolia stepped through the door. "Pretty clever, Senator," he said. Magnolia's scowl disappeared momentarily, giving way to a quizzical look.

"What?"

"The decoy," he laughed. "The whole media gaggle chased your decoy. You have clear sailing."

Magnolia started to respond, then realized that the decoy had to be Hawke's idea. She forced a smile.

The day was dreary, like her mood. A light mist spattered the windshield of the squad car, and people on the sidewalk hunched into the wet and the wind. Only Seth's constant chatter from the driver's seat relieved the gloom. Nothing seemed to sully his sunny, contagious outlook. Magnolia wished the ride to the St. James Hotel was longer than four blocks.

FOURTH SESSION

Magnolia was her usual recalcitrant self. Despite Pollock's persistence, the session didn't seem to be progressing toward anything meaningful.

Pollock asked Magnolia another question. She shifted her position on the chair, and swiveled her neck to try and relieve her headache, which had reappeared the moment she walked into the hotel room. Ignoring his question completely, she replied, "You said these headaches might be caused by something to do with my heart. If that's true, why am I sitting here talking to you instead of seeing a cardiologist?"

Pollock paused and reminded himself to not let his frustration show. "The frequency of your blackouts is a critical piece of information for a diagnosis of the cause. I'm gathering as much information as possible to give to the cardiologist."

"It's your job to prove I'm a lunatic!" she flared. "Your bullshit doesn't fool me."

Pollock rocked back in his chair, giving Magnolia a moment to regain her composure. "Senator," he said in a conciliatory tone, "the fact that we are still here, talking about important times in your life, means that I have yet to form an opinion about your ability to participate in your own defense. You maintain that you are perfectly normal and this is a waste of time. To provide you with some perspective, everyone in your situation is convinced that they are perfectly normal.

"It's my job to determine whether, in your case, that belief is based in reality. It is of no consequence to me whether you are, or are not, competent to stand trial. It is only my job to listen to what you have to say, and then provide my report to the court. So, please help me do that. Are you willing to have a conversation between two reasonable people, explore what has brought you to this point in your life, and allow me to draw a conclusion based upon my professional training and experience?"

Pollock's brief monologue produced no visible change in Magnolia. She sat on the edge of the chair as if she were about to launch herself somewhere. Her jaw muscles were clenched and her hands were clamped to the edge of the cushion, white-knuckled. She glared at Pollock.

"Don't play the victim card with me," she snarled. "I deal with people smarter than you every day, so don't think your professional games are going to sway me. I want an appointment with a cardiologist, NOW!"

"We're already working on getting you a cardiology appointment at the Mayo Clinic," Pollock responded, his voice soothing. "It's only a few miles down the road, and the best doctors in the world practice there. In the meantime, I need you to answer a few more questions."

Magnolia's eyes bored holes in him, but Pollock chose to interpret the lack of a verbal response as permission to continue.

"Have you had a blackout since the Aaron Feldman incident?" he repeated.

"This whole fucking thing is a blackout!"

"Explain, please."

There was a long pause, followed by a slow exhale from Magnolia. Her shoulders slumped and the rigidity went out of her body. "Could this really have something to do with my heart?" she asked, the venom gone from her voice.

Pollock nodded, using his best empathetic expression.

"I've had several," Magnolia said after a long pause, "and they seem to be coming more frequently."

"When was the last one?"

"A few days ago. I remember eating lunch, and the next thing I remember is a guard banging on my cell telling me it's 'lights out'."

"That would be five or six hours?"

"More like eight."

"And you have no recollection of those eight hours?"

"None."

"Were you sleeping during that time?"

"I don't think so, because when they said lights out, I laid down on my bunk and went to sleep. If I'd been sleeping all afternoon, I wouldn't have been able to sleep at night."

"Did you ask anyone about what went on during that period?"

"Who's to ask? With the exception of one guy, the guards aren't exactly talkative, and I'm in isolation so I can't talk to the inmates."

Pollock nodded, jotting a note in his book. "Can you remember another recent time when you have no recollection of what happened?"

Magnolia pondered the question, her left hand cupping her chin. "I can't honestly say," she finally said. "I know I have no recollection of the night I was arrested. I only know about it because my lawyers told me. Since then, so much crazy stuff has gone on, I'm not sure what's real and what's my imagination. Honestly, it feels like I'm missing things. I just can't tell you what…or when…or where."

Pollock let Magnolia's revelation linger in the air. Contrary to her first hostile reaction, his appeal to her was working. Apparently motivated by concerns for her physical health, she had become more cooperative, and in the process, had disclosed critical information. It was clear that his next step was to rule out a physical reason for her blackouts.

"Senator," he said, "I think we should end today's session early. The increased frequency of your blackouts has me concerned. We'll get you in for a cardiology appointment at Mayo as soon as possible."

⌒

SESSION NOTES – DAY 4, MK/BP

1. MK doesn't recognize herself as an inmate. Denial.
2. Narcissistic PD?
3. Blackout frequency increasing/get immediate cardiology appointment.
4. Get back to high school/start of blackouts.

Magnolia's mood improved slightly when she noticed the sky was brighter and the drizzle had stopped. Better yet, when they drove past the jail entrance, there was no sign of the media. The driver made a second loop around the block before stopping in front of the courthouse. To her surprise, Seth was waiting on the curb. He helped Magnolia get out of the car.

"Quick one today," he said. "I think the reporters are still out chasing your decoy."

Magnolia responded with a smile and a nod. Hawke had apparently put her money to quick use.

"Have you been assigned as my personal bodyguard?" she asked, as the deputy accompanied her into the courthouse. "You're the only deputy I've talked to in the last few days."

"Just a scheduling coincidence. I go back on nights next week."

"That must be hard on your family, working nights."

"Yeah. I don't get to see my daughter much when I'm on nights."

"How old is your daughter?"

"Three." They stopped in the corridor for a moment as Seth pulled out his billfold and showed Magnolia a picture of his daughter, dressed in a ruffled pink dress. "It was her birthday party," he said. Her coffee-with-cream skin color suggested her mother was White.

"What a lovely child," Magnolia said.

As she passed through security, she asked, "Before I go back to my cell, could I go to the infirmary. I need something for this headache."

Back in her cell, Magnolia lay on her bed, waiting for the aspirin to take hold. She thought of Seth and his family, and she thought of her own son. *What is he like? Does he have a family? How did he end up in a wheelchair?* She got up, took the French court order off the table, laid back down and read it again. When she awoke the headache was gone, but there lingered a hazy memory of a dream; a mashup of Hamilton and Seth, a cute child, a happy gathering, and a discordant work of art.

It took a moment for her head to clear. Then she rolled off the bed and pushed the intercom buzzer. "I'd like to speak with the captain when she has a moment," Magnolia said.

After lunch, her food tray was picked up by a new guard who informed Magnolia that the clothes in her cell were going to be removed that afternoon. "I'll come back and get them and take them to the jail waiting room. Someone is picking them up there," she said. "That work for you?"

Magnolia nodded and spent the rest of the afternoon gathering and folding her clothes, listening to the radio, and reading. She was startled when the intercom came to life. "Senator Kanaranzi. This is Captain Sharpe. You wanted to speak with me?"

"Yes. Thank you for getting back to me. It's about this young guard, Seth Johnson."

"Has there been a problem?"

"No. No. He's been very nice. I'd like to request that he be assigned to me, so he can work days. He has a young family, and I understand that he's going back on the night shift. That means he won't be able to see his daughter hardly at all."

"Senator, I appreciate your concern for my staff," Captain Sharpe responded, "but we just don't have the manpower to assign specific guards to specific prisoners."

Magnolia paused. "Could you have him work only days? Not assigned to me, but just work days?"

"Deputy Johnson is one of our least senior deputies. As such, he ends up working nights quite often. That's the framework we have to work in. I can't make individual exceptions. I understand you own a business. You know what kind of a morale problem it would create if I played favorites."

Again, Magnolia paused, trying to think of something to help the young deputy and his family, but nothing came to mind. "I understand," she finally said. "I want you to know, though, that Seth, Deputy Johnson, doesn't know I asked you. It was my idea."

"It never crossed my mind. It would be totally out of character for Deputy Johnson to ask for a favor. Since I have you on the phone," Captain Sharpe continued, "two quick things. First, I'd like to thank you for the contribution you made so that indigent inmates can get the same amenities as everyone else. It's the first time that I'm aware of that someone has done anything like that. That was extremely generous of you. Second, you have an appointment at the Mayo Clinic in Rochester tomorrow morning. Your wakeup call will be an hour earlier than usual."

That evening, Magnolia and Samantha met again through the computer monitors.

"Thanks for taking care of my clothes, but I'm not sure how much I'm going to need them. Things have changed."

"What do you mean?" Samantha asked.

"I have an appointment at the Mayo Clinic tomorrow. Depending on what they find, I may no longer be going to see the psychologist." Magnolia purposefully failed to mention Hawke's misdirection ruse that required her to wear her prison clothes.

"What's your appointment for?"

"I've had a couple memory-loss episodes, and the psychologist thinks it might be because of reduced blood flow to my brain. I'm going to see a cardiac specialist to have it checked out. Have you already hired someone to take care of my clothes?"

"Not yet. I have the hotel room rented, and I moved the clothes there earlier today. I thought I'd hire someone local to care for and watch over the clothing."

"Hold off on the hiring until we get the results from tomorrow's appointment. Any news out of Washington?" Magnolia asked, changing the subject.

"I haven't heard or seen anything. *The Globe* ran an article about you yesterday, but that's about it."

"What was it about?"

"Your lawyers raising the issue of competency. It was a short news piece. No opinions."

"I'm sure it will be picked up by the media fiends soon enough. What about Meredith Glenn? Did you talk to her?"

"She said they haven't made up their mind about *The Reaper*."

Thoughts of Hamilton and of Deputy Johnson and his family flashed through Magnolia's mind. "Call Meredith and ask her to talk to me before they finalize any plans for the painting. Tell her I've got some ideas."

FIFTH SESSION – TWO DAYS LATER

She sat on the chair in her blue prison uniform, legs crossed, her foot bouncing as if keeping time to a quick-step. Across the coffee table, Pollock held an open book and a pen, and observed her over his half-glasses.

He was certain that the diagnosis from the Mayo cardiologists would effectively end any cooperation from Magnolia. The Mayo doctors had concluded that there was nothing wrong with her physically that would account for her blackouts. Without concerns about her heart, Pollock was sure she would go back to being uncooperative and belligerent. He decided to temporarily delay divulging the result of her cardio exam and get as much as he could from the day's session.

"Tell me about your family," he stated.

"I have a sister, but we don't talk about her."

Pollock's eyebrows arched in surprise. "Tell me about your sister."

"I can't. We don't talk about her."

"Why not?"

Magnolia shifted on the chair and reached in the pocket of her jump suit, pulling out a stick of gum. She unwrapped it, folded it, and put it in her mouth. She leaned forward and put the crumpled wrapper on the table in front of her.

"Because she does things," she finally answered.

"What kind of things?"

She looked down at her hands. She slid them under her thighs so Pollock couldn't see them. She looked at the tan carpet on the floor and bit the inside of her lip. Pollock wrote something in his book.

"What kind of things?" he pressed gently.

"Bad things." She kept her gaze fixed on the carpet and chewed her gum.

"Can you describe the bad things?"

She shook her head.

"How do you know about these bad things?"

"Just do."

"Okay," Pollock said. "Let's not talk about the bad things your sister does. Let's talk about you."

She looked up. On the surface, she was an attractive and wealthy 60-year-old woman. But today, at this moment, Pollock suspected, she wasn't any of those things.

"I noticed you're sitting on your hands. I am wondering why you're doing that."

She blushed. "Cuz, I chew my nails."

"Can I see?"

Hesitantly, she drew out one hand and held it out to Pollock. The nails were long, their color a vivid blue to match her eyes. The manicure was impeccable.

"Thanks," he said, indicating she could put her hand back. "Let's talk about high school. Please tell me about the first thing you can remember."

She was back in her high school gymnasium, her toes rhythmically touching the wood floor as she floated in the arms of Mr. Freeman, the Dancing Janitor. His left hand held hers gently as he guided her to the sounds of The Righteous Brothers, *Unchained Melody*. Mr. Freeman had been teaching freshmen at the Zumbrota High School how to dance for the last twelve years.

Mary knew all about Mr. Freeman. One day he had spontaneously leaned his push-broom against the wall and twirled a cafeteria worker around the gymnasium floor to show the joy and beauty of dance to a group of reluctant students, and he had been a legend ever since. The regular physical education teachers happily relinquished dance instruction to him, and Mr. Freeman made it fun. The students quickly took to his love for dance. Even the unwilling fourteen-year-old boys learned to dance and, when pressed, admitted they enjoyed it.

Mr. Freeman made high school less scary for Mary. He was the unofficial school greeter who met her the first day (and every day after) with a smile and a "looks like you're going to have a great day" welcome. She soon learned that he did the same for every student, but it didn't matter. First impressions last.

Only a few days into the school year, she also learned that when Mr. Freeman sensed you weren't having a good day, he was willing to take the time to listen, his sad eyes and concerned look giving the impression that you were the only person in the world at the moment. Mary had a few of those days and came to trust Mr. Freeman. He was kind of small for a man, nondescript in appearance, and he smelled kind of peculiar, from a cheap brand of cologne she found out years later, but he made her feel important. And he never broke a confidence.

This particular day he had randomly chosen her to help him demonstrate how to do a simple box step. Embarrassed, as only a thirteen-year-old can be, she hesitantly stepped out of the secure anonymity of the clustered students and joined him on the gym floor. She was nervous as he took her hand and showed the students the proper position to start the dance, but as the first notes of *Unchained Melody* filled the gym, her discomfort disappeared. Mary found herself moving in perfect harmony with Mr. Freeman as the world around her fell away.

As they danced, he talked, instructing the students standing on the sidelines, but they were only opaque statues in her mind, hazy images that faded as the music bathed her. It may have lasted an eternity, or just a few minutes, but whatever the time, Mary had never been in a place that felt so free. So enchanted. So safe.

"Mary. Mary."

The music had ended and the sound of her name brought her back from dreamland. She realized some of the students were clapping their hands.

"Yes, Mr. Freeman?"

"Where did you learn to dance?" he asked.

Flustered, Mary stuttered: "I ... I ... didn't."

"You're an excellent dancer. A natural." All four-foot-ten of Mary blushed.

Mr. Freeman stepped back and took an exaggerated pose. "From this point forward," he said with a serious voice and a twinkle in his eye, "you shall be known as Tiny Dancer. At least in dance class."

Mary should have been mortified, but she wasn't. She wore the nickname proudly and, although Mr. Freeman never picked her to be his dance partner again, the nickname stuck.

"And that's how I got my name," she said, looking earnestly at Pollock.

"So, your name is Tiny Dancer?"

She nodded.

There was a knock on the door, and the guard stuck his head in the room. "Sorry to interrupt you doctor, but there's an emergency phone call for you."

Pollock apologized and excused himself. Fifteen minutes later he came back into the room and apologized again as he sat down. He looked at his notes and then repeated the question he had asked before the interruption. "So, you said your name is Tiny Dancer."

"What?" Her eyes flashed.

"Tell me about Tiny Dancer."

"You mean the Elton John song?" she scoffed. The tone of her voice was derisive.

"Magnolia?"

"What!"

"Can you tell me about Tiny Dancer? The person, not the song."

"I have no idea what you're talking about," she said looking at him in disgust. She spat the gum out of her mouth into a tissue and looked at it like it was a foreign substance. She placed it on the coffee table and gently rubbed her hands on her pants.

SESSION NOTES – DAY 5, MK/BP

1. *Radical personality shift*
2. *Actions and vocabulary suggest teen*
3. *Tiny Dancer???? Pursue.*
4. *Shift back to MK, immediate or gradual?*
5. *What triggered personality shift?*
6. *Rule out DID.*

The guard, an older man she didn't recognize, shackled her before they left the room. It was raining as they stepped out onto the sidewalk outside the hotel.

"Could you put my sweatshirt hood up?" Magnolia nodded toward her restricted hands that prevented her from doing it herself. The guard, who was wearing a raincoat, didn't respond, instead giving her a slight shove in the direction of the waiting squad car. She shuffled across the street, getting soaked by the steady rain. The guard opened the door of the car and placed his hand on the top of her wet head, shoving her into the back seat. He got in front.

"We're not taking you through the courthouse today," he growled.

Magnolia suppressed the urge to call him out and instead hunkered down in the back seat, wet and fuming.

"Bunch of crap," he said as the car pulled away from the curb. "All this cloak and dagger shit. Perps who think they should get special treatment." He turned and glared menacingly at Magnolia.

The driver maneuvered the car into the traffic lane.

"Prisoners have rights now," the guard laughed meanly. "Break the law, come to prison, and suddenly you got rights! Good damn thing I retired. I'd shove their rights right up their ass."

Minutes later, they pulled up to the jail entrance with no further conversation. To Magnolia's relief, there were no TV trucks in the parking lot. No one loitered by the entrance with a microphone or a pen and notepad. Whatever Hawke was doing to divert the media was working. The guard and the driver looked around as the car stopped. They both looked disappointed.

"Get out," the guard ordered. Magnolia slid across the car seat and managed to leverage herself out of the back seat without assistance.

Back in her cell, Magnolia's first intention was to call and complain about the guard, but she was distracted by a folded copy of *USA Today*, with a post-it note attached. "Thought you might want to see this. Sorry. Seth."

She unfolded the newspaper. The headline read, "Senate Moves to Expel Kanaranzi." The story was based on the allegation that she had conspired to kill her mother, and that she had shot and killed a campaign worker. It brought up her struggle with drugs early in her life, and insinuated that there was something nefarious about her rise to the top of Kincaid Media. By the time she was done reading it, Magnolia was seething, even though it was only a regurgitation of all the bad things the media had already said about her. Despite the headline, there was no mention that the Senate had started any proceedings.

Now, angry at the media for muckraking, angry at the Senate for its hypocrisy, and angry at her situation in general, Magnolia exploded. She threw the newspaper across her cell, then picked up her food tray and smashed it against the wall. She screamed, then grabbed the table and flipped it over, scattering pencils and paper around the room. She screamed again and grabbed the pillow from her bed. She beat the pillow against the toilet until it split at the seams, then threw it across the room at the intercom. With nothing left to vent her rage on, she leaned against the wall, her chest heaving.

The tantrum subsided, and her breathing eventually returned to normal. She surveyed the mess she had created and sighed.

She stood the table back on its legs and righted the chair. She picked up a piece of blank paper and a pencil, then sat down and began to write. At the top of the page, she wrote "Collateral Damage." Down the left side of the page, she wrote the numbers one through 20. After No. 1 she wrote Harvey Findley. No. 2 was Senator Bradford Styles. Napoleon Taft was No. 3. Then she skipped down to No. 19 and wrote Henri Hawke. At number 20 she hesitated, then wrote Hamilton Blethen.

I'll fill in the rest later. She signed the bottom of the page: *Maggie*

Taft leaned closer to his computer screen. "How much longer?" he asked.

"I wish I could be more specific," Pollock answered, "but maybe three or four more sessions. I need to be certain that the separate personality wasn't feigned. And if it is legitimate, which I think it is, then I'll need to determine whether there is a direct link between what we've been viewing as blackouts compared to when she is in her alter."

"How do you do that?"

"I'll need to figure out what the trigger mechanisms are that switch her from one personality to another."

"You said 'another.' Could she have more than one alternative identity?"

"It's possible," Pollock answered, "but for the purpose of determining whether she is competent to participate in her own defense, we only need to be able to show she has at least one alter and that there is no communication between the alter and her real personality."

"And you can prove that?" Taft probed.

"I think I've already proven it. We just have to tie up the loose ends so I can render an opinion that can withstand cross examination."

SIXTH SESSION

"In our last session, I asked you about your family," Pollock said, watching closely for Magnolia's reaction.

A scowl crossed her face. "I don't remember that," she said.

"Maybe I'm mistaken," Pollock said. "Tell me about your family."

"I don't have any…well, I have a son…," her voice trailed off.

"Tell me about your son."

"I can't, really. I don't know him. I left him when he was three or four. He'd be about 40 now."

"When was the last time you saw him?"

"I don't know. Maybe about five or six years ago. I think I saw him in Barcelona."

"You aren't sure?"

"Well, I was told it was him. I didn't talk to him. Just saw him from a distance."

"When was the last time you talked to him?"

"Never. Not since I dropped him off with my mother. He was four, I think."

"Didn't he visit you two or three weeks ago? At the jail?"

Magnolia looked at Pollock in confusion. "You mean when I was arrested. In Boston. I was told he was there, but I didn't see him."

"The Goodhue County Detention Center records say that Hamilton Blethen visited you on March 18 at 1:30 p.m." Magnolia shook her head slowly. "Could this be another of those episodes you can't remember?" Magnolia didn't answer.

"Do you have any siblings?" Pollock changed directions, deciding there was no further purpose in pursuing Magnolia's relationship with her son for now.

"No. I was an only child. Thank God. My mother was a tyrant."

"What about your father?"

"My mother kicked him out when I was little. Maybe six or seven. Maybe younger. I don't remember. I don't remember anything about him, except my mother bad-mouthing him all the time."

"It sounds like your early years were not happy."

Magnolia, relatively calm until then, flared. "What's that got to do with my competency to stand trial? I'm not going to talk about my childhood."

"How about high school?"

"We already talked about that. You're wasting my time."

Pollock backed off, nodding. "Okay. Let's change subjects. You'll be happy to know that the doctors at Mayo have given you a clean bill of health," he said. "There was nothing in their examination that indicated any link between your blackouts and a heart condition."

Magnolia stood up and straightened her jump suit. "What's the bad news?"

"There isn't any bad news."

"There's always bad news." She sat back down.

Pollock took his finger off the panic button fastened to the underside of his chair, and decided to go all in. "Do you remember our last session?" he asked.

"You got me an appointment at Mayo Clinic."

"There was one after that. Do you remember that one?"

Magnolia looked puzzled.

"Do you remember me asking you about someone named Tiny Dancer?"

"Vaguely."

"Do you remember anything else from our last session?"

"It was short. I thought it was just part of the session when you got me the cardio appointment. Are you saying that it was a different session?"

Pollock nodded. "Do you remember Mr. Freeman, the dancing janitor from back in high school?" he asked.

Her puzzled frown grew deeper. "Yeaaaah. Why?"

"Tell me what you remember about him."

"He was a nice guy. He taught us how to dance," she said as her voice drifted off.

Pollock watched as something clicked in Magnolia's memory.

"Oh, that's why you were asking about Tiny Dancer," she said. "He gave me that nickname in dance class. How did you know about that?"

"Because I met Tiny Dancer at our last session."

"*What?*"

Pollock leaned forward, placing his hands flat on the coffee table. "I met your alter ego at our last session. It confirmed what I had suspected for some time. You have a condition known as D.I.D."

"What's that?" she scoffed. "Another of your made-up disorders?"

"Dissociative Identity Disorder," he answered. "It used to be known as multiple personality disorder. Basically, it's where a person has multiple, distinct personalities. There is the primary, dominant personality, which is you, but there is also another, secondary, personality, or sometimes more than one. We call these secondary personalities alter egos or alters, for short. When one of them temporarily becomes the dominant, visible personality, the person has no memory of that, or of what happens during the time when the alter is the dominant personality. I believe it explains how and why your blackouts occur."

"And you claim you've met my alter ego."

Pollock nodded.

"And her name is Tiny Dancer. How convenient."

"Tell me what else you remember about Mr. Freeman."

"Listen!" she barked, "I don't know how you found out about Mr. Freeman, but this whole D.I.D. thing is a hoax. I remember the movie, *Sybil*, that was supposed to be a true story, and I also remember the PBS story debunking the whole thing."

"I'm not ...," Pollack started, but Magnolia's tirade continued.

"I've said from the beginning this whole psychoanalysis thing is a scam. You and your fellow shrinks make up these bogus maladies, and then you diagnose people with your made-up disorder so they'll pay you for counseling sessions to cure them of a nonexistent disease. Why somebody doesn't put you all in jail…," she exhaled hard to show her disgust.

"And yet you have blackouts that aren't connected with any physical issue," Pollack countered. "Yes, we've come up with the D.I.D. label, but regardless of what it's called, the underlying psychological disorder is still there, and it is very real. The person who sat on that chair in our last session was not you. She inhabited your body, but she was definitely not you."

"Who am I now?"

The question caught Pollock by surprise. "Ah," he smiled, "only you can tell me that."

"Exactly. I might be one of those alter egos making believe I'm Magnolia Kanaranzi. You wouldn't know the difference. Just like in that *Sybil* case where the patient was making up multiple personalities just to get her shrink's attention."

"I don't want to debate the fact or fiction of *Sybil*. I'm only interested in you, and I *have* met an alter ego of yours. I'd like to keep exploring to see if there may be others."

"You mean you'd like the opportunity to make up more fictional characters so you can convince the judge of how smart you are and that I'm a looney tune. Well, fuck you. I'm not going to play your little game anymore."

Magnolia stood up, glaring at Pollock. His hand immediately reached for the panic button, but she turned and walked to the door, opened it, and yelled at the policeman sitting outside in the hallway. "Take me back to the jail. I'm done here. Permanently."

Pollock watched her go. He sat at his desk for several minutes, processing what just happened, then picked up the phone and punched in the number for Taft. A phone operator, an administrative assistant, and several minutes later, Taft answered.

"Taft here."

"Mr. Taft, it's Bishop Pollock, again. Do you have a minute?"

For the next half hour Pollock related the events of his session with Magnolia. "I'm certain she didn't fake the Tiny Dancer personality," he said. "Her reactions to my questions were too genuine. There is no doubt in my mind that, in her normal state, she is unaware that a second personality exists. She stormed out of my office denying such a personality exists and vowed never to come back. That's not an uncommon reaction, but it also creates a problem. I need you to convince her to come back one more time. I have to trigger her alter so I can determine with certainty that her personalities don't communicate with each other."

"How does that show she's incompetent to stand trial?" Taft asked.

"Because, if she has D.I.D. you can never be sure which of the personalities you are dealing with. It's impossible to know which one your advice is being heard by, Magnolia or her alter, so it impossible to be sure she can weigh alternatives and make choices."

"Sounds great, but to my knowledge I've never had a conversation with any alter ego, and the first thing the judge is going to ask me is if I can identify any time when I was speaking to someone other than Senator Kanaranzi. Talk to this alter ego again and see if she's ever had a conversation with me. Maybe, set up a meeting so I can meet this alter character."

"That's not how it works," Pollock explained. "Her appearance in my office as Tiny Dancer came completely out of the blue. When I first started talking to her, I thought it was Magnolia. Only after a few questions did it become apparent she was someone else."

Not happy that he was being talked to like a child, Taft's voice took on an edge. "You're the renowned expert in this area. I'll get her back in to see you. You do your job. Let me know when you've figured it out." He hung up.

Pollock watched his phone screen evolve back into its home page. *God, how I hate lawyers. Just get through this case. Eyes on the prize. Catch the brass ring. But what's the trigger that will bring back Tiny Dancer?* The trial, and his reputation, were hanging on the answer.

Samantha waited for Magnolia to appear on-screen for their regular Friday visit. The face, when it appeared, looked haggard.

"Are you okay?" she asked.

"I'm having trouble sleeping," Magnolia groused. "I can't get any sleeping pills. They don't give them out without a prescription, and I'm waiting to see the doctor."

Magnolia sighed dramatically. "And that asshole, Taft, is pressuring me to go back to the shrink. I've had a billion sessions already, but apparently that isn't enough."

"What are you going to do?" Samantha asked.

"I haven't made up my mind yet. Do you have any good news for me?"

"Yes. I've consolidated all your accounts, and about 90 percent of your Kincaid stock has been sold. I'm expecting proceeds from the most recent sales to land in the account in the next day or two."

"What's the balance?"

"At the moment?" Samantha paused. "About 58 million. I'm expecting another five million next week. The last 10 percent of the Kincaid stock should be sold within the next two weeks. I'll have the proceeds the week after."

"Good. Contact Henri and find out where he's planning to set up the new account. Don't transfer anything to him yet. I'll have further instructions next week."

Samantha smiled. "Before I go, I have lottery numbers for you," she said. "Henri says he'll be playing these for you tomorrow."

"Any news about the motion to expel me?" Magnolia asked as she got out a pen to write down the numbers.

"Just what you see in the media. Neither the state party chair nor Senator Styles' office will communicate with me."

"Hire a lobbyist," Magnolia ordered. "We need someone on the inside, or close to the inside."

Hawke's coded message simply said, *plans developing will call on Sunday.*

"They're trying to force me back into meeting again with the shrink," Magnolia complained when she got Hawke's call. "This is bullshit."

"Do it," was Hawke's terse answer. "It will all work out in your favor."

The squad car was stopped at an intersection waiting for the light to turn green, and Magnolia was brooding in the back seat over her forced re-engagement with Pollock. A young white woman, holding a brown baby, crossed in front of the car, catching Magnolia's attention.

I'll bet that's Seth Thomas's wife and baby girl. She watched them cross to the other side, where the woman put down the child. They walked away, down the street hand-in-hand. Magnolia realized the gloom she had been feeling had disappeared. She smiled.

SEVENTH SESSION

"I have given a great deal of thought to what you said the last time we were together," Pollock started. "You said D.I.D. is a hoax, and that I am just making up things. I know you're here involuntarily, and I'm sorry about that, but I think you should have the opportunity to prove to me that I'm wrong, and maybe in the process we can tie up a few loose ends from our earlier sessions."

Magnolia sat stiffly in the seafoam green wingback chair, her jaw clamped shut, staring out the window.

"I promise I won't ask about your childhood or your high school years. Instead, let's start by going back to your relationship with Arthur Kincaid. Tell me about your relationship after you left Las Vegas."

Magnolia's eyes darted toward Pollock and then back to the window.

"What did you do for Kincaid when you went to work for him?"

She exhaled, but still didn't respond.

"Why do you think he took you under his wing?"

She seemed to relax a little.

"Did he make a habit of adopting lost souls, or were you the only one?"

Tears welled in the corner of one eye. "I was the only one," Magnolia murmured.

"Why do you think he chose you?"

"I don't know. I've wondered about that. Maybe I was just in the right place at the right time."

"Maybe," Pollock responded, "but he must have seen something in you that compelled him to take what some would consider extreme measures to assure you were given a chance, first by getting you a job in Las Vegas, and then by hiring you as his personal assistant. What do you think he saw in you that distinguished you from other young women he must have met?"

"I don't know," she repeated. "Maybe he'd never met anyone coming off a high who needed a meal and a shower."

"And you repaid him with decades of loyalty."

Magnolia nodded, a tear now trickling down her cheek. "I was rewarded, too," she said, her voice barely more than a whisper.

"Do you expect that same kind of loyalty from the people around you?"

She thought for a moment. "No. Maybe. Depends on the situation."

"Let's talk about your son," Pollock said, switching subjects abruptly. "Do you expect loyalty from him?"

Magnolia sat back in the chair and blinked. "I… I…," her words wouldn't come, but the tears did. "I was a failure at being a mother," she finally said, her voice cracking. "I *am* a failure."

Magnolia wiped the tears away with the back of her hand as Pollock offered her a tissue.

"What can you tell me about your son?"

Magnolia shook her head. "Nothing. I know nothing about him."

"Let's take a five-minute break," Pollock offered. "Can I get you something? Water or coffee?"

First time she's let herself be vulnerable, Pollock thought. *Kincaid and her son. Who else?*

Five minutes later the session resumed.

"Can you tell me more about your sister," Pollock asked.

"I don't have a sister," Magnolia said blankly. "I don't have any siblings. You obviously have me mixed up with someone else." The roll of her eyes told Pollock she was back to her usual self.

Pollock flipped through his notes. "Ah, yes. Tell me about your mother."

"Are you serious?"

"I'm very serious. There is a great deal at stake here. We have the better part of an hour, so take your time."

Magnolia glared at the persistent psychologist, suddenly struggling to contain her temper. "I don't remember much about my mother except that I hated her," she said through clenched teeth. "I left home the day I graduated from high school. I remember that she was strict, and that we clashed a lot."

"What did you clash about?"

"Everything."

"Can you be more specific?" Pollock asked. Then, not waiting for the answer, he turned in his chair toward a small table on which sat a portable music player. "Do you mind?" he asked over his shoulder. "I find that background music sometimes helps people relax and remember."

"Please yourself," Magnolia replied caustically.

The sounds of The Righteous Brothers' *Unchained Melody* drifted from the speaker. Pollock turned back to face Magnolia, and watched as the tension visibly left her body. A winsome smile replaced the scowl.

"Tiny Dancer?" Pollock asked.

She nodded.

"You were going to tell me about your sister."

She nodded.

"Let's start with her name."

"She didn't have a name. Then she got named Maggie."

"How did she get named Maggie?"

"Don't remember." She tucked her hands under her legs and looked at the floor.

"Don't or is there something that makes you feel like you don't want to remember?"

Tiny Dancer's shoulders hunched over and pinched in, as if to protect herself from Pollock's question. He waited, and when no response came, he tried a different approach.

"It's hard to talk about things we don't like to remember. I wonder, can you recall how long she didn't have a name?"

"Awhile. Years I think."

"When you first met her, did she have a name?"

"No."

"How would you describe her?"

"I can't."

"Why not?"

"She is always kind of in the shadows, or her back is to me."

"Have you ever seen her face?"

She thought for a moment. "Not really. It's always blurry." She rubbed her left hand, curled into a fist in her lap. Pollock wrote something in his notebook. She hunched her shoulders even further and made an effort to stop rubbing her hand.

"I'm curious about what your sister looks like. What do you remember about her?" he asked.

"She's tall, not like me. And strong," she said. "I think her hair is brown or gray."

"Why do you think she's strong? Have you seen her do something that would take a lot of strength?"

She looked down at her lap, and began rubbing her balled fist again.

"You're doing a great job. Sometimes there are people in our lives who are so strong it can be scary. Did your sister ever make you feel afraid, or hurt you in any way?"

Tiny Dancer shook her head in short, quick jerks.

"Are you saying 'no'?"

She nodded.

Pollock shifted gears. "What was she wearing the last time you saw her?"

"Fancy clothes."

"Can you describe them to me?"

"Blue. A dress. She likes blue."

"Where did you see her in her blue dress?"

"Don't remember."

"Can you tell me how long ago it was?"

"Don't remember."

"The last time you saw her, when she was wearing her blue dress, what did you say to her?"

"We don't talk."

"How often do you see her?"

"She's around sometimes, but we don't like her so we don't talk to her." Her eyes returned to her lap.

Pollock sat back smiling. *We don't like her.* He looked at the clock. "We still have a few minutes," he said. "I would like to talk about your *other* sister with the time we have left."

Tiny Dancer looked at him suspiciously. "What other sister?" she asked.

"You said *we* don't talk about Maggie. Who is *we*?"

"I can't tell you."

"Do you have another sibling, besides Maggie?"

She hesitated. She furrowed her brow, then eventually she shook her head and said, "No. I don't have another sister."

"You said your sister Maggie always appears to you in the shadows. Do you have a feeling that there is someone else in the shadows?"

Tiny Dancer's head slowly turned back and forth, her stare vacant, as she tried to summon memories. After a minute she stopped and looked at Pollock. "I don't think so, but there's a word."

Pollock cocked his head. "A word?"

She nodded. "Yes. There's always a word in the shadows when Maggie is there."

"What is the word?"

"I don't want to say it. It makes me feel bad."

"It's okay for you to say the word," Pollock coaxed, leaning forward in his chair.

"I don't want to."

"I am wondering if it might help us understand Maggie better."

"I don't want to understand Maggie. I don't like her, and I don't like the word."

﹌

SESSION NOTES – DAY 7, MK/BP

1. *Music trigger worked.*
2. *Maggie/Third alter – continue. Try to draw out.*

3. *Probe TD for Kincaid and Hamilton Blethen memories*
4. *Intro MK to TD???*
5. *More alters?*
6. *"Word" trigger to Maggie alter?*

Tiny Dancer stood by the exit door to the hotel and watched a woman who looked just like her get into a car and speed away. Tiny Dancer shook her head, trying to understand what she had just seen. *Inmates must stay in this hotel,* she thought, then realized that didn't make sense.

A uniformed policeman, who kept referring to her as "Senator," guided her to a car that looked like the one the other woman had gotten into, and helped Tiny Dancer into the back seat. He got in the front passenger seat and looked at his watch impatiently. "Give them a couple of minutes," he said to the driver.

Five minutes later they drove through the parking lot of a large building where a gaggle of people were standing near the entrance, a few holding large cameras like the ones used to make movies. Tiny Dancer faded away.

"Don't stop," Magnolia cried out as she ducked down into the back seat, shocked to find herself in a car passing through the Goodhue County Adult Correction Center parking lot.

"We'll take you in through the courthouse," the driver answered. Magnolia was thankful to have her regular driver back today. The other driver would have kicked her to the curb just for the pleasure of watching her get devoured by the media.

As they left the parking lot, Magnolia peeked up over the back seat. An identical car was stopped at the jail entrance. A woman, who looked remarkably like Magnolia, got out of the car, holding something over her head to shield her face.

By the time Magnolia's driver circled the block and stopped at the courthouse entrance, Magnolia's confusion was gone. She recognized Hawke's work - the decoy - although the timing had been a little off. *How did I get in the back seat of this car?* She tried to retrace her steps from the time she left the jail for her meeting with Pollock. The last thing she could remember was Pollock asking a question about her mother.

Back in her cell, she sat at the table frantically flipping through pages of the *World Almanac*. She began to write words on a piece of paper with three numbers beside each word. Lunch came and went. By mid-afternoon she had finished her message: *Finish money transfer fast new identity new look needed Get me out of here Soon will transfer half of money.*

Now she just needed a visit from Samantha.

She folded the paper and put it under her mattress, then gathered the papers scattered on the table and placed them in a pile on the corner. One caught her eye. Across the top it said "Collateral Damage" and five names were listed below it.

Hmm. Interesting concept, she thought as she tucked it under the mattress with the *Almanac*.

EIGHTH SESSION

She sat quietly, listening to the music and thinking of Mr. Freeman. Pollock would arrive soon.

Seth had volunteered to be on Magnolia's security detail today and was standing by the door. They had chatted briefly on their way from the jail. He confirmed that his wife and daughter had dropped by to visit him over lunch the day before, and that it was probably them Magnolia had seen. The conversation ceased the moment they entered the hotel room and Magnolia heard the music.

Pollock appeared a couple of minutes later, and Seth took his place standing guard in the hallway.

"Sorry to keep you waiting," Pollock said as he greeted her.

"You shouldn't smoke," she replied as he sat down. "It's bad for you."

Pollock looked surprised. "I smoke a pipe," he said before he could catch himself. He never felt comfortable talking to patients about his personal life.

"I know. It smells nice, but you shouldn't smoke."

"You're right," he said, quickly adding, "I never smoke in the office, or at work."

She nodded, and smiled as she watched him discreetly turn his head to sniff the shoulder of his jacket.

"Let's get to it, shall we?" he said, satisfied that he didn't smell of pipe smoke. "I'd like you to tell me more about Mr. Freeman."

"He was nice. He listened. Sometimes I would go to him when I was…I was…when something bad happened."

"When something bad happened," Pollock repeated, smiling gently and nodding. "Can you tell me what you mean?"

"When I'd have a fight with my mom."

"Did that happen often?"

She gave a slight nod. "But I didn't talk to Mr. Freeman every time."

"When you did talk to him, what did you talk about?"

"I just told him about…about what was going on."

"Did he ever do anything like offer help, or hug you, or talk to your mother, or…," Pollock trailed off, leaving open air between them.

"No…once."

"I would like to hear more about that."

Tiny Dancer shifted in her chair and looked at the carpet. "My mother screamed at him. Blamed him."

"Blamed him for what? Did Mr. Freeman do something to you?" Pollock's words were gentle and careful.

"No!" Her head snapped up, and she shook it in short, sharp jerks.

Pollock watched as his client slowly folded into a fetal position, pulling her legs up to her chest, as if withdrawing into an invisible shell. Pollock asked several more questions but was met with silence. Finally, he changed the subject.

"Are you acquainted with a man named Napoleon Taft?"

"Hmmm. Yes. He's my lawyer, I think. I've only met him once."

"Tell me about your meeting with Mr. Taft."

"We were in court, a courtroom. There was a judge. Mr. Taft talked to the judge and the judge asked me a question."

"Why were you in the courtroom with Mr. Taft and the judge?"

She thought for a moment, then shook her head slowly. "I don't remember."

"Do you remember what question the judge asked you?"

Again, she paused. "Sort of. He asked it twice. Something about waiving something."

"Extradition?" Pollock offered.

"Yeah. That's it. Extradition."

"Did you agree to waive extradition?"

"I guess so. I don't know what extradition is. Mr. Taft told me to, so I just said yes."

Pollock realized he had been leaning a little farther forward in his chair with each answer. He sat back. *This could seal the deal.* He pressed on.

"Did you know a man named Arthur Kincaid?"

Tiny Dancer shook her head. "No."

"How about Hamilton Blethen?"

At this, she paused and looked at Pollock curiously. "That name sounds familiar." There was another pause. "Oh, he's the man who came to see me in jail."

"How long ago was that?"

"I don't remember."

"Can you describe him for me?"

"He was a foreigner, maybe from Egypt or India or someplace like that. He had dark skin and really black eyes, black like in the color of his eyes, not like he'd been punched in the eye."

"What did you talk about?"

"I don't remember. Nothing, really. He just disappeared. He must have left."

"Have you met Hamilton any other time?"

"Maybe. I think I remember seeing him in the courtroom with Mr. Taft and the judge," she said, shrugging noncommittally. "But maybe it wasn't him. I remember that guy being in a wheelchair."

Pollock made a show of stretching and looking at this watch. "Do you mind if we take a short break?" he asked. Tiny Dancer nodded. He nonchalantly restarted *Unchained Melody* as he got up to leave. He didn't want Tiny Dancer to disappear.

When he returned, the woman was sitting upright in the chair with her hands in her lap, a smile on her face.

"Tiny Dancer?"

She nodded, and her smile changed from happy to curious.

"Can we talk about your mother a little bit?"

The smile disappeared. She shrugged.

"Tell me the first thing you remember about your mother."

There was a pause. Tiny Dancer's fingers stroked the hair behind her right ear as she thought. "A birthday party. She told me I didn't deserve it. I was five."

She paused and looked thoughtful for a minute. "She had it hard. We were poor. Once she bought me a new dress. I think she didn't eat for a week so she could buy me that dress."

"How old were you when you got the new dress?"

"I think I was eight. It was blue and had short sleeves. It was beautiful. Blue has been my favorite color ever since. When I got too big for the dress my mother hollered at me, like she blamed me because the dress was too small."

"How old were you then?"

"Nine. No, ten."

"Was your sister Maggie there when your mom hollered at you?"

"No. Maggie came later."

"So, you're older than Maggie," Dr. Pollock stated, drawing the logical conclusion.

"I think she's older than me. Maggie and my mother were never around at the same time. Maggie came after my mother was gone."

Pollock nodded, his forehead furrowed. "Do you mean after your mother died?"

"No. After I left home. My mother was still alive."

"So, who named Maggie? Was it your mother?"

"No, I don't think so." She wrinkled up her forehead as if trying to remember.

"Mr. Freeman named you Tiny Dancer. Did he also name Maggie?"

"No. I think some other guy."

"Okay. You're doing great," Pollock gave her an encouraging smile. "Maggie is older than you, but you don't know her well because she's always in the shadows. When you first met her, you didn't know her name, but some man gave her the name, Maggie. Do I have that right?"

She nodded, so he continued. "I'd like to know more about this person who named Maggie. Can you describe him?"

"Just a guy. I remember a suit. He wasn't very tall. Smelled like hair, like the stuff you put in your hair to make it stay in place."

"Do you remember his name?"

"No."

Pollack relaxed back into his chair. "I wonder why he named your sister Maggie?" he said, looking like he was just thinking out loud. "Does the name have any special meaning to your family?"

"No," she shrugged.

"Were you there when he named her Maggie?"

A flicker of memory danced across Tiny Dancer's face. "It's like we were both there when he named her Maggie. She didn't like it."

"Did Maggie tell you she didn't like the name?"

"No. We don't talk."

"Then how do you know she didn't like it?"

"I…just…do." Her jaw muscles were suddenly tight, and she looked him square in the eye. She was clearly done answering questions about her sister.

Pollock looked at the clock.

"Next time I'd like to try something different," he said. "I'd like to try hypnosis to see if it helps you remember some things. Would you be willing to try that?"

Tiny Dancer shrugged.

⤻

SESSION NOTES—DAY 8, MK/BP

1. *Fetal position withdrawal. Hiding something re. Freeman?*
2. *BINGO! Alter was at extradition hearing.*
3. *Cross memory erratic. Kincaid, no. Blethen, yes—dream state.*
4. *Maggie—dream state.*
5. *Hypnosis/no.*

NINTH SESSION – THE NEXT DAY

The door to the hotel room was partially open when Pollock arrived for their session. He stopped in the hallway to observe his patient. She was wearing her regular blue prison uniform, talking to a guard who was sitting in the chair that Pollock normally occupied. There were signs of decline. Her silver-white hair, no longer perfectly coifed, was showing gray at the roots. No lipstick. Chipped fingernail polish. The jumpsuit looked too large for her diminutive frame, like she had lost weight. *Incarceration is taking its toll on her.*

He gathered himself and entered the room.

The guard jumped up from the chair. "Sorry," he said to Pollock, and then left the room.

"Tiny Dancer?" Pollock confirmed, offering a smile. "How are we doing today?"

"Same," she said with a nod and a pixie-like expression. She looked past him, as if searching for someone. "I thought you said something about hypnotizing me today," she said, looking around the room. "Are you the hypnotist?"

"No, I'm not. I'll have her come next time," he said, jotting down a note. "Today, I'd like to go back to the beginning and put together a timeline so I can get a better understanding of when things happened, and I can put them in their proper context. Can you help me do that?"

"Sure."

"The earliest memory we've talked about was a birthday party when you were five or six years old. Is that correct?" She nodded. "Do you remember anything earlier than that?"

She chewed on the inside of her lip as her eyes darted around the room as if searching for a memory. She shook her head.

"You told me about getting a blue dress when you were eight. Was that a birthday present?"

"No. I got that for first communion." Tiny Dancer did a little flounce on the chair as if she was rearranging her blue dress.

"Where did you go to church?"

She scowled, and puckered her lips. "I don't remember. We stopped going because my mother got upset with some people at church. She was always upset with somebody."

"How old were you then?"

"Maybe nine."

"What's the last thing you remember about your mother?" Pollock asked after jotting a few more notes in his book.

"Hating her," she replied without hesitation.

"Let me rephrase that. When was the last time you remember being physically in her presence?"

The clock on the wall ticked as time passed. One minute, two, Tiny Dancer staring at her hands, folded in her lap. Three minutes.

"Tiny Dancer?" Pollock broke the silence.

She jumped, startled. "I remember when she screamed at me and Mr. Freeman," she said suddenly.

"Why did she scream at Mr. Freeman?" Pollock asked, choosing his words carefully to avoid the shutdown that had occurred the last time this subject came up.

"Because she always saw the worst in everybody. All he was doing was helping me."

"How old were you when that happened?"

"I don't know. Fourteen?"

"So, you have no memory of your mother after fourteen?"

Again, there was a long pause. Tiny Dancer crossed then un-crossed her legs. She looked up at the ceiling, a grimace on her face, then back at Pollock. "I have memories, but she wasn't there."

"Tell me about those memories."

"Maggie was saying mean things about her."

"When was that?"

She thought for a moment. "I don't know," she shrugged. She sat back in the chair and reached in her jumpsuit pocket. "Mind if I chew gum?"

"Not at all." Pollock waited patiently while she unwrapped a stick of gum, folded it and popped it in her mouth.

"What mean things was Maggie saying about your mother?" he asked.

"She wanted to kill her."

Pollock couldn't keep the surprise off his face, but quickly collected his thoughts. "Maggie wanted to kill your mother? Did she say why she wanted to kill her?"

"No."

"What did you say when Maggie told you she wanted to kill your mother?"

"She didn't tell me. I just heard it," she said with a smug look on her face.

"Help me understand. Maggie didn't tell you directly, but you heard her say it, correct?"

"Uhuh. Sort of."

"When you heard her say it, did you think that she was serious? That she might actually try to kill your mother?"

"Maggie is strong. She could kill anybody," Tiny Dancer responded, an almost-cheerful look on her face.

Pollock's brow furrowed as he leaned across the table between them. "But did you think she was serious about killing your mother?"

"Yes, but I knew she wouldn't do it."

"How did you know she wouldn't?"

"Because I said she shouldn't." The smug look returned.

"Who did you say that to?"

"Nobody."

Pollock paused the rapid-fire question sequence. "Help me understand," he said slowly. "Did you say it—that Maggie shouldn't kill your mother—out loud, or did you just think it?"

Tiny Dancer shrugged.

"Who was with you when Maggie said she wanted to kill your mother?"

Tiny Dancer clamped her lower lip between her teeth and looked up at the ceiling without raising her head. "I was. Don't remember *anyone* else." The smirk was gone.

Her inflection in the word "anyone" got Pollock's attention. He gambled. "Was the *word* there?"

Her head snapped up. She nodded and whispered, "Yes." Pollock could see the tension building in her neck and shoulders. Her left hand curled into a fist, and she rubbed it hard with the heel of her right hand.

"How old were you when Maggie said she wanted to kill your mother," Pollock asked.

"Maybe fourteen," she replied.

He thought for a moment. "How old are you now?"

"Fourteen," she said in a surprised voice, apparently perplexed by his question.

Pollock again wrote a note on his pad, then lapsed into silence. *This is strange, an alter in control of another alter. Never heard of it before.* He thought about where to go next. *Maybe I should end the session?* But the potential to delve into something extraordinary pushed him forward.

"Why do you always have a police escort when you see me?" he asked.

"Because they don't trust me," she replied, the tension now visibly gone from her body.

"Who doesn't trust you?"

"The people at the place I'm staying." She uncoiled her left hand and put both hands under her thighs.

"Where are you staying?"

"The county jail," she responded with an impish smile. "I must have done something really bad to get arrested."

"Why do you think that?"

"Because people don't stay at the county jail unless they've been arrested," she rolled her eyes at him.

"Do you remember being arrested?"

"No."

"Do you remember going to a court hearing?"

"Duh. I already told you about that yesterday." Like a normal teenager, she was getting bored with him.

Pollock nodded, reminding himself that he wasn't dealing with an adult at the moment. "Of course. I do remember," he said smiling. "Did they ask you, when you were at the hearing, anything about moving or staying in Boston?"

"Nobody asked me anything except the judge. Otherwise, I just sat at a table. A bunch of lawyers were arguing."

"Who else was sitting at the table?"

"Lawyers."

"How many?"

"Two."

"Was one of them Mr. Taft?"

"Yes."

"Was Maggie there? In the courtroom?"

"No."

"Okay. So, you're sitting at the table with two lawyers. Do you remember arriving at the courthouse?"

Tiny Dancer grimaced. "There were a bunch of people shouting, and a man grabbed my arm and pulled me up the steps and pushed me into the courthouse."

"Did you know the man?"

"He was a policeman. I don't know his name."

"Do you remember leaving the courthouse?"

Tiny Dancer thought for a long time.

"Um. I don't know. I remember the judge saying something to the lawyer guy. That's the last thing I remember." She looked at Pollock expectantly.

"Do you remember coming here, to Minnesota?"

"No," she said raising her eyebrows.

"What's the first thing you remember about being in Minnesota?"

"Talking to some women in the jail."

SESSION NOTES, DAY 9, MK/BP

1. *Hypnosis/yes.*
2. *TD stuck at age 14. Cause.*
3. *Maggie alt—possible murder of mother.*
4. *Confirmed extradition hearing presence.*

Taft squinted and scratched the bridge of his nose. "You really think that it was this Tiny Dancer alter that was at the extradition hearing?" he said.

"She's confirmed it in two separate sessions. Her memory is sufficiently consistent without being rote. It's nearly impossible to fake," Pollock answered.

The two men faced each other through the monitors, Taft with his head cocked, thinking. "I remember that she was late for the hearing; she came in at the last minute with a tall Black woman, whom I later learned was her press secretary. We only had a minute before the hearing started. Magnolia was adamantly against extradition when we met the day before, but at the hearing she suddenly changed her mind and waived her opposition."

"Do you know why she changed her mind?"

"To be perfectly frank with you, I was quite surprised."

"Okay. Here's the real question," Pollock countered. "Did you tell Magnolia Kanaranzi about the potential federal prosecution or did you tell Tiny Dancer?"

"Until today, I would have been one hundred percent certain I was talking to Magnolia. Now I'm not sure," Taft admitted. "We should talk to the press secretary. It's my understanding that she visits Magnolia every week."

The buzz of the intercom interrupted Magnolia's mid-afternoon nap.

"You have a call from your lawyer," the voice announced over the speaker. "I'll be there in a minute to get you."

The walk across the day room was tense, as always. Magnolia tried to look nonchalant as her eyes darted around the room, accounting for each inmate who was present. When they reached the phone room, she turned to the guard. "Can you wait outside the door for me?"

The guard looked surprised. "What's going on?" she asked.

"Nothing. Just a premonition," Magnolia said.

"I can't wait, but I'll lock the door after you go in the room," the guard said, "and come get you after you hang up. Just wait for me."

Magnolia nodded and picked up the phone. Taft was on the line. Pleasantries aside, Taft jumped right to the point.

"I want to let you know that we are communicating with Ms. Jones."

"Why do you want to talk to Samantha?" Magnolia asked in surprise.

"We need her to verify something that happened at the extradition hearing. You know, an independent, objective witness." He paused. "Are you regularly in contact with her?"

"Of course I am. She visits me every week."

"Then I'd rather not disclose what we need verified," Taft said. "I don't want to take the chance that she'd be influenced by anything you might say, unintentionally of course, that might affect the independence of her recollection. Tell me what you remember about the extradition hearing."

Taft's cat-and-mouse game didn't please Magnolia, but she answered rather than carp at him. "I remember that you said something about a threat that the federal government might get involved, and that meant the death penalty was a possibility."

"What else?"

Magnolia thought for a long moment. "The next thing I remember is being handcuffed and pushed into a plane. Somebody, I think it was you, or maybe Laura, said that I had agreed to be extradited."

"Do you remember the judge asking you to waive your opposition to extradition?"

"No."

Samantha's phone rang just as she was getting out of an Uber in front of Durgin-Park Restaurant. She didn't recognize the number. "Hello?"

"Is this Samantha Jones?"

"Yes."

"Ms. Jones, this is Napoleon Taft, Magnolia Kanaranzi's lawyer."

"Of course! I remember you Mr. Taft. What can I do for you?"

"If you have a few of minutes, I have a couple of questions about the day of Senator Kanaranzi's extradition hearing. You were there."

"Yes. Can we make it quick? I have people waiting for me."

"When did you first see the Senator on that day?" Taft asked.

"I picked her up to go to the courthouse. It was insane. We were running extremely late and were mobbed the second we got out of the car."

"How did the Senator seem when you picked her up. Did she seem like her usual self?"

"Yes," Samantha said, sounding perplexed. "I guess I don't know what you mean by that. She was tense and nervous about the hearing, if that's what you mean?"

"You're aware that the Senator's competence to stand trial is being challenged."

"I'm aware that you're the one who is challenging it."

"That is correct." Taft sensed Samantha's hostility but pressed on. "We have evidence that the Senator has multiple personalities, and we believe that it was an alter-ego who was present at the extradition hearing. I apologize for being blunt, but that's the reason for my earlier question."

"What?" Samantha nearly dropped the phone.

"Under psychiatric examination it has been discovered that the Senator has at least two distinct personalities and, perhaps, three." Taft knew he wasn't being very humane with Ms. Jones, but he was running out time. Ms. Jones would have to work out her surprise and shock on her own time. "One of those alter egos may have been in court the day of the extradition hearing. When you brought Magnolia to the courtroom, did she seem like her usual self?"

"Yes," Samantha stammered. "When I left her in the room with you, she seemed perfectly normal to me."

Taft thanked her and hung up.

Samantha stood on the street and puzzled over the call. She thought back to the times when the campaign staffers wondered which Magnolia was going to show up. *Could she actually have more than one personality? It might explain some of her behavior.*

TENTH SESSION

Pollock was not pleased that Taft had called Samantha Jones. Taft had bumbled his way through that conversation and, in the process, had thrown doubt on whether Tiny Dancer was in fact present at the extradition hearing. Hopefully, the hypnosis session would repair the damage Taft had done.

A couch and a third chair were added to the hotel room's furnishings for today's session, giving it a slightly crowded feel. Pollock arrived early. He was, hoping to get a word with Carrie Waters before they started, but she was not yet there. He turned on the music players in both the hotel room and in the hallway, making sure the latter was loud enough to be heard at the elevators. *Unchained Melody* wafted through the mezzanine of the St. James Hotel.

Magnolia and her police escort, Deputy Johnson again today, arrived at exactly 9:00 o'clock, followed less than a minute later by Carrie. Pollock considered pulling her aside to talk about the extradition issue but decided it would take too long to explain. Instead, he made introductions and watched as the two women sized each other up. Seth retreated to guard duty outside the door.

In jeans, canvas slip-ons and a long-sleeved pullover, Waters had intentionally dressed in a manner that would make a fourteen-year-old feel comfortable. Although of average height, she dwarfed the petite woman dressed in a blue prison jumpsuit. *Tiny, indeed,* Waters thought. *So small, yet harboring so much.* She leaned forward and stuck out her hand. "Nice to meet you."

Tiny Dancer hesitantly reached out to take Waters' hand only to be startled when, instead of shaking hands, the hypnotist jerked her forward, throwing her off-balance. "We're going to go back in time together," Waters exclaimed. Tiny Dancer, her mouth agape in surprise, could only nod.

"What do you want me to call you?" Waters asked in a soft, pleasant monotone voice intended to defuse the stress created by the unorthodox greeting.

"Tiny Dancer is fine," she murmured.

Satisfied that her use of the Ericksonian handshake method of trance inducement had generated its desired effect, Waters motioned to the couch, and Tiny Dancer sat down.

"Dr. Pollock told me you have agreed to be hypnotized. Is that correct?"

Tiny Dancer nodded.

"Have you ever been hypnotized before?"

"No"

"First, let me assure you that it's entirely safe. Second, you will not be asked to do anything that you would not agree to do if you were not hypnotized. When the session is over, I will clap my hands twice and you will wake up. Until then you will remain sleeping. When you wake up you will not remember anything that happened while you were sleeping, but we are recording this session so you can listen to it whenever you want to. Do you understand?"

Tiny Dancer nodded timidly.

"Do you understand the reason you are being hypnotized today?"

"It helps me remember things."

"Good," Waters nodded.

"What if I don't want to remember?"

"Even when you're asleep, you can refuse to answer a question. If you truly don't want to remember something, your subconscious will override the hypnosis and prevent you from remembering. Ready to give it a try?"

Waters pulled her chair closer as Tiny Dancer stretched out on the full couch. Her soft voice took on a sing-song lilt. "Make sure nothing is binding or feeling lumpy. I want you to be conscious of your breathing. Nice even breaths."

"Now close your eyes," Waters continued. "Starting at the top of your head, let your consciousness drift slowly down your body, savoring every sensation: the dried sweat on your forehead, the sound in your ears, the pressure of the couch on your back. Be sure to travel down your arms, hands, fingers, legs and feet, feeling each of them separately. When you've reached your toes, reverse the trip, moving back up your body, but this time count backwards from 25."

Waters watched as Tiny Dancer's steady breathing slowed until it reached about half its normal rate.

"Tiny Dancer, can you hear me?" she asked, her voice gentle.

"Yes."

"Are you asleep?"

"Yes."

"Let's go to the time and place where your sister Maggie first got her name."

A pause. "Are you there?"

"Yes."

"Where are you?"

"I'm in a hotel room."

"Good. Now tell me what you see."

Tiny Dancer hesitated. "I see a man, and I see a woman." She paused. "They're coming into the hotel room."

Waters kept a quiet cadence to her voice. "Are either you or Maggie in the room?" she asked softly.

"I am."

"Is Maggie?"

"No."

"Do you know who the man and the woman are?"

"I might know the man. He smells like...," Tiny Dancer gasped. A look of panic crossed her face.

"It's all right. It's all right. It's not him. You're safe," Water's silky soft voice cut in. She waited a moment and then asked, "Are you okay? Do you want to continue?"

Tiny Dancer nodded.

"Do they, the man and the woman, see you?"

"No. I'm hiding from them."

"That's very smart. Can you tell me what's happening now?"

"He's pushing the lady against the wall, pressing himself against her. She's trying to push him away."

"You're doing great, Tiny Dancer," Carrie gently prodded.

"I hear the word. See the word."

"What word do you hear, Tiny Dancer?"

"*Bitch.*"

Tiny Dancer's body tensed and her breathing intensified.

"Maggie is there, beating the man with some kind of metal stick. Oh, no," Tiny Dancer gasped. "The man is on the floor bleeding and shouting."

"Can you tell what words the man is shouting?"

"He's shouting 'Maggie! Stop!'"

"And does Maggie stop?"

Suddenly Tiny Dancer cried out. "Stop! Maggie! Stop!" Slowly Tiny Dancer's body relaxed back into the couch, and Waters waited until her breathing slowed back to a calm, resting rate.

"What's happening now that Maggie has stopped hitting the man?"

"He's just lying there. He's not moving. There's lots of blood." Tiny Dancer fell silent and a blank look appeared on her face. She gave a small shake of her head. "We're not in the room anymore. I don't know what happened."

"Let's return to when you saw the man and the woman first enter the hotel room. Can you do that?"

Tiny Dancer nodded.

"Are you already in the room as they come in?" Waters asked, her voice soothing.

"No. I come in at the same time as the man and the woman."

"So, you were with them earlier, before they went to the hotel room?"

Again, Tiny Dancer hesitated. She exhaled deeply. "I must have been. I remember the smell of his cologne from somewhere else."

Waters stopped for a moment, thinking.

"You mentioned before how the man smelled," she resumed. "I'm going to ask you a few questions about that, but I don't want you to get upset. Nothing can hurt you, and if you want me to stop at any time, just tell me. Okay?"

Tiny Dancer nodded. "Okay."

"You said you 'might' know the man. Do you know him?"

"No."

"When do you realize you don't know him?"

"When he is on the floor."

"Why do you think you might have known him?"

"Because of the way he smelled. The cologne."

Tiny Dancer balled her left hand into a fist and rubbed it with her right hand.

"Do you want to stop?" Waters asked.

Tiny Dancer nodded yes then no.

"It's okay. We can talk about something else," Waters said soothingly. "Let's go back to the first time you saw Maggie."

Tiny Dancer lay on the couch, a sanguine look on her face, breathing evenly, not answering. "I can't. I don't remember," she finally said.

"At one of your sessions with Doctor Pollock, you said that your sister, who was later named Maggie, was not around when you were in high school. Is that correct?"

"Yes."

"You graduated from high school in 1971?"

"Yes."

"And the incident you just described occurred while you were living in Las Vegas several years after you left home."

"I guess so."

"When did Maggie threaten to kill your mother? Do you remember when that was?"

"It was a long time later."

"Can we go to that time now? The first time she threatened to kill your mother?"

"Okay."

Waters paused her questioning, waiting for Tiny Dancer to relocate in time.

"Where are you?"

"I'm flying to Boston. No. Barcelona. One or the other. I'm not sure. I'm on an airplane."

"And Maggie is with you?"

"Yes."

"Seated next to you?"

"No. She never lets me see her. She's in a different row."

"Then, how do you know she is threatening to kill your mother?"

"I just know. It's like I can read her thoughts. And she can read mine. I think she may have made a threat before. This might be the second time. I'm sorry. I'm getting mixed up."

"It's okay. You're doing a good job. Take your time," Waters paused briefly. "Were you there the first time Maggie threatened to kill your mother?"

"Yes. I stopped her."

"How did you do that?"

"I told her not to."

"Does Maggie always do what you tell her to do?"

A worried look crossed Tiny Dancer's face. She shrugged.

Again, Waters paused, scribbling notes on a tablet.

"Does it make you happy when Maggie does what you tell her?"

Tiny Dancer's smile disappeared. Waters waited, but there was no answer.

"Do you know who killed your mother?" Carrie asked in almost a whisper.

"No."

"But you're sure Maggie didn't."

"Yes. I know she didn't."

"Let's talk about Magnolia Kanaranzi. Could she have killed your mother?"

"I don't know who that is," Tiny Dancer responded without emotion.

Waters looked at Dr. Pollock and signaled him, with a nod of her head, to join her outside the room. "Anything else?" she asked after she closed the hotel room door.

Pollock thought for a moment, absent-mindedly scratching his ear. "From a purely clinical stand point, I'd love to know what the smell thing is all about, but that's outside the scope of what we're charged to do."

"I believe it's related to a rape," Waters responded. "Mary Blethen was violently raped when she was a freshman in high school. Is it possible that the trauma from the rape unleashed her multiple personalities?"

"That's not the way D.I.D. usually presents," Pollock said, "but I suppose it is possible a single event could be the trigger. How old was she when she was raped?"

"Fourteen."

"Hmm. This Tiny Dancer alter is stuck in the year of her rape," Pollock said, feeling sad and helpless for Tiny Dancer. *I can only hope that someday she gets the help she needs to heal from that.* He sighed. "I guess the only other thing we need for the report is information from the extradition hearing that took place last February in Boston."

Pollock provided the details of the extradition, then added, "Nice job on the Maggie alter. That helps me a lot."

"Thanks," Waters responded. "I'm no psychologist, but I think it's tragic that she might not get the help she needs. Maybe you could get your client to authorize treatment."

"Maybe, but I doubt it," Pollock replied. "She hates psychiatrists. She will never agree to therapy as a means to healing because she thinks it's a bunch of hooey. Yet, there she is, lying on the couch with another person inhabiting her body without her knowing it."

Waters nodded. "What about Maggie? Has she made an appearance on your couch?"

"I don't think so. We have a final session on Monday, and now that I know the trigger word, maybe I will get to meet her," he said nonchalantly. He knew he had to keep his professional and personal curiosity tightly in check.

"Be careful. Maggie sounds violent," Waters warned.

Pollock nodded. "As long as she doesn't have a weapon, I should be fine. Plus, I have a panic button and a guard just outside the door. Ready to go back in?" Waters nodded.

"I have a few more questions if you're willing to continue for a few more minutes," Waters said to Tiny Dancer, who was now sitting up on the couch. "Would you like to lie down again?"

"No. I'm good."

"Are you still asleep?"

"Yes."

"I'd like you to go back to the extradition hearing that took place in Boston. You told Dr. Pollock in an earlier session that you were there. Can you tell me how you got to the courthouse that day?"

"Hmmm. I don't remember."

"Do you remember entering the courthouse?"

Tiny Dancer scrunched up her face. "I don't remember."

"What's the first thing you do remember from that day?"

The clock on the wall ticked as Tiny Dancer thought. Thirty seconds passed; a minute. "I remember," she started then paused, thinking hard. "I am in the courtroom. I think I just got here," she paused again. "I see a man in a wheelchair. I feel like I *know* him." Tiny Dancer was visibly excited.

"Does he say anything to you?"

"No."

"Are you trying to talk to him?"

"No, but I feel so happy right now."

Tiny Dancer paused. A genuine smile spread over her restful face.

"I think he's related to me," Tiny Dancer continued tentatively.

Waters paused, not wanting to rush this moment away from the fragile woman sitting on the couch. Pollock nodded at her, and Waters pressed on.

"What do you see next?"

"I am at a table with my lawyers, and Taft is asking me if I want to waive extradition."

"What do you say?"

"I am saying it's okay."

"Does Tiny Dancer understand what extradition is?"

"No. I'm just saying yes because I think it's what Mr. Taft wants me to say. He seems pleased but surprised with me."

"Is Maggie there? At the extradition hearing?"

"No."

Waters looked over at Pollock with a *should-I-continue?* gesture.

"We're good," he whispered.

Waters looked back at Tiny Dancer and clapped her hands twice.

Tiny Dancer raised her head and arched her eyebrows, blinking. "Did I do good?"

"You were just great," Waters answered.

"Can you stick around for a minute?" Pollock asked.

"Of course."

Pollock turned off the sound machine, then opened the door and turned off the music in the hallway. He came back into the room and sat down, all the while looking at Tiny Dancer. He waited, raising his finger to shush Carrie when she started to say something. They waited and watched together.

Tiny Dancer shifted in her seat, uncomfortable under their stare. Her head swiveled back and forth looking first at Pollock and then at Carrie. After a minute the head-swiveling stopped. She glared at Pollock. "What's going on here," she snapped.

"Magnolia?" he inquired.

"Were you expecting someone else?" she asked rudely.

"I'd like you to meet a friend of mine, Carrie Waters. Carrie, this is Senator Magnolia Kanaranzi."

"Nice to meet you, Madam Senator," Waters said extending her hand and then quickly pulling it back.

Magnolia glared. "What do you want?"

"Just to meet you," Waters said. "I've followed your career for a long time."

⌣

SESSION NOTES—DAY 10, MK/BP/CW

1. *Maggie alt-violent.*
2. *TD has some measure of control over Maggie-pursue. Telepathic communication?*
3. ***BITCH!*** *Maggie trigger???*
4. *Rape/14/time lock.*
5. *Extradition confirmation again.*
6. *TD recognizes family connection to Hamilton Blethen.*
7. *Accomplished transition—TD to MK.*

"The trigger word is *bitch,*" Pollock said. "I'm going to do at least one more session to see if I can draw out her second alter."

Taft frowned on the other end of a video call with Pollock and Carrie Waters. "Is that necessary? From what you and…what's your name again?"

"Carrie. Carrie Waters."

"From what you and Ms. Waters have just told me, you should have enough to render an opinion that Senator Kanaranzi has D.I.D."

"I do," Pollock agreed, "but proof of a second alter would certainly strengthen my opinion."

"We're starting to run short on time. If it's not necessary…"

"There may be a secondary benefit," Pollock interrupted. "If I can get the alter, Maggie, to admit she wanted to kill her mother, and tie that in with a finding that there is no line of communication between Magnolia and Maggie, you may have the basis for a claim that Maggie was the real conspirator, and Senator Kanaranzi was, in fact, insane at the time of her mother's murder. It might give you an insanity defense."

Taft thought for a moment. Even with Pollock's opinion that Magnolia suffered from D.I.D. there was no guarantee the judge would buy the argument. The judge already seemed skeptical about Pollock, or maybe it was just about the legitimacy of psychological evaluation in general. Either way, having an insanity defense to fall back on was a good idea.

"You'll have to get this Maggie alter to admit she was involved, maybe admit that she ordered the appliances," Taft said.

"There weren't any appliances," Waters cut in. "That was just a ruse to get the killers in the door."

"I know that," Taft answered, his voice flat, "but if you go straight at her and ask if she hired someone to kill her mother, I expect - he paused dramatically - she'll deny it. However, if you ask her if she ordered appliances for her mother, you may be able to lead her to an admission she otherwise wouldn't make. You may be a hypnotist, Ms. Waters, but it's apparent you know nothing about the art of cross examination."

An uncomfortable silence stretched on until Pollock looked directly at Taft and said in an authoritative voice, "I'm going to go ahead with at least one more session."

"You go ahead and do that, but make it happen sooner rather than later. We have less than two weeks before your opinion has to be filed, and I'm going to want to go over it with a fine-tooth comb. We'll need at least a week for review and revisions."

Taft leaned forward and ended the call without another word. He rocked back in his plush office chair. Wouldn't that be a feather in his cap, beating a five-year old conspiracy case with an insanity defense. With a U.S. Senator as a defendant. Taft smiled. Only *he* was capable of doing that.

"You saved his ass, Carrie," Pollock consoled a quiet Waters. "He messed it up, and you saved him by getting Tiny Dancer to confirm she'd been at the extradition hearing. He's such a prick."

Waters nodded. "Yup. He is. I get tired of being put down by jerks like him. If you need a hypnotist to testify, you'll have to get someone else. I'm not going to testify if he's going to ask me questions."

"I understand," Pollock said, "but let's not make any rash decisions."

Samantha looked different, wary, like she didn't want to get too close to a caged animal.

"Is something wrong?" Magnolia asked.

"No. I'm fine," was Samantha's tense reply.

"Is the sale of my Kincaid stock finished?"

"Yes."

Magnolia peered at Samantha through the screen. "Have you received all the proceeds?"

"Not yet." Samantha looked over Magnolia's shoulder, then down at her hands.

Magnolia paused. "Samantha, what's wrong. Talk to me. Did Henri do something?"

Samantha shook her head.

"What is it?" Magnolia asked again, her voice rising. Samantha put her hand to her mouth, clearly struggling.

Finally, she blurted, "I got a call from your lawyer. Not Henri. The other one. He said…he said…," Samantha's voice caught in her throat. "He said you're suffering from a mental disease; you have multiple personalities."

Magnolia exhaled. "Is that all. Don't worry about it. They tried to tell me that, too, Taft and his psycho quack, but it's all B.S. They're just trumping up a case so that the judge finds me incompetent to stand trial. I gave Taft your number. He said he wanted to verify something at the extradition hearing, but he wouldn't tell me what. What did he ask you?"

"Just about how you were acting when I picked you up and took you to the courthouse in Boston; whether you were acting funny."

"What did you tell him?" Magnolia asked, genuinely curious.

"That you were acting normally. You were the person I've always known. Are you?" she asked sheepishly, finally looking directly at Magnolia. "The same person?"

Magnolia laughed. "I'm the same mean person you've always known," she joked. "Can you imagine if there were two of me? Nope, you'll just have to be satisfied with only me."

"Thank God," Samantha exhaled.

"Now, let's get down to business." Magnolia cut to another subject. "How much of the Kincaid stock sales proceeds are yet to come in?"

"About five million dollars. It should be in my account early next week."

"Have you made any transfers to Henri?"

"No, but he said the new account would be..."

"Don't tell me where," Magnolia stopped her. "This is not a secure line, and I don't want everyone in the western world knowing where my money is invested."

"Absolutely."

"I want you to transfer $13 million to Artemis Blazing's trust account." Magnolia instructed. "Hang on to the remainder for now. Did you hire a lobbyist to keep track of what's going on in the Senate?"

"I hate to spend your money on stuff I should be able to do for you," Samantha said. "So, I spent some time digging around this week and found an aide in Senator Steinberg's office who, for a small stipend, has agreed to feed me information on a daily basis with respect to any activity to expel you from the Senate."

"How did you find this person?" Magnolia asked.

"I learned that Steinberg and Senator Styles don't get along very well, so I thought there might be a hole in the dike there. I made a couple phone calls to friends in New York, who called some of their friends, and before I knew it, I was talking to one of Steinberg's aides. It's a woman, in case you're curious."

"Good. Have you learned anything?"

"That they're probably a couple of weeks away from starting the proceeding to expel you. My contact said it's being delayed because they're struggling to find enough votes."

"Good." Magnolia exhaled. "On a more pleasant subject, have you talked to Henri since last Saturday. Did I win the lottery?"

"I'm afraid not, but he said you were close," Samantha laughed. "You had one number right out of ten tickets. He said he didn't have any."

"We'll try again," Magnolia laughed. "Get him these numbers tonight. I'm feeling lucky. And ask him to call me this weekend."

They spent the last five minutes chatting about politics and Boston society events. With less than a minute left in the visit, Magnolia said, "Please set up a visit with Meredith Glenn. Try to have it on Monday. Tell her I'd like to talk to her about *The Reaper*."

Magnolia returned to her cell, satisfied with her visit with Samantha. She spent the rest of the time, until lights out, crafting a letter to Artemis Blazing.

Hawke's call came mid-morning on Saturday.

"I received your message," he said. "Everything is proceeding nicely. A few more days and all the pieces will be in place."

"You're referring to the liquidation of my stock and investment of my assets, I presume."

"Exactly."

"I think I may be done with Dr. Pollock."

"But you still have a session with the other psychiatrist, no? The one appointed by the court?" Hawke asked.

"Yes. I don't think it's been scheduled yet."

"Will it be at the same location?"

"I assume so."

"You must confirm that, and I must know at least 48 hours beforehand."

"Are you coming to visit me?".

"Not me, personally, but I'll send someone you know."

"Oh," Magnolia tried to sound disappointed. "I was hoping it was going to be you," she said with feigned playfulness.

"Not this time, *mon amie*," he replied, "but we need to communicate more frequently. Weekly is not often enough. I will call you Monday evening at 7:00."

"That will be two in the morning, your time."

"My day is just starting," Hawke chuckled.

"Will you be sober?"

"Sober enough. Tell me now, what is happening with your Senate seat?" he asked, changing the subject. "I do not hear any news on the international newscasts."

Magnolia simmered for a moment before she answered. "The pompous asses who promised to have my back have all abandoned me. They're looking for someone to replace me."

"But you have not been removed from the Senate?"

"I might as well be," she flared. "I don't think my party is trying very hard to get the votes necessary to stop my expulsion."

"Ah, I am sorry, but I must say I warned you about politicians." There was no gloating in his statement, just the sound of sincere sadness.

"I hope they all burn in hell!"

"Or, maybe, hell here on earth," Hawke suggested.

ELEVENTH SESSION

Pollock spent the weekend ruminating over the events of Friday's session. The part that bothered him the most was not the prospect of facing the Maggie alt, nor even Taft's belittling of Carrie. What bothered him was the revelation that Magnolia had been raped when she was 14.

He was confident in his diagnosis that the Senator suffered from D.I.D. even though that affliction ordinarily was caused by repetitive traumatic occurrences, not from a single event. Add to that her sudden shifts from one alter to another, which occurred in less than five percent of all D.I.D. cases, and the question would inevitably be raised on cross examination whether she was fabricating her condition. With Magnolia presenting both characteristics, he needed at least one more session to pin down his opinion.

He decided that before he tried to summon Maggie, he would take a deep dive into the 50-year-old rape. Even though it did not deal directly with the question of her competence to stand trial, it might provide a foundation for an opinion that a judge could understand. Because of the critical nature of the session, he decided to video record it.

"Let's talk a little more about Mr. Freeman and your mother," he said after he had confirmed it was Tiny Dancer and not Magnolia sitting with him today. "You said that your mother blamed Mr. Freeman. What did she blame him for?"

"For hurting me," she replied.

"Did he hurt you?"

"No, he was helping me, but all my mother could see was that I was to blame and that Mr. Freeman was somehow involved. She said I brought it on myself. By the way I acted."

Pollock rocked back in his chair, stroking his chin. "If Mr. Freeman didn't hurt you, who did?" he asked.

"Mac. A boy from school."

"How did he hurt you?"

Tiny Dancer's expression froze. She chewed her gum faster as she lifted her left hand to her chest and curled it into a fist. With her right hand she rubbed the curled fist harder and harder.

"It's okay," Pollack quickly interjected, trying to calm her. "You don't have to answer that question." It took several minutes for her agitation to subside. Pollock sat patiently, watching Tiny Dancer rock back and forth. When she stopped rubbing her fist and rocking, Pollock apologized. "I'm sorry my questions upset you. We can move on to something different."

"He smelled," she continued following her own thought stream. "He said he borrowed his dad's cologne. He said it made him smell manly, but it made me want to gag. When I laughed, he got mad and called me names. Said I wouldn't know a man if I saw one. Then he called Mr. Freeman names. I got out of the car, but he chased me and knocked me down."

Tiny Dancer stopped talking. Tears began to well in her eyes.

"Did he rape you?" Pollock whispered.

She nodded as the tears crept over her lower eyelids and streamed down her cheeks. Pollock picked up a box of tissue, holding it out to her. "I'm sorry this happened to you," he said compassionately.

"And he beat me up," Tiny Dancer whispered after her tears subsided.

"Do you have dreams about that?"

She nodded. "All the time." She clasped her hands together and shoved them between her legs. Her sobs overwhelmed her momentarily. "I relive it all the time," she finally gasped.

Pollock waited, knowing his next question could have explosive results. Finally, he asked, "Did he call you a bitch?"

Her reaction was immediate. Her jaw muscles tightened, and her eyes grew hard. Her back arched as she pulled herself to a fully upright position. Both hands were balled into fists. She gave the appearance of having doubled in size, even though the blue jumpsuit was still at least a size too large.

"Maggie?" Pollock asked calmly.

She glared at him.

"Maggie, my name is Dr. Pollock. I'm a friend of Tiny Dancer's."

"I hate Tiny Dancer," she growled.

"Why do you hate Tiny Dancer?" he asked, appearing calm while, at the same, using his left hand to locate the panic button concealed on the underside of his chair.

"Because she thinks she knows everything," Maggie snarled, still standing and glaring at Pollock. "She's always telling me what to do."

"Can you..."

"I am not. I'm going to kill your motherfucking *friend*."

Pollock realized that she was no longer talking to him. He opened the drawer in the table that was between them, and put his hand on the taser he had placed there before the session. He watched as Maggie's expression changed to one of disappointment. She sat back down in the chair.

"I'm not going to answer his fucking questions," she groused.

"Are you talking to Tiny Dancer?" Pollock asked. Maggie glared back at him, not answering.

"I think you and I could become friends," he said. "Tell Tiny Dancer she can go. You and I can handle this."

"I don't have friends," the snarl in Maggie's voice hadn't changed, but her posture was less aggressive. "She won't leave. She never leaves. That's why I hate her."

"She's always present? Always?"

The only response was an intense glare and a guttural grunt.

"Tell me what Tiny Dancer looks like."

"She's a little shit, always...wait, you said she was your friend. YOU tell ME what she looks like. What kind of crap are you trying to pull on me?" Again, Maggie was halfway out of the chair, only to sit back down with a loud snort. "Fuck you. Okay. Okay."

Pollock continued to watch the phenomenon of Maggie talking to her invisible alter ego.

"What do you want to know?" she asked, this time directing the question at Pollock.

"So, Tiny Dancer is always present, and she tells you what to do."

"I already told you that!"

"Does she tell you when you have to leave?"

Maggie scowled; nodded.

"What does she say?"

"Time to go, Maggie," she said in a mocking sing-song voice. "But some day...," she trailed off.

This time it was Pollock's turn to nod. The thought of Maggie unleashed was frightening. "Do you have any other sisters?"

"No. Maybe."

"Do you have a sister named Mary?"

"Maybe. I don't know her."

"Why do you think you *might* have a sister named Mary?"

"I don't know."

"Do you have any brothers?"

She shrugged. "No."

"What can you tell me about a person named Mary Blethen?"

"Hmmm. Nothing. I don't know who that is."

"How about Magnolia Kanaranzi? Do you know her?"

"I might have met her once," Maggie said mysteriously.

"What happened when you met her?"

"Nothing. I think she went and hid in a corner. Maybe."

"Did you meet Magnolia any other times?"

Maggie paused. "Maybe one other time."

"Have you ever talked to her?"

"I told you, I don't know her!" she snarled.

"Do you and Tiny Dancer have the same mother?" he asked.

Maggie hesitated, scratching her nose. She shrugged and shook her head. "I don't know. Maybe," she said. "I don't remember my mother."

"Tiny Dancer told me you threatened to kill *her* mother? Is that true?"

"Tiny Dancer's a liar."

"So, you didn't threaten to kill her mother?"

"I would have."

"You would have killed her mother?"

She nodded. "She deserved it."

"Why did she deserve it?"

The muscles in Maggie's jaw pulsed. She didn't answer.

"Why did you buy your mother new appliances?" Pollock asked, hoping the quick transition would catch her off guard.

"What? I didn't buy her any appliances."

"Someone bought her new appliances just before she was killed," Pollock said. "I thought it was you."

"Who told you that?" Maggie shouted. "Nobody bought her no new appliances."

"How do you know that, that no one bought her new appliances?"

"I don't know that. I just know I didn't buy her any."

Pollock cocked his head and raised his eyebrows. "Did you send someone to her house pretending that they had new appliances for her?"

"I didn't send nobody nowhere."

"When was the last time you were in her house?"

"Long time ago."

"What do you remember?"

"Crying."

"Why were you crying?"

She shook her head and shrugged, all at the same time. Her lips were firmly clamped shut.

"Did it have anything to do with you wanting to kill her?"

Maggie came out of the chair, screaming. "She fucked up everyone and everything!"

"Okay. Okay." Pollock reacted, holding his hands up, palms out. The gesture worked. Maggie sat back in her chair.

"We can come back to that, but for now, someone killed her and it wasn't you. Do you know who did kill her?"

"Yeah. Sort of."

"Do you know their name?"

"No, but I know who hired him," she smiled wickedly.

Pollock watched as his client's hunched shoulders relaxed and the hard edges disappeared from her face. A winsome smile replaced the scowl.

"Tiny Dancer?" Pollock asked. She nodded. "Why did you tell Maggie to leave?"

"Can't say," Tiny Dancer responded, a twinkle in her eye. "It was just time."

〜

SESSION NOTES--DAY 11, BP/MK (VIDEO RECORDED)

1. *Rape reaction valid, single cause verified.*
2. *Maggie: TD alter?*
3. *TD controls Maggie. Research alter having own alter. May be landmark case.*
4. *Need session with MK*
5. *Second opinion?*

Magnolia woke up from a fitful nap by the delivery of her lunch tray and the news that she had a 3:00 o'clock visitor, Meredith Glenn, and a 7:00 o'clock phone call with one of her lawyers. She was troubled as she pushed the food around her tray, troubled because she never napped in the morning and did not remember lying down to take a nap, and troubled because of a dream that was quickly fading.

Her son had been in the dream, she was sure of that; and there was a hideous creature with a giant head, holding a curved blade hacking at her son. She couldn't move; she couldn't save him. She tried to grasp the tendrils of the dream to hold it in place so she could see it more clearly, remember it, but it slithered away, leaving only shadows. Soon the memory was completely gone, but her unsettled feeling remained.

The three hours until her meeting with Meredith dragged. Magnolia tried reading, then crossword puzzles, then finally gave up. She stretched out on her bed and looked at the gray ceiling. She thought about Deputy Seth Johnson and his family, and about her own son and whether he had any children. She wondered what they might look like. She tried to bring back images of her son, but they were as vague as the dream.

Finally, at 3:00 o'clock she was escorted to the electronic visitor center. The room was empty.

"No one else has visitors?" she asked the guard in surprise.

"Regular visiting hours are from six to eight," he replied. "Your visits are outside those hours for security reasons."

She nodded and sat down at the monitor the guard indicated. A press of a button and Meredith Glenn appeared on the screen.

"Thanks for agreeing to meet with me," Magnolia said.

"Sorry I haven't visited before," Meredith replied. Her tone was sincere, but her passive expression suggested otherwise. They made small talk about the upcoming museum shows, news of the art world, and the terrible things that were going on in Washington, all the while dancing around the subject of Magnolia's incarceration, mental health, and pending trial. Finally, as the banal chatter started to become labored, Meredith said, "Your assistant said you wanted to talk to me about *The Reaper*."

"I do," Magnolia acknowledged. "Have you made any decision about what you're going to do with it?"

"We have a meeting next week, but it looks like we're going to have to start a lawsuit to rescind the deal and get our money back."

"You're absolutely sure it's a forgery?"

"It really doesn't matter anymore if it is or it isn't," Meredith responded. "With its provenance in question and all the bad press about it, there will always be a question of its authenticity, even if we stack up 20 experts who say it's the real thing. The painting has been devalued to such a degree that it's unlikely we could ever recoup our investment. If we don't do something, it will likely end up in the basement archives, a $13-million boondoggle."

"A lawsuit is just going to bring more bad press," Magnolia observed.

Meredith nodded in agreement. "And that will have a negative impact on donors in the next few years. It's damned if we do, and damned if we don't, but I'd rather be proactive in trying to rectify a mistake than be the fool who got scammed and did nothing."

"It's a bad situation," Magnolia agreed, "but I may have a way for the museum to recoup its investment and avoid the bad press."

Meredith raised an eyebrow.

"I haven't worked out all the details yet, but don't do anything with the painting until you check with me first. I think I may be able to make you look like a hero, or at least a genius."

"I could use some of that," the beleaguered museum curator acknowledged.

A message came with Magnolia's dinner tray. Another session with Pollock was scheduled for Wednesday at 3:30. It put her in a foul mood, which she unleashed on Hawke when he called that evening.

He listened patiently to her rant for half an hour as she took out her frustration in equal proportions on psychologists, lawyers, judges, and politicians. He offered only the occasional grunt of recognition or word of empathy. When her ire finally began to ebb, Hawke turned the conversation to more immediate concerns.

"I understand your frustration," he said, "but don't concern yourself with Pollock. We assume he's going to write an opinion that says you're incompetent to stand trial, but that's of little consequence. What's most important is your meeting with the court-appointed psychiatrist."

Magnolia mulled Hawke's words. "What should I do to prepare?" she finally asked.

"As soon as we find out when you're going to meet the other psychiatrist, I'll send someone to help you. In the meantime, go to your scheduled session with Pollock. Hopefully, it will be the last time you'll see him."

"So, what's the strategy for this meeting with the court's appointed shrink?" Magnolia asked.

"That will depend upon how you want this to turn out."

"I do not want to spend the rest of my life in some mental institution!"

"Then we will need to make the most of the opportunity presented to us by the State's psychiatrist."

Magnolia didn't respond immediately, mulling over Hawke's statement. *Was he being intentionally evasive because someone might be listening? Did he even have a plan? If he does, can I trust him? Do I have a choice?*

"I have new lottery numbers for you," Hawke said, breaking the silence. "I bought these tickets for you yesterday. Do you have something to write them down?"

Magnolia recorded the numbers and inquired about the progress of setting up her investment portfolio.

"I'm working through a bank in Zurich," Hawke said. "Very discreet. When can I expect to receive the funds?"

"I want the account set up so that you can direct investment decisions, but no withdrawals can be made without Samantha's approval," Magnolia said, ignoring his question.

"Very prudent," Hawke answered. "I assume you don't expect Ms. Jones to travel to Zurich each time there is to be a withdrawal. We can set up an account that requires either a thumb print or a retinal scan. I'll ask the banker which technology is best transmitted electronically so that an authorization can be made from anyplace."

"I'll have Samantha meet you in Zurich next week. You can set up the account and she can transfer funds."

"I presume she will authorize my payment at that time?"

"She will bring the funds with her to pay your fee. I want the new account to be intact, invested in something conservative and tax free."

"Of course, Madam," Hawke said, "but I advise you leave some amount liquid in case you have an immediate need, perhaps a political contribution or future legal expenses. May I suggest $5 million?"

Back in her cell, Magnolia waited for the outer door to click shut, then sat down at the table to decode Hawke's message. It read; *French papers complete. Buy or rent at destination like Boy Scouts be prepared. Sending Is a Bell a happen Soon*

Magnolia spent the next several hours composing her response to Hawke's cryptic message. She double-checked her work. *Open new account in new name rent buy later if satisfied am prepared will need new look weapon and documents.*

TWELFTH SESSION

Magnolia had tidied herself up since their last session. The blue prison uniform was a new one that fit her better, and it was clean and pressed; her hair was fixed, and the gray roots were gone; the chipped nail polish had been replaced with a metallic royal blue to match her eyes. *Somebody got paid off,* Pollock thought.

"How are you, Senator?" he asked in a conversational tone.

"Thrilled to be back here talking to you," she replied sarcastically.

"I know. I know. But other than being here, how are they treating you?"

"I'm managing."

"Well, I have some good news," Pollock said. "This will be our last session. There are just a couple more things I'd like to ask you."

"Oh, goody gumdrops," she said. "Don't you have enough dirt on me already to tell the judge I'm crazy? Everyone wants to put me away in some asylum."

"No, Senator, I don't believe you are, as you say, 'crazy'," Pollock responded. "But let's do this. The quicker we get started, the sooner you'll be done with me."

"That will be a pleasure," she said.

"First," Pollock started, "I'd like you to write down the time." He handed her a notepad and a pen. The clock on the wall read ten minutes after three. "Next, I would like you to write every name by which you have been known during your life."

Magnolia shook her head in disbelief. "Stupid," she muttered, but she picked up the pen and began to write. In less than a minute she looked up. "Done. Now what?"

Pollock, his back to Magnolia, turned on his sound system. As he turned to face her, the sounds of *Unchained Melody* filled the room. He watched her transition seamlessly to Tiny Dancer. The lines of her face softened and her body relaxed. Her eyes lost their dark thunder and reflected the mirth of youth.

"Nice to see you again, Tiny Dancer," he said with a smile.

"I thought you were mad at me," she said in a mock pout, tucking her legs under her on the chair.

"Why would I be mad at you?"

"Because I told Maggie to go away." She stuck her tongue out at him playfully, then took a stick of gum from her pocket, unwrapped it, folded it over and popped it in her mouth. She looked up at Pollock with a mischievous smile.

"Oh, that," he laughed. "Why *did* you tell her to go away?"

"Because it was time for her to go home."

"Where is *home*?"

The question caused Tiny Dancer to pause and cock her head. "The jail, I guess," she said, sounding unsure.

"Do you see Maggie at the jail?"

Again, Tiny Dancer looked confused. "Nnnnoo," she said, drawing out the word, "but I've only been there a couple of times."

"I see," Pollock said. "Where are you when you're not at the jail?"

"Here."

"Anywhere else?"

She shook her head in quick, erratic jerks; her expression a puzzled frown.

"Does that mean you don't know?"

"It means I don't remember," she corrected.

Pollock let silence settle over the room. Only the music and the ticking of the wall clock could be heard. He could see, through the movement of her eyes, that Tiny Dancer was trying to reconcile the conundrum that faced her: where was she when she wasn't at the jail or in his office? He was certain she had never grappled with that question before.

"Let's try something," he said, breaking the silence, extending a pad and pen to her. "Flip to a blank page and write down every name by which you have been known during your life."

She picked up the pad and sat back on the chair, tucking her legs under her in cross-cross style. She rested the pad on one knee and began to write. In a few minutes she stopped, put her feet back on the floor and handed the pad to Pollock.

"Just leave it there," he said, motioning to the table between the chairs. "I'll look at it in a minute." Tiny Dancer set the pad and pen down and settled back in the chair. She began fiddling with her hair, rolling a few strands between her thumb and finger. She looked at Pollock with a bored "what's next" look.

"At our last session, when I was talking to Maggie, were you in the room the whole time?"

She gave a little head nod. "Yup."

"So, you heard the entire conversation between Maggie and me?"

"Yup."

"Good," he said. "Maybe you can clarify a couple of things for me. Maggie said she wasn't your sister, and she didn't seem sure if she had any siblings. Can you help me out here?"

He looked at her expectantly, a fixed helpless expression on his face.

"Maggie *is* my sister, or maybe half-sister. I'm not sure," Tiny Dancer answered. "I wish she wasn't because I don't like her."

"Why don't you like her?"

"Because she's always mean, sometimes scary mean."

"But you control her. She seems to do what you tell her to do," Pollock observed.

She nodded. "When I'm there, I can."

"Are you aware of any time when Maggie has gone off on her own without you?"

Tiny Dancer pursed her lips and shook her head "no" authoritatively, but her expression conveyed a different answer. She wasn't sure.

"Let's take a look at that pad," Pollock said, leaning forward to take it off the table. He flipped to the second page, making a mental note of the juvenile handwriting in comparison with Magnolia's eloquent script on the first page.

"I see you listed only two names," he said. "Tiny Dancer and Mary Blethen. Tell me about Mary Blethen."

"You already know that was my name before Tiny Dancer," she said.

"Do some people still call you Mary?"

"No. My mother is dead. She was the only one who called me Mary."

"What about your classmates? Your teachers?"

"Hmmm." She thought for a moment. "Not anymore."

"So now you're only known as Tiny Dancer."

"Yup."

"Did your mother call you any other names besides Mary?"

Again, she paused. "She called me lots of names when she was mad at me," she said, color rising in her cheeks. "Prostitute, whore, and…"

"Did she ever call you a bitch?" Pollock interrupted.

Her eyes went flat, deadly, and she seemed to grow inside the jumpsuit. The color that had begun to rise in her cheeks now encompassed her entire face. She sat forward on the chair; she was suddenly a tightly-wound spring waiting to be uncoiled.

"Hello, Maggie," Pollock said in a friendly tone. "Thanks for stopping in."

She seethed in her chair, unable to sit still but holding back as if she was shackled.

"Can I get you something?" Pollock offered. "A soft drink or water?"

"Coke."

He got up and walked to the mini refrigerator tucked into the cabinet that also held a television set. Turning to Maggie he asked, "Would you like ice?"

"No, just the can."

"How have you been feeling since I saw you last?" he asked as he handed Maggie the can and sat back on the chair across from her.

Maggie shrugged. She opened the can and took a long, noisy sip, then set the can down with an "ahhhh." "I haven't had a Coke in a long time," she said.

"Take your time and enjoy it. We're in no hurry." The Coke and Pollock's soothing voice reduced the tension in the room. "I do have a couple of questions I'd like to ask, though, as a follow-up to the last time we met. Would that be okay?"

Maggie eyed him suspiciously. "Do I have a choice?"

Pollock ignored her question and continued. "Where do you live?"

"Boston."

"Do you know where you are now?"

"You think I'm stupid? We're in a hotel room disguised as your office."

"And where is my 'office' located?" he asked, making air quotes and smiling.

"How the hell should I know. Nobody tells me nothin'."

"Are you referring to Tiny Dancer?"

"Fuckin' right I'm referring to that little shit. Someday I'm going to…" She didn't complete her sentence, interrupted by a voice that only she could hear.

"Do other people tell you things? Tell you what to do?"

"I make other people do things. They don't tell me."

"Like the man in the hotel room in Las Vegas?"

"Yeah. He won't be tellin' nobody what to do anymore," she laughed menacingly.

"Have there been others?"

"Damn right."

"Recently?"

"Hmph." She snorted in acknowledgment.

"Can you tell me about the most recent one?"

"Not much to tell. I shot the motherfucker. Killed him before little miss know-it-all could stop me."

"Where did this happen?"

"Somebody's house, I think. Sprayed blood everywhere," she chuckled in satisfaction.

"Why did you shoot him?"

She paused and fixed Pollock with a serious stare. "He kicked the kitten."

"The kitten named *Houppette*?"

She shrugged. "Maybe…I don't know."

Pollock was at a fork in the road. He had already gotten more from Maggie than he had hoped, but now he had to make a choice: continue to follow Maggie's violent past or focus on her knowledge of the existing trial. Either way, it would probably end the session, and he would never get to follow the other fork. He chose the risky path; one that had the potential to derail his opinion.

"Did they arrest you after you shot the man in Boston?" he asked.

"They'll never catch me," she said, an abundance of arrogance in her voice. "I disappear."

"And where do you disappear to?"

"My secret place."

"Can you tell me about it?"

Maggie looked at Pollock. "I'd have to kill you." There was no mirth in her voice. She was dead serious.

"You said last time that you didn't know a person named Magnolia Kanaranzi," Pollock asked without missing a beat. "She has been charged with murder, and there is a legal proceeding pending. Do you know anything about the murder or the legal proceeding?"

"Did she get arrested because I offed that guy?" she laughed.

"No. She's charged with a different murder. The murder of her mother."

"Just like Tiny Dancer's mother," Maggie said with a smirk.

"Speaking of Tiny Dancer, is she here right now?"

"She's always here."

"You mean, literally always, as in wherever you are, she is there too?"

"Yeah, for now. That's going to change. It is, too, you little fuck. I'm going to crush you like a seed."

Pollock watched as Magnolia's two alters verbally battered each other. He could only hear Maggie, but it was clear that Tiny Dancer was in her head, still in control.

"Wait. Wait. Wait a minute," he said, trying to intervene in the argument. He got Maggie's attention. "One last question. Have you met with any lawyers since you shot that man?"

"Why would I meet with lawyers?"

"I take it that's a 'no'."

"Fuckin' right it's a no. I hate lawyers almost as much as I hate shrinks."

Pollock turned in his chair and turned the music up a little louder. "Tiny Dancer," he said. "Please tell Maggie it's time to go."

A menacing scowl momentarily crossed Maggie's face and then, like someone flipped a light switch, the teenage countenance of Tiny Dancer appeared.

Pollock didn't hesitate. "How often have you seen Maggie since you've been in Minnesota?" he asked.

She paused, biting her lower lip. "I don't know. A couple of times maybe, but it's hard to keep track of time." She fidgeted, playing with her hair again.

"Just a couple more questions," he said, knowing that he was running out of time. "Have you been in meetings with lawyers outside the courtroom?"

Tiny Dancer nodded.

"How many times?"

"Two. Maybe three."

"And what did you talk about?"

"They asked me a bunch of questions," she said, "but I didn't know what they were talking about."

Pollock turned and switched off the music. "I think we're done, but let me step out and check on something. I'll be back in a couple of minutes." She nodded.

Pollock walked out of the room and closed the door. *I hope this works,* he thought as he nodded to the policeman by the door and then headed down the hall to the bathroom. Five minutes later he walked back into the examining room.

"Senator?" he inquired.

"Feel better?" she asked sarcastically. "Bad enough that I have to come here, but then I have to wait while you go relieve yourself in the bathroom."

Pollock sat down, internally rejoicing in his victory.

"Sorry to make you wait," he said. "Remind me. What was the last thing we were talking about?"

"You made me write down all the names that I've gone by."

"Oh, yeah. Now," he said, pointing at the pad on the coffee table, "would you please write down the time on the bottom of the page."

Magnolia rolled her eyes, but glanced at the wall clock and then wrote down 3:58. She looked puzzled for a moment.

"Well, our time's about up."

"That's it!" she shrieked. "You made me come here just to write down my names? You are absolutely incompetent. I don't care what your opinion is, you are incompetent!"

Pollock's pleasant expression didn't change as he walked Magnolia to the door. She stormed out of the room, slamming the door behind her. Pollock said a silent apology to the policeman in the hallway.

He reached over and took the pad off the table, perusing the names Magnolia had written. The last one on the list caught his attention: Bitch.

SESSION NOTES--DAY 12, BP/MK+ALTERS (VIDEO RECORDED)

1. *Warn Taft/Court of triggers.*
2. *More alters? Referral to ???? after commitment.*
3. *Publish? Carrie as co-author?*

"That may be great for an academic publication, but it will open a door big enough for the county prosecutor to run a freight train over you on cross examination," was Taft's response after Pollock explained his theory that Maggie was a sub-alter of Tiny Dancer, and not a direct alter of Magnolia.

"This is not a standard D.I.D. case," Pollock complained. "It's much more complicated."

"I understand that, but the judge already believes this whole incompetence thing is B.S.," Taft answered. "You're not going to convince her with some esoteric new theory when she's already skeptical about the old one. Keep your opinion simple. It will give the prosecutor fewer things to pick apart."

"I'll have a draft to you by Monday," Pollock grumbled, knowing that Taft was right. The interstices of the legal system would once again triumph over scientific advancement. "But I want you to understand what I mean. I'll send along the video tapes of the last two sessions when I send my report."

"Fine. That gives us a week before we have to file it."

Pollock was about to end the phone call when Taft raised a different issue. "I've been thinking about what you said. I'm going to add an insanity defense, just in case the judge denies our incompetency motion, if you're sure she had alter egos six years ago when her mother was killed?"

"I have no doubt."

"Do you think that one of the alters killed her mother?"

"It's possible. Maggie certainly might have, and I wouldn't rule out the possibility that Tiny Dancer could have done it," Pollock answered. "I'd have to delve deeper into it. It could take years to be sure."

"So, do you think I should put her on the witness stand?"

"That's a decision you'll have to make. It would be risky. Wait until you see the videos, and you can draw your own conclusions."

Taft ended the call and buzzed Avery. "C'mon in. I want to brainstorm an insanity defense for Magnolia." Moments later the two lawyers sat across from each other.

"It would at least raise a reasonable doubt about her culpability," Avery offered after listening to Taft explain Pollock's findings.

"That's not how it works," Taft counseled his young associate. "An insanity defense is all or nothing. She would change her plea to not guilty by reason of insanity. She would, essentially, be admitting that she killed her mother. The only question is whether her mental function was such that she did not know or understand what she was doing."

"And this psychologist thinks he can prove what her state of mind was six years ago?"

Taft shrugged. "We'll know more when we get his report. In the meantime, draft a motion to reconsider her plea."

"Would we file it before the incompetency hearing?" Avery asked. "Would we even *have* an incompetency hearing?"

"I have to think about that. The judge has made it clear she's dubious about our motion, and if Pollock gives us a reasonable chance, it might be in Magnolia's best interest to change to an insanity plea."

"How do they treat someone with multiple personalities?" Avery wondered out loud. "How can that person ever return to society? Particularly when one of the personalities is violent."

"I have no idea," Taft said. "That's not our problem."

On Friday, Magnolia had her regular weekly visit with Samantha. The last proceeds from the sale of Kincaid Media stock had come in, completing the liquidation of Magnolia's investments.

"I've transferred $13 million to Mr. Blazing's trust account, as you instructed," Samantha reported. "I told him you'd be giving him instructions on what to do with the money."

"Good. Tell him you're also going to need him to review some foreign banking documents," Magnolia instructed, "and tell him I'll mail him instructions on what to do with the $13 million. Have you transferred anything to Henri, yet?"

"No."

"What's the balance in the account?"

"Fifty-five million in round numbers."

"I want you to go to Zurich and meet Henri. The two of you will set up a new account at an investment bank there. Henri will direct the investments, but only you can authorize transfers or make withdrawals.

There will be an electronic device, some kind of scanner, that only you will be able to activate. Once activated, the investment bank will contact you for confirmation, and then you'll be able to transfer funds. I want all of the documents related to that account sent to Blazing for review before you sign."

"How much do you want me to put in the new account?"

"Fifty million," Magnolia answered. "Pay Blazing from the remaining balance and get a cashier's check payable to Henri for one million. Leave the rest in my existing account."

Samantha nodded as she wrote down the various sums.

"One more thing. *The* most important. Make absolutely certain that only you can access the funds. Henri is a long-time adviser, but $50 million is a big temptation for someone with his extravagant tastes. You I trust. Him, well, not entirely. If you have any questions or feel at all uncomfortable with how the account is being set up, stop the process and do not transfer the money. Get in touch with me immediately."

For the next two days, Magnolia found herself revved up with no place to go. She learned that the jail library's offering of things French was limited to an outdated encyclopedia. The talking heads on the 24-hour news channels reported nothing related to her expulsion from the Senate nor anything else that interested her. Her concentration wandered when she tried to read or do a crossword puzzle.

As she straightened sheets on her bed, a sheet from a yellow legal pad tucked under the mattress caught her attention. At the top of the page were the words "Collateral Damage." She had seen it before. With time on her hands, she finally had something to keep her occupied.

She considered the list and then sat down to consider who should join Findley, Bradford, and Taft at the top of the list: Judge Weber became No. 4, followed by Dr. Pollock at No. 5. Several industry competitors and hostile media personalities were added, as was, at No. 11 "that pain in the ass private detective, Veronica Brilliant." Seven empty lines separated Brilliant from the last two names on the list.

Magnolia erased the names she had previously written at No's. 19 and 20, moving them up the list: Henri Hawke was now at No. 12, and her son, Hamilton, followed. *Perfect,* she thought. *Unlucky 13.*

Hawke called in the late afternoon with the message that he and "the lovely Ms. Jones" were meeting in Zurich on Tuesday. He also had new lottery numbers for her. Decoding them gave Magnolia something to do.

Taft and Pollock sparred over the wording of Pollock's report, with Taft winning on most points. The result was a report that both served Taft's desire for a simplistic approach to support his incompetency motion, while also paving the way for an insanity plea if the motion failed.

"Two bites at the apple" was the way Taft put it, as he explained to Avery why he had elected not to cancel the incompetency motion. "If the judge denies the motion, we can still change her plea to insanity for the trial."

That was also how Avery tried to justify it to a distracted Magnolia in an early morning Wednesday phone call.

"Either way, I end up in an asylum," Magnolia said with a shrug. "Just a different kind of prison. Make sure you send the final version of Pollock's report to Henri. I want him to review it before it's filed with the Court."

"I've already sent him a draft," Avery answered, "but I haven't heard back from him yet. I told him we have to file it on Monday."

"What about the other shrink? Do we know when I have to go see him?"

"He's a *her*," Avery corrected. "Amanda Pappenfuss. I assume it will be sometime next week. She has two weeks from Monday to file her report." Avery checked her email. "Nothing from her yet. I'll let you know as soon as I hear something."

"Will I meet with Pollock or Taft before that session, to prep me?" Magnolia asked.

"We haven't talked about that, but we didn't prep you before the Pollock sessions, so I'm guessing we won't before this one, either. I think we'd prefer that you can truthfully answer 'no' when the prosecutor asks you if we coached you, but I'll ask Mr. Taft. He may have changed his mind."

"Please make sure you let Henri know as soon as you find out when I'm going to meet with this Pappenfuss person. He may have some suggestions for me."

Throughout the remainder of the day Magnolia kept reminding herself that no news was good news. As long as Samantha didn't call, everything must be going as planned in Zurich, but that didn't stop her from pacing in her cell and worrying. By dinner time (midnight in Zurich) there was still no call from Samantha. There would also be no sleep.

Thursday morning came and went. Magnolia played spider solitaire on the prison-issued tablet and realized, a little too late, that she was chewing her fingernails. She hadn't done that since junior high.

A call finally came after lunch, but it was Avery, not Samantha.

"Your session with Dr. Pappenfuss has been scheduled for next Wednesday morning at 10 o'clock," she said.

"Same place?" Magnolia asked.

"Yes," Avery answered. "Same routine as with the Pollock visits."

"Have you heard from Henri? Any comments on Pollock's report?"

"Nothing yet. I'll send him a reminder when I let him know about your Pappenfuss appointment."

"Do that right away, please."

Tedium. Magnolia was trying to compose a coded message to Hawke, but she couldn't find the word in the *World Almanac.* His last message had been friendly, newsy, and had told her to be patient. She wanted to respond with *fuck you.* He wasn't the one sitting in a 12x12 cell, accused of murder, with nothing to do. But those words weren't in the almanac either.

As the day turned into evening with no word from either Samantha or Hawke, Magnolia's thoughts went to the dark side. *Did Henri seduce Samantha, convincing her to join him to steal my money? Had he killed Samantha and cut off her finger so that he could access the account? Was he holding her hostage? Torturing her? How could I have been so stupid, to trust him; to think Samantha could do this on her own.*

"STUPID BITCH!" she screamed at herself, the epithet punctuated by the splattering of coffee on the floor as she swept everything off the table. She screamed again, her arms rigid, and her fists clenched at her side. Then, as the scream ran out of air, she snatched the folding chair and flung it against the wall. She wanted to kill something, someone. She could envision Hawke with blood on his shirt, toppling backwards, blood spattering against the wall. *Die, you sonovabitch, die!* she thought. She lifted the table and sent it careening against the cell door, then snatched papers from the floor and threw them at the wall. The lack of an audible impact fueled her rage even more. She kicked the bent chair, then grabbed it and slammed it again and again against her mattress. Finally, her sides heaving, there was nothing left to absorb her anger. She slid down the wall, gasping for breath, tears of frustration running down her cheeks, until she was only a heap on the floor. "Stupid bitch," she muttered again.

She slouched sideways. She no longer had the strength to hold herself. Slowly, her breathing returned to normal, and her muscles relaxed as exhaustion morphed into sleep.

It was dark outside when she woke up. The dream with the giant head and the curved knife in its claw-like hand had come back. She couldn't run, as if her feet were stuck in cement. *Help me! Help me!* Her dream-self had shouted to the person on the fringes of her dream. But he would not help. As the curved knife came slicing through the air toward her, she woke up, shaking, sweating, terrified.

The rest of the night she lay on her bed, staring at the ceiling, afraid to fall asleep. The gray light of dawn eventually seeped through the narrow window at the top of the cell, followed soon thereafter by a rap on the door.

"Breakfast," a familiar voice said. The door lock clicked and Deputy Seth Johnson entered her cell, food tray in hand.

"What happened here?" he blurted, looking around the trashed cell.

Magnolia closed her eyes and shook her head. "I lost it last night. I had a terrible dream."

Seth set the food tray on the floor and tipped the table back on its legs. He picked up the metal folding chair and pried it open, then tried to straighten a bent leg.

"I need to report this," he said apologetically.

"I know."

"Is there anything I can do to help?"

"Get me out of here," she laughed bitterly.

He looked at her sadly.

"I was just kidding," Magnolia sighed. "What are you doing here?"

"I'm back on day shift," Seth replied. "I haven't seen you since your sessions with that psychologist ended, so I thought I'd stop and see how you are doing. Obviously, my timing isn't great."

"I'll be all right. Just a temporary meltdown. Thanks for stopping by. Nice to know there are still people who care."

Seth nodded, an uncomfortable smile on his face.

"I'm happy you're back on days," Magnolia said, "so you can spend more time with your family."

Again, Seth nodded. "I may have you to thank for that. Night shift is usually for a month at a time, but the captain cut mine short."

"Whatever the reason, I'm happy for you. Would you do me a favor? When you report this," Magnolia started, holding her arms out wide to encompass the trashed cell, "please tell them I'm not a suicide risk. I've had enough psychiatric attention for a while."

After Seth left, Magnolia sat down on the wobbly chair and devoured the scrambled eggs and toast, wishing there were more. She searched her cubby for snacks, but there was only an empty peanut bag. She looked at the scattered papers on the floor but decided she was too tired to pick them up. She collapsed on her bed, exhausted.

A couple of hours later, Magnolia woke with a start to the blaring intercom.

"What? What?" she stammered.

"You have a visitor at two o'clock."

"Who?"

"Samantha Jones."

"What time is it now?"

"Eleven-thirty."

"Is it too late to take a shower?"

"I'll see if I can arrange it after lunch."

At two o'clock Samantha appeared on the visiting room monitor, a look of concern filled her face. "Are you all right?"

Magnolia ignored the question. "Is the account set up?"

"Yes. It took longer than I expected, but it's all done. The transfer of funds was confirmed this afternoon."

"Any problems?"

"Only with the retinal scanner. First one didn't work, but I have one that is working now."

"And this scanner will only read your eyes?"

"Just my right one. Both the electronics guy and the banker assured me that it will recognize only my right eye. We ran several tests to make sure."

"Did those tests include making sure that the scanner could read neither of Henri's eyes?"

"Yes, it did. Henri insisted on it."

"Where are you now?"

"I'm still in Zurich. My flight leaves tomorrow morning."

"And where is Henri?"

"He caught a flight back to Barcelona as soon as I gave him his check."

"So," Magnolia inquired, "what do you think of our Mr. Hawke, now that you've met him in person?"

"He's very charming. A little too touchy-feely for my comfort, but when we were with the bankers he acted the same way, so it wasn't just with me. He did ask me if I'd like to go to Barcelona with him, though."

"Were you tempted?"

"Only because I'd like to see Barcelona some time."

"Be careful with him."

"I've been fending off boys from the hood since I was a teenager," Samantha said confidently. "I can handle Mr. Hawke."

"Please have him call me tomorrow. I want to discuss his investment strategy."

The sun beamed through the narrow cell window, stirring Magnolia from a dead sleep. A breakfast tray was on the table, but the food cold and soggy. She looked at her watch. 11:00 a.m. She had slept for 14 hours.

An old, haggard face stared back at her from the mirror. *Holy shit. I need a makeover.* Lines she didn't remember creased her cheeks and neck. Her hair, longer than usual, was a distinct silver and black two-tone with unwanted gray highlights streaking the black. Her thoughts drifted to anti-wrinkle cream, face lifts, hair dye, and aging.

She gave herself a sponge bath and combed her hair. She had just finished putting on clean prison clothes when lunch arrived. She looked at her watch. 11:50 a.m. *Now what? Over two hours to kill before exercise time.* She turned on her tablet and played spider solitaire until 12:38 p.m. She painted her fingernails and toenails. 1:05 p.m.

I need someone to talk to. This protective custody is too protective. Maybe I could go out to the day room. She pressed the intercom button, waited for a deputy to answer, and made her request.

"You can't," he said. "We would need a court order to let you out of protective custody. Even if we could, it's a weekend, and we're short-staffed. We don't have a person available to be with you."

Exercise time finally came. Her hope that another inmate might be in the exercise area so she would have someone to talk to went unfulfilled, and sixty minutes of walking did nothing to improve her mood. She returned to her cell at 3:05. By 3:15 she was drumming her fingers on the table. Still no call from Hawke.

She went back to compiling a coded communique to Hawke, this time omitting the word tedium. When done, she checked her message. *Need make over college age operation if necessary next session May 6, ten am looking forward to it am prepared.*

It was almost five o'clock when she finished. Dinner was typical Saturday night jailhouse fare: pizza and chips. Magnolia waited, wishing her swear-word vocabulary in French and Catalan was more robust.

Hawke's call finally came at 6:10. The silky sound of a single, female voice crooned in the distant background.

"Nice of you to call," Magnolia said, sarcasm dripping from each word.

"It is a reasonable hour where you are, no?" Hawke answered, the slippery sound of alcohol coloring his speech.

"Where are you?" she demanded.

"I am in gay Paree, mademoiselle."

"What are you doing in Paris? I thought you were in Barcelona."

"I am celebrating."

When Hawke offered no further explanation, she barked, "With my money?"

"Non. With the money from my fee. The money was once yours, but now it is mine to do with as I please. Right now, I am pleased to be toasting you with my new friend, Claude." Magnolia could hear the clinking of glasses.

"I need to talk to you about business matters, and you are drunk and with someone."

"Are you not going to ask why I am celebrating?" Hawke asked, ignoring the chastisement.

"I assume it is because you got your million," Magnolia answered, her voice stone cold.

"Non, again, mademoiselle. I am celebrating because I have put in place the last piece of the puzzle today, and topped it off by telling your American attorney Taft to, how do you say it in American, *go fuck himself.*" Hawke said it as if he was doing her a favor. "It has been a most pleasurable day."

"What the hell did you do?"

"I gave your Mr. Taft several incisive recommendations about the report from Dr. Pollock. He insulted me and refused to consider any of them. You might say his attitude was ugly. You know, as in *Ugly American.* And a fellow attorney no less."

Magnolia was silent.

"Are you still there?" Hawke asked after a long minute.

"I'm thinking," she answered. "Can you talk about the puzzle piece?"

"I have given Ms. Jones numbers. She should be calling you tomorrow."

"Do you know that my session with the court's shrink is Wednesday?"

"Yes. May 6, 10:00 a.m. Central Time."

"I need to talk to you about investments. Call tomorrow."

"I will call you on Monday. Tomorrow, Claude and I plan to spend the day in bed."

Magnolia cringed at the visual his words painted in her head. "Well, I hope you and *Claude* have a wonderful time. Call me Monday, 10:00 a.m. my time. Be sober."

"Oh, I shall be, mon amie."

Magnolia hesitated before hanging up. "And Henri. Thank you."

"Eh?"

"I've wanted to tell Taft to go fuck himself from the first day I met him."

On Sunday morning Magnolia did something she hadn't done since she'd left Zumbrota nearly 50 years ago; she went to a church service. *Just to kill time,* she convinced herself, *and see some other people.* There were only a handful of inmates there, none of whom she recognized. A young priest conducted the service. His homily was about forgiveness. Magnolia took communion. *Good to cover all your bases,* she thought. She felt strangely peaceful when she got back to her cell.

Samantha's visit was at 2:00 o'clock, as usual. She related the events from her Zurich trip and turned her computer screen to face the camera so Magnolia could see the electronic banking information, including the account balance: $50,000,000.00.

"Have you tested your ability to transfer funds?" Magnolia asked.

"No. Should I?"

"Yes. We need to make sure there are no glitches. Better to get them ironed out ahead of time, rather than having an important transfer disrupted. Transfer $1,000.00 to your operating account to make sure it works, then wait a day and transfer it back into the Zurich account. Also, I'm going to want you to set up a monthly automatic withdrawal, so check with the bank and see how to do that. Schedule a visit with me for me Tuesday night, and I'll give you more details."

The two women chatted about political news until less than two minutes of visiting time remained, and Magnolia asked, "Did Henri give you my lottery numbers?"

"Oops. I almost forgot," Samantha answered. "Just a minute." She picked up her phone and punched in something, then scrolled until she came up with the numbers, just seconds before the visit ended and the screen went blank.

The message from the decoded numbers was more cryptic than usual. The first seventeen words were gibberish. Only the last three were legible: *bomb threat Wednesday.*

Taft called Monday morning.

"We're filing Pollock's report today and a motion to change your plea," he said. "I'm sending them to you overnight express so that you can review them before your meeting with Dr. Pappenfuss on Wednesday."

"Whatever."

"You need to review them."

"I'll look to see what Pollock said," was Magnolia's sullen reply, "but it really doesn't make any difference. I'm either going to end up in a loony bin or in prison. It's a life sentence either way. Not what I expected when I hired the famous Napoleon Taft."

He was silent.

"I've changed my mind," Magnolia snarled. "I'm not going to plead insanity. I want my time in court. I want the whole world to see how self-serving and incompetent you are!"

Hawke called an hour later.

"What do you want?" she barked.

"You wanted to talk about investments."

"Bullshit. I ain't got no investments."

Hawke paused. "To whom am I speaking?" he asked.

"You called *me*. You don't know who you called?"

Again, he paused. "Perhaps I have the wrong number."

He hung up and looked down at his phone, hoping to find an answer on the screen. He had read Pollock's report. Perhaps Pollock was right about the multiple personalities. Hawke wished it had been a video call so he could have seen what the person he had just spoken to looked like. He thought back to other meetings. Had he ever been with Magnolia when she was a different person? He was confident he'd never been with the personality called Tiny Dancer, but Maggie? Was that who he had just hung up on? Could it have been Maggie, way back at the beginning, when Magnolia asked him to take care of Kincaid's lawyer? And her mother?

A chill ran though him. What if she was in one of her alters on Wednesday?

He took a burner phone from his desk drawer and dialed an international number.

"Isabella? We have a potential problem."

Hawke told Isabella about the phone call he just had with the alter he presumed was Maggie. "According to the psychologist, when she's in this Maggie personality, she is violent, uncontrollable, and extremely dangerous," he warned. He read aloud the "Maggie" part of Pollock's report to give Isabella an idea of what to expect if Magnolia transitioned to her Maggie alter.

"If, at any time the Maggie personality shows up, abandon the extraction," Hawke ordered. "And kill her."

EXTRACTION

Wednesday, May 6, 2015, started with a cloudless sky and a predicted high temperature of 75; it promised to be a beautiful spring day in the peaceful river city of Red Wing, Minnesota.

Magnolia, in shackles as usual, slid into the back seat of the squad car at 9:45 a.m. Excitement, borne of anticipation, coursed through her body.

"You're in good spirits," her guard-for-the-day, Deputy Lou Strand, observed.

"It's my last shrink session, thank God, and it's a beautiful day," Magnolia replied. "Nice to be out in the sunshine, if only for a few minutes." She was also happy that Seth had not been assigned to her security detail for the day.

Five minutes later, Deputy Strand guided her to the bank of elevators that went to the mezzanine level. At 9:55 they entered the familiar Delta Queen Room.

Doctor Amanda Pappenfuss was waiting, seated in the wingback chair that Magnolia had occupied during the dozen sessions with Dr. Pollock. The bright sun streaming through the windows gave a golden glow to the room, creating a nebula around Dr. Pappenfuss. She rose and introduced herself to Magnolia.

"You'll be outside?" she asked the guard.

"Right outside the door."

"Can you take off the shackles?" Magnolia asked. "I didn't have to wear them when I was with Dr. Pollock."

Pappenfuss looked at Strand for confirmation. He nodded. She eyed her petite patient and thought of Pollock's report.

"I'd prefer that they be left on," she said.

Magnolia's happy moment morphed into a chill. With her movement restricted would she be able ... *to do what?* She had no idea what was going to happen. Hawke had just told her to be ready, and she had been ready with the expectation that the shackles would be removed as they had been in the past.

"Please take a seat," the psychiatrist said, motioning to the other wingback chair. "We'll go until noon, then take a 45-minute break for lunch." The woman was in her late 30s or early 40s, maybe five-foot-six and a little overweight. Her mousy hair, streaked with a few gray strands, was pulled back in a tight bun. "Shall we get started?"

No! No! This is not how it's supposed to go. Magnolia could feel sweat on her forehead.

At 10:05 a call came in to the Red Wing Police Department. There was a bomb threat at the local high school. A call went out to the Goodhue County Sheriff's Office for backup, and all available law enforcement personnel were dispatched to the school. Sirens could be heard heading out of downtown in the direction of the high school. Strand, seated outside the Delta Queen Room, called in to dispatch. He had kids at the high school. He was assured that his presence at the high school was not needed and was ordered to stay at the St. James.

At 10:15, shouting could be heard in the Mark Twain Room, just two doors from the Delta Queen. The door swung open and a

Hispanic woman darted out, turned back toward the room and yelled, "Get away from me!"

An arm shot out the door and grabbed her by the hair. "Get back in here *la puta!*" a man's voice snarled. The woman screamed as she stumbled back into the room.

Strand, still on edge from the bomb threat, launched himself out of the chair, pulling his sidearm. "What's going on here?" he shouted as he stuck his head through the open door where the woman had just disappeared. It was the last thing he remembered.

At 10:18 there was a knock on the Delta Queen Room door, and a uniformed man stepped in. "Security," he said in a loud voice. "We have a bomb threat. We're evacuating the building. Let's go!" He held the door open. "Down the stairs," he said, motioning with his head at a door immediately across the hall. "You first," he said, indicating Magnolia. "Leave your stuff," he shouted at Dr. Pappenfuss. "Hurry."

Magnolia shuffled toward the door as fast as she could, but the ankle shackles tripped her. The security guard grabbed her by the arm and lifted her to her feet. "Go!" he yelled at Pappenfuss who had stopped to help Magnolia. As the psychiatrist stepped into the hallway, a second man, dressed in jeans and a muscle shirt, stepped behind her, wrapping one arm around her neck and placing his other hand over her mouth. "Don't make a sound," he growled into the psychiatrist's ear.

Isabella emerged through the stairwell door, as the man dragged the shocked psychiatrist down the hallway and into the Mark Twain Room. Isabella held a finger to her lips. "Sssshhh," she said as she and the security guard helped Magnolia into the stairwell.

"Get these off her," Isabella ordered, pointing at the shackles.

"The cop must have a key," the security guard said. He raced out of the stairwell just as the second man emerged from the Mark Twain room. "Get the guards keys," the security guard said in a loud whisper. "I'm going to start the car."

A minute passed that felt like an hour.

"Where the hell is he?" Isabella muttered just as the second man came through the stairwell door.

"I had a helluva time getting his keys," he said as he tried to locate the one to unlock Magnolia. "Hold still."

Magnolia was shaking. She could feel time draining away. The walls were closing in. *Why did I agree to do this?*

Finally free of the shackles, the three of them scrambled down a single flight of stairs and out an exit door into the garage. A silver SUV with darkly tinted windows, passenger side doors open and its motor running, waited. The security guard had discarded his uniform jacket and was sitting behind the wheel.

They dove into the SUV and headed down a ramp and out of the parking garage.

"*Bien hecho*," Isabella said.

"*Esta todo bien?*" the driver answered in Spanish.

"Everything is good," Isabella said looking to Magnolia.

"No one was hurt?" Magnolia asked, still shaking.

"The cop will have a headache for a day or two," the second man, seated in the front passenger seat, said over his shoulder. "Otherwise, they're tied and gagged but nice and comfortable."

The SUV turned right out of the parking ramp, then right again at the end of the block. It stopped at a red light. "Stay calm," Isabella said. Magnolia stared straight ahead, afraid to look. She clenched her muscles to keep from wetting herself.

The light turned green after an eternity, and they turned left onto Main Street. In two blocks they drove under the interstate bridge, then did a loop up onto the bridge. In a minute they were on Highway 63, crossing the Mississippi River into Wisconsin. The silver SUV turned into a parking lot and came to a stop in a row of cars parked on the side of a large building. The sign in the parking lot said "Woodshed Liquor Store."

"What are we doing?" Magnolia's voice was brittle but shrill.

"Switching cars," Isabella said, her voice calm.

Parked next to them was a white Ford Escape, screened from Highway 63 by a large pickup truck. Isabella took a key fob out of a cup holder and pushed a button. The Escape's lights flashed and the engine started. The two women got out.

"Get in back," Isabella directed Magnolia. "There's a change of clothes."

They waited as Magnolia took off her prison garb. A man came out of the liquor store and Magnolia froze, but he walked across the parking lot without paying them any attention, got in a car, and left. Magnolia finished changing into baggy jeans and a long-sleeved pullover. Isabella handed her a plastic bag and instructed her to put the prison clothes in it.

"Give them to Felipe," Isabella said gesturing to the passenger in the front seat. Then she turned to the driver of the silver SUV and said, "Put them in a dumpster some place near the Twin Cities airport."

The two women got in the Escape. In a few seconds they were back on Highway 63 and headed deeper into Wisconsin. Isabella looked at her watch. 10:42. It was unlikely anyone would find the two people bound and gagged in the Mark Twain Room until at least noon.

By then, they should be at their destination.

EXTINCTION

A minute later Isabella turned right on Highway 35, headed south parallel with the Mississippi River.

"Where are we going?" Magnolia asked.

"We're going to get you a makeover," Isabella answered. "For the next three weeks you're my daughter. You just enrolled at Viterbo University in La Crosse, Wisconsin. Your name is Rosa Mendez."

Magnolia flipped down the visor and squinted at herself in the mirror. Then she looked at Isabella. "I'm going to be *your* daughter? I'm 20 years older than you." She looked back in the mirror. "And I look it."

"You're going to lose 40 years. You told Hawke you wanted to be a college student. He has taken great pains to make sure you become one, at least temporarily."

"What do you mean?"

"Look in the glove compartment," Isabella said, motioning with a tilt of her head.

Magnolia popped open the glove box and took out a folder. Inside was a course catalog for Viterbo University. "I'm going to a Catholic university? That's almost laughable," she scoffed.

"You, or rather we, are from Argentina. Everyone is Catholic in Argentina. When you get a chance, read up on the ethics, culture, and society program. You're enrolled in what they call the 'art track'."

The folder also contained a student ID card, a passport, and a student visa, all in the name of Rosa Mendez. The picture on the passport was of a young woman, about 20, with short black hair, brown eyes, and a tattoo of a feather on her neck. Magnolia stared at the picture and reflexively touched her neck. "That's supposed to be me?" she asked.

"It is you, or will be very soon." Isabella smiled and leaned back against the head rest. "Relax and enjoy the ride, *hija*. We have about an hour before we reach our destination."

They drove mostly in silence, eating sandwiches and drinking bottled water from a cooler that had been stashed in the backseat. Magnolia marveled at the beauty of the river valley and the small towns that dotted the east bank of the Mississippi.

"This is beautiful, but you haven't told me where we're going," Magnolia said as Highway 35 strayed from the river, meandering into farm country.

"We bought a trailer house in a town called Tremplo. We've been living in it since mid-April. We'll be there in about 20 minutes."

"Who's we?"

"You and me."

"What?"

"Your doppelganger," Isabella laughed. "The person in the picture of your college ID. You'll meet her in a few minutes." Isabella's confident smile reflected her command of the situation. It irked Magnolia, who was still feeling the stress of the escape. She chafed at not being in control.

They turned off Highway 35 and made their way through residential streets until turning into Pinewood Court, a well-kept mobile home park on the edge of town. They zig-zagged through the park and pulled into a driveway at the end of a white mobile home with black shutters and a side awning.

The girl from the college ID, Rosa, met them at the door. Five feet tall. One hundred pounds. Same skin tone. Magnolia, 40 years ago.

"Explain this to me," Magnolia said, after she and Isabella got settled. "Why this place?"

"Small-town, low-tech police department, no news media, and quiet location," Isabella answered, "plus we wanted to be off the road by the time they realized the cop and the psychiatrist were missing. It's a good place to lay low for a couple of weeks until the furor over your escape simmers down."

"Speaking of Escape, I get to take it, right?" Rosa asked, looking out the window at the SUV in the driveway.

"That's the deal," Isabella said, "but you need to leave your clothes. Take just enough to get you back to Florida." Isabella turned to Magnolia and said, "Rosa will be leaving tomorrow. Before then, she'll show you your new wardrobe and fill you in on a few more details of your new life. I've got to get ready for work."

"Work?" Magnolia said. "Henri doesn't pay you enough? You have to work?"

"I got a job at a local restaurant a week ago for the same reason Rosa has made herself visible around this town for the past three weeks. We needed to be familiar faces in the community *before* your escape. You, with a little touch up here and there, will look enough like Rosa that no one will question you, as long as you keep a low profile."

"For how long?"

"You'll be on your way to Europe in two weeks," Isabella explained. "You'll fly out of La Crosse on the Memorial Day weekend, along with a lot of other college students."

"What about the tattoo?" Magnolia asked, nodding toward the feather on Rosa's neck. "I'm not going to walk around with a feather on my neck the rest of my life."

"It's Henna," Rosa said. "I'll give you an identical one tonight, and I'll remove mine. I'll show you how to do it."

"It's not permanent?" Magnolia asked, surprised, and then felt stupid as soon as the words left her mouth. She hated looking stupid, especially in front of the hired help.

"No," Rosa replied, with no indication she thought Magnolia's comment was stupid. "Henna lasts a couple weeks, but if you mix lemon juice and sugar and put it on the tattoo every day, it will last longer. I'll mix some and put it in the fridge for you before I leave. I'll also cut and color your hair tonight to match mine."

An hour later, Rosa and Magnolia were laying clothes out on the bed, choosing which would go home with Rosa and which would stay.

"How did you get involved in this?" Magnolia asked. "You're so young, and..."

"Isabella is my cousin," Rosa interrupted.

"Nice cousin. She gets you involved in illegal activity?"

"She gets jobs for me so I don't have to prostitute myself or work for the cartels."

Rosa's answer jolted Magnolia. "Women are always the victims," she muttered, more to herself than to Rosa.

Rosa shrugged. "I do okay, and I don't really do anything dangerous."

At five o'clock they turned the TV to national news. Magnolia's escape was the headline story on every network. A massive manhunt was underway, and speculation ranged from "she's still in Red Wing" to "she's already out of the country." Some speculated she was headed to

Canada, others thought Mexico, and one claimed she'd commandeered a private jet to South America.

"No one said anything about Tremplo," Rosa giggled. "Isabella's really smart."

Rosa left the next morning before Magnolia got out of bed, leaving behind an old, brown pickup and a college-age wardrobe. Magnolia spent the morning reading the Viterbo catalog and adjusting to new contact lenses, tinted dark brown, while Isabella watched the news on TV.

After lunch, there was a knock on the door and a stunningly beautiful woman with flawless skin came in. Isabella introduced her as Dr. Karen Tremont. Her specialty: dermatology. For an hour she questioned Magnolia about her skin care habits, then spent another several minutes carefully examining her skin.

When she was done, she turned and addressed Isabella as if Magnolia wasn't in the room. "You said she doesn't smoke and her diet appears to contain sufficient fats and amino acids that are good for the skin; for the most part her skin appears to have little sun damage. Overall, her skin appears healthy for a person of her age, so I don't think you'll need to resort to surgery."

Tremont went to her car and brought back a case filled with bottles and tubes and boxes of wipes. She doled out a series of medications, giving Magnolia directions on use and application as if she was instructing a six-year-old.

"Do not overuse these," she remonstrated. "They are more potent than the ordinary prescription or over-the-counter treatments and could burn your skin if you put on too much. Do it exactly as I say, and you should start seeing results in three or four days. If you burn yourself, don't call me."

Magnolia made a mental note to add Dr. Tremont to her collateral damage list.

"She broke out of jail," Ham shouted to Toni. "Unbelievable." He was looking at the morning newspaper. The headline blared "Senator Escapes!"

"Are you serious?" Toni exclaimed as she came from the bedroom where she had been packing boxes.

"Yesterday, during a psychiatric session. It says that she had outside accomplices. They tied up a guard and the psychiatrist. They think she got away by car, although they haven't ruled out that she may have escaped by boat. The hotel where it happened was only a couple of blocks from the Mississippi River."

"All the more reason for us to move," Toni said, "before the news media puts two and two together and figures out that you're her son."

"If they figure it out, they'll find me in Winona just as easily as they will here."

"Maybe, but I'll feel better when we're out of the Twin Cities. It's farther away from a media hub, and you'll be less accessible."

Ham shrugged.

"Plus," Toni continued, "I keep having this feeling that someone is watching me...us. I'll just feel better when we're out of this city."

"So will Barca," Ham said, smiling at his aging golden retriever. "You're going to love that big backyard, aren't you, old buddy?"

Shortly after Toni had accepted the job at the Minnesota Marine Art Museum, they went house hunting in Winona, a college town nestled between the Mississippi River and bluffs created by prehistoric glaciers. They settled on a 1,500-square-foot ranch-style home in Goodview, a suburb named, presumably, because you could see both the bluffs and the river from there. As their luck often went, from Ham and Toni's new home you could see neither.

The new house did, however, provide single-level living, including a small den that would serve as a studio for Ham. It was also only a 10-minute drive from their friends, Jim and Melissa Benson, and was convenient to both the museum and to the Winona State University campus where Ham would have his permanent office.

They were scheduled to move the next day, giving them the weekend to get their new home a bit organized before Toni started work on Monday. Ham would have more time to get acclimated because his official duties as a traveling lecturer didn't start until after Memorial Day. It also allowed time for his new handicapped van to be delivered.

Todd D'Anselmo sat in a parking lot just off Hennepin Avenue on Friday morning, watching the main entrance to Atrium Apartments. He had spent countless hours over the past month sitting in this exact parking spot. On two occasions he had seen Toni leave the apartment building. The first time she got into a car and drove away with what appeared to be a group of girlfriends. The other time he followed her to Whole Foods but lost her in the crowded store. Numerous times he saw *him*, always taking his dog for a walk.

Now, as D'Anselmo watched and waited, he fantasized over Toni Chapereaux, refusing to think of her by her married name. He would become her savior, her hero, caring for her, protecting her. They would finally be together, like back in grad school when he would sit beside her at lectures, when students would gather at places like the Artist's Quarter and he would be near her. He would make it that way again. The way it was before this other guy took her away. Before he beat *him* within an inch of his life and put him in that wheelchair. Before he had to go into hiding to avoid the police, and before he had to take menial jobs. He would release Toni from the prison she was living in; a prison in which the guy in the wheelchair was the warden.

A week earlier he had followed Hamilton, hoping the wheelchair would turn down a deserted alley or some quiet street; he wanted a place where he could finish the job he'd started years ago. But it didn't happen. Hamilton, as always, had that big dog with him, like a bodyguard.

Still, D'Anselmo daydreamed about the moment he would get his second chance. *I won't use a baseball bat like last time. This time will be different.*

He bought a gun, a used Walther PPS M2. It used nine-millimeter rounds and would fit easily into his pocket. And it was cheap. He went to a shooting range to practice, and learned that either he wasn't a good shot or the gun wasn't very accurate. He didn't have enough money to buy another one.

I'll just have to get close enough to not miss, he thought to himself.

Eventually, D'Anselmo came up with two sure-fire plans. When Hamilton took his dog for their daily walk, he would follow them, and at the right time when no one was around, he would simply walk up behind them and put a single shot in the back of *his* head and nonchalantly walk away. By the time anyone knew what had happened, including that damned dog, he would be lost in the crowd. The second plan was to stake out the apartment and wait until Toni went out. Then he would simply buzz their apartment and announce a delivery for Toni that had to be signed for. This time, a single shot in the forehead would do the trick. Simple. And then Toni would finally be his.

D'Anselmo was waiting for the right moment to implement one of his plans when a moving van pulled into the Atrium Apartments parking lot and obstructed his view of the front doors. A few minutes later furniture and boxes were being loaded. Suddenly Toni was there, dressed in a cropped tee shirt and shorts. She was barefoot. Her orange curls waved in the breeze, beckoning D'Anselmo. *She knows I'm here. She's coming to me!*

But she stopped to talk to one of the people loading the van. She turned and went back inside the building.

She's moving!

Hamilton was sitting in the empty living room with the morning newspaper on the floor by his wheelchair.

"They're almost done," Toni said, walking back into their apartment. She absentmindedly picked up the newspaper. "The driver said they should be in Goodview, unloading, by five. If we catch lunch on the road, we should get there close to the same time, maybe have time to get some groceries."

"They haven't found her yet," Hamilton said. "According to the newspaper, there were at least two accomplices. They faked a bomb threat and used that to flush the guard and the psychiatrist out of the room so they could overpower them. Investigators think another bomb threat at the local high school around the same time, was a diversion to occupy the police while she pulled off the escape."

"They'll catch her," Toni said. "It might be in a week, or in a month, but the cops will find her."

"I'm not so sure," Ham responded. "It's been 48 hours. With her resources, she could be in China by now." In the back of his mind, he was hoping he was right.

D'Anselmo waited, expecting Toni to come out again. Fifteen minutes went by. Half an hour. Then the workmen shut the moving van's back doors. *Where is she? What should he do?* He could follow the truck, but he only had $10 in his billfold, and his car was running on fumes. *Shit!* He hadn't picked up his paycheck.

He had to do something *now*! He needed to get inside the building and see her before she left him again. He got out of his car and forced himself to walk slowly to the entrance of the apartment building. He jerked and yanked the locked inside door in frustration, raising a ruckus, but no one responded. Cursing under his breath, he sat on a bench in the vestibule. He would wait for someone to come and then walk in behind them before the door closed. Or, he could buzz Toni's apartment. Maybe she'd let him in. He scrolled down the directory until he found H. and A. Blethen. He dialed the number. It rang. And rang. And rang.

He hung up and redialed, jamming his fingers hard into the keys as if the force would somehow make the numbers more effective. Still no answer. He slammed down the receiver.

As he returned to the bench, a van with a handicapped license plate left the parking ramp and crossed the lot, stopping at the entrance to Hennepin Avenue. A large golden dog looked out the back window.

D'Anselmo raced out the door, sprinting toward his car, fumbling for his keys. The engine roared to life, but he had to wait as another car turned from Hennepin Avenue into the lot. When the other car cleared, he squealed out of the parking space and came to an abrupt stop at the parking lot exit. Frantically, he looked up and down Hennepin Avenue. He heard a warning beep and looked down. His gas gauge was blinking, indicating that there was less than 25 miles before it was empty.

He screamed and pounded the steering wheel with both fists.

The movers were already unloading when Ham and Toni pulled up to their new home on 39th Avenue. Jim and Melissa Benson met them with a bottle of champagne, and after Jim tousled Barca's fur and took him for a short walk, they gathered on the small patio in the back yard. Melissa handed out plastic champagne glasses, and they toasted to new beginnings.

Later in the evening, after the movers were gone, the small party moved inside to the kitchen table to eat carry-out from a local restaurant. Eventually, the conversation turned to art.

"What's the situation with *The Reaper*?" Jim asked.

"We don't know," Toni answered. "We haven't heard anything."

"I expect to get served with a lawsuit," Ham added, "but it hasn't happened yet. They paid us for a painting they have hidden in their basement. I don't see how they can avoid suing us."

"Maybe they're still trying to figure out whether it's the real thing," Jim offered, "or whether they can prove it's a forgery. If they start a lawsuit and lose it would be a PR disaster for the museum, not to mention the legal costs. It would probably cost someone their job."

"Yeah. Maybe. But just in case, we've parked the bulk of the money they paid us," Ham said.

"For now, though," Toni added, "No news is good news."

"Speaking of news," Benson said, looking at Ham, "we're going to put you to work a little earlier than expected. If it's okay with you."

"What's up?"

"The popularity of your lectures last October has not gone unnoticed in the Winona arts community," Benson said. "The local arts council would like you to reprise those lectures and make them open to the public. Of course, they'd give you some sort of stipend."

"When do they want to do it?"

"Before summer session starts, so sometime within the next month."

Ham looked at Toni with a happy questioning cocked eyebrow. She was grinning from ear to ear.

"Give us a week to get settled a little," Ham said. "Maybe we could do it the week before Memorial Day? And they don't need to pay us a stipend. It will be a good warmup for the school year."

For two days Magnolia stayed inside the mobile home carefully tending to her skin and her tattoo, sorting through her new clothes, and watching Spanish-speaking television to sharpen her language skills.

On Saturday morning, she sat at the kitchen table listening to an oldies station on the radio while Isabella made breakfast. Holding a mirror close to her face to examine her skin, Magnolia was certain some of the lines that had been around the corners of her eyes and mouth two days earlier were gone. Dr. Tremont may have been arrogant, but her prescriptions seemed to be doing their job.

"What do you think?" she asked Isabella in Spanish. "Am I looking younger?"

"*Sí*. You're getting there. Keep at it for the next ten days, and you'll look sixteen again," Isabella teased over her shoulder. "And, stay inside. The less sun on your skin, the better, and it's safer."

"No big deal. I'm used to being on the *inside,*" Magnolia sniggered at her own humor. "I think I need some sunglasses, though. And a hat. For when I do go out."

"I don't think you should go out," Isabella said loud enough to be heard over the music, "but if you have to, wear a baseball cap. Remember, you're a teenager." She flipped the eggs, waited a moment, then took a potholder from the counter and picked up the hot frying pan. With a spatula in her other hand, she turned. "One egg or two?" Magnolia was not at the table.

"Two, thanks," came the response from down the hallway. "Be there in just a minute."

The voice, like Magnolia's skin, had become younger. Minutes later she walked out of the hallway in bare feet, wearing distressed jeans and a crop top.

"Thank you, ma'am, for making me breakfast," she said politely to Isabella.

Isabella eyed Magnolia and slid two eggs out of the pan onto a plate, then backed away from the table. Hawke's word came back to her. "If the Maggie personality shows up, kill her." This was definitely a different personality, but she didn't appear to be dangerous.

"My name's Isabella," Isabella said carefully, setting the frying pan on the stove.

"I'm Tiny Dancer. It's nice to meet you. Thanks again for the breakfast."

"Excuse me," Isabella said abruptly. She left the kitchen and walked down the hallway toward her bedroom. She took her Glock 32 from the dresser drawer and checked the 13-round clip. It was full.

She tucked the gun under her belt, against her back, making sure her blouse covered it.

"What did you say your name is?" Isabella asked as she returned to the kitchen, trying to sound friendly.

"Tiny Dancer," she mumbled through a mouth full of eggs and toast.

"Where did Magnolia go?"

The woman, still chewing, cocked her head. "Who's Magnolia?"

"She's…uh…never mind," Isabella said. "When did you get here, Tiny Dancer?"

"Just a few minutes ago."

"Anyone else come with you?"

Tiny Dancer hesitated, looking around. "No. Just me."

"How long are you staying?"

Tiny Dancer shrugged. "Until I wanna go, I guess."

"You know, you have to stay in the trailer. No going outside."

Tiny Dancer frowned. "Why?"

"It's dangerous," Isabella answered. "There are people looking for us. You have to wait here until your plane leaves."

"I get to go on a plane?" Tiny Dancer asked excitedly. "I've never been on a plane."

Isabella nodded. "In about two weeks."

Tiny Dancer enthusiastically chewed her food until a puzzled look crossed her face. "Why are people looking for us?" she asked.

Isabella hesitated, thinking. "They want to kidnap you," she finally said.

"Oh." Tiny Dancer cocked her head a second time. "Okay. Can I have another egg?"

Isabella cracked another egg in the frying pan, standing straight to make sure the outline of the gun against her back was not visible. *What do I do now?* She needed to call Hawke.

Isabella wasn't the only one with a dilemma.

Samantha's world had turned upside down the moment Magnolia's escape became public knowledge. Calls poured in from the media, from Washington, D.C., from local party officials, and from her friends and family. Deny. Deny. Deny. That's all she could do in response to the torrent of questions about her knowledge of the escape. Finally, she stopped taking calls.

Now she was standing in the living room of Magnolia' penthouse, the events of the last few months cycling through her memory. She knew she looked guilty as sin, but she didn't know anything about the escape. The doormen had buzzed a minute earlier, informing her that there were federal agents there to see her. They were on their way up. She was sure they wouldn't believe her.

She answered the knock. A man and a woman in suits flashed their FBI credentials, introducing themselves as agents Guy DeBrukk and Marian Stone. The man gave a low whistle. "Pretty fancy for a press secretary," he said, looking around.

"It's not mine," Samantha blurted. "I'm just taking care of it for her while she's in jail."

"But she's not in jail, is she?" DeBrukk said sharply.

It was clear that they were going to try and intimidate her, but Samantha was ready.

"Apparently not," she answered curtly, "or you wouldn't be here."

"When was the last time you spoke to Kanaranzi?" DeBrukk asked.

"Am I a suspect?" Samantha countered, ignoring his question.

"Everyone's a suspect at this stage," Agent Stone said. Her tone was firm, but not unkind.

Good cop, Samantha thought. "Are you here to arrest me?" she asked.

"No, we just want to ask you some questions and look around a little," Stone answered.

"Do you have a search warrant?"

"Not yet," DeBrukk snapped.

"Then I'm going to ask you to leave. I need to speak to my lawyer before I talk to you about anything." Samantha stepped past the two agents and motioned toward the still-open door.

"That's as good as admitting you're guilty," DeBrukk thundered.

"We just have a few questions," Stone intervened.

Samantha jerked her head toward the door. "Out," she said. She was surprised at how calm her voice sounded.

The two agents left, with promises to return with a warrant. Samantha looked at her watch. It was 9:00 p.m. in Barcelona. She called Hawke.

If the calls had come in reverse order, his response may have been entirely different, but they did not, which left Hawke deep in thought, oblivious to the white noise of traffic and the cacophony of languages being spoken at the packed sidewalk bistro in Barcelona.

The first call was from Isabella. She called and told him of Tiny Dancer's appearance, and Hawke replied, "We've always known this could happen, but according to the psychologist, this Tiny Dancer personality is not dangerous. Just continue on the same course."

"But the report said that this Tiny Dancer might control the dangerous personality," Isabella said.

"You'll have to keep a very close watch on her, and as I said before, if the Maggie alter emerges, dispose of her.

Isabella suggested moving up Magnolia's departure date.

"The escape is still too much in the news," he said. "Our biggest risk is someone recognizing her when she's out in public. We'll stick with the original plan to have her fly out of La Crosse on May 22 when students will be flying home for the holiday. She'll blend in at the airport. Until then, you need to keep her out of sight. If this Tiny Dancer won't cooperate, you'll have to subdue her."

The biggest risk, Isabella thought, *is that these alters will blow our cover and we'll all end up in prison.* She didn't express that opinion to Hawke.

While the call from Isabella was a little unsettling, the subsequent, unexpected call from Samantha was full of opportunity. *Perhaps,* he thought, *she is going to accept my offer to come to Barcelona.* The panic in her voice and her disclosure that the FBI had paid her a visit quickly derailed his thought.

He calmed her, assured her he knew nothing about Magnolia's escape, and gave her the name of a criminal defense attorney in Boston who could help her.

"You have nothing to worry about," he said soothingly, "unless, of course, you arranged her escape."

"I didn't! I first learned about it when I got a call from a reporter." Samantha was nearly hysterical.

"I was only teasing," Hawke said in his most contrite voice. "I am sorry. I shouldn't treat this so cavalierly, but I am accustomed to things of this nature. You are not, and that puts you in a delicate state. Remember, you and I are on the FBI's radar only because we were close to Magnolia. We did nothing illegal. Contact the attorney I gave you, and don't say anything until you talk to him. Again, I apologize, but you'll be fine."

Hawke had always avoided doing anything that might involve the FBI or Interpol. He hadn't considered it when he arranged for Magnolia's escape, but perhaps he had crossed the line. He would need to distance himself from this as soon as possible.

On the other hand, Samantha had called *him*. Surely, she must have friends in Boston to whom she could reach out, but she had called him. And she controlled $50 million of Magnolia's money. With $50 million, he could disappear to places even Interpol couldn't find.

There was a play to be made here. He just had to figure it out.

Isabella called in sick. She could not go to work and take the chance that this new personality would so something foolish. Tiny Dancer spent the evening watching television and eating potato chips. Isabella spent the evening watching Tiny Dancer. Sometime after midnight, Tiny Dancer went to bed.

Isabella lay on the couch with one hand wrapped tightly around her Glock. Twelve more days. Without sleep. Isabella hoped she could make it.

The eastern sky began to show light, and Isabella dragged herself off the couch and put on a pot of coffee. Two cups later the caffeine kicked in. She looked at her phone. Magnolia's escape was still leading the national news. Quietly she opened the door to Magnolia's bedroom and peeked in. She was still sleeping.

Who would she be when she woke up?

"That didn't take long," Ham said, deflated. He had just picked up a telephone message from Allison Long, an old college classmate who now worked for *The Boston Globe*. Long had been instrumental in the investigation that revealed that Magnolia was Ham's mother. She had also set up the sting where Kanaranzi's arrest took place. Now, Long was in Minnesota to interview him about his mother's escape.

"How did she find you?" Toni asked, incredulous. "We moved here *three days ago!*"

"We kept the same phone numbers. And there was that newspaper article about me being hired by MNSCU. It probably wasn't that difficult."

"If she found you, others will too."

"And so will the police," Ham said. "Maybe I need to get a lawyer. I'm going to call Jim." Benson recommended a local attorney, but her office was closed on Saturday. Ham left a message.

"What should we do about Allison?" he asked Toni. "She wants to meet this afternoon."

"If you don't agree to meet with her it will seem like you're hiding something. Besides, she's a friend. She's likely to be less critical than some random reporter."

"Okay," Ham sighed. "I'll call her back and set it up. I'd like you to be there."

"I'll be there," Toni answered. "Actually, why don't you have her come here?"

Ham thought about it for a moment. "Do you think it's wise to let her know where we live?"

"She'll find out, if she wants to. It would be a lot more convenient here, and we wouldn't have to rummage through boxes to find something to wear. If she wants to come for dinner, we can order out."

It was almost noon when Magnolia got out of bed. She went through her morning routine, showering, applying the skin ointments and swabbing the tattoo on her neck with the concoction Rosa had made for her. She checked her hair. No signs of roots beginning to show, but she would need to have it colored again before she left for France. She could not be a college student if she had graying roots.

She dressed in loose-fitting capri pants, capitulating for the moment to the changes her body had undergone from lack of exercise, and the starchy food, at the jail. She put on a square-neck T and gray sneakers. She needed to go for a run.

"Magnolia?" Isabella queried, putting her book down as Magnolia walked toward the front door of the trailer.

"I'm going for a run."

"You can't."

Magnolia bristled. "What do you mean 'I can't.' I'm not your prisoner. I'm actually your employer."

"Rosa didn't run," Isabella tried to explain. "For you to go running would be completely out of character and would raise suspicion. We've got less than two weeks until you leave. Don't risk it."

"You said Rosa made herself visible around town," Magnolia argued. "Wouldn't it be suspicious if she *didn't* make a few appearances?"

"We can do a drive-by or two, so that people can catch a glimpse of you. We don't want you to be in a position where someone can get a clear look at you."

Magnolia exhaled an audible huff of air. "I've got to be able to do something. I can't just sit here in this tin can for two more weeks."

"I've got tomorrow off. Maybe we can do a road trip to La Crosse. Drive around the city, see the college campus. There's a good Mexican restaurant there. We can stop and have lunch."

Isabella's offer gave Magnolia something to look forward to. "That sounds good," she agreed, "but I'd still like to go running. Maybe after dark?"

Isabella's jaw muscles were tense. "I don't advise it," was all she said.

Magnolia made herself a sandwich and turned on the TV. Her escape was still in the news. She went into her room after she was done eating and came back out with a pen and sheet of paper.

Isabella, still on the couch reading, cocked an eyebrow. "What are you doing?"

"It's really none of your business, but if you must know, I'm writing instructions to my personal attorney. I plan to mail it just before I get on the plane."

"Until you get on that plane, everything you do is my business," Isabella snapped and immediately regretted her outburst. "I'm sorry. Of course, you can write your letter, but let me see it when you're done to make sure you don't give away anything. We'll mail it to Rosa. She can mail it to your attorney from Florida."

"We can mail it to Rosa," Magnolia allowed, "but you will not be reading it. I am giving him instructions on what to do with some of my funds that are in his trust account. I am not so stupid as to write anything that might enable him to locate me."

They sat in mutual silence, staring at the TV. Isabella considered pressing the issue of the letter, but decided against it. At least it was Magnolia that she was talking to, and she didn't want to take a chance that arguing with her might bring out a different personality. *God, just get me to May 22nd*, she prayed silently.

At 3:30 Isabella left for work. "Do not answer the door, and do not go out," she warned. "I'll be home by midnight."

Ham's reunion with Allison Long lasted several hours, starting out as two old friends getting caught up. The serious questioning began in the late afternoon and continued through a dinner of Chinese takeout. Eventually, the interview focused on the virtual meeting between Ham and his mother after she had been extradited to Minnesota.

"As you describe it, she sounded really erratic," Allison said. "She was undergoing psychiatric examination because her lawyers are saying she is unfit to stand trial. Do you think her lashing out at you might have had something to do with that?"

"I have no idea," he said. "I just know she got really hostile when the subject of *The Reaper* came up."

The interview turned to the painting, and the allegation that it was a forgery.

"Don't you have a deadline or something?" Ham asked, deflecting the questions. The clock was approaching 9:00 p.m.

"I'll file the story tomorrow, and it will run on Monday," she said. "Monday is always a slow news day, so this will get above-the-fold placement, either on the front page or the first page of the local section. Either way, I get the scoop."

"Maybe a Pulitzer," Ham joked.

"Maybe." Allison wasn't joking.

"Are you going to mention *The Reaper* in your story?" he asked.

"I think I have to," she said. "It's part of the investigation that led us to her."

"Just don't make me look like an art forger."

"I'll be completely neutral on that issue."

"I was hoping for more," he said. "For old time's sake."

Magnolia looked at the kitchen clock. 10:18. It was dark out, although the streets of Pinewood Court were well lit. *Screw it.* Isabella wouldn't be home for almost two hours. She pulled on her gray sneakers.

The evening air was crisp in her lungs as she jogged down Westwood Road, turning right on Evergreen Drive. Two more quick turns, and she was on 11th Street, the mobile home court receding behind her. She picked up the pace as she headed south, away from the street lights and houses that dotted the edge of the village. It felt good to be running free. At an intersection a half-mile south of the park, she turned and started back. Suddenly headlights turned out of Pinewood Court, glaring in her direction. A pickup truck slowed as it approached, then sped up as it passed.

She slowed to a walk as she reached the edge of the park. Street lights absorbed the headlights coming up from behind her. The pickup glided alongside.

"Hey!" called a young, male voice. "Wanna go for a ride?"

Magnolia didn't look and picked up her pace to a trot.

"I could give you a ride home," he shouted from the driver's seat as the truck stayed even with her.

She guessed he was in his teens. "No, gracias," she said, careful not to look directly at him. She turned into Pinewood Court. The truck followed.

"Hey, you live here? I do too. What's your name?"

She broke into a run, swerving between two mobile homes. She made a hard right, running in a grassy area between two rows of trailers. Lights were on in nearly every one, but she didn't stop. She could see the truck on the street 100 feet away, driving slowly. She ducked behind a small out-building to shield herself and hunched over, hands on her knees, her sides heaving.

She waited, trying to listen over her rapid breathing. A vehicle passed at the end of the block, and a moment later she could see lights coming from the opposite direction on the parallel street. She eased around to the other side of the out-building before the lights reached her. Moments later she heard the truck accelerate, the exhaust sound diminishing as it turned the corner. Her breathing slowly returned to normal.

A door opened at the far end of the grass corridor. She turned and walked in the opposite direction, hunched over to keep the out-building between her and whoever had just come outside. She made it to a small tree at the corner of a garage, slipped behind it and looked back. There was no sign of anyone. In the distance a dog yapped.

Magnolia slid alongside the garage wall and the edge of the driveway until she was back on the street. No signs of headlights or moving vehicles. She picked up her jog. She was sweating.

It took her a half hour, most of which was spent in the panic of being lost, before she found her trailer. It was nearly midnight. She locked the doors and shakily put three ice cubes in a water glass and filled it with tequila. Minutes later Isabella pulled into the driveway.

"Dammit. I should just leave and let you go back to jail on your own," Isabella bellowed at her moments later as they stood in the kitchen. "Do you have some kind of death wish?"

Magnolia gulped the tequila, her hands shaking. "Sorry," she said. "It was stupid. But he didn't see me clearly."

"But he knows you live here. If you can't follow orders, you're going to get us caught. I'm not going down just because you don't have the sense to stay put." Isabella stormed down the hallway and into her bedroom, slamming the door.

Hamilton was up before the sun Monday morning, anxious to see *The Boston Globe* article. Shortly after 5:00 a.m. the notice appeared in his email, telling him the edition was ready. He clicked on the icon and the front page appeared before him.

Allison's story hadn't made it above the fold, but it covered the bottom four inches of the front page, edge-to-edge. Actually, it was two stories: one a brief synopsis of Magnolia's escape and the second, much larger story titled "The Senator's Secret Son." He didn't care for the headline.

The story cast him in a sympathetic light, first recounting his abandonment at age four, being raised by his grandmother, his education, his stint in the military, and his brief flirtation with professional baseball. The story then moved to his grandmother's murder in 2009, the investigation that led to the arrest of Senator Magnolia Kanaranzi, and to the revelation that the Senator, now a fugitive from justice, was the mother who had abandoned Hamilton nearly 40 years ago.

Ham was quoted in the article about his mother's arrest, his attempts to meet with her, and her continual refusal to acknowledge him as her son. The issue of *The Reaper* was mentioned briefly, and only in the context of Magnolia's anger directed at him for allegedly selling a forged version of a painting. The article, of course, included his denial. Allison had not mentioned the name of the painting nor the museum to which it had been sold. She also omitted the $13 million sale price, for which Ham silently thanked her.

There were two parts of the story for which he was not so thankful.

Allison had pointed out the coincidence that Ham had accepted a job and moved to Minnesota at the same time his mother was being extradited to the same state. She also mentioned that he moved to Winona, a town only 60 miles from Red Wing, from where his mother had escaped just three days before his move. She did not make any accusations, but a reader could easily infer complicity between mother and son if they were looking for something to connect him to Magnolia's escape.

To add fuel to that fire, Allison closed the story with a quote; it was a statement which Ham had regretted the moment he said it, not because it wasn't how he felt, but because he knew how it would sound. He tried to get her to agree not to use it, but Allison had carefully inferred she *might not* use it, while never stating that she wouldn't.

The quote: "I don't know where she is, but deep down, I kind of hope she's out of the country and this whole thing will go away."

Isabella and Magnolia were unaware of the story as they left Pinewood Court, headed for La Crosse and a lunch at Las Margaritas. Magnolia was dressed in tight jeans, knee boots, a white shell and a holey brown top that was long enough to cover her butt. Isabella had bought her a knit hat to complete the ensemble. Thanks to her diminutive size and slim hips, Magnolia could easily pass for sixteen.

They spoke little as they approached La Crosse. Finally, Isabella said, "We'll speak only in Spanish on the trip. Today, you are Rosa. Don't screw it up."

They toured the city, slowly circling Viterbo University twice so that Magnolia could get familiar with the campus. They swung past a post office and express mailed Magnolia's letter to the real Rosa, then took I-90 across one of the Mississippi River channels to the airport.

As they approached the terminal, Magnolia realized her breathing was rapid and shallow. Her palms were clammy. She exhaled noisily to relieve the tension.

"If you can't handle a test run, how will you survive the real thing?" Isabella scolded gently, laughing a little to take the sting out of the words.

"I'll be all right," Magnolia retorted. "I'm not as experienced as you are with being a criminal."

The rebuke made the hairs on the back of Isabella's neck stand up, but she said nothing more. They returned to the downtown area and arrived at Las Margaritas at 1:00 o'clock.

"From this point, we are a happy mother and daughter," Isabella said before they went into the restaurant. "Time to see if you have the *gondolas* to pull this off."

Their college-age waiter flirted with Magnolia, his interest peaking when he learned she had just enrolled at Viterbo. Magnolia played the shy maiden, turning her face away and acting coy.

"You passed that test," Isabella said as they drove out of La Crosse. "If you can maintain that same composure, the airport should be simple." She wished that day was much closer.

By mid-afternoon, Allison's story had been picked up by the national news networks, and by the time Isabella and "Rosa" got back to Pinewood Court and turned on the TV, every newscast contained a story about the Senator's lost son.

Magnolia watched, transfixed, until Isabella flipped to a news channel where Allison Long was being interviewed. Anger welled up inside Magnolia. The same con artist who had lured her into a trap was now spewing trash about her and making it sound like her son had been complicit in her escape.

"I want to read her story," Magnolia barked. Isabella hunted it down on the internet, and the two of them read it together.

Ham's closing quote surprised Magnolia. "How far is Winona from here?" she asked.

"About 15 miles. A 20-minute drive," Isabella answered. "Don't even think about trying to see him."

"No chance. Why would I want to see him? He's a thief and a liar," but Magnolia was no longer certain.

Ham hired the attorney that Benson recommended, both to have someone to shield him from the media and for the inevitable police investigation. To keep the media hounds at bay, Ham shut off his phone. Both the attorney and Benson were instructed to call Toni's number if they needed to reach him.

The no-phone-gambit worked for less than four hours. By five o'clock there were three news trucks parked in front of their house and a gaggle of reporters on the lawn.

"Oh, God. The neighbors are going to love us," Toni said as she peeked through the living room curtains.

"Just wait until the police show up with their lights and sirens," Ham quipped. "There'll be for sale signs on every lawn by next week."

"Seriously, how are we even going to walk Barca?"

"He'll have to do his business in the back yard for now," Ham answered. "He's okay. He thinks it's a health spa after living in an apartment for the last couple months."

Ham called the lawyer, and a news conference was set up for 8:00 p.m. Ham would appear on the front steps, make a short statement, and take no questions. This would give all the media equal information and something for the evening news.

By 8:00 o'clock the media throng had doubled in size. Ham's lawyer started the press conference by explaining the ground rules. Then he introduced Ham.

Ham told them he had seen his mother only three or four times since he was four years old, that their last conversation was when he visited her in jail and it had ended unpleasantly. He had had no communication with her since then, knew nothing about her escape, and had no idea where she was.

When he was done, reporters shouted questions at him, asking whether his moves to Minneapolis and then to Winona, which paralleled his mother's extradition and escape, were "purely coincidental" or whether there were ulterior motives. And what did he mean when he said "I hope she's out of the country"? Without answering, Ham turned his wheelchair back toward the house, but one question from a local reporter caught his attention. "Are you still going to do the series of lectures for the Winona Arts Council?"

Ham spun back around.

"I have every intention of doing the series. The dates haven't been fixed, but it will be before Memorial Day."

"Isn't your series all about art forgery?"

"Yes, that is the primary focus of the lectures," Ham answered. "I've been accused of being an art forger, which I'm not, but in the process of defending myself I've learned a lot about art forgery. I invite you all to attend the lectures. I've been told they are both informative and entertaining."

There was another deluge of questions related to *The Reaper* and the allegations that had been made against him. Ham turned and went into the house without responding.

"That should generate some buzz," he grinned as the front door closed behind him.

An icy smile crept across D'Anselmo's face as he watched the evening news in his one-room apartment. Hamilton Blethen had appeared on the TV screen, proclaiming innocence in his mother's jailbreak. Then the camera focused on the station's reporter. D'Anselmo didn't care what she had to say. He had learned she was reporting from Winona.

Magnolia replayed the segment of the evening news that featured Ham, pausing it so she could study him, trying to find something, anything, that bore a resemblance to her. He was handsome, with dark skin, flashing eyes, and black hair flecked with gray. He appeared calm and comfortable in front of the cameras, even injecting a little humor.

But she was confused by his mention of a jailhouse visit. She didn't remember him visiting her in jail. In fact, she didn't remember meeting him three or four times, as he claimed. She only remembered seeing him twice: once in Barcelona at a restaurant where she watched only from a distance, and once at the Museum of Visual Arts in Boston.

After watching the segment several times, she turned off the TV, wishing he had said something about hoping she was safe, or had repeated the last line of the *Globe* story. At least he didn't blame her for the "unpleasant" part of his alleged visit.

Have we really met more times than I can remember? Again, she was faced with the prospect that parts of her life had happened without her knowing participation.

Anthony Dykstra, Assistant Special Agent in Charge of the Minnesota office of the Federal Bureau of Investigation, also watched the newscasts. "Blood runs thick," he said to Agent Doug Atkins. "We need to keep a close watch on this guy."

Atkins shrugged. "I'll go talk to him, but we don't have any reason to believe that she's in that area."

"Other than none of our other leads have panned out," Dykstra answered. "I have a hunch she's still in the area. As I said, blood runs thick. He's her only child."

The "buzz" that Ham's news conference created almost resulted in cancellation of the lecture series. The Winona Arts Council had a limited appetite for controversy, but after much deliberation and urging by Jim Benson, it agreed to go forward with the program, reducing it to a single three-hour talk. The date was set for Wednesday, May 20, from 7-10 p.m., at the DuFresne Performing Arts Center located on the Winona State University campus.

An announcement of the event appeared in the *Winona Daily News* the next afternoon, one week before the event, as part of a follow-up story recounting Ham's press conference and the most current news on the whereabouts of the "Fugitive Senator," as Magnolia was becoming known in the media.

The newspaper arrived at Ham and Toni's front door at the same time FBI Agent Atkins was knocking on it. A hurried phone call to their local attorney resulted in an agreement that they would all convene in an hour at the Blethen residence.

"The FBI has taken the lead in this case," Atkins announced as they sat in the cluttered living room. He looked like he was right out of central casting, dark suit, striped tie, black shoes, military haircut. "If you're contacted by any other law enforcement agency, let me know immediately," he said, handing Ham, Toni, and their attorney a business card. Atkins settled into his chair with a notepad and pen.

"When is the last time you saw your mother?"

For the next two hours Ham answered Atkins' questions, often the same question phrased in a different way. For the most part, his answers were the same. "I don't know anything about my mother except what I've seen on television." "I had nothing to do with her escape." "Our moves to Minnesota and Winona were coincidental."

Finally, Atkins seemed satisfied. "If you think of anything else, any little detail, please get in touch with me," he said just as his phone rang. "Excuse me," he said. He took the call outside. Two minutes later he came back in the house.

"Have you ever been to Florida?"

"What? No," Ham answered reflexively. "Well, actually yes. I went to spring training there with the Mets."

The revelation disrupted Atkins' usual stoic demeanor. "Uh. What?"

"I played professional baseball for a couple of years, before *this*," Ham said, nodding toward his wheelchair. "I was in the Mets' system. Our spring training was in Port St. Luce, Florida."

"When was that?"

"Right out of college, I guess about twenty years ago."

"Do you have any friends or family in Florida?"

"No, we pretty much played baseball and hung out with teammates. I haven't been back since," Ham answered. "Uh, wait a minute. I had a customer in Tampa that I did a painting for once," he said blushing. He suddenly felt like he was full of holes that the agent could see right through.

"When was that?"

"Ten, twelve years ago?"

"Did you go to Florida to do the painting?"

"No. I painted it from a photo. I was living in St. Paul at the time. I shipped it to the guy. I never went to Florida for the painting. Just the baseball stuff," he added weakly.

"What's your customer's name?"

"I don't remember, but I could try to look it up for you."

"Can you look it up right now?" Atkins asked

"We just moved," Toni interjected, motioning toward the boxes still stacked along walls. "It will take some time to find anything in the chaos, particularly something that old. We've had three moves since then. I'm not sure we even have records going back that far."

The agent nodded. "I understand, but please try. Let me know if you find it."

"What's with Florida?" Ham asked. "Is that where you think she is?"

"Just covering all our bases," he answered.

When Artemis Blazing received the overnight courier envelope from Florida, he didn't give it much thought. He had many clients who wintered in Florida, and several who had made it their permanent home after retirement.

It wasn't until the end of the work day that he opened the envelope and took out two sheets of handwritten notes. He looked at the signature, *Magnolia Kanaranzi,* then dove into the waste basket next to his desk to retrieve the envelope. It had come from Miami.

He struggled for only a moment with ethical considerations before picking up the phone and dialing the local FBI office. He was certain there must be some exception in the canons of ethics related to attorney-client privilege for situations like this.

He told the FBI about receiving the letter from Miami, but he refused to tell them the letter's content or the nature of his representation of Magnolia. *Attorney-client privilege,* he reasoned, *applies unless a crime is being committed.* There was nothing in Magnolia's letter that was criminal *per se*, nor did it direct him to do anything that broke the law. It only gave instructions related to her estate plan and the distribution of the funds he held in his trust account.

I hope I'm not being asked to distribute laundered money? he thought, quickly washing the idea from his mind.

Atkins looked across the desk at his boss. "Their move to Minnesota was because of a legitimate job offer. It appears coincidental that it came at the same time as his mother's extradition. And the move from

Minneapolis to Winona took place after she escaped, and after we found her prison uniform in a dumpster near the airport."

"Maybe he's clean," Dykstra said, "but don't lose sight of this guy. Even if he wasn't involved in the escape, she might try to contact him."

"I don't know. He's only seen her four times in 40 years, and each time he was the one who instigated the meeting," Atkins countered, "but I'll keep an eye on him. What about the Florida lead? Anything come out of that?"

"Nothing yet. We're scouring hotels and transportation hubs in the Miami area. So far, all dead ends."

"Think it might be a red herring?"

"Could be. Just like her prison uniform dumped near the airport might be. We're still reviewing flight information, but so far it doesn't appear she's boarded any flights out of MSP or any of the local airports."

"You think it's possible she's still in the area?" Atkins asked.

"Possible, maybe laying low until the hubbub dies down," Dykstra answered. "We're reasonably certain she hasn't crossed into either Canada or Mexico, but by now she could have driven to Chicago or Dallas or Atlanta and flown out of the country. We've also called our Boston office to lean on that lawyer, Blazing. There might be something in that letter that could lead us to her."

In the Boston office of the FBI, the conversation was similar.

"Should we bring Samantha Jones in for questioning?" Stone asked the Assistant Special Agent in Charge.

"Who's her lawyer?" the ASAC asked.

"I'll find out and set something up through them," Stone said.

"We really need to search Kanaranzi's place before we do that," DeBrukk cut in.

"We don't have enough to get a search warrant," the ASAC replied. "Get in touch with the jail in Red Wing. They should have recordings of Ms. Jones' visits with Kanaranzi. Maybe that will give us enough to get a warrant. Stone, I want you to talk to Kanaranzi's lawyer, the one who gave us the Miami lead. Remind him he has a duty to cooperate. There is no attorney-client privilege when it relates to a crime that is in progress, and this escape is a continuing crime as long as Kanaranzi's still on the loose."

"Kanaranzi's trial lawyers are from Taft, Hartman and Lowinski. I understand she's also retained an international lawyer from some place in Europe," Stone said. "Barcelona, I think. Or maybe Paris."

"I'll send some folks over to Taft to talk to those lawyers, and I'll get in touch with INTERPOL to see if they can track down the one in Europe."

"What about all these Magnolia-sightings?" DeBrukk asked. "Anything there?"

"The usual. A lot of well-meaning citizens and a few crazies, but none of them have led to anything."

It was a typical, chilly May evening in the small river community. When the sun went down, the temperature went with it, and the uninsulated floor of the mobile home quickly turned cold. Magnolia dug through Isabella's dresser, searching for an extra pair of socks when her hand hit metal. She moved the socks and stared at a handgun.

She picked it up, turned it over in her hand, and felt a familiar thrill of power. She checked the safety, then clasped both hands around the handle and aimed it at the lamp on the nightstand. "Pow. Pow. Pow," she said out loud. Then she smiled.

She ejected the magazine. All 13 slots were loaded. She pulled the slide back. There was another shell in the barrel. Carefully she slid the slide back in place and placed the magazine back into the handle. She put the gun back in the drawer, covering it with socks, and started to close the drawer, then stopped and felt around the drawer under the socks until she found a box. It was half full of .357 hollow point bullets. She arranged the socks to cover the gun and the box of ammunition, then closed the drawer.

Magnolia went back to the living room with cold feet. She put on her shoes and turned on the TV. Someday she might need that gun.

On the advice of her counsel, Samantha refused to talk to the FBI, invoking her Fifth Amendment right not to incriminate herself.

"I didn't do anything illegal," she argued with her lawyer. "I didn't have anything to do with Magnolia's escape. I don't know anything about it."

"You handled her money," he said, "and you met with her every week while she was in jail. *You* don't even *know* what you might have said or done that was illegal, or at least the FBI will make it look that way. You've got to plead the Fifth."

She called Hawke. He agreed with her lawyer.

"You should have come with me to Barcelona," he said. "The FBI wouldn't have found you here."

"Have they found you?" she asked.

"No. And even if they do, I will invoke attorney-client privilege. Neither of us has anything to worry about."

Samantha ended the call, thinking of the millions of dollars she had transferred to the Swiss account. *Magnolia must have been planning her escape when she told me to do that. Is Henri in on it, or is he just a pawn, like me?*

She began to think Hawke's advice might have merit. Maybe she should disappear.

There was a persistent drizzle Saturday morning, just enough to keep the windshield wipers busy as D'Anselmo cruised into the outskirts of Winona. He stopped at a coffee shop and purged his early morning cup in the restroom, then ordered another and found a table in the corner. He took out his phone and located the address of the local newspaper.

The newspaper staff, busy putting out the weekend edition, paid little attention to the man who asked to look at the past week's newspapers. He found the story about Hamilton Blethen, and the sidebar about the upcoming lecture. The story didn't give Blethen's address, but it did have a byline. The reporter was busy pounding away at his keyboard when D'Anselmo approached.

"You're the guy who wrote the story about the fugitive Senator's son, right?" he asked, interrupting the reporter's train of thought.

"Yeah," the reporter said without looking up.

"Can you tell me where he lives?"

"Why do you want to know?"

"I went to grad school with his wife. I didn't know they were living here until I saw your story. I'd like to go see them, but your story didn't give an address."

"It's on 39th Street in Goodview, don't remember the exact address," the reporter said. "I think his wife works at the maritime museum. You might find her there."

The museum's admission charge was $7.00 which would put a dent in D'Anselmo's meager resources. Rather than buy a ticket, he asked the woman selling tickets whether Toni was working. She had no idea who Toni was. "I only volunteer on weekends," she said. "I don't think there's anyone here named Toni. Would you like to buy a ticket?"

"You open tomorrow?"

"Yes. We're open on Sundays from 10 to five."

"I'll come back then."

The rain was coming down harder as he got back in his car and sat for several minutes listening to the patter on the car's roof. *Where the hell is Goodview?* He tried to find it on MapQuest, but the map was too small to read on his phone. He needed a computer. He looked up the location of the public library.

It took him only a few minutes to find 39th Avenue on the computerized map. To his surprise, he had driven through Goodview on his way into Winona. Thirty-ninth Avenue was only five and a half blocks long. *This should be easy.*

He stopped counting at thirty as he slowly drove north on 39th Avenue. There were more houses than he had expected, and none of them had mail boxes or any other clue to who occupied the homes. To complicate things even more, the street had two jogs that prevented him from seeing more than two blocks at a time.

Randomly patrolling the street would likely draw attention because of his car, so he drove the length of 39th Avenue only one more time looking for an unobtrusive place where he could park and watch. He found nothing. This was not going to be as easy as he thought. He considered waiting until the next day to see if Toni was working at the museum, but sleeping in his car didn't appeal to him. He decided to drive back to Minneapolis and come back Wednesday night, when he knew he could find Blethen at his lecture. Then he would follow him home.

Buoyed by a pep talk from Hawke in the wee hours of Sunday morning, Isabella woke up refreshed. She went to the kitchen to make coffee, passing Magnolia's closed bedroom door on the way. With the coffee percolating, she retrieved a tube of cinnamon rolls from the refrigerator. She opened the tube, placed the rolls on a baking sheet, and put them in the oven. The smell of the baking rolls made her mouth water.

Only six days to go. Might as well make nice. She rapped on the bedroom door. "Come join me for coffee and cinnamon rolls," she called. No answer. She rapped again and opened the door. No Magnolia. *What the... Where the hell is she?*

She found Magnolia reclining in a lawn chair on the driveway, soaking up the late morning sun. A tube of suntan lotion and sunglasses stuck out of a tote bag beside the lawn chair. "Thought I'd get a little color," Magnolia said.

"Are you insane?" Isabella said, her voice somewhere between a scream and a whisper. "You need to keep out of the sun. Your skin will..."

"I'm wearing a visor," Magnolia interrupted, "to keep my face shielded.

"You have to stay inside, both for your skin and for *our* safety."

"Nobody comes by here," Magnolia answered, brushing off Isabella's warning. "I'm going to lay here for another hour. Actually, do we have any ice tea?"

"Get your ass in the house!" Isabella shrieked, "or I'm leaving."

Magnolia ignored her.

As Isabella turned to go back in the trailer, an old pickup truck drove past. Isabella watched it go down the street; Wisconsin license plates, one occupant. *Probably someone who lives here.*

She stormed to her bedroom, yanked her suitcase out of the closet, and threw it on the bed.

She stopped and exhaled. Her deal with Hawke was to get Magnolia to the plane on Friday. *Maybe I should just shoot her and leave. I can tell Hawke she turned into Maggie.* She let out a long breathe and stood there, not opening the suitcase. *Shit!* Isabella threw the suitcase back in the closet and went to the kitchen to pour a cup of coffee and eat a cinnamon roll.

Through the kitchen window she saw the same pickup, approaching from the opposite direction. It stopped, blocking their driveway. Isabella bolted for the door.

"Hi. I saw you the other night," a young male voice said from inside the pickup just as Isabella came out the trailer door. Magnolia looked up, then tilted her head downward so the visor blocked her face.

"Excuse me," Isabella shouted, drawing the young man's attention. "My daughter and I do not want to be bothered, so please leave."

He looked back at Magnolia. "Maybe we could go out some time," he said, ignoring Isabella.

Magnolia raised her head again. "You heard what the lady said," her tone was condescending, no trace of a Spanish accent. "Get the hell out of here!"

"Geez. You could of just said no. You don't have to be such a bitch about it."

Magnolia flew off the chair and charged the pickup. Isabella momentarily froze, then raced after her. The surprised boy also hesitated, just long enough for "Rosa" to reach the pickup and slam her fist against the fender. "I'll kill you!" she screamed. The boy reacted as she reached for the passenger door handle, slamming the accelerator to the floor. Maggie screamed another threat as he sped away.

Isabella caught up from behind, wrapping both arms around her. "C'mon. We've got to go inside."

"Get your hands off me!" she spat and spun out of Isabella's grip. "Touch me again, and I'll kill you." A chill coursed down Isabella's backbone. She backed away. The person she was looking at was not Magnolia, and it wasn't Tiny Dancer. This had to be Maggie.

Isabella backed toward the door of the trailer, feeling for the railing behind her, as Maggie reached down for the tote bag. Isabella turned and raced up the steps into the trailer and down the hall to her bedroom. She pulled open her dresser drawer and rummaged under the socks, then threw them on the floor emptying the drawer. Her gun was gone.

She heard the trailer door slam shut.

Maggie sat at the kitchen table, sipping lemonade while loading the Glock 32. "Shut the fuck up, or you'll be next," she growled at the voice in her head. "No. No. I don't want to go." She slammed the clip on the table next to the gun and Isabella's cellphone. Slowly her muscles relaxed and her eyes softened.

"You've really put us in a predicament this time, Maggie," Tiny Dancer said. "I suppose I'll have to clean up your mess…again."

Tiny Dancer slid the loaded clip into the handle of the Glock until it snapped into place, then walked to the back of the trailer and put the gun on the nightstand next to her bed. She stopped at the door of Isabella's bedroom and looked in. The rusty odor of fresh blood mingled with the acrid smell of gun powder. Isabella's body lay on the blood-soaked bed. A pillow ravaged with bullet holes lay over her face. Tiny Dancer scrunched up her face in disgust. She went into the bathroom and looked under the sink for cleaning supplies.

Magnolia woke up groggy, feeling like she'd been on a week-long bender. Slowly, she swung her feet out of bed and sat up. Her back and shoulders hurt, aching as if she'd over-exercised. There was a strange, antiseptic smell in the air. She did a double take. *How did that gun get on the nightstand?* She opened the nightstand drawer and put it inside.

The pulsating hot water from the shower felt good pounding on her sore muscles. She stood for a long time, letting the water wash away her sleep and some of the pain, but her arms still throbbed as she washed her hair. *I should dye my hair again tonight. Maybe Isabella will help. She doesn't work on Mondays. Why do my arms hurt?*

She stood in front of the mirror, dripping. Most of her wrinkles were no longer visible, and her tan looked good. With a baseball cap, and the sun glasses Isabella still needed to get her, she could easily pass for a college student. She dried herself, got dressed, and went into the kitchen. A set of keys and Isabella's cell phone lay on the table. She looked out the window. The brown truck was sitting in the driveway. *Isabella must be outside.* She took the potion Rosa had made for her out of the refrigerator and applied it to the henna tattoo on her neck. The tattoo still looked fresh.

As Magnolia searched the refrigerator for something to eat, Isabella's phone rang. She looked at the caller ID. It wasn't an international number, so it wasn't Hawke. On the fourth ring Magnolia answered.

"Isabella?"

"No. This is her daughter." Magnolia was careful to inflect a Spanish accent.

"Is she there?"

"Not right now. Can I give her a message?"

"Sure. Tell her she doesn't have to come in to work tonight."

"Tonight? She doesn't work on Mondays."

There was a pause. "This is Tuesday, honey. Just tell her she doesn't have to come to work."

Tuesday? Magnolia clicked off the call and looked at the phone's screen. It confirmed that it was Tuesday.

What happened to Monday…and where is Isabella?

She tapped on Isabella's bedroom door and called her name. There was no answer. She tapped again and waited a moment, then opened the door. The smell of household cleaner was strong. The bed was made, but it looked odd, lower, as if someone had removed the mattress. She opened the closet. Everything looked normal. She opened the sock drawer and rummaged through it even though she knew the gun wasn't there. She opened the other drawers and did the same. Everything seemed in place.

Puzzled, Magnolia went outside. *Where would she have gone? She was mad at me. Did she just leave? That doesn't make sense, her clothes are still here, and so is her phone and the truck.* She walked around the trailer, then went back inside. *What the hell? Where did she go, and how did I lose a day?* She wanted to call Hawke, but Isabella's phone was password protected. *Damn it!*

She would just have to wait. He was bound to call Isabella in the next day or two. *But where is she? Did she get arrested?* The thought worried Magnolia. *Maybe I should leave…but where would I go? What about my flight out of here? There must be tickets.*

She went to Isabella's room and searched the dresser again, then went through the closet thoroughly. Nothing. Finally, in a bedside table she hit pay dirt: a purse with packets of hundred-dollar bills and an airline ticket to Paris, by way of Chicago O'Hare, in the name of Rosa Mendez. She exhaled. *I can handle the flight to Paris on my own, without Isabella's help.*

Later, with no food in the refrigerator and no Isabella to stop her, Magnolia decided to go someplace to eat. Maybe she'd buy herself sunglasses and a few groceries. It would be good for the town people to see Rosa, but actually eating at a local restaurant would be too big a risk, she reasoned. Someone might see her and realize she wasn't Rosa. A safer place would be Winona, only 15 miles away and a college town so she wouldn't stand out. And maybe she would see her son.

With the help of Isabella's computer, she found directions to Winona. Cautiously, she drove out of Pinewood Court, watching for the pickup and the young man who had stopped and asked her for a date. She snorted at the thought, but when she saw the truck parked in a driveway, she pulled her knit hat further down around her face and turned the opposite direction.

Outside of the village, a car passed her and honked. Both startled and puzzled by the other driver's actions, Magnolia concentrated even harder on the road ahead. The pickup's speedometer read 35-miles-per-hour. Soon there was another car in her rearview mirror. Again, there was a honk and the car zipped around her. This time the driver gave her a one-fingered salute. *What is wrong with these people?* It had been years since she'd driven a car, and she'd never driven a pickup.

She eased the speed up to 50 miles per hour. To her, it felt like 100. *All this, and I'm going to die in a car accident,* she thought, but by the time she was halfway to Winona, she was more comfortable.

The river bridge that linked Wisconsin to Minnesota was a big challenge. The guard rails seemed so close, and her still-aching muscles were tense, but she reached the end of the bridge with a relieved sigh and pulled in to a parking lot next to The Boat House restaurant. She sat in the truck for several minutes waiting for the restaurant to open, and was seated on the patio by 4:00 p.m.

The restaurant overlooked the river, and on the far bank a young family splashed in the sand, their happy voices heard across the water. In the middle of the river channel a speedboat roared downstream. The shrieks and laughter of the children were drowned out, then emerged again after the sound of the speedboat faded. She thought of her son. *Do I have grandchildren? Could those be my grandchildren?* She strained to see the children across the river.

Her fish and chips arrived, along with a complimentary copy of the hot-off-the-press *Winona Daily News.* Magnolia browsed the first few pages, happy to see that she had slipped to the third page of the news section. Hawke's plan to let things simmer down before she left the country was working.

On page five, an advertisement drew her attention. The Winona Arts Council was sponsoring an event that featured Hamilton Blethen. It was scheduled for the next evening, May 20. She wrote down the time and location, her heart suddenly pounding.

"You going to go?" asked a voice behind her. Magnolia jumped. It was her waiter.

"No. No."

"You go to school here?" he asked conversationally.

"No. I go to Viterbo in La Crosse," she answered, realizing too late she had forgotten to use her Spanish accent. "I just enrolled there."

"Where're you from?"

Magnolia hesitated. "Argentina." This time she made sure the accent was thick.

She left hurriedly just as the dinner crowd was starting to build. Two blocks away was a grocery store where she picked up enough food for the rest of the week. The store had a rack of sunglasses and, after trying on several pair, she chose one and checked out. By the time the brown pickup was re-crossing the river bridge, Magnolia had made up her mind. *I'm coming back to Winona tomorrow night.* She was going to see her son one last time before she left the country.

Wednesday morning broke cold and windy with a drab sky that threatened rain, but it was business as usual in the Minneapolis office of the FBI.

"Got another Magnolia sighting from Winona this morning," the SAC told Agent Atkins.

"That makes what, a dozen or more for Winona?" Atkins responded sardonically. "Over a thousand total?"

"At least, but this one might be worth a follow-up. Waiter at a local restaurant saw a woman with a fake accent jotting down info from an advertisement for a lecture by Hamilton Blethen. When he asked her about attending the lecture, she acted really weird and said she wasn't going."

"Why would she need the information for the event if she wasn't interested in going?"

"That's what I was thinking, plus his description of her is a match for Kanaranzi: five-foot, a hundred pounds. He said she was young, though, college age, but she acted strange when he asked her."

"Pretty detailed observations for a waiter," Atkins observed skeptically.

"He's getting a degree in criminology at Winona State," the SAC laughed.

Atkins scratched his ear, wrinkling up his face. "We got anyone we can send down there?"

"Only you."

"Yeah. A hundred-to-one it's another wild goose chase."

D'Anselmo left the bookstore at noon, telling them he had to go out of town and might not be back until Friday. The store manager told him not to come back at all. She wrote him his final paycheck on the spot.

Getting fired was not a new experience for him, and he was not totally unhappy about it. Being a clerk at a bookstore was demeaning, beneath someone who had a graduate degree in visual arts. He could always get another job. Maybe he'd find one in Winona. Besides, he now had cash for his trip.

He threw extra clothes in a duffle bag, found his one un-maxed credit card, filled up his car with gas, and was eating gas station food on his way to Winona by 2:30. A detailed plan blossomed in his mind as he drove south on Highway 61 along the river: he'd stop at a grocery store to buy flowers for Toni, and to grab something to eat from the deli counter. Then he'd park close to the highway. From that vantage point he could see most of the houses on 39th Avenue, and if someone was going to the university, they would most likely go on Highway 61. Blethen's handicapped van would drive right past him. If Toni wasn't in the van, he would go directly to the house and give her the flowers.

Maybe I should wait on the flowers, he thought, rethinking his plan. *I'll get rid of him first. Then I can use the flowers to show my sympathy.*

He pictured Toni gratefully falling into his arms.

Magnolia felt giddy, like the day of the escape, but without the stress. She wanted to go for a run but decided against it, in fear of seeing the boy in the truck again. She turned on the TV and switched between cable channels. It was just two weeks after her escape, and she was no longer on national news. She turned the TV off and paced the length of the mobile home several times. At noon she fixed herself a sandwich. As she ate, she wrote another letter to Blazing. She addressed the envelope to Rosa Mendez in Florida and included instructions to mail the letter to Blazing's office in Boston. She didn't mention that Isabella had disappeared. *Only a couple days to go. No sense muddying the waters.*

She changed several times, trying to decide which of the college-student clothes were most appropriate for the event, and then went to the drawer where she had stashed the money. She took out ten fresh $100.00 bills, her passport and her student ID, and put them in a backpack. She added Isabella's laptop, and an extra sweatshirt to fend off the evening chill. She hesitated, then took the handgun out of the drawer, wrapped the sweatshirt around it, and put it in the backpack. She was on the road by 2:15 p.m.

Magnolia's mind was on autopilot, her thoughts occupied by the prospect of seeing her son, making the trip to Winona was less stressful than the day before. Even crossing the interstate bridge was easier.

She made several loops around the Winona State campus before finding DuFresne Center, located on a dead-end street in the heart of the university. There was street parking and a parking lot a block away. She would have no trouble finding a parking space for the evening lecture.

She pulled out the laptop and found directions to the local post office where she paid to over-night the letter to Rosa. Her next stop was a coffee shop on the edge of the university campus. She ordered coffee and sat in the corner, watching a trickle of customers come and go in the late afternoon while she absent-mindedly paged through a bevy of publications that were on the table next to her. Nothing held her attention.

The absence of Isabella was still a puzzle, but it was also a relief not to have her watching every minute and dictating what to do. *The only logical explanation is that she got caught by the police. But why hasn't it been all over the news? Unless they were keeping her arrest quiet, trying to break her, make her give me up. I need to get out of the trailer park. Maybe I'll go find a hotel room in La Crosse tomorrow. I'll dump the truck and take a cab to the airport.*

The longer she sat, the more paranoid her thoughts became. *This whole lecture thing could be a trap. Just like when I got arrested. Maybe my bastard son is setting me up, just like back in Boston.* Suddenly, she needed to get out of the coffee shop.

She slid from behind the table, leaving a half cup of coffee behind, and slung her backpack over her shoulder. The DuFresne Center was only a couple of blocks away, so she decided to leave the truck parked and walk.

Walking, and the brisk spring air, helped deflate her paranoia. *Am I imagining things? Would they really set this up just to try and catch me? Do they even think I'm still in this area? They should be looking for me in Florida.*

Standing at the end of Johnson Street, Magnolia looked at the DuFresne Center a half-block away. Should she go? She looked at her watch: 5:00 o'clock. Two hours until the lecture was scheduled to begin. She walked back to where she had parked the truck.

"You've heard this lecture before. No need for you to sit through it again," Ham said, trying to persuade Toni that it wasn't necessary for her to go with him.

She frowned. "I'm perfectly happy to go with you."

"I'm going to start making this drive on a daily basis beginning in June, so I might as well get used to it. And you have plenty to do here."

"I worry. You're still getting used to driving the new van and getting in and out of it. I'd feel better if you had someone with you."

"How about if I take Barca?" Ham grinned.

"Oh, *that* would be a lot of help," Toni said in mock sarcasm.

"Seriously, he's good company, and the people at the lecture will love him. Besides, he could use an outing."

At 6:15, Ham rolled into the van, happily followed by Barca. "See you later, Love," Ham called out. "I should be home by 10:30. If it's going to be later than that, I'll call."

Using a joystick as a steering mechanism, Ham maneuvered the van out of the driveway, turned left on 39th Avenue, did a short right-left jog on 7th Street, and then turned right on 6th.

D'Anselmo watched from the edge of Highway 61 as Ham's van turned in the opposite direction. He started the Trans Am with a rumble and followed, stopping momentarily across the street from the driveway where the van had just exited to write down the address. For a moment he considered whether to knock on the door to see if Toni was home, then changed his mind and accelerated down 39th, turning right on 7th in pursuit of the van. In a heartbeat he was lost, with no van in sight.

A string of expletives ramped up his temper. *You think you're so smart. I know where that lecture place is. I'll find you there. Your ass is mine!*

Agent Atkins steered his navy-blue, government-issue sedan out of the McDonald's parking lot, eating a handful of French fries and thinking how trips of this nature were going to give him a fast-food induced heart attack. He checked his GPS, and in 10 minutes he was sitting in a parking lot, kitty-corner from the DuFresne Performing Arts Center, with a clear view of the entrance. It was 6:20 p.m.

Five minutes later, a white van with handicapped plates pulled into a parking spot a half dozen spaces away. Ham got out, followed by his golden retriever.

Atkins intercepted them as they headed toward the DuFresne Center. "Hey Hamilton," he called out in a friendly voice.

Ham turned his head, a surprised looked on his face. "Wow. I didn't think my lectures were this big a draw," he laughed as he recognized Atkins.

"We figured if you're here, maybe your mother will be, too."

"She's never come to see me before," Ham said. "You remember Barca." The dog leaned against the FBI agent, waiting to be petted.

"I remember Barca," Atkins said, ruffling the dog's fur. "I'm just going to hang out here to see who comes to listen to you."

"Knock yourself out." Ham and Barca continued toward the art center.

Man, I hope she doesn't come, Ham thought as he crossed the street and rolled toward the DuFresne Center entrance. *I hope she's nowhere near here.*

Atkins returned to his car to wait and watch. Ham had shown no alarm at Atkins' presence. It was clear that he was not expecting his mother. Atkins nodded. *Yup. Just another wild goose chase.*

Magnolia's brown pickup was parked on Johnson Street across from the DuFresne Center entrance. She watched through the truck's back window as Hamilton got out of his van and was approached by a man in a dark suit. After a short conversation, the man in the suit returned to his car, while Hamilton and his dog continued toward DuFresne Center. There was no doubt in Magnolia's mind that the man in the suit was a cop.

"You bastard," she muttered to herself, her anger rising. "You're setting me up again."

She pulled the sweatshirt out of her duffel bag and unrolled it. The gun felt heavy in her hand. She checked to see if it was loaded, made sure the safety was on, then tucked it against her back, the way she'd seen it done in television shows.

Magnolia rolled down the window to get a clearer look at the man in the wheelchair, just as D'Anselmo's car turned the corner.

As he turned on to Johnson Street, D'Anselmo saw the man in the wheelchair. *I have you now, you sonovabitch!* He jammed down on the accelerator and jerked the steering wheel to the left. With a roar and a screech of tires, the car jumped the curb, accelerating straight for Ham. *You're a dead man!*

"Look out!" Magnolia screamed out the truck window.

Ham heard the sound of the rapidly approaching car and the scream at the same time. He swerved his wheelchair toward the building, too late. The car roared past, the front fender striking the wheelchair a glancing blow that sent the chair and Ham spinning through the air. For a nanosecond Ham saw the gold firebird on the car's hood, and memories of three years ago flashed through his mind. The impact sent him sprawling, face down on the grass beside a row of bushes.

D'Anselmo felt the impact and saw Ham fly out of the spinning wheelchair as he flew past. He got on the brakes hard, then cranked the wheel and accelerated just before the car reached the Johnson Street dead end. Tires smoked and squealed as he did a U-turn and roared back down Johnson Street. *You're not getting away this time, you sonovabitch.* He brought the car to a sliding stop just past the turned-over wheelchair.

"You're a dead man!" he shouted as he jumped out of the car, brandishing a gun in his right hand.

Magnolia, shocked at what had just happened, sat in the truck until the screech of D'Anselmo's car doing a U-turn snapped her out of it. She started out of the truck, pulling the pistol from her waistband, just as the car skidded to a stop.

Ham managed to roll his head sideways at the sound of the screeching tires. He heard the shouted threat as the driver came around the back of the car waving a gun. He sensed movement in the street behind the man, and then, out of nowhere, Barca lunged, clamping his jaws on the gunman's arm.

D'Anselmo reacted to Barca's attack, reflexively spinning his body, trying to shake the dog loose. The centrifugal force created by the dog being attached to his extended, spinning arm slammed Barca hard against the side of the car. At impact, Barca yelped, released his bite, and sagged to the ground.

"You sonovabitch!" a woman's voice screamed from behind him. He spun and fired in the direction of the voice.

The bullet hit her in the thigh, knocking her to the pavement. She could see the man in the dark suit running toward them from the parking lot. The man who shot her was yelling and pointing his gun at the man lying on the ground.

Adrenalin drove her to a standing position, both hands wrapped around the pistol grip, her arms extended, unwavering. "You sonovabitch," she repeated, ice in her voice. Thirteen times she pulled the trigger, the last one clicking on an empty chamber.

The man convulsed, then jerked twice more before he crashed to the pavement. Hamilton saw the surprise on his face and then the light go out in his eyes. Ham's focus slid to the woman on the street firing the gun. They locked eyes, and he saw recognition on her face. *I know her.* The thought flashed through his mind just before he passed out.

Atkins had seen the car turn the corner and then accelerate, but it didn't register what was happening until the car sent the wheelchair and its occupant flying. He bolted out of his car and began running across the parking lot, pulling his gun from his shoulder holster as he ran.

"Drop your gun," Atkins shouted as he ran, his voice drowned out by the repeated *POP! POP! POP!* of the Glock. He shouted again, just as the hammer went *click* on the empty chamber.

The woman looked at D'Anselmo's body on the pavement, then at Hamilton lying by the wheelchair. She lowered her gun and took one step toward her son. Her leg buckled. She looked down and watched the blood pump out of the wound in her thigh. "Sonovabitch," she repeated. Her eyes rolled back in her head, and she collapsed in the middle of the street.

Magnolia Kanaranzi, a.k.a. Tiny Dancer, a.k.a. Maggie, died before the ambulance arrived. Todd D'Anselmo's bullet had destroyed her femoral artery, and she bled out in minutes.

She had needed less than one of those minutes to end Todd D'Anselmo's life. The coroner counted 11 bullets in his body, coincidentally, the same number that had killed Aaron Feldman just seven months earlier.

Two days later, Hamilton sat propped up in his hospital bed, reading newspaper stories about his mother, Magnolia Kanaranzi, formerly known as Mary Blethen. Her escape from jail and the shooting were detailed, as was her D.I.D. diagnosis and the three personalities that had been identified. There was also much speculation about which of the personalities had been in control when she shot D'Anselmo, and one editorial suggested that, just as cruelty to the kitten, Houpette, had triggered the shooting of Aaron Feldman, the injury inflicted on the dog, *Barca,* had triggered a switch to the Maggie personality, which resulted in the shooting of Todd D'Anselmo.

For Hamilton, it didn't matter, and the injuries he had suffered--a broken femur, bruises, and lacerations—were inconsequential. His mother had come to see him. She had given her life. He chose to believe that she had done it for him. He was released from the hospital just after Memorial Day, mended in heart and body.

Barca also recovered. Although he walked with a permanent limp for the rest of his life, he remained a loyal companion and attended every one of Ham's lectures.

A week after the shooting, Artemis Blazing opened an express letter from Miami.

> *Dear Artemis,*
>
> *Please disregard the letter I sent you a few days ago. I want you to implement the directives in this letter with haste and without variation.*
>
> 1. *I have reached an agreement to purchase the painting known as "The Reaper" from the Boston Museum of Visual Arts. The price is $12 million to be paid from the funds on deposit in your trust account. Contact Meredith Glenn, the museum's curator, to arrange for payment and delivery of the painting. She will also deliver a signed agreement stating the Museum will not bring any litigation with respect to "The Reaper".*
>
> 2. *The painting should be delivered to Winona State University as a gift from Hamilton Blethen.*

3. *The remaining funds in your trust account should be distributed as follows:*

    a. *$500,000 to the animal humane societies of the Greater Boston Area.*

    b. *$500,000 to be placed in an education fund for the children of Deputy Seth Johnson of the Goodhue County Sheriff's Office, Red Wing, Minnesota, and the children of Hamilton and Antoinette Blethen.*

    c. *My penthouse at Pier 4 in Boston should go to Samantha Jones of Boston, Massachusetts.*

    Senator Magnolia Kanaranzi

At about the same time that the letter arrived in Blazing's office, Cheryl Belton declared her candidacy for the now-vacant Massachusetts Senate seat. In her announcement, Belton praised the heroism of Magnolia Kanaranzi and lamented the tragedy that had prevented Magnolia from fulfilling her Senate term "which she so richly deserved." Senate Minority Leader Bradford Styles, in attendance to introduce Belton, let it be known that he and the national party would give Belton "the same unwavering support" which they had given the late Senator Kanaranzi.

EPILOGUE

The dance floor at The MOOG was crowded. In the center of the mass of gyrating bodies was a couple lost in their own little world – a short, round, bald white man sweating profusely, and a tall, lithe black woman who never perspired a drop.

Hawke was notorious in the Barcelona dance clubs. Despite his physique, he was a superb dancer, and in the past, there were many, both women and men, who had benefited from his generosity toward his dance partners. Recently, however, his eyes were only for this partner, Samantha Jones of Boston, Massachusetts.

When the DJ took a break and the music stopped, Hawke led Samantha by the hand toward a table-for-two along the wall. A waiter appeared with a Pernod for Mr. Hawke, and Prosecco for his lady.

"I have something special for you tonight," Hawke said, wiping his face delicately with a linen handkerchief.

"What could be more special than this?" Samantha answered, sweeping her hand in an arc to encompass the entire club. "A wonderful evening at a wonderful club with a wonderful man, in Barcelona. And a glass of prosecco," she added, raising her glass.

"Oh, we have far more wonderful places to go, you and I, and things to do," Hawke answered. With a flourish, he removed a small velvet box from his pocket. Turning it toward Samantha, he opened it to display a five-carat solitaire diamond.

"I think we should get married."

ACKNOWLEDGMENTS

While writing, itself, is a solitary task, it takes a crowd to craft a story that is worthy of you, the reader, and for that, I give immense credit and huge thanks to....

The Goodhue County Sheriff's Department, and particularly Sheriff Marty Kelly, Captain Heather Stephens, Deputy Jen Hofschulte and the entire staff of the Goodhue County Adult Correctional Facility, for their unselfish willingness to help me understand the location, sights, sounds and procedures so that I could write this book in a plausible manner.

Retired federal prosecutor Kevin Reisenauer and Goodhue County Attorney Steve O'Keefe for schooling me on practices and procedures of the criminal law system.

Irma Upsahl, Morgan and Oliver, and the entire staff at the St. James Hotel for giving me access and information that made the setting a real and vibrant part of this book.

The people who made my writing better and the story more compelling: my editor—Heidi Burns; my critique group—Kelly Langdon, Charlotte Babler, Brian Lutterman and Dennis Johnston; my beta readers—Paul Becker, Shel Mahannah Kubitz Nan DeMars, and my beloved wife, Kathy; my forever medical consultant, Dr. Jon Wogensen; my producer—Tiffany Harelik, and my cover designer—Jun Ares.

Rachel Anderson, my publicist, who has the unenviable task of trying to make the publishing industry aware of the work of this independent author.

Ashley Junghans-Rutelonis, PhD, doctor of psychology and my youngest daughter, of whom I am so proud and to whom this book is dedicated.

ABOUT THE AUTHOR

Born in the wine country of California; raised in a beautiful, little Mississippi River town in Wisconsin; educated in the Minnesota State University system and Harvard Law School, Rob Jung now lives the writer's life in suburban St. Paul, Minnesota, with his wife, Kathy. A life-long student of history, geography and religion, Jung has traveled in every continent except Antarctica, and his stories often find their origin in his travels.

Judgment Day is his fourth novel, and the third and final book of the *Chimera Chronicles Trilogy* that started with *The Reaper* and continued with *The Sower.*

Jung is a member of The Loft Literary Society, Sisters in Crime, Mystery Writers of America and a founding member of Midwest Mystery Works and Minnesota Mystery Night.

He is the father of three grown children, four grandchildren and one (+2) great-grandchildren, in addition to a countless number of "adopted" children of all ages. In addition to writing and lawyering, Jung likes to cook, garden, read, fish, travel, watch baseball and football, attend classic car auctions, drink wine and tell stories.

He can be found at www.robjungwriter.com, where you can sign up for his blog, *The View from Middle Spunk Creek.* He is also on Facebook and LinkedIn.

*Rob Jung is the pen name of Robert W. Junghans who also writes limericks and tells stories under pseudonym "C.J. Rakham".

CPSIA information can be obtained
at www.ICGtesting.com
Printed in the USA
JSHW020909160623
43338JS00003B/19